Ludmila's Broken English

DBC Pierre won the MAN Booker Prize, the Whitbread First Novel Award and the Bollinger Everyman Wodehouse Award for Comic Writing in 2003. *Ludmila's Broken English* is his second novel. He lives in County Leitrim, Ireland.

by the same author

VERNON GOD LITTLE

DBC PIERRE
Ludmila's Broken English

ff

faber and faber

First published in 2006
by Faber and Faber Limited
3 Queen Square London WC1N 3AU
This export paperback edition published in 2006

Typeset by Faber and Faber Limited
Printed in England by Mackays of Chatham, plc

A CIP record for this book
is available from the British Library

ISBN 0–571–23165–9
ISBN 978–0–571–23165–2

2 4 6 8 10 9 7 5 3

To the good people of Chambarak, Hayastan

For one of us was born a twin
And not a soul knew which.

H. S. Leigh

Prologue

The shocker came in the nursery. Matron tried to distract the Heath twins that first morning, whisked folds of dusty light around them, ruffled the stink of milk with her antics. But her clucking was wasted. The boys couldn't help but notice none of the other children were conjoined.

It sparked a plummeting feeling like being squeezed from a sponge.

Even as infants, the essence and the algorithm of the Heaths' situation dawned clearly on them, almost came with its own little flourish of harps. Blair Albert and Gordon-Marie Heath were omphalopagus: conjoined anteriorly at the trunk. They shared certain organs, but not a heart. In a different age or culture we might have wondered what past-life crime, what sin of the parents, had called such a sentence upon two otherwise bright and healthy lads.

A bobby-dazzler, it must have been.

Even in enlightened Britain, doctors would not separate the twins at birth. Indeed, the boys were among few undivided monozygotes to survive their birth; a curious enough thing that it merited a photograph in the newspaper. You might have seen that photograph, if you opened a newspaper all those years ago. There they were, a snarl of raw sausages with hopeful puppy eyes.

After the picture was taken, they were bundled up in terry towelling and sent to an institution. Authorities deemed it the kindest thing. Though it was never said aloud, the sum of everyone's behaviour told the Heaths they were powerful in their uncanniness. It must have been true, given the lengths everyone went to in shielding them from the world's curiosity.

Still, for all that, they were just lads. Lads who would never take a wicket at Lord's. Who would never fly Dagger fighter-bombers out of Leeming. Who would never even be dustmen. This creeping knowledge bled the shine from their eyes. Action posters came down off their walls, leaving Sellotape scabs to curl on the plaster, reminders of all they should reasonably expect.

Most crushing of all – their parents never came to see them again.

With the perfect wisdom of the choiceless, the twins deployed themselves inwards to shepherd the tics and protocols of strange coexistence. Theirs was a hell divided into the levels imagined by Dante – *forza* and *forda*. While Blair possessed the twins' physical power – *forza* – their cunning resided in Gordon, making him dominant in most situations, despite being the weaker twin.

Beyond these clinical glimpses, the boys' deeper unfolding remained obscure. It was in nobody's interest to publicise their life's progress; official strife even attended the publication of that first baby picture. Thereafter, nothing was really known outside of Albion House Institution, the centuries-old jumble of menacing architectures crouched deep in the northern countryside, in whose alternating smells of antiseptic and stewed cauliflower they spent their days.

In her favour, Albion seemed always to marinate in a silvery light like cloudlight bounced off the bell of a horn. And certain pleasures dotted her routine: we know the boys had access to Smarties, for instance, and that Gordon developed a mathematical model to apportion them according to relationships of colours as they fell into the hand. We know that behind Gordon's back – as was the only way – Blair played with dolls, though he never admitted this, and these were later confiscated after his application of unsavoury unguents to their intimate crannies. There was even jocularity enough at Albion for Gordon to be nicknamed Bunny, owing to his generous ears and snaggle teeth.

But after this, nothing more was known of the Heath twins.

Nothing more really happened until the spring before last – that dark, close spring – when the newly privatised health service decided Bunny was leeching resources from his brother. This parasitism would only worsen with age, placing both in jeopardy. Health chiefs decided – as they should have thirty-three years earlier – to try and salvage at least one worthwhile Englishman from the pair. Surely one robust, independent life was better than two lives half-lived.

And so the Heaths were cut free.

Quickly, and in secret.

It was late in life for the procedure. Unprecedented even in Great Ormond Street Hospital, London, where a palette of rare surgical skills was assembled from across the British Isles. One Tuesday in May, expert teams bustled like chefs for fourteen hours and twenty-three minutes over a rotating cage built purposely for the twins.

But it was late. In the first post-operative week it became clear that the Heaths' true interdependence hadn't even been guessed at. They remained terra incognita, a tangle of severed tendrils like the ivy that strangled Albion's turrets and gargoyles.

Within a fortnight of separation, the twins' personalities began to diverge profoundly. Within six weeks, the very flesh they inhabited began to change, furnishing an entire branch of clinical science with unimagined findings. Their unfurling was at once splendid and grisly, a ballet of sticky hatchlings in time-lapse.

But it all came late.

3

As predicted, Bunny fared the poorer, no longer able to siphon vitality from his twin. He never fully recovered from the operation. Both sensed he wouldn't survive that first Christmas. Blair, meanwhile, crackled like gunfire out of Bunny's dominion. He found himself in a world churning with opportunity, rowdy with chatter of freedom, globalisation, self-empowerment.

Sex.

In their first December as individuals, the twins were among a number of care clients given four weeks' leave in the community. They were sent to London. The leave came as a final flurry of privatisations sent Albion House Institution – England's last public healthcare facility, said to have been founded for an illegitimate son of Charles II – into private hands for the first time since paupers were locked up for being poor. Nobody seemed to know why the leave came about. Some rumoured it to be an assessment for future release into the community, the harbinger of a new era in long-term care. Others said it was the lid flying off the Establishment's waste bin, a flushing out of embarrassing care cases before privatised Britain's new information laws allowed media access to case histories. So-called broadsheet newspapers supported the former rumour, while so-called tabloids gleefully touted the latter, citing a rich British history of awkward human accidents conveniently shut away under former asylum laws.

Whatever caused the leave, the Heaths were suddenly at large for the first time in their lives. Nobody could predict how they would get on. Their first bewildering weeks in the new world are a study of human states in secession, burning brightly and swiftly as only the long-frustrated can, unhindered by the learned disciplines of the free. The speed of their enmeshing with the world was breathtaking. And it is ironic, and still much dis-

4

cussed – perhaps as an illustration of mutually attractive energies – that their instincts quickly dragged them into the very
whirlpool-spout of global conjoining and secession.

Into a maelstrom of spirits on parallel journeys.

Far away to the east.

I

ARGUMENTS FROM THE OLD WORLD

UBLILSK–KUZHNISKIA
ADMINISTRATIVE DISTRICT FORTY-ONE
THE DEREV FAMILY

LUDMILA IVANOVA ❧ The Girl

IRINA ALEKSANDROVNA ❧ Her Mother

OLGA VLADIMIROVNA ❧ Her Grandmother

MAKSIMILIAN IVANOV ❧ Her Brother

KISKA IVANOVA ❧ Her Sister

ALEKSANDR VASILIEV ❧ Her Grandfather

MICHAEL 'MISHA' BUKINOV ❧ Her Lover

I

Ludmila paused to watch the sun idle. Her escape would begin when it fell. But it just hung, tediously, shimmering as if through egg white. The night stayed an urgent eternity away.

A helicopter gunship drummed in and out of tune near by. Ludmila stifled a shiver.

Five more hours to discuss the obvious and inane, and sigh in the usual way, and look morose and sceptical. She would hide her excitement, bide her last moments until the family yawned itself in dribs and drabs to bed.

Then she would run.

The mountains threw a shadow beside her, an early consulate of night. She stiffened into the breeze, felt her lips fuller than usual, her vulva fuller, and slick. A curious arousal, one that defied the cold. That night, Misha Bukinov would slip away from his patrol as it skirted the foot of her mountain. She would meet him in the dark between dunes of snow that folded off the slope beneath her shack. He wasn't the prince she had dreamt of as a girl, but he was more than she could hope for in Ublilsk.

And he was her ticket to the west.

Hers would be a harsh departure. The family would wake to find her bedding cold. She knew that all their foibles – most of them, anyway – would become sentimental barbs in her mind once she was gone. They threatened to become so already. She would cry whenever silence caught up with her. But Ludmila clung to the hope that in the west she would find a way for the family to join her.

They would surely forgive her when this was understood.

An icy gust ran its fingers through her hair, flicked it high around her face, to seem like ravens abducting a cherub. Behind her the sky was a pool getting deeper, though not deep enough to contain her excitement and resolve.

She would flee to where there were no bullets or explosions. She sensed it might be a country where these were designed, where the very energies behind them were invoked, where whole armies and wars were contracted by the very rich. She sensed that only the fountainhead of strife would be peaceful. While they lived from war, those very rich wouldn't tolerate the inconvenience of war in the place where they lived.

That's where she would run with Misha.

Ludmila never wanted to see another gun, or hear one bark. Not after learning their value in the equation of power. She saw that they were as addictive as orgasm, through their power to nurture pride. Watching men, she had learnt that pride was a whisper from evil's voice, making cultural pride, by the number of whispers involved, its yell. She never wanted to meet another man spoiled by that whisper. Because, even without a gun in their hands, the instinct to prevail at all cost always lived in the spoilt. This much was clear. She had seen it. The equation never left their minds.

The thought that Misha's Kalashnikov might infect him with its romance made their escape all the more compelling.

Ludmila's grandfather, Aleksandr Vasiliev, was a man spoilt by munitions. He said he cared less about the second person he killed than the first. And the third he cared less about still. After a small number of killings, he came not to care about much at all. And finally not to care about himself. Ludmila remembered the day this knowing fell to him. She saw it dilute the colour of his eyes. They dulled from vivid ponds to glasses of tea as she watched. She remembered perfectly because it was the day her first menstrual episode introduced itself with spatterings on the shack's earth floor; an awkward day with hot cheeks and a sense that she smelt of goat's cheese and beetroot jam.

'More blood on these mountains!' her grandmother Olga had railed. 'As if the place wasn't already a Persian carpet of blood! Pay close attention to what I say: blood is no welcome portent, in the place where you sleep.'

On top of Ludmila's relegation from nymphet to blight, the day marked the beginning of a dirty, tactical life, lived alongside her grandfather; he seemed to sniff her flow each month, and make transparent detours to linger in her air. The four other sour kin who shared the dwelling were only useful to Ludmila at those times, and then only as distractions.

But no more, after that night.

Ludmila shook herself into the present, and hurried through the snow to fetch home her grandfather. She wasn't to know things were about to change. Perhaps it was her excitement that lured change near; because it's in the nature of sudden change to look first for invitations. Whatever the cause, let's be clear: the equation was about to take a savage swing. And it wasn't that Ludmila went looking for trouble, least of all on that precious day. But in the aura known to rise off brutal shifts of fortune, known to lace its gas with arabesques like squealings of Armenian clarinet, she should've sensed trouble's nest was made.

The first sign came in her choice of words.

'What you devour devours you,' she called up the track to Aleksandr. 'Stand down the bottle, Grandpapa, before you join the martyrs.'

'The martyrs can have the smoke off my piss,' Aleksandr's

voice flopped out on a string of saliva, joining limbs to dangle stirring in the breeze. Patches of ginger shone from the fuzz on his face, black shade made huge eyes of his sockets. He was like a bee hung leering in the sun.

'Grandpapa, your wife's voice is broken from asking after you.' Ludmila turned a slender edge to the wind, let it carve her hair off her face. 'Walk back with me, don't make the day too hard – the sun's too low for hard games.'

'Pah! Like pigs, you only send noise in my direction when you're hungry.'

'But we revere you for taking care of us. You're a saint in the house, we would sniff the dust of our bones without you. Come, honour the household that honours you.'

'The household can have the steam off my shit.'

Lavender sunlight spilled like syrup over corrugations of snow, framing the high pasture as a theatre; its stage a dazzling swatch curtained by mountains to the west, and dark flannels of sky to the east. Fluffs of dung smoke hung over the village a thousand feet below, daubed on a flat of glassy air. The line that ran behind it like a frayed electrical cord was the Uvila road. Ludmila watched a lime-green van inch up it like a toy to the far horizon.

'Anyway, your boy doesn't even have a cock.' Aleksandr threw an accusing finger. 'The goat has more grunt than your lover, and is frankly prettier, even looked at into its arse.'

'Everything is as it should be with Misha, Grandpapa, thank you for your concern. Anyway, I can't think why you cough up his memory now, when I haven't troubled your house with his face in a month. So please, enough distemper. Stand down the bottle – the mothers will lash us if we miss the depot again.'

'He has no cock, and he's ugly. And his brain would sit small in a maggot. These two facts are true of your little friend. And his name is of a girl.'

12

Ludmila folded her arms across her chest, scowling. A scowl was an important tool in Ublilsk, taught early and practised often. Hers came with stabbing green eyes like spears of young bamboo. 'Well, it's not of a girl at all. Michael has, because of his friendly nature, simply earned an abbreviation to Misha.' She strode across that crystal stage to her grandfather. 'So, come, before they send the tractor –'

'Pah!' Aleksandr's fist catapulted from his sleeve. He punched her face, and when she didn't flinch, he punched it again.

A filament of blood flew wriggling through Ludmila's lips, bright as a neon vein. She crumpled under it, falling to light the snow with her eyes.

'And don't think I'll beg for your goat's arse of a hole. I'll show you cock – I'll demonstrate cock like the trunk of a tree. Open the pouch for your provider, be thankful I don't sell you to the nearest Gnez.' The old man threw down the bottle, and tripped to his knees. He crushed her breasts with a slab of forearm, wrenching down the trousers beneath her skirts.

Ludmila bucked and squealed.

The equation was suddenly this: if Aleksandr sodomised her, he would more quickly be persuaded to sign his pension voucher, and bread would appear on the family table that night. If her buggery was easily had – she crouching small, glowing rude against the snow, or bent over standing, spreading her bottom with her hands – there might appear pork as well. And if she wet the air with lusty squeaks, there might even be orange Fanta.

Ludmila clenched her eyes, and felt his hands steady her as a child on a donkey, pictured his gurn hanging after a joke, heard the tiny whines that slithered out to hunt stray laughter. It stirred an instinct to hug him close, leach away his hurt, bring him back to rights; she fought the instinct, but it thrashed her back.

13

Aleksandr popped the button on his trousers, and ripped off one of her gloves. 'Hold the thing in your hand – squeeze it, pilot your saviour in.' Turning her face-down, he slapped time on her buttocks, made them blush like nectarines against the ice.

But as Ludmila felt the paste of his breath on her neck, heard the moans that come with closed eyes, something inside her shattered. She spun under him, snatched up her glove, and stuffed it down his throat.

Aleksandr gagged, gasping it deeper. She watched him arch, inflate, vomit inwardly. His brow flickered up, he tightened, and torsioned. She threw him off like a snake found in her bed, and tossed up a broken sob.

Now: whether she slid a finger inside him, tried to remove the obstruction, and if she did, whether she made much effort – she can't remember. She only remembers his hair blowing stiff like dead lawn, and an icy sting on edges of eyeball not usually exposed. However long the moment of that personal border lasted – because it was a border in the grandest sense, a crucial evolution for her and the culture around her – the very next moment she looked down to see Aleksandr lying still. His head was just another rock on the pillow of the Caucasus. Sweat dampened her.

It wasn't long before the family tractor sent chugs over the rise. It stopped for a moment, listening; then started up again. Her brother Maksimilian finally appeared under ghosts of its smoke, a rangy weasel in carpet-like coats.

'Milochka, are you squeaking noises from there?' he shouted. 'Do I have to come all the way and carry you on my back? Your family is seeing spots from hunger, waiting for you.'

Ludmila wiped her face with a sleeve, and twisted Aleksandr's gape into the snow. 'Well, can't you hurry?' she called. She

14

replaced his weeping penis, tied back his trousers, and glanced a hand over his hair.

'Hoh! And listen to me: if you only make the generic noises of a gerbil how do you expect I will know to hurry?'

'They're not generic, grandpapa is fallen.'

'How do you mean, he's fallen?'

'Smack your cuckoo! He's fallen and won't move.'

Maksimilian squeezed an empty roar from the motor, which came as a complaint on the breeze. The old red machine didn't crawl any faster. His eyes met his sister's and stuck for the minute it took the tractor to bring them together. 'We can't even dispatch you to fetch an old man from a hill. What have you done to him?'

'Nothing, he fell where he stood.'

'And why then does the snow around him look like a shell exploded?'

'From trying to investigate his condition.'

'Hoh.' Maks stepped up to the corpse, tapped it with a boot. 'Well, his condition won't improve with his face mashed like that in the snow.' He dug a space around Aleksandr's head, twisting it back until nose and mouth appeared.

'Look!' Ludmila pointed away from the body. 'It must have been the *dzuz*!'

Maks followed Ludmila's finger. He reached for the bottle of home-made vodka, and studied it against the sky. 'He almost finished it – it must be less poisonous than usual. Pilo's been cheating the still.' He lifted the bottle and took a long draught, tickling it over his tongue. Then he turned to his sister. 'And what possesses your mongoloid senses to blame the *dzuz*?'

'I'm in shock to discover the cause, that's all.'

'Well, hoh, with good reason. I won't contemplate what will be the outcome if he's dead. And I won't contemplate what you'll say to your mothers. If he's dead, Milochka, I won't even set out to contemplate.'

'Tss! He might hear you, and waste his last memories in dismay – he might lose his confidence to fight.'

Maks spat a breath. 'Looking at him I wouldn't say confidence is his main challenge. Not the way you've left him.'

'What! What! He fell where he stood! I'm trying to save his life!'

Maks's chin pointed out the body. 'Save him then. Save his life, go on.'

'Tsst! Ears can still hear after death!'

'I thought you were saving his life.'

The sky bruised behind Ludmila. She arched her back against the wind like a child awaiting trouble, let its tongue lick her clothes flat against her, whip her face with her hair. Underneath, from the vortex of this whipping, and the shadow of her eyes, came a shiny rose-tip of nose, like a drop from a hot candle. A tear ran down it for the warmth of a nostril, but blew away sparkling as ice.

'We should lay him in the mud pool,' she sniffed.

Maks sent his most insulting eye. 'And this is a fine concept of yours, that we should make it look even more like a crime, so we both can have blame. You are going to have a prize for this concept.'

'Don't spray shit at me, Maksimilian. You goose. I'm just saying to do the humane thing.'

'Hoh! Charity! Dump a man in freezing mud just to prove your spastic feminine notions.'

'Well, he might have some last words to tell us.'

Maks looked down at the old man's body. 'This is all he had to tell us. Such a witty man, he took fifty-nine years to tell us this.'

16

'But he could sign some vouchers.'

'Hoh, yes! Bring a pen with him to the mud.' Maks puffed a mocking nut of air at the heavens. 'Well – you're the one saving him.'

'I didn't say I was saving him, I said we could get him to the mud if you would help.'

'And, of course – because it is the miracle of ages, carried secretly in the tit of the woman – the mud will save him.'

'Look: if you don't like the concept of trying everything to save him, let you be the one to tell the mothers it was so.' Ludmila went on to her knees to tidy her grandfather's collar. 'Already the colour of his face has turned like borscht.' Out of Maks's view, in a hollow of snow around the head, she explored Aleksandr's throat with her fingertips. He had inhaled the glove finger-first, leaving its back in a hump beyond grasping. As Maks stepped closer, she tried to force the mouth shut, but found it locked agape. Sweat sucked another chill to her.

Maks scowled down. 'A Russian's face might turn like borscht. A Ukrainian's might. Ours won't. If you're asking my assessment, his heart's burst. His heart's burst and all the blood has risen up, it's clear to see.'

'Then take his legs. Maks? He can be wrapped in cloth and put lying in mud, in the dark, where consciousness survives longer. Later we can sew new eyes and fingers on to the body, it's true. Wait while I wrap my coat around his head.'

'Save your tit miracles for the bread queue.'

'But he mustn't die.' Ludmila peeled off her outer coat, wrapping it over Aleksandr's head, tying its sleeves around his neck.

'And cut your mouth if you can only whine like a Russian.' Maks pulled the body by its legs to the rear of the tractor. 'We can take him to the mud, stick new parts on later, like I said.'

17

'Or you could bring him to the clinic at Nevinnomyssk!'

'Are you soft? The tractor will use a month to reach Nevinnomyssk.' With a grunt Maks hoisted the legs on to the tractor's rear forks.

'Put the tractor on the train, is what I said – take him on the train to the clinic.'

Maks turned a withering eye. 'Try, please, for me, to climb back to your midget senses. If you had one eye in your face you would have observed that he doesn't breathe. Do you think he'll hold his breath between here and Nevinnomyssk? Will the clinic just fill him with air like a tyre? And think the curses your mothers will blow if I transport the body out of their sight.'

'Well, but –'

'Anyway, the train passed.'

'That's the bread train. Today passes the big train.' Ludmila went to relieve Maks of the upper body as he pulled it along the forks. 'Have care, if his heart's exploded.'

'I told you it hasn't exploded yet. Why don't you listen? He's had a bubble in the head. Or a worm. If we can stand him up, other blood will absorb it. In the case of a worm, it's known they can't scale vertical surfaces. We could trap it at the neck.'

'Don't unwrap his neck!'

Ice-dust rose in sudden shapes off the snow, only to be smacked to pieces by the wind. And perhaps on that freezing perch the same happened to souls trying to rise from the body. Ludmila hugged her remaining coat around her. In the course of a tight little squirm she practised running away, racing to a place where herbs were kept on window sills for fragrance's sake alone, where life enough existed to support a children's clown. She faced the horizon and closed her eyes. In the place of her dreams she had an egg-yolk-coloured apartment with skirting sharp to the floor. Her prince stepped warm over its threshold each night. She laid him out a gift, in her dreams, of fancy meats in greaseproof paper, or a favourite pie given her with a wink by her colleague Katyrine, or Debie, or Suzan – or whoever the foreign girls would be who shared with her the rolled eyes and snorted giggles of a day at the sunlit offices where she would work. She would be a secretary, or even an administrator, as she could be quite sullen. Big, clean men with square hands would work alongside her and marvel at their progress in her care.

But her eyes opened to Ublilsk Administrative District Forty-One: a mountainous, gale-swept outback whose borders shifted daily due to war; neither yet a country nor still a province; a roofless limbo where sounds rang clear like coins dropped in a cathedral, where mortar fire thumped the pulses of a dozen foetal republics near by.

Maks turned to his sister and spat into the snow. 'So look what you've done. We're damned.'

'Cut your hatch, it was more likely your sloth that weakened him. Look at you, even still wasting fuel from the tractor to come this small distance!'

'Hoh! And I'd laugh to see you carry the body without a tractor.'

'You didn't know there would be a body!'

'Still. You're guilty of the death of a man! For isn't it a person closely reminiscent of you who is discovered beside him?'

'Don't toss gas, I can be seen near his body all the days of the year.'

'But on those other days his body is in possession of breath. *You're guilty of the death of a man*! And you invite me to offend the saints by not pelting a lash at your snout. Just make the sign, before more sour meals are served in your name.'

'Hoh! And you –'

'Just make the sign!'

An aeroplane spun a shining thread across the sky, on its way west to somewhere effervescent, too high to see the young uprights without shadows who held out their arms to form standing crosses. They did it so that Aleksandr's ghost might be snuck into the garden of any vaguely interested God. That model pair of young ethnic Ublis – he with the airs of a dangerous puppy, she with a filthy and knowing innocence – stood until their arms fell nearly broken under Heaven's weight, hissing whispers in their language of crackles and slices like criss-crossing dance steps on ice. Kabardo-Cherkess-tongued people, as well as Azeris, Hayastanis, and Georgians, all suspect that curious tongue to be, if not a massacre, surely a kidnapping of their own language.

But Ubli is unique to Ublilsk.

It is said to be the language most exquisitely tailored to the expression of disdain. Soviet scholars once reasoned that slow death was so vibrant a part of Ubli culture that it had not only to scorn it, but to scorn it decoratively, with high ironic art. To scorn death, however, they also had to scorn life. So that linguistic adaptation of a culture to its environment was, ironically, its final evolution: it soldered hopelessness into a closed circuit that prevented further life.

Soviet scholars reasoned this, back when they were paid. Now nobody is paid to reason anything about Ublilsk, or indeed, about any but three of the dozen warring fragments of that true human border between east and west: those glorious Caucasus.

Ludmila watched gunmetal clouds darken over the mountains, sucking the shine from the snow. 'Well,' she sighed. 'Well then, so.'

'Well then, so what?'

'We should travel back.'

'Hoh!' Maks tossed his chin at the sky. 'And you're in a fine hurry to get back. You're in an uncontrolled passion to get back, and tell your mothers that you've killed the provider.'

'Cut your bile, we'll have to return sooner or later. There are other things still in the world to do after telling the news.'

'What! We'll be lighting candles over his body for a month, is what there'll be to do, thanks to you. Nothing more will be to do until we starve and freeze in our beds – thanks to you.'

A tremble took Ludmila's lip. 'Don't spray such shit – he fell where he stood, Maksimilian. He fell, and he's gone, and some kind of life will have to continue, even as we mourn.'

Maks turned a sneer on his sister. 'Of course,' he mused, looking her up and down. 'Some life will have to continue. Clouds will have to continue to fly. Defence patrols will have to continue to pass under the mountain, in the night.' He stopped, impaling her on a stare. 'Some little species of romance you imagined was going to continue as well, in the dunes, tonight? With an intrepid goose's arse highly resemblant of the young Misha Bukinov? You forget I meet the patrol each day on my travels.' Maks clasped his hands behind his back, and sauntered to the tractor, nodding thoughtfully. 'Well, well, so. Perhaps not everything will have to continue. Perhaps we've discovered a thing that won't be having to continue at all, in the new light of things.'

2

'Something with arugula?' called Blair.

'Is that not an inflammatory disease?'

'Well, what do you bloody want?'

'Bacon,' croaked Bunny.

'You're supposed to stay off the fats. There's couscous.'

'Is there not just some bacon?'

'There's a scrap of jamón serrano.'

Bunny craned out of the bath like a badger, speckled eyes darting into the bed-sitting room, whose shadow-lit spaces spoke of newly installed students in digs. 'Is there not just something that hasn't been flayed off the back of a wog cadaver?'

'Well I take exception to that,' snapped Blair. 'I'm sorry, but if that's the only level you can find to deal on, you can get your own.'

'Are you some sort of cunt? Is there not something English? Just fetch us owt suitable for deployment in a bap. Something bap-ready. Prêt à bapper.'

A week earlier, cooked breakfasts would have whispered into the morning with the squeak of the tea urn on its way from the green lounge, distant clattering from the kitchens. Bunny would have kissed a first Rothmans, lit it with a match. Before its burn had reached the maker's name, fatty smells would have roamed Albion's Dreadnought wing, glistening a promise of fried bread. Bunny would have entertained himself with idle mental projects, such as his ongoing categorisation of facial types, in which he had reached people who resembled pigs and squirrels, having closed the reptilian phase of the endeavour by deciding his brother had become a salamander.

All this would have been routine only days before. But now the twins were on leave in London, alone in a basement flat like a tank of dishwater, even down to its floating detritus. Freedom, Blair called it. To Bunny this so-called freedom was a song made of notes that ended in tight little screams, a Hindi song accompanied by a bandsaw.

'I mean to say,' he called from the bath. In the interests of morale, he used his everyday inflection: a faintly disbelieving tone with the dryness of a biscuit snapping.

'You mean to say what?' called Blair. 'You had a curry Monday night, and that's not bloody English.'

'It is.'

A thump from the kitchenette twanged the floorboards. Blair broke into the bathroom's fog, an elfin pharaoh seeming through Bunny's dark glasses to drag horns of light from his brow. It was the sort of thing that happened through Bunny's sunglasses; his sensitivity to light made all the world an impressionist tone-poem. Blair kicked aside some dressing gowns piled like a waiting camel on the floor, and thrust a glossy bag over the bath. 'This is what there is, take it or leave it. I've better things to be getting on with.'

'Such as?'

'Such as getting those forms into the register office, like you haven't found it in yourself to do.'

Bunny manoeuvred a finger under a floating slick of soap, and burst it like a shark attacking. 'I spoke to them on the phone.'

'Well, they don't give out birth certificates on the phone, you have to materialise the forms in a physical way. I'm sorry if it's inconvenient.'

23

'I mean to say. Getting me nads blown off by a terrorist, or getting shot to fuck by the anti-terrorist squad, might be a tad out of me way. Might take more than the odd cup of tea to get over. I'm not going out unless I bloody have to.'

'For God's sake. Anyway, if you'd just mow your hair, and stop wearing those manky dressing gowns, you'd look much less of a threat.'

'But I'm English.'

'The terrorists are English, Bunny.'

'Anyhow, there's not much point applying down here, is there? We'll do it when we get back up north.'

'We were born in London, Buns. This is where the hospital is that deals with people like us, I'm sorry if it's confusing.'

'I don't see what the hurry is. We've been a while now without a birth certificate.'

'Well, but can you exist in this absurd vacuum of self-knowledge?' Blair stared distastefully at Bunny's body, wobbling gently in the swell like a blancmange. He huffed a sigh. 'Never mind, I'll do it.'

Bunny clicked his tongue. Pushing his sunglasses on to his head, he reached out of the bath and took the food bag suspiciously between thumb and finger. 'Romany Fig Polenta with Cuitlacoche Tips and Sorrel-Smoked Bushmeat Lardons,' he read. 'For the love of God.'

'Right, get your own.' Blair tramped out through the door.

'I mean to fucking say. Don't be taken in by that TV chef twat – you don't think he got so cocky eating this fucking shite? Off-camera'll be littered with Scotch-egg crumbs, mark my words.'

Bunny peeled a long straggle of hair from his neck and threw it over his shoulder. It slapped stuck to the bath's enamel. He replaced his glasses. Contrary to his belief, the dimness of life through sunglasses didn't make his other senses more acute. Rather, they dimmed as well. His nostrils twitched, hunting the fleecy sense of renewal known to lurk in a bathroom's steam. None was found. Instead a salt-and-vinegar gust poked the overhead light, dicing from the bathwater the sort of dapple sent by the seabed on unlucky days.

One eye curled to the door. 'Is this how we're supposed to be now, for ever?'

'Well, you be how you want.'

'I mean to say. A fiver for this bollocks? They're taking no end of widdle. I think I'd best have a crack at the shopping.'

'Well, I'm sorry but we can't just live on frozen breaded things. That's just not on.'

'Would it be on if I jammed a lardon up your bastard chuff?'

'I won't even dignify that.'

'I mean to say. Is there not just a crumpet? I'm at a loss to grasp you since we came down. Complete bloody loss.'

'Well, it's called a life,' spat Blair. 'You wouldn't know.'

'Another post-modern lozenge, how *au fait*.'

'It's nothing to do with post-modern, it's about informed choices.'

'Describe for me then – a Cuitlacoche Tip.'

'Oh piss off.'

'Petit bourgeois intimidated by the cappuccino menu, that's you, sunshine. Northern man of mystery out of his fucking depth.'

No reply. The television in the sitting room was on, though it sounded unwatched. Still it squeaked frights from December's medley of perils – the Al-Masur virus, neo-natal depression, and, even as Bunny rankled in the bath, the jagged harmonies of either the 'If You Care – Beware!' anti-terrorist campaign, or an old Boris Karloff film. Bunny craned a little farther out of the bath. 'Just fetch us something common or garden, to take me tablets with. Mate?'

No reply.

'I say, Blair? Me chest's a bit dicky this morning – best get me tablets down.'

No reply. Blair would be at the mirror again, beside the kitchen night-light. Its glow warmed the scornful penis his face had become. Then sounded a creak from the computer chair. Blair was on the internet. Bunny tossed the bag out through the door. 'Bollocks then. And try and not spaff the desk, I've writing to do later.'

'Well, that's bang out of order, I'm looking something up for work.'

'No, pet, you carry on,' Bunny's drone coiled into a whine. 'Have yourself a fiddle, you've been up nearly an hour. It's a wonder you haven't jizzed yourself involuntarily.'

'It's for bloody work!'

'Diversifying, are they? Rear-action Teens?'

Blair jumped so forcefully from his chair that it left the ground in his wake. He crashed to the bathroom door, and stabbed a finger into the mist. 'I'll bloody have you in a minute.'

Bunny's eyebrows popped like crusts of toast. 'How urban,' he said, reaching for his Stephenson's *Rocket* nail brush. 'How street-credible.'

'I mean it, Buns. This is the end. You've done my head in.'

'I mean to say – you can wank yourself into a coma for all I care.' Bunny leant away into a corner of the gothic tub. 'How are you so prickly all of a sudden?'

'Well, it's called privacy. A basic global human bloody right.'

'Global, eh?' sniffed Bunny. 'Off you go then.'

'And don't come the sacrificial lamb over it either.'

'Fine, off you go.'

An explosive sigh shunted Blair to the edge of the bath. 'I'm not playing any more, Bunny. We're thirty-three. This is our first real crack at life and I'm sorry if I've given the impression I might spend it withering away with you, but I've heard a clock ticking and it bloody ticks for me.'

'*Tolls* for me.'

'*I'm speaking*!'

'Sorry, it's actually a bell that tolls. Tolls for *thee*, my mistake. "Send not to ask for whom –"'

'*Shut up*!' Blair smacked a bottle of detergent into the water, whipping up a mighty splash. 'I'm not allowing you away with this. We're here now. It's the world. I don't know what your hang-up is, but I'm jumping in.'

'You're the one with the hang-up, pal.'

'No, Bunny, you're the one with the hang-up – every step I take sends you into a bloody panic. Look at yourself. You should be happy I'm off out to make a future, you should be overjoyed we're finally free.'

'Don't be daft, we'll be back next month. Ahh, Albion, verdant cradle –'

'I'll not be back. Make no mistake.'

'We're on four weeks' supervision, Blair. Don't run away with your bloody self. I'm not even unpacking me bag.'

'Nice one, Bunny, very clever. You're just going to sit there and pretend that whole discussion with the facilitator never happened. That's how you're going to pass it off, by just spinning things out of the picture. Because you listen to me: I'll never forget a word of that meeting.'

Bunny began opening and closing his legs, forcing little tsunamis over his belly. 'I only said we're on four weeks' supervision. Not much equivocal about that.'

'Say what you like, we were told to go out and integrate. Why do you think I've been found a job? Do you honestly think they'd place me in a job if I were off back into care in four weeks' time?'

'What, that sandwich activator bollocks? Making sandwich activators is hardly –'

'They're sandwich *applicators*, and they're made overseas. We're head office, we only do the global market strategies.'

'I mean to say, you've only shown up once. Jammy bit of graft, that. Anyway, what would you bloody know about it?'

'Well, that's not the point – the point is it's a job. Don't confuse us with the hard cases, Bunny. Under privatisation it's just not profitable to keep everyone in care, the government just won't come at it. They've lowered the overflow valve, whether you can deal with it or not. And I, for one, intend to overflow.'

Bunny chuckled darkly. 'Soft cases now, are we? Talk to me about spinning things out of the picture.'

'Well, what I'm telling you is we're perfectly rational and ambulant – at least I bloody am. There's nothing to say I can't join the wider community. The governors are clearly waiting to see who takes the initiative and gets a life up and running, and who flounders about crying to go back. I, for one, intend to count myself among the former.'

'Count yourself among the former, eh? Is that the sort of bollocks you'll tell the assessor on Saturday?'

'Well, nobody's even said he's an assessor! It's the day of the social, he's probably just an escort.'

'He can still assess us over sandwiches and Ribena.'

'Rubbish, the social's an introduction to the local care scene, a friendly drink. And I doubt it'll be Ribena. For God's sake, you're acting like an escaped prisoner.'

'I feel like one and all. Prisoner of bloody war. Shouldn't wonder they'd assess us for post-traumatic fucking stress, sending us to London.'

'Oh stop it, there's not been an incident all week.'

'There has, last Friday.'

'Well, I mean, this is the state of play in the world, you can't just cower away. We have to get involved, exercise our rights, stamp out the scourge of terrorism. I'm sorry if it's not soothing.'

'Be a good lad, then – after you've stamped out tourism, can you grab us a pork pie and a bottle of Gordon's at Patel's?'

'God, you're such a pathetic liberal. Have you heard yourself lately? You've become such an absurd hippie, it's a joke. And after the sacrifices this country's made for your safety – you should be bloody ashamed.'

'You're the one should be ashamed, sunshine. It's your type made the fucking tourists in the first place.'

'Well, no actually, Bunny, it was *your* kind of piss-weak complacency. If your type hadn't been so busy rescuing foxes, we could've jumped on the threat while we had a fighting chance!'

'Jumped on it, eh? Where?'

'Well, I mean – the Middle East, for bloody starters.'

'I think we did that, mate, to be honest. I think we poked them with a fucking great stick, then ran back home and expected them to think they deserved it for being poor and not letting their women flash their arses on the street.'

'Such a pathetic little hippie, Bunny, I can't believe it.'

'You want fucking assessing, you do.'

'You're the one wants assessing.'

Bunny sat up and blinked. 'You admit he'll be an assessor then, this man on Saturday?'

A yard of breath collapsed through Blair's nose. 'For God's sake! Nobody cares about assessments! They only want to stop these nasty special-needs stories running in the papers! I mean, it's just so clear, Bunny. If anything, I'd say Saturday's visit is to ensure we're not only comfortable but bloody ecstatic. They need us to be a success, to set an example. They'll do anything to make that happen.'

'Crap, they're only worried about royal baby stories.' Bunny clapped the bones of his knees together, squirting a wave up his chest that lapped into his ears. 'Every bugger knows it. Do you honestly think they give a toss about the rest of our stories? A few mad raspberries with slightly wrong paperwork? No, mate. Royal baby. Smell it a mile off. I'd say we're only out because we had the room by the stairs. Handy view of Dreadnought security door.'

'Right, forget it, there's no point bloody talking to you.'

'Look, royalty's always parked dicky bairns in the country-side, out of the way. It's what the Establishment's all about, covering things up for one another.'

'Well, the Establishment's been privatised, Bunny. Get used to it.'

'And what do you think the annexe is for, round the back of Albion? Fucking bingo? Mate – dodgy royal babies. Stories like that don't come from nothing, you know, you don't get smoke without fire.'

'Honestly, Bunny, for God's sake. And I suppose this theory's seeped out of the *Mail*.'

'Don't knock the *Daily Mail*, pal – they've got your kind read like a fucking dictionary.'

'Well, just you tell me when, in thirty-odd years at Albion, you've ever seen a royal baby.'

'Well, they're not going to fucking tell you which one it is, are they? Do you think they'll stamp a royal warrant on its head?'

'What I'm bloody saying to you is that as a resident of the institution where all this is supposed to be happening, I haven't heard a single credible rumour about a royal bloody baby.'

'If you ask me it'll be the lass down the dark end of

Dreadnought, with all the machines. The one that's just a head with sort of gills.' Bunny put a finger to his cheek, dragged down a solemn eyelid. 'Mark my words: royal bairn.'

'Oh very funny, and that's why they've released a thousand residents across Britain, because of what some of us might know about one bloody baby? For Christ's sake, Bunny. It's absurd. There are enough curiosities locked away in these places to keep the papers going for a century, never mind royal babies. I mean, for God's sake, there's been a high-functioning, fully ambulant human spider on Empire wing for at least two decades, *and* they dress it in black fur for the Hallowe'en party – what do you think the papers'd make of that?'

'Her name's Eva, Blair, before you run away with yourself. And she'll not get in the papers just for being disadvantaged.'

'What I am saying to you is that half these people's files expose embarrassing if not criminal healthcare mistakes dating back to their births. Ours as well: can you imagine the fuss – healthy twins waiting thirty-three years to be separated? Healthy lads, institutionalised for life? They'd never hear the end of it. Now look at the sequence of events: privatisation throws up the files for all to see; we're suddenly sent on leave. Does that not suggest something to you?'

'Gammy royal bairn.'

'Oh piss off.'

Bunny rested a gaunt arm along the rim of the bath, and settled back with a knowing air. 'Look, pal, if they were so worried about us telling stories to the papers, d'you think they'd set us loose in London? Up the road from fucking Fleet Street? Give over, I mean to say. They'd have us overseas in a flash, they'd concoct an excuse for a holiday, or some other bollocks. Face it: you could tell any bugger our story and he'd not bat an eye. Nobody cares about our stories, Blair. We're just decoys.'

'Well, first of all there aren't any papers left on bloody Fleet Street, so there's that argument shot down in flames. And anyway, don't let your twisted assessment of things lull you into thinking you can swan about telling our story, do you hear?'

'And why not? There's no shame in it. I should think we'd be better off getting things out in the open, we'll only get sussed out.'

'Well, we've been pointedly warned not to. And if you'd just behave normally for a minute, we wouldn't get sussed out at all.'

'And what is there in my behaviour that'd give our background away? Fucking nothing. You tell me one thing that says anything about our background.'

'Ballroom dancing for a bloody start.'

'Oh, now, Blair, I mean to say – is that why I've not had you up the last five Saturdays?'

'Three Saturdays.'

'It's five Saturdays, pal, ever since that bloody meeting. I should've known. Tango not butch enough for you any more? Does it not fit your dashing new Biggles-type image?'

Blair snapped at the waist and hung emptying words like chunks of litter into the bath. 'Well, I mean, I'm sorry, but come on, what would people think? It's unnatural. And if you ever bring it up in front of third parties I will bin your sodding disc collection, do you hear?'

'Mind, you'd be hard pressed to find a royal bairn as light on its feet as us.'

'Give over! The bloody point is, having let everyone out, for whatever reason, do you think the governors would rather we integrated and got on with building a constructive future, or lolled about in the bath all day whining for a cooked breakfast?'

'Aye, cracking future you'll build in four weeks.' Bunny reached for the hot tap, grunting. 'Probably have your own polenta factory after a fortnight.'

'You just haven't a bloody clue, have you? It's all too much for Buns. Threatened a bit, are we, Bun-Marie? On the hobble from ourselves? Because let me tell you something: they've not let us out to be the way you are. They've let us out to find a genuine sort of social integration.'

'A shag, you mean.'

'I mean the establishment of emotional connections other than the tedious psychological loops you've designed to prove to yourself that you're better off not bloody doing anything!'

'Save a fortune on tissues, a shag.'

'Right, that's it.' Blair stamped a pointless circle without quite exiting the bathroom.

Bunny lifted his glasses, rolled his eyeballs to his brother. 'Blair – I mean to say. Be serious for a minute. I know what skips through your little mind. Forget it, right? Don't get hurt. You'll not be a cosy nuclear family by the end of four weeks. You'll not be out shopping for fabrics. And they'll not leave care patients swanning about indefinitely, will they bollocks. They'll round us up when the heat's off in the papers, if we haven't wafted back through the courts. I mean to say – whose bed-sit do you think this is? We've been parked here, Blair. It's just another care room. Mark my words: if you start prancing about like a twat you'll be the first one back. Do us both a favour. You'll have a smashing time if you just fucking lighten up, and take the thing for what it is: a month's laff in the Big Smoke.'

Blair's face tightened to bone. 'Well, first of all we're care clients, not patients.'

'Are you going to be a wanker all your life?'

'And I'm sorry but I'll tell you this only once: stand clear of me, Bunny, I'm on the move.'

Bunny returned a volley of blinks. He gave his lips an exploratory chew. 'Well, I'm glad we sorted that out.' He went back to scrubbing his fingertips. 'Just to recap: it's a shag, Blair. You've three and a bit more weeks to get your end wet.'

Blair stood twitching with friction. With a grunt he erupted, sweeping a bedpan from under the sink, and hurling it at his brother. Bunny crashed underwater with a clang, unleashing a wave that crested over the lip of the bath and clapped across the floor, engulfing the dressing-gown camel. Blair pulled himself back and hung a stare on his brother's hair, swirling in the choppy bathwater. Then he turned and thundered out.

A pain twinkled in Bunny's chest when he surfaced. He spun about to smooth the flannel that clung to the tub's rim like a slice of ragged ham.

The pain twinkled on.

3

Irina Aleksandrovna sagged at the door of her shack, just another globular patch among wood and tin scraps. She was grubby and blank-faced, a rag doll run over by a pram. Her breasts and belly, and the fat that hung from her cheeks and neck, travelled downwards to sniff her grave. Her lashes flickered waiting for noise from the tractor.

Irina nursed bad news at the door for her father Aleksandr and her children Ludmila and Maksimilian. The news was routinely bad, about food and weather, about the rooster's dripping eye, about the new closeness of gunfire. It was ordinary for her to pass the minutes after such newses came on the local breeze – which was to say on the Kalashnikov breath of Nadezhda Krupskaya, the passing oracle – inventing dressings to sweeten their telling. But that day she neglected her lies. It was the day Aleksandr's pension voucher rode his hand into Ublilsk village, and returned in shapes of meat and bread.

On a good day there might be orange Fanta.

'Have they run away laughing, these children?' her mother Olga wheezed from the dark of the shack. 'The depot will be empty of bread!' Shocks of black eyebrow bristled over her words.

'Well, your husband with a bottle in his hand can invite some labour to shift,' sighed Irina, standing her eyes on the peaks behind the shack.

Those mountains had started to claim back their dwelling. Selected boards had been torn from the shack's cladding and burnt as firewood on the worst winter nights, nights when even dung was scarce. Such nights had a cumulative effect, measured in draughts that vacuumed the hovel from three sides, replacing any stray warmth with animal damp. Added to this was Olga's increasingly cheesy smell, and the various and growing incontinences which Irina suspected were not entirely involuntary, but part of the price she would extract from the world for the disappointment of her birth. In those days it seemed everyone in the district was busy exacting such tolls, it was evident before the war started, before the propeller factory closed. Even allowing for their traditional delight in hardship, their respect for the sweet ecstasy of suffering, emotional tolls were two a kopek in Ublilsk that December.

More long minutes passed before the tractor popped over the horizon. Bent smoke puffed banging from its pipe. Irina wiped her nose on the arm of her dress, and stepped into the yard to see Ludmila fly like a boy towards her. As her daughter's colours emerged from the mist and grew warm, Maksimilian and the tractor growled into the yard behind her. Aleksandr's corpse lay face-down on its forks, legs bouncing jauntily.

Irina's features scattered from the middle of her face. She took a step closer, slapped a hand to her mouth.

'He fell where he stood,' sobbed Ludmila. 'I barely found him when he just fell.'

'Does he breathe?'

'No.'

'And too late to take him to the mud. Oh saints in heaven. Oh my saints.' Irina parted calves like oak trunks to keep her balance. She looked up at Ludmila and frowned, pointing. 'And bring your face to me.'

'I tell you he just fell with his bottle.'

'Present me your face!' Irina grabbed her daughter's coat and pulled her close. Her eyes flicked over the painful shine on her cheek. 'And don't let the day swallow any stories. Tell me them now.'

Ludmila tucked her gloveless hand under an arm, and stood panting bullets of fog. 'I slipped on the way up, and then, when I saw him, I tell you –'

'Pah! Then don't make another sound.'

Ludmila fell quiet. Anything she said would only complete a circuit of dead-end psychologies. She fixed her mind instead on Misha Bukinov, his sensitive hands, and her escape in their warmth.

Six-year-old Kiska came like a wasp to the nectar of pain. Her eyes beamed wide, plotting each corner of the scene, anxious, like all Ubli children, to learn where to hunt her own pain one day. Maks shut off the tractor with a clatter, and strode to his family by the doorstep. Behind him a last puddle of sun soaked under the horizon.

'And so,' Irina sniffed, 'now arrives the day.'

'Before you set out to ask my assessment,' Maks frowned gravely, 'I'll tell you squarely that mobile telephones are the answer. With such a commerce, made mainly by long hours of intelligence and sharp thinking, and not depending on the malice of soil or weather, or the unpredictable clenchings of an animal's gut, I can still be here to guard you, now the house has no man.'

Irina's cheeks surged colour like an octopus slapped. 'His heart's scarcely cold before you paint me geese in the sky!'

'I only attempt to say –'

'And what money will you use to buy them! Who is even left to dial on your telephones! You're right to say the house has no man!'

'There's no other work!'

With a finger Irina gashed a hole through the wind. 'Look at this land and tell me there's no work. *Look at it*! *Hit, kill, and eat, Maks!*'

Maks was clever enough to stay quiet. His eyes seeped bile into the eve.

Olga rolled through the door, absorbing Kiska into her skirts like a wool amoeba. She squealed when she saw her husband's body, and threw desperate cupped hands at the sky – 'Served the saints a sour meal.' But although the sight was a year's licence to wail, her reaction was short. In this way, and in the changing of her eyes into finger holes in a dumpling, and in the empty chewing that went on behind the hairs of her chin, the family knew that, without waiting for another cloud to pass, they must decide how to live without Aleksandr's pension.

Maksimilian moved like an upholstered whip of muscle, dragging an oil drum into the tractor's lea, lighting dung bricks in it, and carrying chairs from the shack. To consult and respect Aleksandr, the mothers ordered the chairs put in a semicircle around his body. Maks sat on the tractor's step. The Derevs were a dark nativity, bleeding steam into a purple sky.

As they sat, Misha Bukinov would be making his way to the dunes. Ludmila looked around. Even the latrine was visible from most corners of the yard. She had no cover, and no excuse left to slip away.

'The house needs a man, Iri,' said Olga. 'Look what's happening in the Forty-One. We're four females alone, the only next visitors walk with guns.'

Maks lifted his head to half the height it would stand if he were asked to take charge. He puffed his chest, in waiting.

Irina looked up to the sky, pursing her lips as if to sip an answer from the breeze. 'But a man in these districts brings nothing but strife and appetite. It's clear through my eyes that the house will not by itself travel the way of any benefit. One of us must go for work to the munitions factory in Kuzhnisk. It must be Maksimilian, saints help us. Or who otherwise?'

38

Olga half-spat and half-sucked the answer through drapes of lip and cheek. 'Well, we can't send Maksimilian – he's a goose's arse, you might as well tie his wages to a rocket and fire it at the sun. And he'd be snatched by soldiers, even before he passed the bridge.'

Maks jumped from the tractor to storm away muttering. Olga tossed her chin after him, raising her voice. 'No, Maksimilian should stay and collect wood and turds. He's useful to us as a dog is useful.'

'And more costly than a Gnezvar wedding,' sighed Irina. 'Anyway, let's not quickly seal such a decision – it has many edges to consider, and we still have the tractor to bargain with.'

'No!' Olga's knotty finger struck the air. 'Let's do seal it. As it is, we'll have to kill one of the animals, or sleep hungry again – and who around here do you think has cake enough to buy tractors? Let's quickly enter an assessment of the thing, in the following sensible way: who, first of all, is the eldest? Maksimilian is just twenty-one; Ludmila is twenty-three. By which I say: see, please, what's clear in front of your face. Ludmila Ivanova is the correct pilgrim. And if the munitions plant won't have her, well, I say – she has other opportunities to explore.' Olga reached to Ludmila's nearest breast and squeezed it like a pomegranate.

'And but, Mama, she can assist with other things than her tits!'

'Hoh!' shrilled Olga. 'If times were so sweet that I could choose my work and penance! Only the fortunes will direct what she can do, but hear this: she must leave her idle dreams and do everything possible to save us, and herself.'

'I won't send her to that!' Irina wagged a finger back.

'And I'm not going to the munitions plant,' Ludmila sniffled.

'But it's not just munitions, said Irina. 'They also make speciality articles for the food industry.'

'Yes, to avoid tax on the plant. Anyway, whatever they make, I'm not going.'

'What! Then you're telling me you'd rather sell pleasure to lorry drivers by the road!'

'I won't do that either. There must be more choices than munitions and sex.'

Olga threw up her hands. 'On such a dark day I have to be put in the way of foul slogans! Such a word for God's deepest manifestation of love!'

'It's the laboratory word, Mama,' said Irina. 'There's nothing wrong with the word "sex", licensed doctors use it. Get back to the theme.'

'Hoh, well.' Olga leant out of her chair. 'The theme for Ludmila Ivanova is this simple fact: she will do as we say!'

'But also consider if the factory won't take her. A river of people has been absorbed by the factory, they might not take any more, especially unskilled like this one.'

'Well, but she has other skills. I can think of a skill she has, I'm sure I can.'

Ludmila leant forward to catch her mothers' eyes. She took her final gamble. 'I may know a way, a much quicker way than munitions and pleasure.'

'Oh yes?' Irina raised an eyebrow. 'And would this be gathering snow, or digging up land-mines to resell to the Gnez?'

'It's an opportunity I don't yet know the shape of, one to still discover – but if I could hurry now, into the village, I might still be in time to learn of it.'

'Hoh yes,' said Irina. 'Clearly if you go to the village they will build an international airport, build a shopping centre just to employ you. I haven't sent my cuckoos to the seaside, Milochka. A much better idea, for the immediate future, is for you to tell me what possible opportunity is left in Ublilsk village that my ears have somehow missed in forty years of living its slow death.'

'I didn't say it was in the village. I didn't say it was in the village at all, why can't you listen? I said I could go in that direction to hear about it – and it's an action I can take immediately, tonight. Much quicker than applying to the plant in Kuzhnisk.'

'Hoh, and –'

'No, please listen!' Ludmila gathered a hand each from her mothers, and squeezed them in hers. 'I can spend half the night playing interrogations with you, or I can immediately test an opportunity.'

'And you listen to me,' said Irina. 'This wouldn't, by some extraordinary outbreak of fortune, be a romantic opportunity? Because you should know: I haven't survived these mountains by having slow eyes. How often is it, do you think, that I see all your clothes washed clean at the same time? You insult us, Milochka, with your stupidity.'

Heat rose from Ludmila's gut to scald the back of her eyes. She blinked at each woman in turn.

'And don't think you'll find the bag tonight, that you packed with your clothes. You'll be staying here to pay the correct respect to your grandfather.' Irina turned to wag a finger at her mother. 'And I'll tell you, Mama, that my daughter isn't wrong to say there are more available labours than just selling pleasure to soldiers.'

'Cut your mouth, hear what I have to say,' Olga raised a hand. 'Like all things, there's a floor of opportunity, which you can imagine looking at this dripping ripe plum of a girl, and there's a sky. Ludmila will have to bargain with fortune to climb above the floor. And this suits us, because in the heights of a situation is where our rescue most quickly lives.' Olga's eyes twinkled fire from the drum. 'Don't spill your eyes in the snow, Iri. She can proceed to the munitions factory, as we have now discussed. But if they don't take her, you will see there is a higher possibility still. Watch how clear it sits before you, this unexpected gift from your husband. Because the least stupid thing Ivan Andreyevich ever did from this place – saints forgive me for making the noise of his name on such a day – was to allow Ludmila to superior school.'

'And you're right,' said Irina, looking up. 'She even learnt some English.'

'Yes!' Olga's eyes sharpened into cuts. 'We have Ludmila's English.'

4

Instead of a cooked breakfast, streaky rashers of pain crackled through Bunny's chest. Organs like sausages popped and spat. He lay still in the bath as a full English heart attack fetched up inside him. His sense of things began to warp. Soap bubbles popped as dry salts; the plonk of tap water became dredger chain banging on iron.

'Blair?'

No reply. His throat tightened. He doubled forward, and slapped the water. 'Blair!'

'Shut up. And where's the birth certificate form?' A drawer scraped open in the kitchenette.

'Here, I'm poorly.' Bunny's snaggle teeth seemed to crawl in the light.

Blair smashed shut the kitchen drawer, and brought a slow smirk to the doorway. 'You're sweating like a rapist, Buns. Massive stroke, is it?'

'Heart.'

'Well, I'm sorry, but you've only yourself to blame.'

'Get the phone.' Bunny flapped a hand.

Blair leant into the door frame. From that angle he spied a box of England's Glory matches, and a pile of its blackened dead on the ledge beside the bath. Alongside them lay a browned tip of paper like a tiny half-eaten sausage roll recently shot off as a flare. 'Hang on – is that a spliff?' he pointed.

'What?'

'Well, I mean, come on.'

43

Bunny's sunglasses twitched.

'I mean, I'm sorry,' said Blair, 'I'm not going to embark on a systematic campaign of concealment on your behalf. That's just not on.'

'I'm having a cardiac event.'

'Well, you might say that, Buns, but is it not just a fear event? Is it not just a physical manifestation of your fear of moving forward, of leaving the old ways behind?'

'Are you some sort of cunt? My heart's manifesting a fucking cardiac event.'

'Well, you should have thought of that before you started breaking the law.'

'Will you not get the phone?'

'I mean, come on – you'd be carted off under whatever phonetic code they use for overdoses. Oscar Delta, or something. You'd be identified as a junkie. Then I'd be stigmatised too. I'll not be having it, Buns, I'm sorry.'

'It's only a spliff, for Christ's sake – paramedics don't give a toss, they're just medical people.'

'Well, I'm sorry but I don't think they just are any more. I think they're also charged with keeping the peace. And quite frankly, Buns, for what it's worth, in this day and age, if they're not, they should be. Especially in cases like yours.'

Bunny's face swivelled to Blair. It was the face of a pensioner kicked from his bath-chair. 'Why, mate? What's it all about? This is murder.'

'Don't be naïvely absurd. Anyway, I doubt parasiticide's a crime. You can probably buy a spray for it at Patel's.'

'This is well out of order. We've only got each other, I mean to say.'

'Well, I haven't only got you. After today I might never have to see you again.'

44

'How's that then?'

'Never you mind.'

Bunny looked down, then up again. His lips trembled. 'Can you not put yourself in my position for one minute? You might feel suddenly free, but spare a thought for old Bunny. You and me and a bit twirl of a Saturday night is all I've got in the world. Mate? Blair?'

Blair ran a hand over the starchy remains of his coif. 'Well, realistically, Buns, if you can say all that you can't be too badly off.' He strode through the doorway, bristling erect with fresh power. 'I'm off to the register office, then I'm out for the rest of the day with Nicki. And if this does turn into my lucky day, and I bring her back here to find that you're not dead, or at very least in a profound vegetative state, I will kill you myself. Do you hear?'

Bunny paused mid-wince. 'You're not going to try and pull our Nicolah?'

'Never you mind.'

'Get away, you can't poach Nickers.'

'Well, I can, actually. And I'll not have you using pejorative names for her.'

'I mean to say, Blair. She's only come down as a courtesy – it's probably on carer expenses.'

'Well, if you're dead you won't mind, will you?'

'But she's our bloody carer, have some grace.'

'Not any more. Anyway, I mean that's just the point: the ice is broken, we understand and respect each other. I know it might be slightly above your capacity to reason.'

'She knows you haven't got a belly button, you mean. Tad less explaining to do before Albion Sports Day. Bit of a soft target there, sunshine. Did Matron turn you down then?'

'You just get on with your coronary.' Blair lanced his new

45

leather coat off the kitchen bench, jangled his keys in his jeans pocket, and burst upstairs like a suicide bomber. 'And if work phones, I'm off doing research.'

'Are you bollocks.'

'Well, I'd bloody call it research.' The front door crashed behind him.

Bunny's eyes fell. The sight of his body in the bath – a rippling white mouse on browned enamel – didn't invite reality's pea to its cup. What's more, a silkworm buoyed up from his pelvis, cheerful to be drowned.

He pulled some straggles of hair from his face, and peered through the doorway. Night's gravy was thinning. Although the basement's tiny street-level window was shut, its net curtain wavered, hoovering air from the road: a road spread like toast with a Marmite of diesel soot and pigeon shit. Bunny tried to ignore the hoot of car alarms and sirens starting to rise like banshee cries across the borough. They unnerved him, made him mindful of the violent tangle around him, the city of lurid reflections on fetid tarmac, the hamster-wheel of never-quites. From what he'd seen of it, and the crossfire of air-kisses that drove it, he could easily imagine women's loins also sported siren packs – mound-enhancing quim klaxons whose notes rasped or chirped the day's pubic airs, just for fashion's sake. Just for Blair.

Bunny sighed.

He hunched like a grub in a bath in a basement of a city with a bosom not only big enough to support pan-pipe minstrels from Ecuador, but to suckle so many that some wore Red Indian costumes to gain a competitive edge. A world of children playing adults, and adults playing children, a place too busy watching itself in the mirror to be bothered with the likes of him.

Each lonely musing brought a thrust of plasma, and each thrust of plasma spurted words into Bunny's mind. Syllables

46

clotted into scornful pearls like 'Myocardial Infarction' and 'Cardiac Arrest'. Purulent whores like 'Superior Vena Cava' skewed and tore like puff-pastry petals before his mind's eye.

'Stay this side of the gate,' he whispered.

The Gate was a concept of Bunny's, a mental tool he had devised to help him cope with the world around him. It described the gate of acceptance, where one collected new instructions for a reduced life. For example: a man with good eyes might be grateful for his sight in a philosophical way. The thought of becoming blind might chill him, but he would hate the thought in a simple way, because he knew nothing of the peculiarities of blindness. For all he knew there might be a hundred species of blindness. He might think you simply went blind, but once his sight had left him, and he passed through the gate, he would find a new book of odds to accept, a new raft of things to wish for, or worry about. There might be a kind of blindness where one's eyes stayed bright, and looked normal to others. Once the man accepted he was blind at all, this would be a good kind of blindness. Or there might be a kind where one's eyes turned milky, or their pupils darted painfully about. This kind would be bad. A healthy man would not have to imagine these sub-species of dismay, wouldn't imagine the relief of having good compared to bad blindness. Until he passed through the gate, where glossy young experts peddled new realities, made you feel engaged in the upper-middle order of a game of endless scope, with people worse off beneath you, and possibilities ahead for gain.

When the truth would just be: you were blind.

How Bunny wished they had stayed up north. Oh for the tea-stained water-colour that was Albion House Institution; her still corridors; her stately grounds, which summer's explosion made into a kind of Borneo without monkeys; her gentle routines

47

attended by the sort of disappointed birdsong that comes like a sigh after silence, that lives only to lament the tinkle of cutlery on china.

To some, Albion was just a receptacle for the grossly unfortunate, a sinister presence behind ancient trees. But she was the only home the boys had ever known. They had fluttered strangely out of Albion. Butterflies released as bats. Nobody really knew what would happen.

The optimistic presumed there would be a great devouring of life.

Bunny sighed again, and dragged a hand over his face. Apart from his health, and fears about his health, and growing fears about those fears, he knew if he survived the day he had but one labour before him: to put Blair in his proper place. And it seemed there was a new instrument in the equation of power: the care worker, Nicolah Wilson.

Bunny chewed his lip.

Nicolah Wilson dreamt of a life of chilled guanabana kisses. Of careless urban spunk to an ethnic groove. Hers were the dreams of New Britannia, a fluorescent whirlwind, a mad-for-it merry-go-round of effortless cool and truth, of wide-jawed laughter at not very much at all.

Whereas Blair's urges had the flush of an angry mandrill's arse.

Perhaps Bunny had best wait up for them.

5

'Because somebody must examine him for a cause of death, you can't just bury a person without papers. That would be murder.' Irina sent a testy push of her chin to the shack.

'Well, it might sound clever to you as it steps from your mouth, but it brings to my ears the wingbeats of money flying away.' Olga chewed emptily in her chair by the stove.

'It won't cost us what we haven't got! It just has to be done, to rule out malicious killing.'

'What I'm trying to put before your face are the obvious facts – the district is cultivating dead soldiers like peas, do you think a man follows them all around to make papers?'

'And listen to me: if Aleks fails to redeem his pension they will send an inspector to see. And then the whole flock of beetles will be loose. Can you imagine the business we would give an inspector if he came?'

'But, Irina –'

'Anyway, it's too late, I've sent for the man through Nadezhda. He'll come up just now. The questions will only grow harder the longer we wait.'

'Hoh, well, if it's Nadezhda you've sent, be sure and leave a note on your grave for the man.'

'Well, she still has some sense, Mama! Don't waste another breath with your rabies, I've also now heard the Uvila road is under attack from Gnezvariks. We must get Ludmila out before real dark falls. This is the last day for travel east.'

As she said it, a chill wriggled through her. Winds gathered strength in the gullies, howling gales of change.

'And are you just going to leave Aleksandr lying on the tractor like a missed potato?' Olga called from the gloom. 'Shall we dump hay and shit on him as well, to show how we honour our beloved? You were probably hoping a few good bites were taken out of him by wolves in the night, to demonstrate how graciously we live in these mountains! Some good wolf-bites taken out of him, so everyone can suspect us of insulting nature due to hunger!'

'Mama!' Irina shouted. 'You're making the day too hard! Kindly collect your senses. Because we revere Aleksandr, we have kept him outside where he is best preserved. It was only one night, wolves won't cross the fence. And to leave the body there until the examiner comes is pure intelligence – because he will imagine the death is just after happening.'

'Hoh! His own death will probably be long after happening if it's Nadezhda you've sent to fetch him.'

'Mama!'

'Well, at least bring those sacks off his face!'

'Those aren't sacks, it's Milochka's coat that she has kindly assigned to serve her grandpapa's dignity. Listen to me: when his death is properly written, he'll come inside for a bit. Now please don't steal everyone's ears away from the day's important business. The front is nearly here, let's get Ludmila away.'

Maksimilian loped smoking up the hillside track. He huddled deep in his coats, and wore a fuzzy military hat pilfered on an excursion near the front.

Irina tossed her chin as he entered the yard. 'And how do we only now see your miserable face?'

'And didn't you prefer not to see it?'

'Don't let me find you've wasted the morning anywhere in the

50

vicinity of Viktor Pilosanov. Or anyone whose name starts with Pilo. And where have you found cigarettes?'

Maks stopped and glared through a pall of tobacco smoke that hung stationary around his head, a buffer between him and the bastard world. 'And if it's not a crime to ask, how is it that by simply treading footsteps I can attract the collected blames of history?'

His mother flapped her hands to her hips. 'If you'd been to the village you would know the roads are falling. Ludmila has to go!'

'Well, I wish her good travels.'

'And you are to carry her!'

'Hoh, yes,' spat Maks, 'on the tractor so that she can be old and dead when she arrives to even the nearest city, to find a very important job as an old and dead person.'

Irina spared herself the boredom of a sigh. She wrung her hands in her apron, and beached a fat eye on her son. Beyond the yard, through a traffic of rolling mist, came Ludmila. She carried two buckets stuffed with shrub branches. She looked around, imagining her lover behind every crest. Then she looked into the yard. From afar she sensed another fissure of hostility, and slowed her trudge to a loiter.

'Maksimilian,' Irina squared up to her son, 'misery has invited itself into the house, it falls to us to be astute hosts. The big train won't be back until next week. We could all be dead by then. There's only the goat and two chickens, we could have eaten them, and every wild animal and insect in the Forty-One, and still be dead.' She paused to let the moment's weight find him. 'But the tractor has fuel. Take it to Kuzhnisk – and sell it. Get the best price. Bring the cake directly back to me. Only that will keep us until Ludmila draws her first pay. Your family counts on you, Maksimilian. The sharp point of our history, and the last

51

drop of our blood, waits for you. This is your time, Maks – hit, kill, and eat.'

'Hoh, so now sell the tractor. Sell the tractor so that our empty bones can be found on the place where they fell without assets to borrow against. Any reasonable person, who is a person not touched by the mania of a woman's grief, would first sell some of this land.'

'Yes, any goose from your world of dreams. They'd sell it to the first of the hundred people who queue here every day to buy ice minefields at the front line.' Irina threw back her head. 'Do you know how big is the district of the Forty-One? Answer me!'

'Big enough.'

'I'll tell you this: it's not much bigger than seventy thousand hectares. But seventy thousand hectares is the area already seized by Gnezvarik military. And do you think they walk with wads of cake, buying up snow as they go? They're sealing the roads around us, strangling us even as I stand wasting my breath on a maggot's arse. This land now belongs to nobody. Maksimilian, I beg you, as the mother who chewed your food for you – honour your blood.'

'Hoh, and of course we're to believe all we hear from the mad Nadezhda, or the mongol Lubov!'

'Maksimilian!'

His brow found some mauve distance. 'And now sell the tractor – hoh! – so future generations can escape the shock of finding our bones somewhere splendid because we managed to escape this hell on our Lipetsk tractor.' His words sped to a tangle, then tangled to a mutter.

Irina stood firm and silent. It was her way of telling him what he already knew: cash alone would save them.

'And why doesn't Ludmila go to Georgi and Yelena, live on jam with her cousins outside Labinsk?'

Irina chuckled darkly. 'As if they would take her, after they've not once spared a kopek for us. Anyway, that's not work, just charity. She must become productive. And you must take her with the tractor, and return here with some weeks' worth of life in cash.'

'Well, at least now you can thank me for the Ubli hat, with which I'll roam the district at my perfect pleasure.'

Irina stared him down. 'And as the soldiers all drive tractors to war you won't look stupid at all! No hat, Maksimilian. In fact, I want the hat buried. These are real men's games now.'

'Hoh! Don't concern yourself with the business of men and guns.'

'I won't – as I have neither in the house.' Irina speared him with an eye.

Maks pretended not to hear. He swaggered a pointless circuit around the yard.

Ludmila crossed in front of him, pausing to shake her boot at the passing goat. When she reached the mishmash of the shack's wall, she rested a hand on one of its tin panels; it bled warmth from the stovepipe behind. 'Don't get worms over me,' she said. 'I can walk.'

'Hoh!' spat Maks. 'And be violated and probably killed, probably violated with the barrel of a gun by some Gnezvar turd-eater. You'll come on the tractor with me, and when the tractor empties of fuel, and I sell it, you'll have the world of Kuzhnisk at your feet, though I wouldn't personally go there so much as to spit.'

'Mama,' said Ludmila, 'why can't we just sign Aleksandr's vouchers? Who needs to know he's dead?'

'You make more of your father's noises each day! And will you be the one to bury Aleksandr and dress in his clothes? And will you be the one answering to the inspectorate? Saints lash sense into you!'

At this, Olga appeared through the door for just long enough to grunt, and shake her head in condemnation. When she shook her head for such purposes, the shake always ended with a quick upward toss of her chin in the condemned's direction. Around Administrative District Forty-One, this was called the Push.

Ludmila folded her arms, and dangled sceptically against the breeze. 'Do you seriously think these voucher paperworks will stay important once bullets start flying up the hill?'

'Cut that mouth!' Irina fetched her daughter a swipe. 'The difference between the crimes that travel with soldiers, and the crime that you ignorantly propose, is that soldiers keep moving on. We, saints please it, will still be here waiting with our crimes to be discovered.'

Another shake, and a push, from Olga, who emptied a bowl of black dishwater beside the step. 'For the chicken,' she snorted, turning back inside. 'That it might have a life like the lives of my family, who live on a holiday of sunshine and jams while I rot in my bed.'

Irina sent a push to Ludmila. 'Indeed, that life of a princess must be grand, to have so much time to stand counting straw on the ground.'

'I don't want to go,' Ludmila scowled.

'Then you make it hard for yourself. Because you are going.'

'Well, I'm not. I should find other avenues, at least until the fighting passes.'

'And what you fail to understand is that the fighting might not pass, it might chase us ahead of it. Then where will we go? And how?' Irina took a step towards Ludmila, swinging a finger at the shack. 'When the door of this house is shut tonight, you will be outside of it. And don't imagine to run away with your little friend – you will go the munitions factory in Kuzhnisk. Your face will not be welcome here until you have a regular wage. Try and

54

think of something other than yourself, this is for all of us, Milochka.'

Ludmila's eyes fell. 'Then I might as well leave now, and never come back.' She stamped up the single flagstone into the shack. 'As you've revealed your joy at the concept.'

'Maks,' Irina chuckled, 'we could use your telephones after all, if this is how long it takes your sister to get the message.' She followed her daughter inside.

'And a question for you,' Maks mused after them. 'Is Aleksandr's body to make the journey as well? Shall we find him a desk at the factory?'

Irina stopped inside the door. 'If the examiner hasn't come by the time you leave, we'll carry him down off the tractor.'

'What examiner?'

'The man to examine for the death. And in the time it takes him to come, you can get the tractor ready to travel, instead of loafing in a smell like the goat.'

'Well, is there piss saved?' Maks shouted after her.

'No! Don't!' came Olga's muffled cry. 'Your grandfather said it definitely doesn't work, and it will even stop the engine for good!'

'I mean from the goat,' called Maks, vacuuming from his throat a spittle projectile destined for the rooster's head.

'That's what I mean! Don't use piss, not any of it.'

Taking careful aim, Maks fired a slug from his mouth that near as well took out the rooster's eye. Still it stood defiant, swayed by a possibility of spilt nutrients by the step. 'Well, it's not what you mean,' shouted Maks, 'because old man Aleks used to piss into the tank himself and then complain it wouldn't run. I mean to add goat's piss, like everyone says to. It even makes the machine faster, or else why would everyone save it in buckets?'

Irina burst through the door. 'Watch me,' she stormed to the tractor, and yanked off the grease tin that served as a fuel cap. She thrust into the tank a long twig that was kept under the seat, the fuel gauge having long since released its ghost – ironically on the day in its life when the tank was full. She pulled out the stick, and held it in Maksimilian's face. 'Is that half a tankful?'

'No,' said Maks without looking.

'Yes it is, so you can at least get to Uvila and beg fuel. No piss. Now go.'

'We're not going to Uvila, it's the wrong way.'

Irina raised the stick and lashed the boy till he hissed. Then she glowered for a moment before bustling away spouting puffs of steam.

'Anyway, we're going direct to Kuzhnisk!' Maks shouted at the rolls of her back.

A curtain separated Ludmila's military bunk from the shack's two rooms; the main room embraced a kitchen corner, with something like a large iron shoe-box that was the dung burner and stove, connected by a pipe to the roof. In its orbit, like ducklings, were a table covered in plastic, three folding chairs, and two petrol drums aspiring to be occasional tables. A small window opposite Ludmila's cubicle threw handfuls of light like grains of pollen on to the floor. The only bedroom held two sagging beds of different heights – the lowest for Irina and, until recently, Kiska, who had since decided she would mature more quickly sleeping in her sister's cubicle, and the tallest bed for Olga and Aleksandr. Maksimilian had taken to sleeping on the floor by the shack's front door. He had vowed never to enter the bedroom again, after his unkind reaction to a glimpse of his grandmother's bare bottom had sparked days of bitter emotional combat the summer before.

Ludmila stood naked behind her curtain, fussing through her clothes in their musty holdall. Irina had hidden it outdoors overnight, dampening its contents. Ludmila rummaged idly, sucking in the malty dark of her home, the smoke of her vanished childhood. A blade of light crossed the room to burn the edge of her curtain; she drew the curtain back to splash herself in the light, flexing before her mirror to make it pool and play around her hollows and curves. She met herself staring, and pouted.

Her eyes threw animals back.

Wriggling into faded, psychedelic briefs, she opened the trunk that formed the base of Kiska's bed, and pulled out a red woollen dress stored in plastic. Her father had bought it for her eighteenth birthday. He said she would never look like a farm girl again. What's more, he declared, she would look like a princess. And he was right, mad Ivan, for once in his life, though he'd been less than usually refreshed when he said it.

An artillery round thudded behind the mountain. For a moment it drowned out the mothers' bickering in the yard, where Maks could be heard defending a plan to steal fuel – or rather, borrow it, as he insisted – from the ironmonger's widow.

Ludmila didn't hear Kiska swish through the curtain behind her. She felt a little hand on her thigh, and spun around.

A cushion of tongue appeared at the gap in Kiska's teeth. She raised a finger to her lips. Ludmila scowled, and followed another little finger through the curtain to the back window.

Misha Bukinov was there.

6

Whistling thunder chased Blair and Nicolah home that night. It trailed the day's first flight rolling low overhead into Heathrow, crackly with sleep from the east. Daylight was hours behind it, barely broken over Kuzhnisk as the pair billowed over the sort of wet that lives on London's pavements without ever having fallen. Whiffs of Blair's new life pulsed through the chill, shone on the wings of parked Mercedes; flashes of hard driving to hard music at night, of sex before breakfast before jetting away on air miles. A life without fastidious thought, a world of charming disarray. London was a power grid churning with such potentials. Blair was electrified by her possibilities. The charge didn't escape Nicolah Wilson.

'I've had worse days than today,' she said, with a squeeze of his arm.

'Don't sound so surprised.' Blair braced his jaw like a yachtsman.

'I had me doubts about you two. Not everyone's got on with relocation.'

'We've only come from the north.'

'You know what I mean.'

'Well, it's a hunting ground, isn't it?' Blair reached for her hand. 'Young man on the move, and what have you.'

'Oh yeah.'

'Well, you know. I mean, I hope I don't have to map out all the details.'

'God help the girl who ends up breaking you in.'

'Now I didn't actually say that. I'm after something more than just that sort of thing.' Blair paused. 'No thoughts of family yourself?'

'Slit me wrists first. Can't be doing with no grief.'

'Still.' Blair took wide, bouncing steps – partly in aid of balance, partly to achieve the correct billow for his oncoming life of cashmere strewn carelessly over teak. 'I mean to say.'

Nicki snorted gently. 'That's just what Bunny'd say.'

'What?'

'"I mean to say." I didn't recognise you when I saw your poncey hairdo, and your bit of weight you've taken off. But you're still Bunny's other half. It's weird.'

A pucker rippled Blair's cheek. 'Well, I haven't come out to discuss the junkie.'

'You what?'

'We've lost Bunny, I'm afraid. Cannabis all over the flat.'

'He hooked up fast. I was going to bring him some down.'

'Well, I'm sorry but I can't dignify that sort of thing any more.'

'What's up with you all of a sudden?'

'I just can't be doing with this absurd co-dependent escapist lark any longer. I'm on a new trajectory.'

Nicki's eyes rose over the horizon. 'Still, eh? Bless. I mean, there's something about Buns, everyone really misses him. And you, of course. But old Bunny, I mean – there's something really timeless. What you going to tell him about the register office?'

'I don't have to tell him anything, it wasn't him I was going for. He's not my master, you know.'

'All right.'

'Well, I mean, it's not up to me if the thing's moved overseas. How am I to know?'

59

'All right!'

The pair bullied a feral supermarket trolley off the road, kicked a fried chicken box into the gutter, and negotiated a trail of pet excreta laid out with the cunning of a show-jumping course. They strolled deep into the maze of Victorian rows, past the Patel brothers' corner shop, where no banknote would be examined against the light for another two hours, under the iron railway bridge, quiet save for the sniff and rustle of sleeping pigeons, to finally skirt the corner of Tooting Common which sixteen weeks earlier had been a hotbed of latte-froth interplay, and which in six months would see a next curiously tanned generation, the previous having bought twin prams and decamped to the counties.

For that was the city's speed. A lurid juggernaut in its gran's old bloomers. Somewhere in London's gizzard stood a lever that drove it, but with no setting for fast or slow, no notch forward or back. Its welded lever read: 'Gone. Mind the fucking gap.'

The pair turned into Scombarton Road. The shining Mercedes of leafier streets gave way to older Mercedes sporting massage-bead seat covers, exotic dashboard trim, and smelling, even through the cold and glass and steel, of taxi deodoriser. A ragged fox dragged swirls of fog into the alley beside number 16A. Nicki tucked herself into the crook of Blair's arm, street-lamp highlights cartooning her gentle creole face.

'Well – we're here,' she said.

'Here we are.' Blair sidled close, sipping the chill of her hair. 'Are you about tomorrow as well?'

'I thought they'd set you up a job?'

'I'm off this week.'

'Your first bloody week? Listen, mate, you're the only ex-resident I've heard of getting straight into a job. Somebody must be pulling strings from the inside, don't chuck it away.'

'Well, I mean, Bunny's not working.'

'That's different, he's not recovered. Anyway, as you ask about my plans, I should give him some time while I'm down. Can't play favourites.' Nicki dragged friendship's limp hand down a non-erogenous panel of Blair's jacket, and stepped up to the door. 'I'd kill for a cuppa just now, though. Try'n not wake Bunny.'

'He's dead,' grunted Blair, foraging for his keys.

'You what?'

'Apparently. Cardiac event.'

'You've not left him having one of his turns?' Nicki batted aside his arms, and snatched out the keys.

Blair followed her through the door, hunched into the dark of his collar. Frayed matting sneezed dust around her trainers as she banged down into the murk. The settees were empty. 'What you done with him?'

'Drowned him in the bath,' Blair shambled after her, careful to visit the stairs' creakier edges. He steadied himself against the banister to kick off a shoe.

'Bloody hell – Buns? Bunny?'

'It's a joke,' huffed Blair, launching a shoe downstairs.

'*You're* a bloody joke. Buns – can you hear me, darling?' Nicolah found the light switch and clicked it on to find Bunny lying on his side on the kitchen floor. He wore his black suit, white shirt, and evergreen dark glasses. The unshorn goat's mop that usually spewed from his head was pulled into a ponytail. He was barefoot. Beside him sat a glass tumbler, a brandy bottle mostly lonely for brandy, and an ashtray overflowing with half-smoked Rothmans – half-smoked because Bunny felt safe, in a cardio-vascular sense, between cigarettes, and always scurried back to the space between them.

He lifted his head an inch and ogled Nicki sideways.

She examined the scene, taking off her coat to squat beside him. Blair watched her buttocks strain shiny against the cloth of her trousers, conjured for himself the view Bunny must have of her, tortured himself imagining the warm cline that might rise to his face.

'You okay, Buns?' she reached a hand to his forehead. 'You shun't be drinking, bloody hell. Christ, mate. You shun't drink at all, what's going on? Bunny? What you doing in the kitchen?'

'Handy for the glassware.'

'But why you all dressed up?'

Bunny's mouth dropped open, dangling teeth over his lip. 'We were due at therapy tonight, Blair and me. But as things go, I've probably done as well to stop in.'

'Well now, hang on,' Blair boomed over the bench, 'have I not made it perfectly clear I won't be doing any more Group? I'm sorry but you can't come that old ruse with Nicki.'

'Ooh, ooh, ooh,' squeaked Bunny, 'he's grown out of his Group. Well, Group's come down to Simon's tonight specially, so we wouldn't have to travel. I hope that makes you feel better. Come all this way down. And Simon was saving back a lid of that skunk for me, so you've completely ballsed up my fucking world as well.'

'Well, you've just talked yourself out of any possible sympathy we might have had. You've completely justified our not having gone.'

'Have I bollocks.'

Nicki flicked a scowl over the bench, then helped Bunny sit with his back to the stove. 'I'm sorry, Buns – he never said you had Group. You knew I was down, why didn't you call?'

'More than me bloody life's worth. Anyway, as I say, I've probably done as well to stop in. I've had what they call a Cardiac Event – bugger knows on what scale.'

'Define the scale then!' shouted Blair. 'Does it range from sudden death, to rolling about the floor bladdered on cooking brandy?'

Bunny twisted his mouth towards the bench. 'High-powered day at work, was it? Graft was it today, at the sandwich activator factory, Blair?'

'Bugger off, you know I haven't properly started. Anyway, we don't make the applicators, we only supply the global markets intelligence.'

Nicolah pouted over the bench at Blair. 'You said you was off for the week!'

'Well, work experience isn't a job, he's just winding you up.'

'You still have to bloody go.'

'I'm off sick this week.'

'Aye,' chuckled Bunny, 'Repetitive Strain – which hand was it?'

'Piss off.' Blair clenched himself shut and stormed to a settee.

Bunny molested his inside pocket for a Rothmans. The cigarette trembled as it touched his lips. Nicki watched, and frowned. 'I'd best call someone.'

'Oh, I've tried the telephone.' Bunny waved a hand. 'There's nobody there.'

Nicki sharpened her gaze. 'How much have you had to drink?'

Bunny threw a volley of blinks into the middle distance.

'Buns, come on,' she tugged at his sleeve, and lifted the bottle. 'Have you had all this?'

Blair bowled into the kitchen, arms flapping. 'Look, he's necked the lot. Leave him, you'll play right into his hands. He's been on the lash all night, look. It's ridiculous.'

Nicki took a swipe at Blair's leg. 'Sod off! Honestly, you two.'

'I mean, it's just not on!' Blair stamped back to his settee.

'Oi!' cried Nicki. 'Both of you – shut it, till we sort this out.'

Bunny sucked a wad of smoke, and swivelled to watch Nicki's ringlets peck her shoulders. The simplicity of her stance always touched him. 'I'm here, and this is bloody me,' it said. His sympathies flew to the curve of her back. 'I'll be all right,' he whispered, patting her smooth brown hand.

'Yeah, but I'm up to me neck in it. We're calling somebody.'

'Well, don't do that,' snapped Blair. 'They'll have us both away, for Christ's sake.'

Bunny clicked his tongue. 'Blair – we're individuals now, you've said it time and again. Nobody'll come for you – it's a clinical concern of mine, I can't just hide away from clinical concerns, I mean to say.'

'You're conspiring,' said Blair. 'You're both conspiring to have us shut away again and I won't have it. I won't have it!'

'Oi!' shrilled Nicki. 'Do you honestly reckon I'll sit about and wait for it all to be my bleeding fault?'

'For Christ's sake! Well, so help me, Bunny, if we're fetched back to Albion because of this I will bloody kill you myself. Do you hear?'

Bunny hung a dull eye on his brother. 'You're obsessed. Try and catch a hold of yourself, Blair?'

'Just you piss well off.'

'You're on the turn, mate. Mark my words, madness there lies.' Bunny tried to twist the bottle from Nicki's hand. She grabbed it away, stretching to stand it on the bench. Her fingertips found the phone, and pulled it down.

'Anyway, I've tried the phone,' said Bunny. 'Nobody's there.'

'Who've you tried?'

'Everyone.'

'You know it's all changed?'

'Yes, in that it has ceased to be.'

'No, I mean it's all Vitaxis now. You have to dial a new system and use your PIN number.'

'Is that the National Health then?'

'Vitaxis, it's what I'm telling you – it's all private now, you have to ring a main number.' Nicki prised Bunny's eyes from the bottle on the bench. 'Honestly, Bunny' – she punched some keys on the telephone, and waited – 'me bleeding granddad barely remembers the National Health. Make yourself useful, put the kettle on.'

On his settee, Blair's face drained of warmth. It drained of two sessions' worth of costly tan. He felt it so. He covered it with his hands, and slumped forward.

Nicki brought the phone and sat beside him. 'Hello? It's Nicolah Wilson here, from Warm Aftercare – six one four nine three nine eight. South-east. Three seven four seven. Wilson. Heath. Is it too early to speak to Doctor Compton?'

There came an instrumental cover of 'Reck ma Skank' by Pirie Jammette, then: 'Yes?' A drowned oboe reed, the doctor's voice. 'What seems to be the matter?'

'Chest pain, and shortness of breath,' hissed Bunny from the kitchen.

'And discomfort in our left arm and shoulder,' Nicki repeated into the phone.

'Which one of them feels unwell?'

'Bunny. I mean Gordon.'

'I see. Can you discern any blue or purple around his lips?'

'No.'

'Is his pulse racing, or irregular?'

'No. But he may have had a drink.'

Bunny gave a naughty shrug at the sink.

Compton paused to clear his throat. 'I see. Is he perspiring, clammy?'

'Not really – he says he had an event earlier.'

65

'I see, I see. Neither of them should drink, you know. Quite apart from their liver function, I'm afraid it might precipitate an emotional episode of some sort. This is still uncharted psychological territory. Has the other one been drinking as well?'

'Just a couple of pints.'

'I see. Well. As for these symptoms, if it were the first time –'

'I hear you, doctor.'

'Don't embarrass him over it, stress can have a surprisingly powerful effect. Perhaps you should put him on.'

Nicolah skipped to the bar and handed the phone to Bunny. He held the handset to his chest while his telephone voice assembled. 'Sorry, Spencer, it's only my old carry-on.'

'The thing is, Gordon, you're in the community now. I'm just concerned that things might get on top of you both, it's still early days. Wouldn't you feel more comfortable back in care, until things are stabilised? I think I'd feel more comfortable with you back in care, or home with your family.'

'We haven't contact with our family.'

'Of course, of course – I'm sorry.'

Blair sprang from the settee, and snatched the handset from Bunny. 'Doctor? Have you not specifically told me not to make a fuss over his turns?'

'The thing is,' said Compton, 'panic's pretty common, and can be highly debilitating. A majority of people will suffer it at some point.'

'But did you not tell me not to fuss?' Blair hit the speaker button, brandishing the phone at Nicolah, then Bunny.

'Well, certainly there's no sense compounding the fright, although –'

'See?' screamed Blair. '*See!*'

'Not to worry, not to worry,' Compton's voice buzzed lonely through the handset. 'It's early days, big change of routine. Once things fall into place in your minds, you'll find these episodes decrease in frequency and severity. Settle yourselves down, not too much tea or coffee. And *no alcohol,* for goodness' sake. I might order an assessment. I'm not at all comfortable with things as they are.'

Blair's eyes narrowed tight. Bunny shuffled out from behind the bench, lifted two cups of milky tea, and floated them towards the settee. A smile flickered over his face. 'So,' he cooed, 'what else did our Spencer say?'

'That you're going to die.'

'Oi!' Nicolah slapped his leg.

Bunny hunched feebly, and turned to rest the teacups on the bench. He curled an eye over his back like Quasimodo, and sent a pitiful shrug to Nicolah. Her eyes cradled him. He smelt on Blair a seething potential: serious conflict, and its shimmer; the twin wraiths of ridicule and remorse that hang waiting above anger's madness. Bunny turned side-on, still hunched like a serf awaiting the cat-o'-nine, and pointed empty eyes at his brother. He sighed. 'I take it you didn't get your snog then.'

'Bunny!' Nicki squealed.

Blair's eyes snapped left. He caught her swallowing a giggle. And that was that. 'Why don't you just shag him?' His eyes didn't pierce, neither burn nor stab her. This was the disquieting thing. They shone unseeing. They drew attention to the whites not only above, but beneath, their pupils. 'Ooh Buns darlin', ooh,' he whined. 'Ooh Bunny this, ooh Bunny that. Well, what about bloody *me!*'

Nicki tightened her arms across her chest. 'I hear you, don't get vex.'

'Ahh, love's a sickness full of woes,' tutted Bunny over his shoulder.

Nicolah watched Blair brooding, balding, puckering like an

anus, on command from middle-English genes, fusty, bile-sodden genes leering envy and fear. Then, like a cable snapping, he snatched up the brandy bottle and flung it across the kitchen. Bunny watched it explode against the stove.

Nicolah's shriek rocked the gloom. She sprang to her feet, snatched her coat, choked curses up each stair to the door, and tossed them over her shoulder all the way up Scombarton Road.

Then came still like the still after a gunfight. A car furrowed the wet outside, a distant siren chirped. And after a moment, Blair's unearthly sobs seized the air. Growing pains, Matron called them. Bunny edged to his brother's side on the settee. Slowly he turned his eyes, then his head, to his brother.

'Well,' he said, 'you've your work cut out for you there.'

Blair snorted, a bubble popped from a nostril. He pointed it up at the window, and tried, as he sucked it back, to suck London's high-voltage coat with it, the mad coat with its pong of reckless camaraderie and brake soot.

But only the naff electric whirr of a milk float wafted down.

Bunny shuffled to the television, and switched it on. A pair of stout, skinheaded young Englishmen appeared, weeping into the camera. The scene of a tragedy. Bunny frowned. As the men's story unfolded over sunburnt tattoos, it transpired that a baggage-handlers' strike had delayed their package flight overnight in Malaga. Puffy children in Millwall kit appeared sniffling beside them: radish-coloured women lurked behind.

'See?' said Bunny. 'There's always someone worse off than yourself.'

Blair crackled some snot.

'Ahh, well,' Bunny switched off the set, and returned to the settee. 'Cheer up, mate. Friday tomorrow: shepherd's pie.'

With a tuneful hum, as the most brazen birds of grey morning took pluck from the light, he put a hand to Blair's heaving back, and ever-so-gently traced a circle. 'Who's a silly sausage?' he said in his softest northern drone. It was the first complete sentence he'd ever learned to say. It throbbed memories of antiseptic and pooey rubber. Bunny rocked back and forth, and traced the first of a hundred gentle circles.

'Who's a silly sausage?'

7

Ludmila clutched the dress to her chest, and flapped a hand at Kiska. 'Go to the door, quickly – sing if anyone comes.'

'And but what song?' Kiska stood writhing with excitement, dangling like a puppet on the spot.

'Anything, just sing loudly.' Ludmila flew to the window, and unlatched it. Misha's face burst through, ears glowing red.

'The railway song, or the mountain-dog song?'

'The railway song – now go! Quick!'

The little girl had scarcely turned when Misha took Ludmila's shoulders through the window, and kissed her three times about the face. She leant across the frame and buried herself into the rough of his military coat. 'Hoh,' she prodded his belly, 'they're turning you into two soldiers.'

Misha scraped his whiskers over her hair, parted it with his nose. 'Because if nobody keeps their appointments with me, I can only linger by the pot and wonder why.'

'Aleks died, they found my bag packed. The mothers are twisted rabid. They're sending me to Kuzhnisk.'

Misha held her head in his hands, brushed a lock of hair from her eyes. 'Did someone strike you on the face? Look at this bruise.'

'I fell, it's nothing.'

'I'm sorry about the old man. Saints speed him. Are you still able to come away? Patrol moves over the mountain in the morning – if we don't do it now –'

'To the front? Mishi, that's not for you.'

'But if we can't get away? I'll only escape lashes for desertion if I leave the country, and I won't go without you.'

'You could wait for me, in a place. I could come in a few days, after my first pay.'

Misha shook his head. 'But gather your cuckoos – the only way we can stay overseas is to ask for asylum at the port of entry. We have to be together – after that you enter a system, we might never find each other again.'

Ludmila thought a moment. 'And who's to say they will even let us in?'

'They have to let you in, once you're there. You get to stay while they investigate your status. We almost definitely would get through – me a deserter, from a place raining bombs.' He ran a finger over her glowing cheek. 'And you, they would usher in immediately, with such a shine on your cheek. They'd fetch a pot of coffee and a table of fruit and chocolates after a look at you.'

Kiska began to sing at the door. Ludmila spun around. The little girl paused, hissing a laugh. 'I'm practising.'

'Goose! Save it for when someone really comes.'

Misha pressed his face to Ludmila's cheekbone, kissing it between words. 'Listen, when are you going to Kuzhnisk?'

'Just now, today. But they're sending Maksimilian all the way on the tractor, I don't know if I'll see a moment to escape.'

'Then here: past the station, on the principal road in Kuzhnisk, on a corner, is the Café-Bar Kaustik. I will come there tomorrow, to arrive after dark. But hear me: times are uncertain, forces are gathering towards the bridge. Travel quickly, and don't worry if I come late – I'll find my way, I tell you with my heart.'

'Men move the trains, and trains move the men!' Kiska screamed from the door.

'And Kiski, in saints' name!' Irina scolded as she neared the step. 'You'll shout the snows off the roof!'

'Go, fat soldier.' Ludmila pecked Misha's lips and pushed the window shut.

'Tell me again tomorrow if I'm fat,' he mouthed, touching a finger to the pane before ducking away.

Ludmila flew behind her curtain. Within ten seconds, Irina's shadow soaked over it, moving to the gap by the wall. She watched with full eyes as Ludmila uncoiled from a crouch, untapping a spring of muscles across her back. Milochka was not a peasant gorgon, thick-boned and lead-footed like so many in the district. Green eyes made her a rarity, as did her strange aloofness and poise. Her bottom had even lost its baby fat, Irina reflected, watching puddles of shade empty and fill the dimples behind her briefs.

She scattered the damp from her eyes with a salvo of blinks, and stepped through the curtain.

'What?' mumbled Ludmila, shrugging herself into the dress. 'Am I not leaving quickly enough?'

'And well,' her mother said huskily, 'I thought to tell you where we all plan to be buried, as you'll clearly still be dawdling after three more generations have gone.'

'Hoh,' Ludmila dressed quickly, without another word to her mother, and stepped into the sunlight with her bag, mussing Kiska's curls at the door as she passed.

'Am I to understand the body is coming down, as your man hasn't shown himself?' Maks yelled to the shack as Ludmila lifted her bag into the tractor.

'What man?' she turned to scan the track.

'Whoever it is left to do examining for deaths,' said Maks. He cupped his hands again and shouted; 'I say – are we bringing grandpapa down from the tractor?'

'Yes, if you see no one on the track,' called Irina. 'And bring that coat off his head, Ludmila will need it.'

'No, leave it with him,' said Ludmila.

'Bring off the coat for yourself, you'll freeze,' Irina scowled from the step.

Ludmila helped lift the body from the hoist and lay it on hard ice beside the fence. She toyed with the coat until Maks turned away, then pulled it off quickly behind her. A glimpse of Aleks's gape still infected her eye.

Butter sunlight bathed the shack as Irina, Olga, and a strangely quiet Kiska watched the tractor bounce through hanging cliffs and caves of mist, away down the hill to the road. Neither Ludmila nor Maks looked back. Their mother stood blinking grit until they vanished. Within four minutes, the thick Ublilsk air – in which words and breaths hung motionless from autumn to spring – had absorbed the tractor's chudder.

'A family torn apart,' grunted Olga, turning back inside. 'Get me a voucher, Iri. If I sign it now, you can still have time to reach the depot.'

'Land Cruiser, or Nissan Patrol,' Maks barked over the motor's clatter. 'That's the best. Long wheelbase, with electric windows. You think that's for rich custards? I'll get one just now.'

Tiger stripes of amber light spilt through leafless trees by the road. Ludmila saw no type of examiner making his way up the hill. She squinted ahead to the shadows where her future lived, and adopted the shell of the internal traveller she was, taster of inner breezes, weigher of imperceptible colours, gatherer of emotional intelligence for which no word or expression existed; the shell nobody could fathom, which was put down to aloofness.

Then a familiar wooden telegraph pole approached, followed by the tufted ruin of a grain silo. Ludmila blinked twice,

73

scowled, and turned to Maks. 'And in which way are you going?'

'For instance,' shouted Maks, 'in the last battle for Grozny, a Nissan Patrol with guns made nearly a whole Russian battalion run shitting like old women.'

'Maks-imil-ian!' Ludmila slapped the back of his head. 'You're going in the wrong way!'

'No, I'm going in the perfect way.' Maks leant out of his sister's reach.

'But you've brought me to the village – I can't get anywhere from Ublilsk!'

Maks shrugged. 'This is as far as I come, Darling of Light.'

'Oh-hoh, and when you return home with the tractor still, in no time, you can tell our mothers that a wind helped you to Kuzhnisk and back.'

'We weren't going to Kuzhnisk.'

'I guessed it. I guessed it because you've come to the stupid village instead!'

'Pilo will give you a ride from here.' Maks steered casually around a crater in the road.

'Oh yes, in an instant. Because he sat in his lonely room for all my years only secretly waiting to carry me away to romantic Kuzhnisk.'

In a violent display of nasal suction, Maks cocked a spit parcel in his mouth and pelted it at a passing road sign. 'No,' he said. 'Because I'll tell him to. Now cut your spastic hatch. Too much woman's shit from you.'

Ludmila sat scowling for nine turns of the tractor's wheels. Then she shouted, 'I have to get work in the city! You have to sell the tractor! Wake up the bird in your head, Maks!'

'Pilo is buying the tractor. And Kuzhnisk isn't a city, don't get airs around your tits.'

74

'Oh-hoh, and this is the same Pilosanov who drank away all his cake and his health with my father, and who is now going to miraculously drive me to the city even though he never had a car in all his long life?'

'He'll have a tractor,' shrugged Maks. 'And Kuzhnisk isn't a city.'

Old Nadezhda Krupskaya stopped at the corner beside the depot. She set down her plastic bag and puffed clouds like empty thought bubbles as the tractor throttled back through the village – more a hamlet, in fact, since its population had dwindled to less than thirty.

Nadezhda was a more visible feature on the road since a stray rocket-propelled grenade smashed through her roof and embedded itself in the kitchen floor a year earlier. It remained unexploded, which meant she not only survived to fulfil her slow and noisy decline to the grave – an achievement all Ublis aspired to, and one they treated with the correct sense of competition and pride – but she had rich grounds for ongoing despair, as well as an impetus to vacate the house whenever possible, and take her miseries on tour. Coupled with increasing forgetfulness, if not dementia, her repertoire was by then a polished monologue, a proper feast of sour meals for the saints.

Still, things weren't all roses: the missile's casing had stuck at an inconvenient angle to the stove door, making kitchen duties especially tiresome. This and the hole in the roof eventually prompted her to move into her tiny outhouse – still within a respectable blast's radius, but not quite the potential calamity she had once enjoyed.

Ludmila watched her without waving, until her old tea-cosy-like form slipped behind a grey Soviet slab comprising thirty-six apartments – all but four of them gutted – which was the only optimistic construction the village had ever seen. Aside from that dire block, Ublilsk appeared to have risen organically from the sludge, as if strewn litter had taken root and grown into a patch of buildings bound together with wreckage from the abandoned propeller factory. No fewer than five buildings along the road had frontages that included parts of the factory's main sign, one of these reading the whole word 'Propeller'.

A radio hit blared across the road, featuring an electric guitar that plinked and plonked like a handful of bullets tossed into a pond. Above it whined the desperate voices of a boy and a girl. 'Obsession' was the lyric that stood out. The song's playing in the heart of Ublilsk gave a wistful, romantic air to its dying throes, a sort of languorous tropical yearning that stirred Ludmila to her toes. Suddenly hers was more than just a physical abandonment of home. It was a broken love as well.

The tractor moved past a faceless pile of coats and a puddle of vomit in the snow – a bed and breakfast, as Ludmila's father used to call it – to the outskirt where Viktor Pilosanov lived. The house was number twelve, and was distinguished by its green door. Pilosanov had one day been compelled to visit a town where green paint was sold, use good money to buy some, then lavish coats of it on his old door. This is what first invited rumours about his alcoholic disease. The diagnosis was upgraded to bachelor's madness the day he bought a pot of red paint and painted the number twelve, then becoming the only numbered address within a ninety-kilometre radius. He maintained that such symbols were the fabric of civilisation, and that only by paying attention to their upkeep would civilisation's nest stay warm for its return.

Pilo's door was ajar. Leaving the tractor sputtering, Maks swaggered over and kicked it. 'Pilo!'

Pilosanov's lumpy nose appeared at the crack, and behind it, under a sparse lawn of whiskers, his pocked and ruddy face. 'What?' he said.

'I've come for the gun. And here's your machine – freshly fuelled to the brim, as agreed.'

Pilosanov edged through the door with a wary eye. Ludmila jumped glaring from the tractor. 'Your bones will roast in hell for this,' she hissed at Maks.

'Pilo, she has to go to Kuzhnisk before the road falls,' Maks smacked his sister quiet. 'Let's do our business quickly, so you don't have to burn the headlamp too much along the way.'

'And what do you mean with "headlamp?" Surely the apparatus has two headlamps?'

'How many roads are you taking at once? One road, one headlamp. If you wanted my Toyota Land Cruiser, with multiple headlamps, you should have said earlier.'

'Pah! You don't have a Toyota Land Cruiser.'

'Listen to me, before I grow bored and smash something closely reminiscent of your head – where is the firearm, as per our agreed business?'

'The gun is not here,' Pilo glanced vaguely up and down the road.

Ludmila fixed a scowl on her brother. Maks knew it was the word 'gun' that piqued her. Rather than explain, he switched off the tractor motor. As its clatter died, he cocked an ear to the rooftops, and pointed. The sound of small-arms fire crackled through the mist. An artillery round shocked the sky. He turned a hard eye on Ludmila by way of full stop.

'I don't know if I can still do the gun,' said Pilo. 'Gnezvariks took the dam yesterday. There's nothing between us and them now. Every goose and goat wants the gun.'

Maks brought the slap of his breath to the man's face. 'Pilo,' he hissed, 'I will bolt the cheeks of your arse to the backs of different trains. There are hills still between the Gnez and us. And remember, you speak to the most able polisher of aeroplane propellers this side of the Caspian. What stronger man will you find to administer defence with the gun?'

'Ha! I took more exercise coming to the door just now than any propeller polisher has had in this district for two years.'

'Well then, before I pelt you down dead with my hands – what about the other, more important business we have between us?'

'That's okay,' Pilo lazily opened his army-issue overcoat to scratch an armpit through his jumper. 'The man will be here after Lubov closes. He knows they're for you.'

'You're saying you don't have them here?'

'And what colour goose do you take me for? Do you think I want your face down here again? Complaining that the things were spoiled by the damp of my house? They'll come clean to your hands, and I'll not be to blame for anything.'

Pilo's words hastened the moment, critical in all local transactions, when the men stood face to face, and promised death into each other's eyes. The stare was a down payment, as no truly brutal revenge could be justified until a man could say his enemy had cheated him through open eyes.

Pilo tossed open eyes at Maks. Maks's glare shifted minutely across Pilo's whiskers, gathering tokens for a grim, well-justified death. 'You leave me stood here with nothing, Pilosanov. You're possessing my tractor early and leaving me at this stupid green door with nothing under the stars to show.'

Pilo's face crumpled with hurt. 'I stand here beside you, so how can you mean?'

'Because you're immediately taking my sister to Kuzhnisk on the tractor.' He raised a slow, upright finger, symbolically gutting the man from crotch to chest. 'And remember, Viktor Illich Pilosanov – my eyes travel with you. Go now before I kill you, but leave me entry to your house with its feminine green door while I wait for the other business to be delivered like you say it will.'

Maks snatched his sister by the arm, shoving her into the side of the tractor. He brought his mouth close up to her ear. 'Watch him. Don't let him bring you anywhere but the main road at Kuzhnisk. I mean it. And see that he goes the Uvila way, you'll need more fuel. He can pay.'

'You're moleshit after you do this to our mothers. I'll bring the tractor back to them and tell them what you did.'

'Then *you* will be moleshit, sweet dewdrop from heaven.'

'Hoh!' said Ludmila.

'Hoh!' replied Maks. He stood a long moment, glowering at her. Then he sent a knowing push of his chin. 'And hark the sour nuggets I have to bear from you, after I went to the trouble of finding a gift for your farewell!'

'Hoh! You mean the gift of watching your arse disappear!'

Maks tutted to himself. Reaching inside his coat pocket, he pulled out Ludmila's missing glove, still sticky from Aleksandr's throat. 'You'll be warmer with this,' he said, levelling a stare from deep under his brow. He nailed her with a final chin-push, turned, and walked away spitting.

Pilo shrugged and climbed into the tractor. 'How does it begin?'

Ludmila's eyes filled with tears. She bit her lip, squeezed in behind the seat, and reached past Pilosanov to press the starter. The machine sneezed itself awake. Maks disappeared through the green door, slamming it behind him.

The headlamp's beam spilt milky tea light over the track out of Ublilsk. Ludmila gathered her coats around her, tightening herself into a knot behind the driver's seat. A lump like a jelly meatball stuck in her throat.

'Ha! Oh my glory, ha ho ho!' Pilosanov roared as the hamlet sank behind them. 'A bigger goose couldn't be born! I left him stood there with nothing. I have his tractor and he's left with

79

nothing under the sky to show!' Pilo's shoulders trembled with laughter. He turned to smirk at Ludmila. 'You're safe now, little cat. No more do you have to assort your creams amongst your family.'

'And don't mistake my family for yours.'

'Hoh! But let's admit the clear truth; that no house with man or dog could stay dry from the juice of such a pear as you, not for a solitary night.'

'And do you see a single mongol face, or so much as a slow eye, born in my family? No! So cut your filthy hole.'

'Well, I can say your brother is none too fast!' Pilo laughed some more, releasing little whines of reflection and enjoyment of the moment in general. Then he reached into his lap, and wrenched the tip of his half-fat penis out through his clothes. 'I'm just proud to finally give you the taste of a real man, as such a sticky girl deserves. Come. Come to lovely Viktor.'

8

Five cats prowled the smut between the corners of Scombarton and Milliner Roads. Three were black. All were uneasy about the basement at 16A.

A man's impending visit made urgent energies churn around the flat. Bunny tried to ignore them, and skulked like a widow between sink and bench. He wore his usual three dressing gowns with business shoes and socks, and a pair of large Balorama sunglasses. An albino Bedouin widow. Light in the room was dull sepia; his voice found a drone to match.

'I mean to say. The most likely scenario is that we're back at Albion for breakfast tomorrow. Best prepare yourself, son – bugger knows what Nicki will have told them. More I think about it, they'll not be sending a man out on a Saturday night just to buy us a pint, he'll have to be an assessor.' Bunny looked up to the light bulb that hung like a dark star over the sitting room, and smiled peacefully to himself.

'Just get those bloody dishes done,' came Blair's muted voice. His legs stuck out from the cupboard under the bench, black suit trousers straining over his buttocks.

Bunny retracted his gaze, and turned over his shoulder. 'Will I find you a headscarf and curlers? Wish I had a bloody camera – can you imagine what the Albion lads'd say, seeing you muck out a cupboard? Can you imagine what Gladdy'd say?'

'Gladstone's blind and autistic,' grunted Blair.

'He chats all right with me. He'll laff when I tell him.'

Grunt.

The men spent another few moments with the gentle clattering and knocking that usually brings warmth to a kitchen at week-ends. Then Bunny paused and put down his cloth. He bit his lip. 'I think I can feel a gin coming on.' Silence hissed loudly between his words. 'Can you not sense a juniper-influenced restorative trend looming?'

Blair's face heaved up from the cupboard. 'Will you get bloody dressed, the man'll be here just now.'

'Don't be daft, I'm not cleaning in me suit.'

'Well staring at teacups isn't cleaning.'

'I mean to bloody say, I look forward to the day I can grasp you. On the one hand you say he won't even be an assessor, that he'll just come and take us out on the lash, and on the other you're cleaning like a bloody charwoman.' Bunny fished another teacup from the sink. 'I mean, I should think any assessment'll be slightly more clinical than the state of the cupboards. Do you honestly think they'd send someone to go through the cup-boards? Have they a sort of char squad?'

'Look, Bunny, just don't talk to me. I'm not doing anything for you. You do what you want, and I'll do what I want. When this chap comes I'm just going to pretend we're separate files.'

'Are we not separate files?'

'Well, if you'd just take stock of half of what goes on around you, you'd know that's one of the crucial administrative and human rights errors that's probably prompted our release. I mean, look what the register office said about the birth certificates.'

'But that doesn't mean we can't have one, just that they could-n't find the record to hand. It's a bureaucracy, Blair.'

'Well, but it's symptomatic. The care file's our life, Bunny. We live and die by the file. For God's sake, why do you think I haven't just told you to bugger off back by yourself? Do I sound

82

like someone who wants to live with you? Now just don't talk to me. You're your own file now.'

'Ta.' Bunny's chest puffed. 'Here, perhaps we could play a sort of bingo with the man, see who wins the most benefits. Wait – I know, when he comes, why don't you discuss the devastation of sharing a file, and I'll mention a royal baby?'

'Don't bait me, Bunny.'

Bunny stopped and put his hands to his hips, stiffly flexing sideways and back. He jerked his shoulders up and down. He hummed for a moment. Then he reached for the gin. 'You're having a major lend of yourself, you know. Wish I had money to put on this man being an assessor.'

Blair's head burst from the cupboard, 'Well, if you're so cocksure, why don't we wager the rest of the month on it? If the man drags us away, you can set the agenda for the next three weeks at Albion. But if, Bunny, his visit benefits us in any way at all, if he just takes us to the Vitaxis social, I'll set the bloody agenda down here.'

'You're joking – would you honour that?'

'Well, that's what I've just bloody told you.'

'Strictly?'

'Strictly.'

Bunny chuckled darkly. 'You're on. Is it too early to have you fix us a gin?'

'And is it too early to have you just shut up? Now don't talk to me again.' Blair disappeared into the next cupboard.

Bunny glided pleasantly around the kitchen for a few more moments, before returning thoughtfully to the bench. He leant an elbow on it, and stared across the sitting room. 'Where do you think our bank's gone then? There's only a machine answers the phone, I mean to say.'

No reply.

83

'Do you think Ray Langton's really coming back to *Coronation Street*? Can they have honestly faked his death?'

No reply.

Bunny leant back. One eye curled down like the feeler on a snail. 'Is this how we're supposed to be now, for ever?'

'You be how you want.'

Bunny lifted a teacup, and ran a teatowel over it. 'Mind,' he mused, 'smashing bum on our Nicki. Hadn't really clocked it out of uniform. Did I tell you she slaps perfume down there?'

Blair poked deadly eyes from the cupboard.

'Crack ruddy walnuts in it, more I think about it,' muttered Bunny.

Blair knelt back and turned a filthy stare on his brother. 'You don't even like girls, so leave it out.'

'I love them, thank you very much. And in a proper, respectful way. Get on with them better than you. Amazing how they respond when you leave off all that tremulous pubescent shite.'

'Well, it's called sex, Bunny, and girls want it too. You're the only one who doesn't want it.'

'I mean to say. Well, it just seems sort of –'

'Leave it out, will you! You'd be struggling to find anything more unhygienic than living with you.'

'I wasn't going to say unhygienic, actually.'

'Honestly, you're like a medieval gnome in post-modern times.'

'Post fucking modern?' Bunny snorted. 'Post-post, you mean. Post-post-fucking-post.'

The mostly ceremonial fussing over the teacups tinkled to a halt, and Bunny turned to lean, thinking, against the bench. The kitchenette and its freshly mopped, chequered floor shone in his sunglasses, then drained away as he lifted them off his nose. 'Listen, mate,' he said, wiping his tongue over his gums, 'you made a right twat of yourself the other night. I hope it's given

84

you an opportunity to suss the vibe. Because the vibe is: fucking lighten up. As it is, we'll probably be carted back tonight. Try and adapt to your likely fate. Things can't be so bad with old Buns, we can still have a laff, you and me. The lads. Take the wee. I mean to bloody say.'

Blair uncoiled from the floor and parked a grimace on Bunny's face, chewing little hisses and spitting them. 'Well, you listen to me, because I'll not say this again: it's over, Bunny. First opportunity comes to that door, whatsoever it may be, I am history. Do you hear? Now don't talk to me again.'

Bunny's brow popped up, making his eyeballs hang like boiled eggs in the sacs of his eyelids. 'Smashing,' he said. 'And no bugger'd be more chuffed than me.' He made a workman's fist, jabbed a thumb into his chest. 'I'd cheer you on to catch that breeze, my son, roger it with all your bristling young energy – however, pal, given that so far we've only had an urchin selling cleaning products and a mobile fishmonger from Tyneside at the door, I'd suggest you stop having a fucking lend of yourself. Best you can hope for is the removals crew in white coats, and I can't say I'll be sorry.'

There came a knock at the door. Bunny's fist wilted. 'Get the sausage rolls on, will you?'

'Piss off,' said Blair.

Bunny rubbed his hair into a more hopeless tangle, retied his outermost dressing gown, and trotted upstairs like a travelling nativity. A stain grew in watery pixels behind the door's frosted-glass panel. He opened it, and peered out into a dull, petrol-scented cold that lacquered his skin like milk scum. In the middle of his field of vision, close but down somewhat, stood a slight man in middle age. Grey slacks flapped around his bones, a twisted school tie threw blobs of shadow between the lapels of a blazer.

Bunny clenched and unclenched his hands by his side.

'Hard night, was it?' The man rolled yellow eyes up to Bunny's sunglasses. He sidled close, undulating like a seahorse. His carriage said that in his world he was hip. Bunny sensed that his world had made a home in 1977. He sensed that in his world he may also have been quite tall.

'Come in, come in,' Bunny showed the man down the stairs.

'You'd have to be Gordon.'

Bunny detected the north in the man's voice, and noted that he only saw his words to the door of his mouth, didn't project them out. Tones were softly served on a wafer of breath which he had to drop his head to catch. He flapped a few blinks. 'Long journey?'

'Battersea, couple of miles away.' The man's eyes rolled up like an ageing baby's.

'You're not from Albion, then?'

'Albion House? No, no.'

Bunny blinked into the kitchenette. Blair was arranging a handful of rustic croutons on beds of something leafy. 'We've some warm *amuse-bouches* to come,' he breezed.

'Afraid my diet's confined to things I can pronounce,' said the man. 'Mind, I wouldn't say no to some liquid refreshment.'

Bunny swallowed a smirk. Blair's eyes probed the man's rumpled form before scurrying up through the window into a drizzle that pulsed like hot plankton under the street lamp. He quietly wiped the croutons back into their bag, and left it puffed open behind the bench rather than rustle it.

'Did you come by the bins?' asked Bunny. 'You could furnish an estate with what's stood in that alley. The council won't touch it, even the charities can't be arsed. We had St Vincent's on the phone and they said, "What is it you have?" and I said, "A perfectly good dresser and a chest of drawers," and they said it wasn't worth their while sending a van for it. I felt like saying,

86

"Well, you tell us what you fancy and we'll order it new and have it sent round." I mean to bloody say.'

The man settled in the sitting room, taking in the scene. 'No, I didn't come past the bins,' he reclined, resting an arm along the back of the settee. Ambient noise died as if in punctuation of the Heaths' first moments with the mysterious functionary.

Blair reached over the bench with a large gin in a child's beaker. 'Sorry about the glassware, we're not fully installed yet.'

'I'm sure you're not. I can only say how pleased we are that you've taken it all on board.'

'Well, as you mention it, can I ask – who's "we"?'

'Sorry, I mean *I'm* pleased.' The man took a sip of his drink.

Blair shifted uncomfortably on his feet. 'You're not an assessor – are you?'

When no answer came, the twins stared at the man. They found a distant, comfortable smile settling on his white, gargoyle-like face. His eyes found them out, unblinking. They were more luminous than the brothers had first thought. His persona grew large before them, his whimsy drained away.

Bunny frowned sympathetically. 'Is there something you want to ask us about Albion House? Something we might've seen? A baby?'

'No,' he finally said.

Blair crossed his arms. 'Well, who are you then?'

The man held his gaze unwaveringly on the pair. 'Donald Lamb,' he said. His head tilted slightly down, his marble eyes slightly up, their pupils lying in wait beneath the hoods of his eyelids. Blair came to the settee opposite, careful to sit out of direct line. Bunny barricaded himself behind the kitchen bench, and peered over Blair's head.

'I see you like your ballroom dancing,' Lamb reached to a stack of music discs beside the settee.

Blair's cheek twitched.

'Tango, tango, tango,' said Lamb, evenly, hypnotically, as he rifled through the discs. 'Tango, tango, tango, tango.'

The lightness and directness of his tone grabbed the men. They tensed. Bunny's teeth crept over his lip. There was suddenly something about Donald Lamb that spoke not just of seniority, but of a higher natural caste.

Lamb lifted two final discs. '"Time To Say Goodbye", Andrea Bocelli and Sarah Brightman. "Jerusalem", Grimethorpe Colliery Band.' He brought his gin to his mouth, gently sipped it, and held it in folded arm, looking from Blair to Bunny. 'Wouldn't Brahms's first piano concerto be more descriptive of your adventure?'

Bunny took a long draught from his glass. 'Well, um. Brahms sets out rather stridently in that first concerto. Almost had a symphony there.'

'He certainly does set out stridently,' said Lamb, softly, monotonously. 'Very stridently indeed.' He narrowed his eyes, and shone them at the men.

The room fell still for a few moments. Blair studied the creases on his trousers. Bunny shifted his weight behind the bench. He pushed his glasses up his nose, and crossed his arms. 'You're having a lend,' he said finally. 'I mean to say, I'm afraid the shark pool's at the cleaners, we hadn't expected an evil genius.'

Lamb's face crinkled affably, and he took a sip of gin. 'Sorry, I'm swept away with the moment – it's been a long week. Here, but listen' – he leant forward, and dropped his voice to a rasp – 'I come bearing gifts.'

Blair flashed an eye at his brother. 'Well, that's very kind, but we still don't know who you are.'

Lamb beamed his eyes around the room, and paused. 'I'll not sod you about – it'll take some time to grasp our relationship in detail. I'm sure you're aware of the upheaval that's come with privatisation.' His face softened back into the ageing child. 'For now just call me Don, or Lamby. I'm from another untidy corner of His Majesty's government.'

'And what's it called, this corner of yours?' Blair leant forward on his settee.

'You've got me there. I've lost track, to be honest – they rebrand the bugger every Tuesday lunchtime.' Don was slow to let go the witticism, sawing three more jerky breaths over his teeth in its memory. 'Anyway,' he said, 'without harping on unduly, roughly in the area you might expect, of social-type concerns. Home Office is my manor, broadly speaking. A little more clout than some of the departments you deal with. Hence this –' A stiff envelope appeared from his inside pocket. He passed it to Blair.

Bunny craned over the bench, lifting up his glasses.

'Passports,' said Blair. 'That's an achievement, given they can't even find a birth certificate.'

'We thought it'd make a nice token of your independence. Don't know if you heard at work, but the new owner of Vitaxis is scouting talent to send on junkets – you might get to meet him tonight, and you never know –'

Blair looked up. 'Is he coming to the social?'

'The social's being held in his entertainment complex.'

'And he's just plucking people out of their jobs, to send on overseas trips? What do they tell their employers?'

Lamb smiled. 'Well, in your case he *is* your employer – you're doing work experience at GL Solutions, aren't you?'

'He owns that as well? Crumbs. And where might he send you, if you were picked to go on a junket?'

'Could be anywhere. I know he has interests in Spain, and Croatia.'

Bunny moved to the end of Lamb's settee, and sat on its edge. His mouth clenched open like the grille of a vintage motor car.

'Mind,' said Lamb, 'if you were picked, you'd both get to go.'

Blair's eyes brightened. 'Well, this all suggests we've more than four weeks out.'

'Actually, I couldn't say,' said Lamb. 'I've nothing to do with your schedule.'

Bunny hunched still on the settee. He stared at a hole in the matting by his feet.

Lamb settled back, and crossed his legs. 'Anyway – how are you getting on?'

'Fine, fine,' said Blair, bouncing sparkles off the passport's security tape.

'Not to harp on unduly, but I trust you've been warned your interests mightn't be best served by revealing your backgrounds?'

'Yeah, they've told us all that.'

An indulgent smile settled on Lamb's face. 'Then, gents' – he flicked his eyes to the stairs – 'shall we go? I've a driver outside.'

Bunny flinched. 'Well – it's a bit late now, isn't it, to be traipsing about? What about the curfew?'

'Only applies to central London – the complexes outside the admission zone will crack on all night.'

Blair's tongue stirred in his cheek. 'Don't panic, Buns – it's a simple drink.'

'I mean to say.' Bunny stiffened like an old lady at a slight. 'Now me portal vein's throbbing.' He pressed two fingers to his gut. 'Blair, I might need you to see what you can suss out on the net. Sorry if my bastard carry-on puts a kibosh on the night.'

Lamb frowned. 'Of course, if you're not up to it –'

'I mean to say, we've gin here,' said Bunny. 'And those sausage rolls'll only spoil.'

'They've not left the freezer, Bunny. Get a hold of yourself – it's a simple drink on a Saturday night.'

'Is it Saturday? Damn.'

'What – ?'

'You know. What we discussed earlier.' Bunny stared at his brother, inviting his complicity in an excuse. He sensed no good would come of their exposure to London's pulsing night.

Blair stood up slowly from his settee. He gazed down at Lamb, then up through the window, to the street outside. 'Bunny,' he said softly, 'opportunities wafting through that door is what we discussed earlier. Opportunities for my independence.'

9

Maksimilian climbed the last hundred metres home, blasting up snow with his boots. The only sign of his dwelling over the rise was the gradually increasing size of the objects half-buried beside the track. First there came a spherical tangle of chicken wire, not thus designed but accidental; the wire had once been the door of a rabbit hutch, dating back to Maks's foray into rabbit breeding for unconscionable profit, which project had lasted one-eighth the lifespan of a pair of Pilosanov's rabbits. These were eaten with potato and onion after both were found to be male. The hutch itself fuelled their braising on the stove.

Next to a gnarled tree twelve metres farther up sat a pile of large, uneven stones, which were to have been the foundation for a new, fully enclosed latrine. That was two years ago, but mortar had become dear, and each winter made the reek of their present hole disappear for a few months, which time they spent resolving to move it at the first whiff of spring.

What stayed buried under the track's snow were the ruts worn in it by a rich history of missions to barter possessions for credit at the depot, each mission also heralding the disappearance of a smell from the house; with the television set went the smell of meat roasting, with the toaster-oven the smell of meat stewing. In the first post-Soviet months even a motorbike and a cement mixer travelled from the house, somehow dragging with them the smells of flat-bread baking and fruits being stewed to preserve. These instruments of credit gradually shrank into clothes, utensils and toys, until every cranny of their lives had given up its treasure, until only dung was left with its smell. Each reminder of their collective past brought distant musings to Maks, such that it took a second to hear the voice piping out from the shack.

'I don't see any bread with him. I don't see it in life, but he might have it hidden in secret.' It was Kiska. Maks couldn't see her, but she had seen him. He cursed her for trumpeting his approach.

'And Kiski, watch me, move away from there,' called Irina. Valves on Maks's heart hardened at the creak of his mother's voice. For all that it tried to sound weary, her tone had taken a weight off its feet, and lolled ready for benefit.

'Send him back away if he has no bread,' chirped Olga from inside the shack. 'Give him the correct thrashing with a branch.'

Maks rounded the last corner, eyes fixed down on the track as it widened over iced churnings from the lost tractor's wheels. When he looked up, he saw Kiska skipping towards him, and his mother standing clean, erect, and insecure at the door, one hand on her hip. She had bathed – something the mothers preferred to do while Maks was out of the house – but more unsettling to Maksimilian was the code beneath the soap: bathing was a tedious, expensive job involving firewood, fresh water, and free time. It was something that only happened in the certainty of new resources. And Irina had also changed her dress. She wore her cream dress with twisted blue fish on it like freezing ghosts by Munch.

A whiff of lipstick ushered Maks to the step. 'Blow on me,' Irina snapped as he neared the door.

'I haven't taken a drop.'

'No,' she said, 'you will have taken a tankful. And where's the bread?'

'What bread?' Maks scraped past her into the house. He was just in time to see Olga scurry behind the curtain with a loaf of bread under her arm.

'You sold your grandfather's tractor and didn't buy bread for today?' hissed Irina. 'Come here so that I can cut the miserable tongue from your head!'

'You have bread. Why buy more bread to rot, when you have already bread?'

'And who says we have bread!'

'Grandma has bread. How did you get it?'

'We'd all be nourishing worms if it were up to you to do anything.'

'Grandmama has fresh bread.' Maks stood over his mother like a cloud. 'How did you get it?'

'Nadezhda brought it for us.' Irina hurriedly turned to the bench to scrape a strip of pig fat into her hand.

'Hoh! And beetroots grow up my arse!'

'And they probably do.'

'You piss fat down my throat for not buying bread when you have it here all along!'

'And why didn't you buy bread, now that we're caked from the tractor?' His mother turned to glower. 'You weren't to know we had been saved by the coincidence of old Nadezhda passing.'

Maks paused a moment, scowling hard, then leant into the smell of his mother's face. 'Because I gave money to the very witch Nadezhda to bring a fat loaf to your door!'

'Hoh!' cried Irina. 'Hoh!'

Maks trod a circle around her, staring at the corners of the rotten ceiling, its blackened beams hung with empty hooks, and lengths of string. 'You've signed one of grandpapa's vouchers! Hoh! Ask me all you like about tractors, and about bread, go on.

And then' – he sliced his eyes into tiny leers – 'I'll ask you all *I* like about obtaining benefit by criminal false pretences against the state!'

'Cut your lid, that boy.' Olga stumbled back past the curtain. 'He should be sent to write chastushki with such a mouth.' She stopped at the table, and raised one trembling arm. A bottle of vodka rose with it from the pocket of her apron. She thumped it hard on to the table. 'This will feed my nerves some sense,' she muttered. 'It's clear now that my family wants to kill me with their disrespect and their antics.'

'Nadezhda has been good to you today,' said Maks. 'What about meat?' He watched Olga lift two shot glasses, and one tin cup, from a petrol drum.

'You have an entire zoological garden of questions today,' she said, 'when, in fact, there's only one tiny bald question to be asked: where is the money from the tractor? Perhaps, if you show us it, we might feed you. But remember this' – she whipped up a finger, hurled it like a javelin at Maks – 'again it was your mothers who had to feed your mouth like a naked bird! Because even with the strength of a square hammer you're too stupid to feed yourself or your family! Our teeth are lost and broken from chewing your food for you, Maksimilian. You're worse than a legless dog!'

'Hoh! What!' sputtered Maks.

'And just cut your goosey flap.' Olga squelched her open palm into his face. 'We saved the most rich part of the meat for you. Show him, Iri.'

Irina smiled weakly, unfurling her fingers like a lover. The strip of cold fat lay coiled in her hand like a slug.

'Now get the cake on to this table!' Olga slammed down a fist. 'If we don't pay back the sum of the voucher before Lubov tries to cash it with the inspectorate, we'll be damned to the worms!'

*

Ludmila saw Pilosanov's dirty penis under the dashboard's light, curled like a finger in his palm. 'Pilo,' she said flatly.

'What, my sweet?'

'A noodle fell on your trouser.'

'Hoh! Hahaha! And she has fire, my new thing!' Pilosanov pulled from the folds of his overcoat a half-full bottle of vodka, drank from it, and passed it back to Ludmila.

She took the bottle without shifting her gaze, tightened her fingers around its neck, and took a long swig.

Pilosanov didn't take the Uvila road. He headed to Kuzhnisk along the Stavropol road. Ludmila knew they hadn't the fuel to get even half-way to Kuzhnisk, but she didn't correct the man. The route suited her in other ways. Soldiers were creeping around the railway bridge when the tractor approached. They were Ublis, and took Pilosanov's boomed greeting and upraised fist in good spirit.

After that, once the tractor chugged alone like a barge through floes of starlit snow, Ludmila was free in the world. Pilo had served to see her through the militarised zone. He didn't think to question the fuel gauge constantly reading full, and cheap vodka made him snake the tractor most uneconomically through the night. Still, he was in fine spirits, and sang for a while, wretchedly, before calling over his shoulder: 'Milochka, in the devil's name! Don't make me ask you again and again – stand beside me and help steer, I find the road twists at every chance.'

Ludmila returned to his side, bracing herself with an arm around the roof pillar, reaching with the other to correct their leisurely hurtle. Before long Pilo's hand found its way to her leg. It rested firmly for a minute before crawling roughly up her thigh. A finger made its way to her warmth.

Ludmila decided not to wait until the bottle emptied. As soon as Pilo passed it back, she took two long swigs, grabbed it by the neck, and smashed it over his head.

He looked up at her like a man just told that his canary had melted, then slumped into the pillar, dark fluids shining to his collar. Ludmila swerved to the edge of the road and pulled the throttle to idle. She rifled through Pilo's pockets as the tractor bumped to a stop, found a wad of roubles, and jumped from the cab to count them in the headlamp's beam. Three hundred and forty. Tucking them into her underwear, she skipped to the side of the machine and pulled Pilosanov out by his sleeve. The snow absorbed him, crunching like meringue.

Ludmila looked down at him, then up at the ceilingless night. It was a crime, wasting so much vodka.

Vacant cold rode with her the rest of the way, seeming benign in Pilosanov's absence, stinging a promise not only of warmth ahead, but of Misha's warmth, perhaps new kinds of warmth, from things they had never done in Ublilsk. She kept the tractor travelling at a fair clip, and, lulled by its toss and chug, came to feel the road and its walls of night as an unexplored hallway, a vacant universe all her own. When the tractor gave its last breath in the middle of nowhere, she felt it a blessing, a chance to savour the quiet, feel the saints behind her. She climbed down from the old Lipetsk and stretched, taking in the sky, realising things were turning out better than she had hoped.

That moment alone with space and snow made itself known as freedom.

A sort of sleep came beside the fading warmth of the tractor's bulkhead, patchy with stirred excitement. Shortly after dawn lit up the flat, empty snowfield where she had come to rest, an old blue lorry lumbered clanking along the icy furrows that passed for a road. Ludmila stepped out and flagged the driver down. 'Are you going to Kuzhnisk?' she called in Russian.

97

Two snow-tanned men, one old and one young, slowed to look at her. 'Are *you* going to Kuzhnisk?' they called back.

'I need to ask you a question.'

'You're very beautiful,' called the young man, 'a goddess, in fact, but we don't have the price of you today.'

'It's not for that, I just have a serious question.'

The lorry hissed to a stop some yards up the road. Ludmila didn't move from her spot. She watched the young man's head poke out of the nearside window and look at her. Then, after a moment, the truck jolted into reverse and pulled alongside.

'Did you travel from the districts, or is this your land here?' asked the young man, studying the tractor in the field behind Ludmila.

'No, I came from Uvila way,' Ludmila lied.

'Oh. Because the road is taken now between here and Ublilsk, we were the last to pass.'

'Who has the road?'

'Gnezvars have a chunk of it, past the quarry. There are some Ubli dead on the road. I didn't mean to insult you suggesting you were Ubli, of course you're much too lovely for that. What question do you have for your servants?'

Ludmila's pulse sharpened on hearing of Ubli dead, even though she had seen them alive, when she passed with Pilosanov, and knew Misha wasn't among them. 'I need fuel,' she said after a moment, 'and to know if there's a market in Kuzhnisk, for the tractor.'

'Are you trying to fix the tractor?' words whistled through a gap in the old man's teeth.

'No, I'm trying to sell the tractor. It's a fine Lipetsk tractor.'

The old man squinted at the rat-eaten machine. 'Yes, it is a fine tractor,' he said. 'You might take it past the agricultural depot on this side of Kuzhnisk. That's all I can think, because the concessionary closed down three years ago next month.'

98

'And is there fuel you can sell?'

'Well, that would be an agricultural diesel you'd need, a coloured diesel, not the kind that we feed the lorry.'

'Then do you think you could tow me? I have rigging in the machine.'

The men looked at each other for a long moment. Eventually the old man leant back to the window. 'No, because the gear ratio is too low, and we'd have to drive too slowly. Because the gearing is much lower in a tractor, see, than in a road vehicle.'

'Yes,' nodded the young man, 'the gearing's all wrong between lorry and tractor, we might pull its wheels off, or worse.'

'It doesn't have to be in gear,' said Ludmila, 'it can float neutrally at any speed you want. And anyway, look at the road, there's no speed in it until summer.'

The men paused again to look at each other. They took longer about it this time, and Ludmila became impatient.

'I can pay you,' she said.

'Five hundred roubles,' the old man called without blinking.

'I only have one hundred,' said Ludmila.

'Four hundred.'

Ludmila cut her voice with a cry. 'My grandfather died and left the tractor, it's all my family has left. You see me on a day at the edge of our deaths, wondering where next to run after Uvila.'

The men consulted each other once more. Then the young man stuffed his head into a tall fur hat, opened his door, and jumped from the cab. 'Let me have a look,' he eyed Ludmila up and down as he went to the tractor, stepping high through uneven snow. 'It's from Lipetsk, you say?'

'Yes,' nodded Ludmila, 'and you'll see the hoist at the back, that's very hard to find on a new tractor.'

The young man stood gouging an ear with a fingertip, and squinting. 'Well, no, in reality there's no shortage of hoists for new tractors, you're wrong there. Anyway, still – two hundred roubles, in advance, and we'll attempt it. If I find the machine is too heavy, or behaves wrongly, I'll pay you a hundred back. That's fair.'

'Yes, that's fair,' nodded the old man with a frown. 'But we assure you we will try our best to move it.'

Like a fat mother and child, the lorry and tractor waddled some grey hours over ice to the outskirts of Kuzhnisk. The town heralded itself with smatterings of fresh dung and straw on the snow and, eventually, a mighty Soviet statue of a superhuman pointing to the sky. The livestock was bigger than in the country, and the town itself, an old mill town of some nine thousand people, rolled out debris and ruins along the road into its sparse bowel. Gradually the road fell under shadow from buildings on both sides, the air hung nutty with dung and wood smoke, and the horizon disappeared as concrete and volcanic stone grew into the town proper: a faded post-Soviet junkyard scattered like a sackful of wooden blocks after a tantrum. A petrol sign hung behind a weave of telegraph cables at the roadside. The lorry slowed up to the pump, which was administered by a dwarf in a small metal booth like a newsstand.

Ludmila argued with the man over the smallest allowed fuel purchase. After some tears, and a mention of her grandfather, she added a revised minimum to the tractor's tank. Then, having waved goodbye to the men in the lorry, she found the town's agricultural depot, sold the Lipetsk to the clerk of the depot himself, who confirmed the going price with a wizened superior, and bowled powerfully into the streets of Kuzhnisk, a coat of optimism shielding her from needles of ice-dust in the wind. Nine thousand roubles was nothing for such a fine tractor; still, it would keep some trouble at bay.

But her optimism lasted ten paces. There was no way to safely send the money home, unless she returned with it herself. She hadn't discussed a contingency with her mothers – they expected Maks to return with it in his hand. Ludmila thought of posting the money to the depot, where mail was kept for the village and its surrounds. But she knew too well that Lubov would rifle through any mail for cash, if it left Kuzhnisk at all.

She tried to varnish these realisations with marvellings at the evening's sparkling ink on the streets of Kuzhnisk, she tried to bustle and flounce full of purpose, but the effect was the sort of attentive familiarity seen only in self-conscious strangers. She walked for a while down Ulitsa Kuzhniskaya – a compacted hump of dung and ice between shadowy Soviet hulks that looked more like abandoned hangars than apartment blocks. They were pimpled with iron prongs that had once secured letters to the signs above their tomb-like entrances. She tried to picture the dynamic grinding of an organism of ambitious cells behind them. She tried to feel seduced by the speed and progress of the city.

But none was there. A pack of ravening half-wolves rattled out of the shadows to spill across the road. She saw that the town belonged to them.

Apart from a battered white car buzzing sideways down the ice, wheels spinning uselessly, it took a purposeful walk of five blocks before Ludmila saw another person. It was a pirozhki seller, bent nearly double, bashing ice off the legs of her stove beside the road, roughly where a curb might sit in milder times. The trader saw Ludmila pause, and called to her offering a left-over pastry for half price. Ludmila shook her head. Around the corner, a café bled orange light on to the sludge.

The Café-Bar Kaustik was named after the famous Volgograd handball team, and was hung with victorious mementos. Beneath these it was simple and wooden, with a light end and a dark end, mottled through with green upholstery and swirling shadow.

Misha was not there when she entered.

Tobacco smoke writhed in listless strands from one end to the other, drained off by the door. A broad, moustachioed man leant beside a stuffed weasel at the farthest end of the bar. Two other men with sandpaper skin and yellowing breath hunched in the darkest corner, nursing beers, and rubbing their whiskers with flat palms. The weasel and the men stared at Ludmila as she emerged through beams and swirls of smoky light. She folded her coat over the backrest of a stool, then had a second thought, and moved it a stool farther away from the weasel. The flurry of folding interrupted a stream of smoke from the barman's cigarette.

'He only bites men,' the man grunted through it.

Ludmila looked up. 'What do you say?'

'I say he only bites men, the polecat. Don't be afraid.' The man's eyes hung unblinking on Ludmila.

'Hoh, excuse me. Do you have a hot drink?'

'Well, no, *I* have a beer. Would *you* like a hot drink?'

Ludmila slung a heavy gaze. 'There's only so much refreshment I can get watching the weasel.'

The barman shrugged, and heaved himself behind the bar with a smile and a shake of the head. 'Another smart Cherkess,' he said. 'Is it coffee or tea you want?'

'Coffee. And I'm not Cherkess.'

'But you're from the west. Which is the same thing.'

'Hoh! And then you're from China.'

The man left his coffee machine to plant both hands on the bar. He poked a knowing breath at Ludmila. 'And listen to me: you say "Hoh!" when you speak – that's a mannerism from the far west. If you're not Cherkess, it just proves that you're all the same, if you all walk around saying, "Hoh!"'

'Well, it proves more about you than about them,' said Ludmila. 'So – hoh!'

The man leant back to his task, tossing a chuckle at the pair huddled in the corner. 'Listen to this one, will you?'

'She's Ublil,' said one of the men, without turning. 'Cherkess don't say "Hoh." And she uses the push, with her chin, did you see? I'll wager she also says "cut your hatch" instead of "shut up". "Cut your hatch and catch down the cuckoos, spastic goose" – that's how they carry on up in the Ublil districts.'

'Ahh, an expert on Cherkess.' The barman slid a coffee across the counter to Ludmila. Its steam ran to play with the other smokes above the bar. 'So, can you tell us – is she from Uvila, or Ublilsk proper?' He came to lean close to Ludmila, as if both were teamed against the men in the corner.

'Don't feel you have to answer on my account,' said Ludmila, sipping hot bubbles at the edge of her cup. 'I know where I'm from.'

'See?' The barman triumphantly squeezed her arm. 'A live one she is, a real mountain girl.'

'Well,' said the man, turning, 'if she were from Uvila, she probably would be at home, and not here with farmyard mud on her boots. So, I'll say she's from the Admin Districts. The Thirty-Nine, or the Forty-One. More likely the Thirty-Nine, because the Forty-One has really gone under, no services are operating. It would be hard to come out.'

'Yes,' said the other man, 'I hear today that Gnezvarik forces have sealed it, except for the railway. And that won't be long falling.'

'Well, and – Christ!' The barman thumped a stony hand on the bar. 'How many republics fit in one place?'

The first man settled back with a philosophical shrug. 'Me, I just say if they want to turn their minefield into a country, and

turn their goat into a president, then let them. It's only the raping and killing that leaves a bad taste.'

The second man shook his head, and took a noisy swig of
beer. 'Well, but killing is the way to get foreign witnesses. What
other reason is there to kill strangers who aren't soldiers? It's the
same with extremists and bombs, they do it because television
sends the terror far and wide, and at a profit.' He leant towards
to Ludmila, 'Isn't that right, miss?'

'What would I know?' shrugged Ludmila. 'I'm from Stavropol.'

'Haha!' bellowed the barman. 'She gets better and better!' He
leant over the bar and rolled twinkling eyes over Ludmila.
'You'll bankrupt me, I won't be able to take your money after
such entertainments!'

'What?' Ludmila said flatly. 'Many people come from
Stavropol. I just wanted to test the countryside for a while, and see
your rustic ways for myself, after all the pressures of the city.' She
stood from her stool and turned a pirouette for the men. 'Look at
this dress, if you don't believe me. Do you think anyone from the
Admin Districts could plough mountains in such a dress?'

'Hahaha!' the barman whipped applause from his hands. 'We
only wish that they would!'

As she settled back on to her stool, the second, contemplative
man in the corner pointed to Ludmila's cheek. 'A hard life it
must be in the city. They have sufficient obstacles to leave such
bruises on their young.'

'Well, it's not only here the ground is icy,' she turned her cheek
away.

Leaning forward, the man tightened his eyes on her. 'Name for
us one street in Stavropol.'

'Ulitsa Stavropolskaya,' she said without blinking.

The man gave a snort, and frosted his lip with a sip of beer.
'That's cheating. Name another.'

'And but listen,' snapped Ludmila. 'Can a person not have a peaceful coffee in your dismal countryside? It's bad enough that I can't walk your streets without farm boots.'

'Anyway,' said the barman, 'I have nothing against Cherkess. Or Ublil, in fact.' He threw his eyes to the ceiling, trying to imagine on a map the protrusion of Ublilsk, pointing west like a teapot spout into the high Caucasus. But other than its notorious mists, which had to be treated as moving topographical solids, and in which whole caravans of people, animals, and even heavy vehicles had been known to vanish without trace, he couldn't spin any romance from its imagining. Instead, he lifted a cloth from a basket behind the bar, and plucked out a hardened pastry. He plopped it on to a saucer and pushed it to Ludmila. 'For your services to mirth,' he smiled, turning to sit by the men in the corner.

Ludmila said nothing. She kept an eye on the approaches to the café, scanning the mist for Misha's gait. Her pastry sat until the coffee was almost drained, then its scent proved too much, and she tore chunks off it with her teeth. Each chunk brought an empty feeling, and a thought that many kilometres away her family sat hungry, waiting for her to act. Then, with the last chunk, a surge of anger pumped through her. The tractor had been Maks's responsibility and he had failed. Moreover, he had abandoned her to the whims of Viktor Pilosanov, and had stolen from her the enjoyment of being full of hot coffee and sweet pastry, looking out on to the ice through warm electric light, waiting for her love. Anyway, she thought, he had apparently traded the tractor for a gun, and God only knew what other asset, so presumably he planned to take care of his mothers. She didn't dare imagine the outcome if not.

Ludmila would keep the money until Misha came, and see how better they could send it home. She leant close to the overhang of the bar, reached under her dress, and pulled out a bank-note, laying it carefully beside her cup.

The barman looked up, then rose to stand beside her at the bar. 'The polecat invites you,' he said, shooing her note away. 'I can't guess where my comrades are from any more, but I know a hungry traveller when I see one. I feel to take the end of my belt to your husband's back for sending you away like this, the modern day being what it is.'

Ludmila didn't take the bait at first, but sat and stared at the old wooden bar. It would have made fine firewood. 'I'm not married,' she finally said. 'And I'd have to slap something closely resembling your face before you took a belt to me.'

'Christ,' chuckled the barman, tossing back his head. 'Your noises might sound big in the west, but you won't last three minutes in this town. Every wayward pig fetches up here. I'm from Volgograd, I know civilisation – and this is not it. The town belongs to Liberty Munitions now, supplying arms to the front line up your way, probably to front lines around the world. It's not good for the soul of a place, to exist only for such things.'

Ludmila stopped to look at him, weighed up his large, droopy face, his thick hands. 'Don't get worms over me. Any wayward pig should pray he doesn't cross paths with a Stavropol girl. Anyway, my fiancé is coming – we'll be moving on, probably even tonight.' She turned back to the bar with a tiny but effective flounce.

'Definite Ublil,' chuckled a man from the corner. 'Exquisite.'

'Definite something,' said the barman. 'Can I get you something more, Miss Ublil?'

'I'm all right, thank you – you don't mind if I stay back and wait awhile? He's meeting me here, in your famous café.'

'Well, you could stay for ever, if it were up to me – but I'm afraid the bar has to close in twenty minutes.'

The approaches to the World & Oyster were asquirm with floaty-type people so contorted by casualness that they seemed driven by internal gusts of wind. Around them flashed the naked circuitry of London: tail-lights splashing down glycerine roads, figures bustling like great-coated trolls past sand-and-soot structures daubed wet on to the night.

Bunny cocked an eye at his brother. 'Is this the bit where you make a twat of yourself in public?'

'Sorry to disappoint you, Buns. This is the bit where I carve a warm niche in somebody's life and have you send my belongings round to her flat.'

'Inside, is she? Miss Right?'

'Well, don't be bitter, you'll get by.' Blair filled his lungs with frosty air, and let out an exhilarated sigh. 'It's my agenda now, Buns. And my first instruction to you is: stand well clear.'

'You're playing with yourself. Who do you think'll come to a healthcare social? Other bloody cripples like us, pal.'

'It's in a pub complex, Buns, we don't even have to go into the social. And speak for yourself about cripples.'

The Heaths felt the first slap of ozone and tonic from the edge of the car park. They looked up. The World & Oyster was a towering Victorian building entombed in smooth, blue concrete, with chimneys and spires sprouting through the top as if a crate had been dropped on to an old hotel – as indeed one sort of had. Blue lights prickled the road behind it at the boundary of the

Central London Admission Zone. The brothers wore black suits with white shirts buttoned at the collar. They pulsed in and out of reflections on the pavement, seeming like holes torn flapping in the street.

'Brought your jammies then?' Bunny tossed a glance at the plastic bag in Blair's hand. Drizzle on his sunglasses made a sequinned cobweb of the scene.

Blair tightened his grip on the bag, cradling its bottom in the crook of an arm. Donald Lamb's fragile silhouette undulated ahead towards the light.

'I mean to say. Or is it a ploughman's you've packed?'

'It's nothing. Just rubbish.' Blair strode ahead. 'It's nearly a week till bin day, thought I'd at least give you a clean start.' He reached to a roadside bin without slowing, and stuffed the bag inside. As Lamb was absorbed into the fray by the club's entrance, Blair slowed back to hiss at his brother. 'Now listen: let me do the talking, for God's sake. He won't have told us about the junkets, and brought passports, if he doesn't think we're in with a chance.'

Bunny clicked his tongue. 'We could've just asked him what his game was, and stopped home.'

'Relax, Bunny. You can also think of it as farewell drinks.'

'I doubt they'll be serving drinks at a healthcare social, Blair, I mean to fucking say.'

'I told you, we don't even have to stay in the social, we'll nip around the other pubs. Honestly, Bunny, lighten up – think of me for a change, there'll be masses of skirt out on a Saturday night.'

Bunny scowled. 'You mind how you go. These aren't your people, son. You'll set yourself up for a fall.'

As if in punctuation, a young woman shot out of the building vomiting yellow chowder into her path. She stopped and hung cramped at the velvet rope while three more compulsive jets smacked her party shoes. As the last umbilical string left her mouth for the puddle, four more girls heaved out of the club wearing fluffy pink antennae. They jostled past the girl, saw the Heaths staring, and flopped out their breasts with shrieks of laughter before scuttling away like a bashed insect in spasm.

'Mark my fucking words.'

'Just you relax.' Blair composed himself and went to join Lamb. He developed a swagger on the way to the World's smoked-glass entrance. Then he saw two large doormen in dinner jackets watching him approach. The swagger collapsed to a shamble. The doormen were of the hairless London type that embody the threat of cruelty, men grown hard on white bread, who would sooner put your head in a chip fryer than untidy their manicures with a blow. The brothers shuffled beside a queue of people as Lamb shared a word with the men. Bunny lit a Rothmans. Eventually one of the doormen slightly creased his face at Lamb, and gathered up the trio's identity cards, swiping them into a hand-held machine. When it chirped three times, he unhooked the rope and waved them into a long entrance hall. One stony eye gave Bunny to understand he should abandon his Rothmans. He planted it in a tray of grit by the door, shook his suit square on to his shoulders, and trundled in behind Lamb and Blair: half rock star, half derelict schoolboy shopping with his gran.

'Me vein's going mental,' he said as a bass thump began to ring through his flesh. 'Should probably head home.'

'Well, don't let me stop you,' Blair said over his shoulder. 'Taxis over the road.'

'Mini-cabs? I don't mean home to bloody Nigeria.'

'Well, that's totally uncalled for, Bunny.'

'What's wrong with that?' Bunny stopped to dangle his snaggles.

'It's utterly racist, for a start. For Christ's sake, this is multicultural London – you'll get yourself put away, or bloody killed.'

'Blair, pet – Nigeria isn't a race.'

'Well, I mean, come on,' Blair turned to scowl from a few paces ahead. Lamb vanished through the doors behind him.

'I mean to bloody say. You tell me, how is it racist to say a mini-cab driver's from Nigeria?'

Blair rolled his eyes. 'Well, it's the inference that they're all mini-cab drivers, and somehow providers of lesser services.'

'Blair – the three mini-cab drivers I've had so far have been smashing lads, I'd join a lottery pool with them. But none of them have been off the plane long enough to know where we're bloody going. I was an hour finding the launderette, and it's only up the road. You tell me how that's racist. It's common fucking sense, I'm only a foreigner here meself, remember. I mean to say.'

'Well, it's pejorative to lump members of the African community together under the heading of one particular place. You were being pointedly snide.'

'Was I bollocks! Anyway, pal, hark at you – "members of the African community" – you've completely buggered them into a different community from yourself, you're the fucking racist.'

'Oh yeah, Bunny – well, I challenge you to show me how that can be true, given that's how they're officially referred to across the English-speaking world.'

'Because if you'd honestly accepted them into the culture, you'd say "African members of the community". Words are concepts, Blair.'

'Well, this is just absurd now.'

'No, pal, it's horribly true. You perpetuate the issue by making it fucking taboo to say anything. And don't pretend to me that knocking about with the likes of Nicki makes you fucking multicultural – she's just a fashion accessory with a knockout bum.

Dark girls have the best arses, you've said it yourself time and again.'

'Well, I take serious bloody exception to that.'

'And well you fucking should. Because for all your swanny airs, you're still just an anal white bourgeois fascist tosspot.'

'Well, you can just piss off home. Take the bloody tube.'

'Oh aye, thanks, a mobile buried-alive experience.'

'You've never bloody tried it.'

'You don't have to try it, just hark at the screeching goes on under the pavement. Those are people, Blair – human organisms screaming.'

Don's ghostly face popped back through the doors. A throbbing musical chill puffed around him, from Sketel One's hit 'Deys ony be one ennifink'. 'Come on, lads, it's carnage,' he shouted. 'The World's a one-stop shop – three main areas down here, members upstairs.' He waited for Sketel's vocal to subside before continuing. 'We could've gone into the social round the back way, where it's quiet, but I thought you'd want to see the likes of this. Stay close, we'll head through this way.'

'Can we not stop here for a minute?' said Blair.

Lamb stopped, studying the pair. 'Are you sure?'

'Why not? We'll be discreet.'

Lamb looked around. 'Aye, there's some lasses knocking about. Go on, lads. Ten minutes.'

'Well actually, it's just me – Bunny's not into girls.'

'I've no problem with that,' shouted Lamb. 'There's lads knocking about too.'

'Well, he's not gay either. He's just sort of – asexual.'

'Sensible man,' shouted Lamb. 'Stay handy, I'll start the trek to the bar.'

Blair nodded, and dotted the room with blinks. He calculated his quickest adhesion to the fizz. Sharp downlights like hanging light-sabres patterned the room, all but one of whose walls were mirrored from floor to ceiling, giving the effect of an endless middle earth, a halogen sperm stadium wriggling with life. Clumps of elastic professionals were silhouetted against a huge aquarium set into the fourth wall. A dull, spotty fish spun dying on its surface. A posse of bright ones pecked at its belly. A group of windswept youths near by also hovered and flitted in a school, and one of them, a turtlenecked man, turned a cheek towards the Heaths, not to acknowledge them, but to report their appearance as a sneering aside to the rest of the school. They flicked furtive eyes and pretended not to notice.

Bunny looked around, shook his head, and stumbled off towards a lavatory sign at the back of the room. Blair watched him pass, but pretended not to notice. Instead he lost himself to a silky creature who was gliding like an elf towards the bar. When she sensed him staring, her tiny mouth and brow twitched self-consciously, and she thrust her nose a little high. She pretended not to notice him. Blair leered to himself; he was a garden of plump synapses, an electric oyster bed all a-tingle. He edged through the comfort zones of women in his orbit, but no matter how close he stood he was buffered from their animal truths by an armour of perfume. Still, at their spinning core, in the eye of their storm, even as they pretended not to notice him, or themselves, which they very much did notice, he felt shimmering the sweet vapour of abandon, the nucleus of opportunity – alcohol. Blair watched it dissolve and reorganise cell walls around groups of people, noting that all were connected by a synaptic web whose links increased with every drink. A real-estate conversation in one group would attract a sympathetic comment from another, and the groups would fuse for as long as the exchange glowed. Even after fusion they stayed in sympathetic, brow-flashing communion.

Lamb returned through a firefly grotto of designer drinks. He carried three pints, and smiled to see Blair so keen. 'Get this down you,' he shouted. 'Where's our lad?'

'Don't know. Cheers.'

'Will I find him?'

'Leave him. If we're lucky he'll be stabbed in the toilets.'

Blair shadowed Lamb out of the first bar, down a corridor, and into a vestige of the original pub; a place where time stood still – the lounge. Here men paid proper attention to drink, and to ruminations whose colour arose from drink, within a comfortable smog of beer-sodden carpet. The music was old, and old in an unfashionable way. Whiskers and broken veins flowered over the bar, pink eyes tracked the barmaid and pretended not to. Football roared from a wall-mounted screen. A man at the bar with a whippet's hunch watched Blair through a shifty eye.

'I'd best have a look for our lad,' said Lamb, pressing a twenty-pound note, and Bunny's pint, into Blair's hands. 'Mine's a Badgers.'

'What?'

'A pint of Badgers Lout, and whatever you want.'

The barmaid was flirting and rinsing glasses some distance away, pretending not to notice Blair by the taps. He turned his back and absorbed the rustic scene. Between his third and fourth sips of beer, Bunny appeared with a large gin in the thoroughfare between bar and corridor. He sidled up to Blair's ear.

'I feel a twat saying, but some lass's just asked after you.'

'Eh?' A jolt ran through Blair. His eyes flicked around.

'Couldn't believe it, meself,' said Bunny. 'Just like that, up she came.'

'Well, how do you know she meant me?'

'Saw us come in together. Said, "Who's the important-looking one – the statesmanlike one."' Bunny grunted ironically.

'Couldn't fucking believe it, meself.'

Blair turned to his brother and locked a stare into his sunglasses. 'Well, what did you say?'

'Said she'd be better off home with a candlestick.'

'Buns, not now, come on. What did you say?'

'Well, you know, I just –'

'Well, no, what words did you use *exactly*?' Blair's mouth fell open with concentration.

'I mean to say, it was only quick.' Bunny looked over his shoulder and dangled a leg back into the thoroughfare. A healthy blonde girl with an arm full of drinks tried to skirt it, but lightly grazed Blair as she passed. 'Sorry,' she said, pausing to steady the lapping pints.

Bunny lifted his glasses and flickered his eyes at Blair. Their expansion and contraction said nothing in particular, but Blair heard them scream, 'That's her!'

He spun around. The girl's belly-button squinted over her denims, her perfume entered his lymph and found out his groin with its hands. With that, and a sudden uptake of beer – indeed, the rest of his pint – a reckless high gale blew through him. He waited for reason to challenge it. No challenge came. He was compelled to covet her. And his instinct wasn't to hammer the fluids out of her, not at first; it was simply to curl up with her, stare into her teeth, tell lies.

She moved on. He turned. She went to a table. Around it sat either her mother or older sister, and a bulky, older man, presumably that lady's husband; beside them a boy slumped morosely, too young to be on drinking business. They were types from up the way, people called Derek and Tracy, not long back from Malaga, starting to save for Salou. Blair marvelled. Such people had only nominally existed in his world. Now his own specimens sat before him in all their knockabout cotton glory.

He watched the girl's mouth squirm wet and pink around her words. She would have a birthmark on her hip, a blemish so faint it could only be found in full Mediterranean sun. But it had been enough to fatally dash her confidence, especially when added to slightly protuberant vaginal lips, and listless hair in adolescence. And so, Blair furiously projected, although she was now physically perfect, the scars of pubescent tragedy meant she hadn't developed the conceits of the early-bloomer, and had thus learnt to cherish the mundane.

The mundane meant taking his penis in her mouth. And doing other things. She would do them at his whim, as well as surprise him with them, in the mundane course of a day in their well-appointed home in the suburbs. It would be a large home, but still her adoration of him, and the things he did to her, would make its walls throb and leak saliva. He would writhe and sleep for ever in the glistening creams by her loins' gate. She would go about the business of cleaning up after this writhing wearing only his rugby jersey over stockings matted with semen.

Blair devoured the texture of that family at the beer-washed table. His dreams lashed the crannies of their lives, composed the awkward confidences her brother would share with him, practised the wisdoms he would expound while the mother looked dotingly on in bright acrylic sportswear too snug for her, cheeks flushed from deep-frying their tea. Blair would banish the aitches from his speech, toss saucy fibs at the mum with a crooked smile and a raffish jerk of his head.

How he soared through the heavens of that forthcoming life. And though he struggled to find reasoning against it, he had to concede that those visions of careless family life embodied all that was great about Britain. All that was great about freedom, about democracy. And on that basis alone, all was surely permitted in their pursuit.

He smirked to himself. To cap things off, he, a newcomer, had discovered the easy way to pull. Hordes of lads competed uselessly in the main bar while he swam in the quiet deep, poached nymphs from the stream of an ordinary day, snared them before their shower, in yesterday's mufti. He flicked his eyes around the lounge. It was true. There was only the one target. She sat waiting for him to make a move, confident enough of it that she spared no further thought.

'So anyway,' said Bunny.

'Never mind, never mind.' Blair tried to hook the girl's eyes across the room. She was the only person that night who didn't pretend not to notice him. Rather, she genuinely didn't notice him. This was a rare and beautiful thing to Blair. Not pretending not to notice him made her shine. Debbie, she'd be called. Debs. Our Debs. Blair 'n' Debs Heath. Blair and Deborah request the pleasure. Round to Blair 'n' Deb's for a knees-up. Seen B & D about? Nah, mate, they're down Florida for the winter. Lucky bleeder, you know how she gets when the sun comes out. Randy little minx. He spooled the words through his mind, played Professor Higgins with the sounds: 'Randy, raindy, rayndie li'oow mincs.'

'Well, you're a barrel of laffs,' said Bunny. 'Where's our Mister Lamb?'

'Don't know.' He flapped a hand. Bunny shuffled away up the corridor. Blair rolled an eye to see him truly gone, then he reached back to the bar, found Bunny's pint with his fingertips, drained it, slammed the glass down, belched inwardly, and lurched to his new family's table. Whippet swung a cheek from the bar.

The family didn't notice Blair until his shadow fell over their pints. Then, one by one, they looked up, eyes snagging on the banknote in his hand. Blair went down on one knee beside the girl.

'Evening,' he said, smiling around the table. He tightened his mouth to stop it trembling, and tried to force a dashing rake on to his brow.

'Yeah?' said the girl, eyes darting to the elder male.

''Orright, mate?' said the man.

'Fine, thanks.' Blair reached out to squeeze the girl's arm. 'Do you know, you'll laugh, I suppose, in retrospect, but this stunning creature –'

''Oo the bloody 'ell's this?' The girl pulled away.

'No, no,' said Blair, slapping her shoulder, 'no, no, I mean, I've not come, that is –' Words fled his mind like lint before the mistral. He found himself scowling at the carpet. One hand flapped hopelessly above the girl's breast.

The elder man stood, heaving his belt up over his gut. Seven yards away the barmaid logged a change in the lounge's rhythm, sensed like a hound that its molecular structure had been violated. She threw an eye to the elder. Tension crystallised across the room. Heads turned, pretending not to notice.

The whippet broke a hole through the chill, turning in his stool to call out, ''Ere, mate – you're s'posed to be puttin' up a round for the little geezer.'

Blair turned to him, then turned back to fawn into his beloved's eyes.

''Oo's this tosser?' she squeaked.

'Look, my friend –' growled the elder, leaning close.

Blair stood – burning, imploding – and shuffled away without a sound.

Whippet smiled crookedly as he approached the bar. 'You ain't pesterin' them people, are ya?' He threw a grin back to the girl's table: ''E don't get out much.'

''E's come out once *too* much, mate,' said the elder, still heavily planted between the tragic lovers. 'Once too bloody much.'

'Well, but wait a minute –' said Blair.

'Look, mate,' said Whippet, 'leave it out, before you get fuckin' glassed.'

The blonde's father sat slowly, and called across the room, 'You wonna watch that one. Very strange. Very strange.'

Sweat trickled down Blair's back. Whippet leant close, cupping a hand to his mouth. 'Best 'ave a tinker with your technique,' he said.

'Well, but you don't understand –'

'Nah, mate, nah. First of all, stick with them what's in the market – see the bird you's chattin' up? She ain't come for that, that's why she's in the lounge. The geezer's her old man. Very dodgy move that, pullin' a bird in front of 'er farver. So first rule: never try 'n' pull from a mixed table.'

'Well, but listen –'

'Yeah, mate, I know, I know. Second rule: the lounge ain't about that. This is where you rest in between that sort of palaver, it's where you bring your mum and dad to tell 'em you been sacked from McDonald's. Anyway, what you gunna do – shag 'er in the back of 'er old man's Transit?'

'Well, but –'

'You won't get better advice than from me.' The man rolled a glance up and down the bar. 'Listen, mate, even if she was up for it, you're going about it all wrong: you 'ave to play 'em like eels – a bit of this 'n' that, then pull back, let 'em run with the bait. Can't come across so keen. As far as any tart should know, you got four better-lookin skirts than 'er waitin home with their Alans round their bleedin' ankles.'

'She stopped to talk to *me*.'

'See, mate' – Whippet leant into Blair's shadow – 'that ain't no grounds to pull 'er. Never, ever try 'n' pull in the lounge. We'll call that off limits. There's masses of apron gaggin' for it next door.'

'No, I'm sorry, I mean, that's why this one's special –'

'And there's more of what makes a bird special in the bar. Because' – Whippet gave a pantomime wink – 'payin' respect to your fox and badger's what makes a bird special, if you get my drift. Bit of Horatio and all.'

'Fine, fine,' said Blair.

'What are you like, eh? What are you bloody like?'

Blair stood chewing the inside of his cheek. As the heat in his face slipped to his collar, he was struck with an image of Bunny. Bunny smiling through his snaggles.

Bunny's stamp was all over the incident.

Lamb returned to find Blair grinding his teeth, eyes smouldering. 'Safety,' he sighed, stepping in from the corridor. 'It's bedlam out front.'

Bunny sauntered in behind him. He looked his brother quickly up and down, pausing to smile through his snaggles. 'Still here? Thought you'd have had her on the twentieth position by now.'

Blair leapt off his feet and tackled his brother into the corridor wall, snarling, hissing, billowing jags in three dimensions. Bunny ducked and feinted as Blair scratched the air around his head. Lamb threw an arm between them, trying to wedge himself into the blur.

In the time it took for the men to turn white and sweaty, a large figure in a dinner jacket swept into the corridor. The stem of a headset microphone curled around one square cheek.

'No bother, it's just a laff,' Lamb said before the man could speak. He reached for his wallet and pulled out a metallic card. 'I'll sort it with Mister Truman – we're attached to the Vitaxis social.'

'Yes, Mister Lamb.' The man studied the card. 'I'm afraid I can't authorise you into the Vitaxis room, but I can find somebody who can. Perhaps you'd like to bring your party through to the members in the meantime? Only we have to keep a close eye out here, Saturdays can be mental. Probably be for the best.'

'Good idea,' said Lamb. 'Let Truman know I'm about, will you?'

'Yes, Mister Lamb.' The bouncer stood a moment, staring down at Blair and Bunny. The vacuum in his eyes delivered a message. They understood, and slumped silent. 'This way, gents.' He unhooked his eyes and rolled up the corridor like a statue on a trolley.

The men were ushered to the corridor's far end, away from the main bars. When the bouncer left them, Lamb turned and nailed both charges in the eye. 'Will we call it a night? I've stuck me neck out here – don't let me down.'

The pair stopped beneath a single, napkin-white spotlight, and rumpled visibly. Their suits drooped sideways towards each other, as if magnetically drawn. They dropped their eyes. Bunny clenched and unclenched his hands by his side, trying to ignore the muffled apocalypse banging through the walls. He reached a hand to Blair's back, and began to trace a gentle circle.

It was four minutes past midnight.

II

'Grandpapa says to find a hat for the goat!' Kiska flew out of the bedroom towards the front door.

'And kindly catch down your brain.' Irina stepped into the rosy projectile's path. 'Your grandpapa has gone away with the saints, and the goat lives quite well without a hat.'

'No, he just told me from his bed, and he himself also cares for a hat.'

Irina reached down and turned the little girl like a clockwork key, patting her towards the bedroom. 'Your grandfather has gone away, little bird. Don't imagine him again, or you'll make him sad.'

Kiska sailed the answer across her eyes. 'Will he even cry?'

'And he might probably even begin to cry. Go back now to mama's bed.'

A pause gripped the dung smoke while Kiska flapped back to the bedroom. Irina, Olga, and Maks drooped at the table by the stove, waiting for the creak of Kiska's bottom on the mattress. Then they went on, huddled like a poker school in the dead of an unfriendly night. Olga's eyes shone alternately wide and narrow with each rusty word. Maks tried hard to focus, but all he could see in her black old sockets were dancing lights from the stove. Undried dungs fizzed a curious smoke. Kiska had twice been up coughing. Again her wheeze could be heard through the bedroom door.

'Anyway, don't piss grease down my throat,' Maks finally

said. 'Nothing you have so far revealed provokes me to tell of the extraordinary success I achieved with the tractor.'

'Well, listen to what else I can tell you about the sacrifices that permit you to sit puffing gas instead of truth!' Olga railed. 'He ate human flesh! He had to, Maksimilian! Great numbers of men ate from dead bodies like wolves! I say men because women hadn't such stomach. Some women did too, though, to survive. Some babies grew up on the softer parts, I won't even tell you what. You were blessed to be born after the end of it. These are the truths of our past that you ignore and disrespect!'

'You're denouncing my great-grandfather as a cannibal,' scowled Maks. 'And where is his son's body? What happened with this examiner of deaths?'

'Your great-grandfather did what he had to do, like an animal, because let me tell you something that you ignore: strong creatures will do anything to survive. When you remove a person's dignity, and subject his blood to generations of aching hunger, so that each morning is a decade away from each night, so that a body can't spare the salt for tears – the strong of spirit have to look for survival. They do it because of a flame that burns in their gut, a hope that if they can survive another minute then God might grow bored pandering to the fancies of the rich and evil to spare the ordinary man a crumb of benefit.'

'Where is Aleks resting?'

'And you listen to me, Maksimilian, with open ears: he did it so that one day you might be born with higher possibilities. He went to his glory with sickly cells from insulting God so that you could loll with your lazy stupidities.'

'You know, Grandmama, that I worship and respect every drop of sweat from my great-grandfather, and the fathers before and after him. And that is why today I have no problem with my position as heir because I have fixed the family's fortune for ever.' He sat back and swigged from the bottle, leaving a mouthful of vodka for each of his mothers. They sat scowling, unable to quite meet his eyes.

'I can read you like a bad poem, Maksimilian,' said Irina. 'Just tell us the story, so we know what torment to face.'

'Pah!' Maks spat on the floor. 'I can only tell you this: that last night, while you bumbled around talking nonsense about the healing properties of mud, and other senseless inutilities about nothing, and probably already lounged with bread and drink while I fought my way through the snows – I secured our first shipment of communication technologies. The result of this action, even as you scorn me to my face, is that within a week – two at most – I predict you'll insult me instead from the balcony of a duplex on the Caspian.'

Irina's head puckered like an old party balloon. 'Just tell us,' she whispered.

'And let me announce' – Maks raised a glorious finger – 'in case you thought it was shit what I now said, that these are the first instruments of their kind anywhere in these republics. Better even than Nokia.'

'Maksimilian,' said Irina. 'Empty me your pockets.'

'What! What! What colour of goose do you take me for? Do you think I'd bring them here, to get mouldy and broken?'

'How much did you get for the tractor?'

'I said, do you just expect that I should bring delicate and high-performance electronic tools for you to rupture like mongols?'

'Maks,' grunted Olga, 'the tractor.'

'I got at least half-price on a whole boxful of the latest handsets. Probably more like three for one, you should've seen me hammer down the deal.'

'Please, God' – Irina curled her eyes up at the ceiling – 'don't let me hear any name at all beginning with Pilo.'

'What! What! Pilosanov knows all the correct people for these affairs. You women wouldn't know in the least!'

'Saints in paradise.' Irina shifted red-rimmed eyes on to her son. 'Where are these telephones?'

'Tomorrow I'm almost definitely picking them up, after this damp weather. That was a good decision, a great decision of mine, in fact, to wait for the damp to pass a bit. The man wanted to foist them on me straight away last night – almost fought with me, but I had the better of him. "You imagine my cuckoos are sleeping, spastic friend," I said to him. "Bring me the instruments fresh and in sunshine, before I smash down something very reminiscent of your face and head." He was nearly shitting where he stood, this man, who was clearly a homosexual from Labinsk, but strong though. Still, anyway' – Maks rapped on the table – 'our investment is now safe.'

Irina's eyes clunked shut. 'So you don't possess the telephones. And where is the tractor?'

'Maksimilian,' said Olga, 'fetch back the tractor.'

'What! What! I should've gone to the navy like Georgi! I should've left you to fester like rats!'

The trio froze, and threw their eyes to the door as the goat bleated outside. A footstep squelched near, then thumped on to the step. 'Aleksandr Vasiliev!' yelled a voice. 'Come to your door!'

'No, I don't like that blue.' Ludmila pushed her chin at the girl. The girl remained unperturbed, perhaps hadn't even taken stock of Ludmila's tone. This riled Ludmila even more.

'Yes, but it's clean and sensual.' The girl raised both legs in front of her. 'The blue of electricity. Come, and I'll show you others in my wardrobe.'

'Later,' said Ludmila.

The girl, Oksana, threw back her head like a whinnying horse, and reached behind her neck to gather her long blonde hair. She sat batting paint-encrusted eyelids in thought, and finally spread her hands in an expansive gesture. 'Yes, but now that my uncle has allowed you to stay in the room, and removed your troubles of accommodation for a day or two, you have the leisure to just look at pretty things!'

Ludmila sat quiet on a wooden chair in a one-room apartment opposite the Kaustik café-bar. From there she could mount a vigil over its door, and wait for Misha's lumbering form to appear. She felt some relief at having secured a room, in the short term at least, and found herself thinking she should be more civil to the barman's niece. She shifted her weight in the chair, calculating how many hours of good firewood it would make. 'Anyway,' she said, 'I paid good cake for the room.'

'Oh dear,' smiled the girl, 'but five hundred roubles is nothing. Look, we even have a boiler for water.' The girl sat back for a moment, toying with a strand of her hair. 'You know,' she said, 'if you weren't wearing that dress my uncle would never have helped you.'

Ludmila levelled a baleful stare. 'And why?'

'Well,' Oksana smiled coyly, 'let's just say it covers some of the soil in you. I don't say it in a bad way, I think you're very pretty for a mountain girl, beautiful even. But if you'd come up here with a headscarf, and socks on the outside of your boots, he would've found the whole idea just too bad.'

Ludmila flashed the sounds of a few choice slaps through her mind. But she said nothing. She listened to the silence on the street outside, and wondered whether to be happy or unhappy about the amount of light that glowed in through the curtain, or the fact there was a flushing toilet that could be used only during two daily hours of water supply.

'What are you thinking?' asked Oksana after a moment.

'That I should be out working instead of taxing myself with the ecstasy of all your Pretty Things.'

Oksana gave a squeaking laugh, her eyes rolling like a child's. 'Yes, but the munitions factory uses only skilled workers, and there are no fields to plough here in Kuzhnisk! What else would you do?'

'I don't mean here in your cockroach-hole of a town. I mean away, in the west, with my fiancé.' Ludmila scratched the inside of a thigh with her fingernails. 'Anyway, my line of work sits far above your miserable factory of death. I'd be a secretary. Or an administrator.'

'Oh dear!' giggled Oksana. 'Can you write? And type?'

'Of course I can write.'

'And type?'

'Listen to me, Oksana Kovalenko, I can speak English. I'm not just any secretary. You think I emerge crawling from a mud field but you don't take into account my family's status in the region. Ask anyone about the name Derev. I speak English. And fly aeroplanes.'

'Oh dear! Speak me some English then.'

'Well – "Ayem plisttomityu."'

'Oh dear!' giggled Oksana.

'Oh dear what!'

'Oh dear!' The girl's smile froze. She searched Ludmila's face. 'You shouldn't be looking to work with such a razor mouth. You should be looking to capture a foreign man to support you. You would cut a foreign man to rags with your hard ways.'

'Yes,' said Ludmila, 'and I'm going to catch one fast sitting here speaking such deep philosophical themes with you. I doubt I can tear myself away from such profound issues as I'm exploring with you, Oksana Kovalenko.'

Oksana's smile withdrew twitching like a caned tentacle. She coiled a thicker strand of hair around her finger, and sat back into her chair, raising her knees up to her chest. Ludmila turned away to study a plastic bath-cage that held a sponge and a lump of perfumed soap. She noticed a lot of perfume in the apartment – the girl herself puffed it every time she moved.

'Yes, it's a shame you don't want to make friends, after all our kindness.' Oksana pulled the strand of hair into her mouth with a sigh.

'I never said I didn't want to make friends,' said Ludmila. 'When did you hear my mouth say those words?'

'Yes, but –'

'Hoh! And listen to me – you assume everything's up to my discretion because I'm the visitor from another place. No! You're the one with the welcome sign hung on your wall, you should see how you have to make friends with *me*. If you'd been anywhere you would know that! If a different type of person comes your way, you have to be ready to bend to their shape. That's how the world is managed, and how you become enriched by different passing souls because you bend to their experience and come away with a new outlook!'

'Oh dear!'

Ludmila swelled majestically in her chair. 'Finally we reach the subject I was too offended and embarrassed to speak of! Finally we can deal with this theme that's been like a smell from under your chair, because let me tell you something, Oksana Kovalenko: I've been sat an hour here making every type of invitation for you to do the correct and worldly thing in respect of our friendship, and all you can do is flap your rubber mouth up and down about your vulgar dresses. Imagine! A new and important visitor and you waste the crucial first hour, the golden hour, with squeakings about yourself!'

'Yes, but I didn't mean to make things awkward.' Oksana hugged her legs tight up to her chin.

'And I'm the elder of us! The elder, and all you can do in place of a correct welcome is hug your legs and wink at me through your clownish red underpants!'

Oksana threw her legs off the chair and crossed them tight, yanking down her hem. 'How can I help the friendship then?'

'By immediately fetching vodka.'

'Well, actually, I already have vodka but it belongs to Uncle Sergei, from when he sometimes comes with clients. I think we could perhaps drink some – do you think we should drink some?'

'Wait while I recoil with astonishment – you suggest to actually *drink* it?'

'I'll get it.' Oksana stood up with a sigh.

Ludmila sat back and smiled as the girl slipped to a cupboard behind them and brought out a branded bottle of vodka. She watched her reach for two small glasses from the shelf beside the room's miniature gas boiler.

'And that's not all we should do,' said Ludmila, 'if we're to create a real friendship between women.'

'What else should we do?'

'If you're serious, and not just leading me up the backside with your innocent city ways – we should drink it with open chests, to display our pride at this crossing of our paths.'

'Oh dear!' Oksana stopped pouring to watch Ludmila hike her dress up over her head, and sit poking alert, defiant breasts, with nipples like tiny dog-snouts quivering up.

'Do it only if you're serious about a deep and enduring friendship,' frowned Ludmila.

'Oh dear!' giggled Oksana, opening her blouse.

'More!' Ludmila slashed a hand through the air. 'You're lucky you don't have to do it naked, which is only for the very deepest relationships to form.'

Oksana squirmed out of her blouse to bare a loose red brassière. She arched forwards to take up its slack.

'And then,' said Ludmila, 'take a drink – drink your whole glass down, and I'll do the same.' Ludmila emptied her glass with a gulp, then turned to watch the girl wince as the drink hit her throat. 'Now,' said Ludmila, 'hand me the bottle, lean back, and close your eyes.'

'What?'

'Do as I say.'

As the girl leant carefully back in her chair, Ludmila reached for the sponge in the bath-cage, held it over the girl's chest, and squeezed it hard. Oksana shrieked as half a cupful of cold water soaked her bra and ran down her belly.

'Oh dear!'

'Now we can be friends.' Ludmila smiled, and filled both their tumblers to the brim.

As the next tumbler of vodka, and the one after it, was drained, Oksana could no longer form sentences through her giggles. Soon after, Ludmila giggled along.

'I know where we could go,' said Oksana, squeaking for air. 'You can thank me later, but this could be your very lucky day.'

'Hsst!' Olga flapped a hand across Maks's face. The family sat frozen in the stove's glow. Such a late call was strange. Whoever approached must have heard their chatter. Whoever it was must be local, and know well that the family was inside. It sounded like Lubov Kaganovich from the depot.

'Aleksandr Vasiliev! Somebody open up this door!' It was Lubov. She was audibly irritated by the walk up the hill. 'Or have you all gone out for the evening? Gone drinking to a lively boulevard club with music and dancing?'

The women held their breath. 'She's in a smell,' hissed Irina. 'We'll have to open.' She wrung her hands until the whites of her knuckles shone.

Olga shrugged, adopting her poker face. It was a face that had seen her through four wars and an alphabetical list of privations with no letters missing, including X if one counted the incorrect X-ray doses she received after giving birth, and from which it was a miracle she hadn't perished years before.

'Aleksandr Vasiliev, I'll break down this door with my hands!' banged Lubov.

As keeper of the bread depot, the last registered business of any kind in the district, Lubov's power was absolute. The depot was a mildewed cockpit from which she piloted the destinies of the district's last mollusc-like inhabitants. Every week, a forlorn box-car was uncoupled from a train on the main line, and pushed on to a disused siding that ran to within four kilometres of Ublilsk. The track had no sleepers, these having vanished before the line was even closed, and so it snaked uneven and invisible beneath a froth of undergrowth and snow. Oafish young men met the wagon each week, carrying metal bars and sharpened chains for security. Rumour had it they now also carried a gun. They were Lubov's retarded son and nephew – for the stigma of feeble blood twice stained her – and they would heave and pull the wagon as far as the track would allow, then unload the bread into sacks, and carry it over their backs to the depot. In milder weather, people sometimes slept on the depot doorstep, waiting. And it didn't have to be much milder. Others would emerge like gnomes from the snows around the box-car, following Lubov's boys from the tracks, shouting enticements to loosen a loaf from their grip. The town had several simple faces rumoured to be the cost of a dirty loaf.

A mighty battle erupted at the depot every bread day, as the last dogged citizens hurled shouts that ricocheted like rusty blades off wet green tiles, splintered over the rough wooden bar where vodka was also sold throughout the week, even on bread day, which didn't help matters. One's slate was the only argument in town, and relentless bickering crowded the day, and the week after it, with conflicts over sums too small to even form the whole denomination of a coin. The depot slate was a magical instrument, in the style of the International Monetary Fund, inspiring little hope that its capital sums would be recovered, but rather involving itself with arbitrary fluctuations of payable interest, and not immune to summary relaxings or tightenings of policy at its master's whim, in this case Lubov Kaganovich's.

Everybody knew she added sums to the slate out of spite.

'I'm opening the door,' whispered Irina.

Maks grabbed the cast-iron stove handle and began to detach it. Olga put a hand to his arm, and shook her head. She tossed her eyes to a crowbar whose tip menaced from behind the wire trolley frame that was their kitchen tidy. Understanding soaked through Maks's eyes.

Lubov burst into the smoke, displacing a cloud of it into the night. The family watched it freeze and sink into the snow as Lubov stamped her feet, huffing billows at the threshold. 'You should thank me – nay, pray at my feet – for making such a filthy journey for no other purpose than to save your miserable names.'

Maks stood out of sight. He weighed the crowbar in his hand. Olga sat back. She defaulted to her seniority as a woman, as a mother of children and grandchildren of strong blood, and twisted her face into a disdainful pucker. 'Knowing it was you, we would have built the road longer, and with deeper holes.'

'Yes, Olga Aleksandrovna,' sneered Lubov, 'you can say that until you hear what trouble I've saved you by coming to your hovel. Anyway, I'm not here for you but for Aleksandr.'

'You have snot on your lip.'

'It's my snot to deal with, thank you very much.' Lubov dragged a sleeve across her moustache. 'Now go and fetch the old man so I don't have to dirty my shoes a moment longer on your animal-trough floor.'

'Rather you mean not to dirty our floor with your hooves,' said Olga, happy to carry on the distraction. From the corner of her eye she saw Maks edging to the wall nearest Lubov.

Lubov clenched her face. 'And I say it to you now: don't make me have to proceed myself and wake your husband.'

'He won't see you,' said Olga. She could see Maks's hand approaching with the crowbar.

'And don't trouble to come at me from behind the wall, you boy!' Lubov thumped the wall behind her. 'Don't think my eyes have stayed empty all these years I've suffered watching you.' She said it rather too boldly for a woman alone in a house full of enemies. The Derevs weighed her tone, glanced at each other, then turned to peer through the kitchen window. Sure enough, a lumpy shadow bobbed outside, then another. Lubov's oafs were there.

Maks carefully parked the crowbar in the corner of the main room. He stepped back into the shadows and emerged into view from a different pocket of gloom. 'And are you so bored raping us at the depot that you now come to pilfer from our beds?'

'Go for your grandfather. Do it before I send my men for him.'

'Hoh!' laughed Maks. 'If they can stop pissing in their boots!'

'Enough!' Irina squared herself up to Lubov. 'Why do you want my father, what has he done?'

'He signed an old voucher, you were supposed to bring me one from the new series.'

'But you cashed it,' said Irina, folding her arms.

'Because God has damned me with the stupidity of trust.'

'It called for no trust, that's a registered coupon still.'

'It's from the old series! I told him about this only last month, he must be losing his cuckoos. Now fetch him here before I catch all your diseases.'

'I'll have him sign two next month,' said Olga.

'No.' Lubov took another step into the room. 'I'm going to find him now.'

Olga held up a hand. 'Tell us why he can't sign one in daylight. He's an old man, he doesn't need your fat jelly face on his bed. He might catch sight of it in the dark and be killed choking on bile.'

Lubov let fly an angry gasp. 'And I'll tell you why: because today the inspector for the region carried your rancid voucher into my depot in his own cold hands and forced me to open out my ledgers dating back to the factory days. For all I know he sits there still, wondering sharp questions about your accounts, even as we stand here like fools.' A hint of fear crept into the back of Lubov's voice. It came by way of a creak.

'Hoh!' chirped Olga. 'And even Kiska Ivanova, who sleeps, bless her future misery, would die laughing to be told that you came to help us in any way at all. What is there in your ledgers that fetches you needing our help? Surely not a thirty-year elegy of crime, a patterned carpet of deceit and callousness to those whose punishment is to depend on you?'

'Fold back your tongue, my ledgers are cleaner than the plates you graze from. I just don't have the same hard face as you to be wasting the man's time with my ledgers when all he came to see about is that one voucher.'

'Hoh!' Maks stepped up to the woman, 'And isn't it rather *your* job to see that the correct vouchers are presented?'

His mother cast him a vixen's eye. 'Tread wisely, for all of us,' it said.

Maks poked a finger at the woman. 'You suggest to waken an old soul who works in a day what you work in a year, when all the time it's your responsibility to assess the vouchers for correctness!'

'Well it's not,' said Lubov.

'You lie to the front of our faces!'

'I'm waking the old man.'

Kiska emerged whining from the bedroom, and ran to her mother's skirts. Maks stepped squarely into Lubov's path, a coil of black hair flopping over his eye. Lubov cupped her hands towards the kitchen window. 'Gregor! Karel!' she called. Carved potatoes with sleepy dog-faces trudged into the shack. One of them carried a rifle. Lubov pointed them to the bedroom door. 'Get the old man.'

'You can't do it!' said Irina. 'I'll set the whole district against you!'

'Pah! Then all you threaten is another day of my normal life.' Lubov whipped an impatient finger at her boys.

Maks stepped scowling into the boys' path. 'Stop there before I smash something closely evocative of your –'

Crack. Gregor smote him with the rifle butt.

12

'That's the long and short of it,' said Blair. He teased the girl's nipple with a strand of her hair. 'Just another global markets consultant in the City.'

'Oh, oh,' said the girl. 'You big man. Rich, clever man.'

A snort popped in Bunny's nose. Blair glowered over the table at the banquette where his brother sat with Donald Lamb. He sent a quick threat with his eyes, then turned back, trying to absorb the girl through his skin, soak her up like gravy into white bread.

She picked Blair's hand off her thigh, and knelt up to make a luscious adjustment of her thong. A clean graduation from pink to brown winked from the cleft of her bottom. 'Will I dance now for you, Mister Big Clever?'

A squeak burst through Bunny's lips. He bit them, and looked around for a distraction. The World & Oyster's members bar was a misty chamber of mirrors, leather, and young womanhood in tiny undergarments that had never entertained an odour or secretion not issued from a bottle. Its size was impossible to calculate. The air pulsed to crisp music, starched light fell in rods away to infinity.

'You don't like dance?' The girl walked fingers over Blair's chest.

He made a quick spatial assessment with his eyes, and drew in the range of his voice. 'Well, I mean, don't dance where everyone can see.'

'You want only me for your whole self?' She fingered an edge of satin at her crotch. 'With nobody, just you, and little me? We can go to special room, just only you and me, alone.'

'I'd like that very much, Natasha. I'd like that more than I can say.'

'Oof, you are special man.' Natasha rolled her eyes. 'In Russia there isn't man like you. Russia man only drinking until fall down, only hit woman. If I see man like you in Russia I never come to England firstly.'

Blair squeezed her hand. 'Well, you've found me now.' He lingered to part her mane with the tip of his nose. 'We need never be apart again.'

Bunny's shoulders began to bounce. A hand jerked up to smother his face, but little whines escaped through his fingers.

Blair flew off his seat. 'Look – I'll bloody have you in a minute!'

'Here, settle,' Lamb frowned across the table. 'We'd best go downstairs, the department'll have me head for bringing you up here.'

Bunny's hands flapped, tears began to stream under his glasses.

'*Piss off, Bunny*! Right, that's it. Bunny's out.'

Lamb half-stood. 'Keep it down, come on.'

'Well, I mean, look at him! It's just not on!'

The girl frowned, and leant away from the disturbance, readjusting her thong over her hips.

Lamb stepped out, and led Blair by the arm to a patch of empty shadow near by. 'Here, settle – it's only a laff. I've misjudged the situation, I apologise. We'll head downstairs, meet the Vitaxis crew.'

'Well, I'm sorry, but it's not just a laugh. I'm on to something here, and this bastard –'

'For heaven's sake, try and remember where you are. I've paid a hundred quid for the young lady to chat with you, don't run off with the ruddy elves.'

'But she's, she's –'

'She's a stripper, Blair. You've known her ten minutes.' Lamb tightened his grip on Blair's arm, levelled a gaze into his face. He met with the eyes of a toddler abandoned in hell. Donald Lamb had indeed miscalculated.

The girl unfolded off the banquette. Blair's eyes slithered to her pubic delta, over her hips, across her belly, and past two handfuls of creamy breast. But he never saw her face again. She turned and walked away with the indifference of a cat.

'Natasha!' he called.

'Leave it,' said Lamb.

'Natasha!'

The girl vanished through a door beside the bar. Blair's face crumpled. He glanced around, dazed. Then his eyes filled with tears. Throbbing music no longer beat time to a young life ascending. Now it hammered boards over future's window.

Lamb put an arm around Blair, led him to Bunny's banquette, and stood back to watch the pair through narrowed eyes. The Heaths sat melded, one face laughing, one face crying: a comedy, a tragedy. Slowly they trembled into synchrony. Bunny traced a circle on his brother's back. His grin began to crack. Come the fifth circle it propped into a silent scream, and with the seventh it collapsed into miseria. He began to sputter and hiss.

Lamb's eyes fell to the floor.

The Heaths' collision with the new world was as shocking to behold as a lorry crashing into a pram.

137

13

'You look like someone pooped on your grave,' said Oksana.

'And what would you know?' Ludmila tossed her head. 'This is love I'm dealing with, not any of your goose's trifles. Real love, with a life waiting in the west.'

'Oh dear. But he won't be coming now, will he? Anyway, there was no benefit in watching the Kaustik all the night through the window, not when it's shut. Won't you have another drink? I'm sure the bar will invite you one.'

'Hoh, well. What's that one, that glows?' Ludmila pointed to a drink that shone like an arctic beacon from the bar.

'Gin,' said Oksana. 'The violet light makes it glow. It's expensive. It has to come from Ukraine.'

'Hoh. Chernobyl tapwater, it looks like. Anyway, I don't need to drink anything from Ukraine.' Ludmila scowled the length of the long velvet cave. 'Or from Moscow, actually, now that I taste your vodka around here. You wouldn't know a good vodka if it came with its own cheese.'

'Don't begin back your complaints,' said Oksana. 'Look – there he is.'

Ludmila leant on to the bar, following Oksana's finger with a scowl. 'Who?'

'My cousin, who owns the Leprikonsi, and has the other business I told you about.'

'*Leprikonsi?*'

'That's the name of this bar, silly. Have you hair in your ears?'

'He needs an administrator?'

'Oh dear! Don't you remember what I said about here?'

'He's a rich foreign man?' Ludmila spied a shapeless man like a thumb with features painted on in miniature. He chattered carelessly at the end of the bar with two over-decorated women, smoothing gelled hair with the palm of his hand, then wiping the hand on a shiny black trouser leg.

'No, silly! He's the technologist for international partnerships – he has waiting hundreds of rich, serious partners from America and Sweden.'

'Hoh. And that explains why I see your streets crowded with rich foreign partners. Listen to me, to address the practical business: can we just have this drink and get going? My man is a soldier, he can arrive at any moment of the day or night.'

'Yes, we can drink.' Oksana motioned the barman. He slid to them and filled two glasses with vodka. No money changed hands. 'Look,' said Oksana, 'there just aren't virtuous girls left in those countries, the traffic of money is so easy that the women have fallen lazy and vulgar. These men are rich, and desperate for a sensitive and correct romance. They have houses, and send gifts, and cash. When Ivan tells you the details, you'll cover him in kisses of thanks, even fat as he is – I know you will.' She squeezed Ludmila's hand, and popped off her stool to fetch the thumb.

'And but listen to me,' called Ludmila, 'what have I only now spent a dozen hours struggling to impress on you? That I have a man!'

Oksana was gone. She wove along the bar, catching the man's attention with a limp, flapping hand that was a materialisation of her giggle. He lowered an ear to her, rolled a black eye along her finger towards Ludmila, then turned to leer at the barman, pointing at the empty glasses of the girls he had surrounded.

He left them with a chuckled word, and followed Oksana back to her stool, stopping by each patron for a nudge and a laugh. Through vodka's shimmer he appeared to Ludmila as a mass of black cloth rolling gyroscopically towards her, a sort of executive tumbleweed.

'Well, save me from hell' – his chubby pink hand unfolded – 'another one from Ossetia.'

'Ublilsk,' Ludmila muttered into her glass.

The man's breath prodded her face, she felt his eyes swarm over her like mice. He motioned the barman, then took her hand and kneaded her fingertips. 'I'm Ivan,' he said.

'A saint-forsaken name if I ever heard one.'

'What!' he bellowed. 'Saint-forgiven is what you mean!'

'See what I told you about her?' giggled Oksana.

'A real mountain goat – but juicy with it.'

'Listen to me,' Ludmila turned her most baleful stare on the man. 'I'm not going to ever see the house of you or your Swiss friends. My man is a soldier who is bigger than three of you tied together, so why don't you go back to the jam pastries you were talking to before?'

'Haaa!' roared Ivan. 'You precious jewel! Well, seeing as you like to speak bluntly, let me put something to you. I'll start with a divination, which is a thing I'm very clever at doing – Oksana, you must need the toilet.' He paused while Oksana captured the idea, stood, and swayed away down the bar. Then he rasped cheerily into Ludmila's ear, 'Let us begin a friendship in the presence of truth. My divination is this: as you sit here emptying a stranger's vodka into your neck, and casting your eyes around for cheap profit, your mother, and probably your grandparents, are in a shack of tin and cardboard wondering what sauce to put on worms. A war is coming which will kill them, and any other family, probably your own children for all I know, unless you send back enough cash to buy their escape. Your soldier friend will be no help, in fact you'll probably more easily find a lump of gold in your soup than ever see his face again. You've tasted a banana only twice in your life, you have hairs growing along the length of your legs like a monkey because there is no salon within a thousand kilometres of your hovel, and you steal used teabags from the bin of your nearest depot to use for your intimate hygiene, which members of your family have afterwards more than once still considered boiling up to drink.'

'Only in case you were passing.'

Ivan didn't move his face, or change his expression at all. He kept his mouth slightly open after his last word. 'So don't suddenly inflate your tits in the big city and pretend you have rainbow-coloured options. This town was eating mountain girls before the first of your bloodline had a pile.' Ivan leant back from Ludmila's face, keeping her nailed with a frown. Then, as she took her glass from the bar, and drank her vodka down, his brow sailed up and up until his features shone with optimism.

'I have made uglier girls than you millionaires,' he hissed brightly. 'I don't lie, on my own immediate grave, and I don't mean from acts of immodesty. I'm telling you, I have on a Monday afternoon taken girls with half your juice, and by Thursday morning been driving them to shop for cars, houses, jewels. And do you know what?' He nudged her, bending his head to her ear. 'They didn't marry for it, or do anything at all!'

'Yes, I believed it as soon as I saw your face,' said Ludmila. 'It's called armed robbery. We see that in the mountains too, you know, in between boiling rags for your visit.'

'Look in my eye, woman.' Ivan nudged her again. 'Take a gun and kill me if what I say isn't one hundred parts true. Oksana has done you the biggest favour of your life. Because I own and

141

manage the most famous internet introduction service in the district, probably in the whole country. Men from all over the world bring their dollars and euros to impress girls half as pretty, and most of them never marry. Do you hear the detail of what I say? And don't think I hunt far for them, don't think I scratch my head wondering where they are: I have an American contact, a man of such power that he can authorise visas within an hour for any girl.'

Ludmila's gaze hardened on Ivan. She filed away the theme of visas to tell Misha. Her eyes glazed over, picturing herself unveiling her research into his ear, perhaps over coffee, perhaps over coffee and cake.

Ivan's fingers snapped in her face. 'Ha, you see! You dream of it even before I finish telling you. Unbelievable, you say to yourself. Unbelievable this opportunity. Yet it's true! Generous men come from countries where women have grown selfish and decadent, come for even the smallest taste of a real woman's spirit, and they pay any sum to do it. And be sure that they come fully armed with cash – this isn't a cheap destination to get to from anywhere, not like the interconnected dots of their own flabby countries, where aeroplanes fly every minute for the price of a hot bath. To fly to Kuzhnisk one must get first to Moscow, or Tblisi, or Yerevan, then fly on an entirely different aeroplane, for more money still, to get to Mineralnyye Vody, or Stavropol. And the same to get back. Over fourteen hundred American dollars it costs to get here, even from London. And do you think such men spend that to come and live poorly?'

'Well, they don't spend it to watch net stockings across a dark street.'

'And they don't spend it to interfere with my girls either! The best they get is to sit across a dinner table with an interpreter and chaperone, hearing about your love of the simple virtues of service. Do you imagine yourself the opportunities lurking in such a combination of softness and wealth?'

'It's not my place to deceive the blind.'

'What do you mean with "blind"?'

'If they had working eyes they would see on a map that there are safer places to find romance.'

'Well, firstly, don't think your Ublil districts stretch to here, we barely get sniping any more in Kuzhnisk. Our last artillery shell fell over a year ago, and didn't even reach the town boundary, it thumped by itself in an empty field. And you ignore the main factor of these men – and in a way I have to admit you're correct, they *are* blind – blind with love! They don't care about geography, and we don't trouble them with details. When you say Russia to an American he thinks only of Moscow.'

'Hoh! They come to Kuzhnisk and think it's Moscow?'

'Well, no, but we don't weigh things hard on their minds either – they're collected from an aeroplane and brought here to a hotel. Do you think we make them hitch-hike by the road? Anyway, my American partner owns businesses here, if he sends men they come knowing full well where they are. They're often functionaries of his own industries, top performers – instead of bonuses, he rewards them with the gift of loving family life. Can you imagine such enlightenment, to make a gift of loving family life?'

Ludmila sat quiet. Ivan was a repulsive man with a dam of sweat in the dimple of his chin. Any visa she tried to secure through him would be a last resort, with Misha's full complicity. From the corner of her eye, she watched Oksana return along the bar, hips swaying with an exaggerated clunk: a function of improbably high-heeled shoes.

Before Oksana reached her stool, Ivan's breath lapped back at Ludmila's ear. 'I have waited up nights and days to drink from your breath again, be in your manly cocoon,' he crooned. 'But my grandmother has taken deadly ill and I must pull her to Moscow on the sled because I'm short of the fare for an autobus.' He paused a moment for effect. 'My darling strongman, I long to be at your side, but the state will not allow me away from the intimate teabag factory unless I pay the eighty thousand roubles they say they will lose if another shift is wasted deepening my fanatical love for you.'

'Oh dear!' Oksana settled back beside them.

Ludmila turned to Ivan, and stared for a moment. Then she tossed him her chin. 'Hoh! And beetroots might grow up my arse.'

'Olga Aleksandrovna!' Lubov screeched from the depths of the shack. 'Your husband can't be woken.'

'I told you he was peaky. I told you he was peaky, and a very sound sleeper, so now that you've shown your hand as a gangster and a ruffian you should know what to do, Lubov Kaganovich. Come out before you kill old Aleksandr and leave me at the mercy of the maggots in the ground!'

'Mama,' Maks crouched down beneath the kitchen window, 'there's a light.'

Irina recoiled out of view of the window, peering around its frame into the night. Headlights lit the mist two hundred metres down the hill. She pulled Kiska into her skirts and stroked her head quiet. The lights flickered out, to be replaced by a bobbing torch beam.

'Well, if you ever deserved any kind of husband at all,' shouted Lubov, 'I'd tell you this one needed to be on his way to the clinic.'

'Tssst!' hissed Olga, monitoring the goings-on at the kitchen window. 'Now another of your gangsters comes, in an automobile.'

'What!' Lubov stepped out of the bedroom. 'Gregor, see about it.'

The larger boy stamped across the floor to the kitchen window. He stopped square and tall in the middle of it to call over his shoulder, 'It might be the inspector.'

'Lucifer!' Lubov scurried out of the bedroom, slamming the door behind her.

Irina and Maks circulated sharp glances. These gathered power until they hit Olga, who twitched with their impact.

'Now he has a torch light and is shining it through the window,' Gregor watched stains of light flicker over his military coat.

'Get down!' snarled Maks. He tugged at one of the boy's epaulettes, but the effect was to make Gregor's head turn an inch, frown at Maks, then turn back to window and crane to follow a man's fur hat to the step.

A slice of light appeared under the door.

'Now he's at the door,' shouted Gregor.

'Listen carefully to me,' whispered Lubov. 'You have to produce the new series vouchers and wake your old dog immediately.'

'He won't be woken,' said Olga. 'Anyway, his fingers are beyond use.'

There came a bang at the door that made the smoke wobble. After a moment's pause, Irina asked, 'Who is it there?'

'Inspector Abakumov for regions Thirty-Nine and Forty-One,' a taut voice called in Russian.

'I'll clear a way for you to come inside,' called Irina, flapping a hand at the others, and scooting Kiska to the bedroom with a slap of her backside. The little form stirred swirls in the shadows, and vanished.

Lubov took Olga's furry face in her hands and hissed thickly at it in Ubli. 'You have to sign a voucher for him. Get one and sign it now.'

Olga threw back her head, 'You're asking me to transform into a criminal like you, Lubov Kaganovich, just to spare your hide?'

'And *your* hide,' hissed Lubov, 'because it's *your* voucher.'

'Everything is correct in my house, I'll not be starting a life of crime on your say-so.' Olga rose from her chair.

'I'm letting him in,' whispered Irina from the door. 'Get that gun out of view, move away!' The boys clomped into the bedroom, and closed the door all but a crack.

'Look at me, Olga,' Lubov moved with the old woman to the table. 'This Abakumov sounds fluffy in his voice, but he's a hard and twisted man. I'm telling it to your bare face.'

'Pah!' spat Olga.

Irina straightened her dress, and opened the door. Outside stood a small, pig-featured man with a sausage mottle. Reflected torchlight gave a muddy tint to his tidy, fair fringe of hair. He shone the torch into the room, settling the beam on Olga, then Irina, before removing his fur hat, sitting his torch in it, still lit, and placing it on the bench to light up the room. It took some moments for his eyes to absorb the sting of dung smoke.

'Sub-agent Kaganovich?' he squinted circles around her form.

'Yes, inspector.' Lubov stepped smartly from the shadows. 'You needn't have travelled all this way, I'm seeing about the document.'

'Do you have it?'

'I'm just now seeing to the matter.'

'Then let us take possession of it – I'll carry it back with me. I was referencing from your ledger and it seems the last review of this Aleksandr Vasiliev Derev was nearly four years ago. I'll make a review tonight and phone it to the department tomorrow morning, or else I could be delayed here for a week.'

'And well!' said Olga in Russian. 'This is some time of the day to be visiting the dirt-poor in their sleep. We should do it tomorrow at the depot, where all your books must be kept. We can come as early as the saints like.'

'You seem to be awake now still,' said Abakumov. 'It will only take as long as Comrade Aleksandr makes it. Fetch him here for me, please.'

'But that's just the problem,' said Olga. 'He's green in his bed and can't be woken.'

'Well, but let's be frank,' Abakumov flashed rounded, widely spaced teeth in a semblance of courteousness. 'Anyone who is still at home in his bed can be troubled to confirm some simple facts.'

'No, that's just the problem, he should be in the clinic but we have no way to go.'

'Since when has he been like this?'

'Since earlier, that is, earlier yesterday. He's gone down and down, it can only be a massive type of worm.'

'So then,' asked Abakumov, 'how did he sign his voucher?'

'No because yes, and this is why he signed the wrong voucher. He was already delirious, he was calling out his mother's name when he signed.'

'Then we must bring him immediately to a clinic. Sub-agent Kaganovich, help me to the old man.'

'You're selling them like bread in a depot!' Ludmila sat gaping as hundreds of lurid faces scrolled down the computer screen. Ivan turned off the light in the box-room above the bar, making the faces on the screen shine brighter still. A pop tune crackled from a radio on the window sill, verses droning up and down in time with the scrolling pictures.

'I'm not selling them at all,' said Ivan. 'They are selling a dream.

They are selling an address to write sweet and daring letters to, which our interpreters will reply to with meaningless nothings. The girls in these pictures are at their homes this minute, waiting for envelopes of cash.'

'You see?' smiled Oksana. 'I told you it was easy. You must think this is the luckiest day of your life.'

'Yes, it is,' said Ludmila. 'Lucky for you both.'

'Here's what we're to do for best results.' Ivan leant over Ludmila, waving both hands like a magician about to make her vanish. 'Tomorrow my assistant will collect you to shop for new clothes. How does that sound? Then you'll go to a salon where they'll do startling new things to your hair and face. Then we'll take professional photographs, and by the afternoon a thousand men around the world will be stabbing themselves with love for you.'

Ludmila sat staring at the faces on the screen. Wide faces, eyes like tractor headlamps, beluga eyes, painted eggs, Svetlanas, Oksanas, Marinas, Tatyanas. Ludmilas. 'Father Jesus!' she pointed. 'That girl used to come around my town – her uncle is the signalman's brother, from Zimovniki!'

'And,' Ivan ran a finger through Ludmila's hair, 'only because of your situation, and your relationship with little Oksana, because you are nearly family, in a way – at least, you should begin to think in that way – I can give you the whole package for three thousand meagre roubles.'

'Aah, aaah.' Ludmila sat back and smiled, looking up from the bottom of her eyes. 'Now is the moment a gun appears.'

'You'll make twenty times that back, at least!'

'Then,' said Ludmila, 'why don't you bring the man, and take three thousand from the twenty he will give you?'

'Watch my face' – Ivan pointed forked fingers at his eyes – 'and see me tell you that there are costs we have to pay first. Do you think the clothes store and the salon and the photographer will work for nothing?'

'And where is the last twenty thousand that came from the foreigner before?'

'That money belongs to the girl!' Ivan's whole body protested. 'Do you think I can hold back the money that's rightfully hers?'

'Aaah, so now I see this is a charity. I see that you are sent by the saints to look after all the farm girls.'

'No, but pay attention – my commission is very small, just enough to pay for power, and the enormous costs of operating such a big computer as this. Do you think so many faces would inhabit a small machine, at no cost? They won't.'

'And what is your commission?'

'It's very, very small,' said Ivan, making his mouth just as small, and pinching his fingers hard together.

'Then I wish you good fortune with your great works of mercy to the farming community. I'm going down to wait for my real man, and to find a drink.' Ludmila rose from the computer chair.

'You've lost your sense!' cried Ivan. 'You're burning away hard currency, dollars, that are now going to pay for lip enlargements or smell-gland refreshments for a fat and stupid foreign girl not a bite as pretty as you.'

'Oh dear!' said Oksana. 'It truly is one of the finest opportunities – I've seen it work over and over.'

'Well, I haven't seen it work,' said Ludmila. 'Bring the man and we'll see together if it still works.'

'But the clothes, the salon –' said Ivan.

'Do you see me sitting here naked? And my hair – what's wrong with my hair? It hangs off my head, as hair is seen to do.'

'And the photographer –'

'I will bring my own photograph. Then, when the lazy man comes, tired of his smell-lipped woman, he will pay your commission. That's how proper business operates. You must have thought I was that lazy foreign girl to believe your fairytales about money.' Ludmila stood up from the screen, and made gracefully for the door.

Ivan stood back, dropped his jowls, and belted wet laughter at the ceiling. He slapped the back of Oksana's head. 'You find some hard ones, Father Jesus, you find them. I presume you've explained the terms of her accommodation?'

'Oh dear! Well, I didn't think I'd have to, I've never seen a girl so wrong-headed.'

'And what is it now?' Ludmila called from the stairs.

'Just to tell you – well, as you probably guessed' – Oksana batted her lashes stickily – 'the room of my uncle is really reserved only for girls in the partnership scheme.'

Ludmila woke next morning with a taste of tin in her mouth, not helped by an acid light through the curtain. She found herself on Oksana's bed, entangled with her. Both women were clothed but for one spiky shoe and two boots that dotted the corners of the apartment. The second shoe dangled from Oksana's foot as she lay belly-down on the bed.

Ludmila unhooked herself with a distasteful curl of her lip, and stood rubbing her face into shape. Then she kicked Oksana's shoe off her foot, clattering it across the polished stone floor, waking her.

'How do you make water for tea?' asked Ludmila.

Oksana grunted, and burrowed deeper into her bedclothes.

Ludmila clicked her tongue, and left the girl sleeping. She smoothed herself down, threw a little of Oksana's perfume on her neck, and left the apartment, heading up the street to eat and drink tea, though not to the Kaustik, or the Leprikonsi.

Then, with coffee and pastry inside her, she strode huddled

against the cold towards the busiest-looking end of the main street, to find a job that had nothing to do with munitions. Misha was clearly delayed. He would come, just as he promised, and she would be there waiting. She would send the tractor money home, she resolved, that day if possible – as much to remove the pressure of guilt, and as much to brighten the hearts of her kin, as to rub their noses in the turd of their decision to send her away while her brother, the most talented young propeller-polisher the region had seen in years, with polishing secrets of his own invention, spun idle tracks in the snow.

She began the task, with a deeper than usual scowl, by identifying the tallest buildings, reasoning these would need the most secretaries and administrators. That day she enquired in nine buildings, waiting as long as it took to speak to someone in a higher position than she wanted for herself. By the ninth building her arms dangled limp.

At the foot of the last building she visited, sunlight already exchanging snow for pink sugar, a round old woman wheeling a mail trolley overheard her enquiry to the porter.

After Ludmila had been turned away, the woman waddled over to her, wheezing because of her weight and its bell-like distribution. 'Darling peach,' she coughed, pulling the trolley near to lean on, 'take the advice of an old woman, and go back to your home where you're needed.'

'I'm a pilot of aeroplanes,' said Ludmila, straightening. Even as she said it she wondered why. 'I'm just looking to fill in some hours on the ground.'

The woman hung open her mouth and flicked her eyes left and right across Ludmila's face. 'Take the advice of an old woman. Look, look out here.' She pointed through the yawn of the building's foyer. Edged with cold sunlight, a young woman with a baby sat begging in a doorway across the street.

'Well, pardon me saying,' said Ludmila, taking in the beggar's shawl and scarf, 'but she's Gnezvarik.'

'She's a girl,' said the old woman. 'A pilot of aeroplanes, with some hours to kill on the ground. With dreams and a shack full of hungry people somewhere far away, people who know nothing of where she is, but wait each minute for her triumphant return in a shiny big car. A big black car is what she'll end up in, lying flat on her bones. Do you know how I say it with such certainty? Because she's the only beggar in Kuzhnisk. Can you imagine? A soul with the tragic misguidance to come to a town too poor even to support a beggar.'

'And but I have skills,' said Ludmila.

'I know,' the woman tutted. 'You're a pilot of aeroplanes.'

'I just need to get some money home, for birthday presents. That's all, a few extra roubles.'

'Well, good luck. Don't be sending anything by post is what I'll tell you, not to Novosibirsk.'

'Ublilsk, I'm talking about.'

'Not to Novosibirsk or anywhere is what I'll tell you, darling peach. If it's to the Admin Districts it must go by the bread train, the guard will accept it.'

'But our depot is worse than the post.'

'Not if you send it on the train. I know that train, the guard will never take bread again to a depot that steals from his consignments. You must pay him, though. A hundred roubles. Better still, take my advice and get back on the train yourself, while you still have clear eyes. Take the advice of an old woman from Kuzhnisk.'

2

ARGUMENTS IN THE NEW WORLD

14

A figure came to Blair's side. No sooner had Lamb stepped out to summon help on his telephone, than a polished man emerged from the club's twilight like a lily breaking the surface of a lake. He could only have been American. An absence of noise and a sense of presence coincided in his gait, and his suit was cleaner and straighter than human manufacture would allow. The twins looked up. They wiped their eyes with the backs of their hands. There glowed this small, perfectly flesh-toned bear, with an over-bite, and a canted smile that suggested he knew much more about things than they did. He pursed his lips, and paused before speaking, as if waiting for the right amusements to well up his throat. Then he said, 'You coming down off of something, or did you get fired from a funeral parlour?'

The twins blinked.

The man reached over the table and offered a hand to Blair. 'Truman.'

Blair held up a hand without looking. 'Hullo,' he croaked.

'Was that Danny you were with, the little guy? Are you his men?'

Blair drew an inward sigh. 'Lamb, you mean?'

'That's the boy – from the Home Office.' Truman reached into his trouser pocket, fumbled in it, then looked up. A door opened in the mirrored wall beside the banquette where the twins hud-dled. A large man in a dinner jacket stepped out.

Truman turned to the men. Through his posture alone, he gave them to understand that they should follow him. Blair looked around for Lamb, glanced at his brother, who was wiping tears off his sunglasses with a shirt tail, and finally rose from his seat. The twins followed the man without a word up a hall, and through another door that swung open with a whirr. Beyond it, a trail of overhead spotlights lit in series down a longer hall, dimming behind the men as they passed. Truman led the twins into a room as big as a supermarket; it was black, stained with satin light, and faced a wall of smoked glass – a one-way mirror – overlooking the main bar, and giving an intimate view of the throng. Bunny pushed his glasses on to his head. He saw they were on a mezzanine. Below them, over an upholstered railing, was a ground floor whose walls were also windows overlooking the various mirrored bars.

'Come into the pit,' said Truman.

Blair became stuck at the window. His eyes rose and fell over the bodies huddled unsuspecting on the other side. 'I mean – is it legal, this kind of voyeurism?'

'Of course it's legal. Ladies' room would be illegal. This is legal. Same as a security camera, only live.' Truman led the twins to an inner office cluttered with photographs of himself with assorted luminaries, some of whom, Bunny thought, must surely have been dead before the American was born.

Truman showed the men to a sofa, and waited, humming to himself, rolling his eyes in the air, while they sat. Then he turned, tugging at his cuffs. 'You boys don't seem to know who I am.'

'No,' said Blair.

The man leant smiling over the pair. 'Do the words Gepetto Global Liberty mean anything to you? Because, how shall I put it' – he unveiled his teeth to the light – 'you are sitting in the nerve centre of European and Near Eastern operations. How's that make you feel?'

Blair stiffened attentively. 'Well, um –'

'I know. Sometimes even I feel it. Not everyone gets to come up here. In fact – nobody gets to come up here. But something tells me you boys are doing good things for the cause. And you should know – I like good things.'

Blair's upper lip twitched as if heralding a sneeze. His eyes flickered up and down. 'Well, um, Bunny doesn't actually work. And I've unfortunately been –'

'Godammit, Bob, you know I'm talking about you. I don't have to tell you that.'

'Well, what I mean is –'

'Where do you work?'

'Oh, um – GL Solutions. But it's just work experience, really, and I've not –'

'GL Solutions?'

'The sandwich applicator project.'

'I'm telling you, Bobby, it's a skyrocket – and it's my brain-child, don't even ask me where the ideas come from. One day, eating lunch, I just thought: why get mayo on my fingers? Kaboom. The sandwich applicator: bite-size access without the mess. Between that, and the entertainment business, and the oil franchise –'

'And the British healthcare system,' said Bunny helpfully.

'And the British healthcare system, and the cocktail mix –' Truman paused. 'Now there's a skyrocket for you: Howitzer, the most uplifting drink in the world, ready-mixed, comes in a packet. It's the way forward, boys – it's going to permanently refocus the way people leisurise, probably the whole way they live.'

'Crikey,' said Bunny, 'do you just mix it with alcohol?'

'No, everything's right there, freeze-dried, in the packet. What kind of host would I be if I didn't rustle one up for my boys?' He stepped away to press a button on his desk. After a moment, a young oriental woman appeared mincing in a satin dress. She was so slim and fine-featured, and with such a delicate long neck, that she seemed of a species of wading bird. She carried a tray with glasses, a jug, and a tea-caddy filled with foil sachets. She beamed at the men.

Blair tensed, and shot an eye at Bunny.

The girl unfastened her dress. It fell away to leave an intimate triangle of white silk, and nothing else, not so much as a hair, or the stubble of a hair, between her legs. With ceremonial precision she poured clear liquid into the glasses, plucked a sachet from the bowl, and emptied it into the drinks. It flashed violently, first red, then blue, before vanishing into the clear. The woman emptied the drink into her mouth, held it without swallowing, and pushed Blair back into his seat to climb astride him. She clamped him about the hips with her knees, arched herself back, and faced him with full mouth.

Blair's eyes jerked to his brother.

'Go with it,' waved Truman. 'It's good.'

Arching to Blair's face, the girl slotted herself over his crotch, gave a sigh through her nose like a bird's first breath, and emptied her mouth into his. Blair's shoulders melted. His hand trembled to her head. He swallowed, sputtered, and coughed.

The girl pulled back, stepping daintily off his lap. She spent a moment conjuring the gaze of one brought to climax in uncommon ways. Then she reset her face, and turned to beam at Bunny.

Snaggles crept on to his lip. 'I'll just sip mine, I think.'

'Wait, Buns,' said Blair. 'We don't even know what it is. I've never seen anything flash like that in a glass, it's liquid fireworks. This has all gotten very weird. Very weird, I'm sorry.'

'Nothing gets past you, pal.'

'Boys, boys, boys.' Truman waved himself a space on the sofa, and settled with a sigh between the men. He looked at each brother in turn. 'You've been out of the loop awhile, and I understand that. I want you to know we're here to help you back in. It's a bright new world, there for the taking. I mean – do you have any idea where we are?'

Four eyes scanned the room. Two heads slowly shook in time with each other. Bunny cleared his throat. 'How do you mean exactly?'

'How do you think? In time and space!'

The twins recoiled.

'Let me make it simple: in your lives, do you seek happiness, or misery?'

The pair thought a moment. Their lashes fluttered. 'Do you mean in an Aristotelian sense?' Bunny ventured. 'As in, for instance, the dramatic –'

'*I mean, do you want to be happy or fucking sad!*'

The twins jolted back. After a long, awkward moment, Bunny cocked an eyebrow. 'Are you having a lend of us?'

Truman squeezed the brothers' hands, pulling them into his lap, gazing patiently up at the ceiling. 'Boys, boys, boys, let me tell you something about our species. It's a non-negotiable fact that the humanoid body, scientifically known as homo saxons, hasn't moved its evolutionary ass in ten thousand years. It's the same as when we left the swamps. But – our brains have developed beyond all comprehension. Do you think that's an accident of nature? No!' Truman leant into Blair's face. 'From here on in, evolution is *mental*. The brain is the way forward. Can we be agreed on that?'

The brothers glanced at each other. 'Aye, fair enough,' said Bunny.

'Good. Now, the pace of our evolution means we're not taking time to dismantle old systems in the brain, we're merely adding new layers on top. Which means redundant circuits – emotional turmoil, inner conflict – are still there underneath. So although we can mix mojitos at forty thousand feet, and download porn between holes at Augusta – we're still basically hard-wired for the swamps. Comprende? It's like trying to run high-end software on a typewriter. Fact of nature. Are we agreed?'

The brothers sat perfectly still. Truman took this to mean yes.

'Which means: manipulation of these mental structures holds the key to our continued success. Right? Embracing the concepts that propel us forward, ditching the routines that hold us back – these are the tools of human progress. Because frankly, boys, the qualities that everyone says make us human are a pain in the ass. Your kid fumbles the ball on the touchline, oh my God, it's only human. My ass. What makes us human is our ability to *not* fumble, *not* cry, *not* move backwards.'

Blair fixed a gaze on the man. 'I see, yes. Mmm.'

'I might nip to the lav,' said Bunny. He reached for his Howitzer, drained it, and tottered across the room. The young hostess appeared before he reached the door. She took him by the arm, and led him off into the dark.

Truman carved a shape in the air with his hand, as if to engage a motion-sensing device. Nothing seemed to happen. He repeated the gesture, forcefully. After a moment, overhead lights dimmed away to nothing, save for one starchy spot over the sofa. The man moved beneath it, face etched hot on to black, eyes lit like mirrors. 'So my question, Bob, is this: do we fulfil the sacred duties of progress better when we're happy or sad?' His eyes narrowed to a squint. 'You know the answer. Sure, you can be liberal, you can be organic, you can whine about the good old days, when nobody was high on sugar, or bombed on burgers. You can take that line. But d'you know what?'

Blair's eyes glistened up like a child's at storytime. 'What?'

'You'd be an asshole. You'd be the hole of an ass.'

Blair's brow twitched. He sat back, and began to nod. 'Yes,' he said, 'the hole of an ass.'

'Because what did the vegans ever give us? A bunch of songs about hair. A bunch of ways to cook tofu. They ride our subways, fly on our airplanes – and bitch about what it does to their chakras. Did a vegan ever build a subway? No, they're too busy lighting candles, eating placenta. Do you hear what I'm saying?'

'Yes, yes, placenta, yes. So I mean, in terms of the broader interrelationships –'

'They only *pretend* to have meaningful relationships, Bobby. Do you hear what I'm saying? Meaningful relationships my ass – they enter relationships just as conditionally as the rest of us. A meaningful relationship is a profitable relationship, it's been that way since the dawn of time. They *pretend* to renounce enmity, but they still save dirt against you. Their contract of friendship is the same as ours: a suspension of open hostilities while the going's good. Watch any pair of 'em arguing, see how exponentially shit escalates to its maximum potential; note with awe the amount of saved hostility they have against each other. Son, I am telling you. Respect the succession of waivers that passes for a relationship, and you're on your way to understanding the ways of this world. And it's the same for countries, corporations, men, women, and children.'

'Waivers,' Blair nodded. 'Mmm.'

'Now, I don't want to preach to you, Bobby. Me, I say, whatever gets you off, gets you off. But if a scientific discovery comes along that cuts through mental bureaucracy, that removes redundant constraints of progress – I say go for it. Objectivity? My ass. There's only consensual inter-subjectivity, Bob – and I say let's play those dice, let's burn 'em up.'

'So what is it I've just drunk exactly?'

'Solipsidrine hydrochloride. I think you had wild cherry flavour.'

'Is it legal?'

'Of course it's legal, what do you think this is? D'you think I'd give you something illegal? Did you ever hear of something illegal that came in wild cherry flavour?'

Blair stared into his lap. A bulge formed there. A smile squirmed over his face. He looked up, rolling his eyes into corners of ceiling, down arches and barrels of dark and light. 'Because I suddenly feel less than entirely depressed.'

Truman slackened his jaw, lolled his tongue. He looked Blair up and down. 'You do, huh?'

'Yes,' said Blair. 'Somehow remote from devastation.' He tried to swallow a laugh, but it escaped in snorts through his nose.

'Attaboy.' Truman slapped a hand on to his leg, dislodging Blair's member, making it thwack against the cloth of his trousers. 'See? Uncle Truman has the fixes. Them old fixes are right here. And you know why I thought I'd share them with you? You know why I said to myself, "This is a man worth saving?" I'll tell you why, Bob: it's because there's something about you. Something that speaks to me of speed, of progress. Of understanding the way things really work. I took one look at you, and I said, "This man has the shine of future on him." I said it just like that. And it's not just the English thing, where you all sound so damn smart – I mean it, Bobby. Sincerely. You're the man.'

Blair flashed him a loving glance.

'And hey,' Truman nudged, 'that little bonus in the boy's zone is a side effect of this shit. Your baby won't know herself tonight, she'll think she's been hit by a fucking rocket.'

Blair clasped his hands over his lap. 'Actually I'm between relationships at the moment. Just starting to sniff around, in fact.'

'You came to the right place. You chasing big game, or do-ables?'

'How do you mean?'

'Local or imported?'

'Not fussy, to be honest.'

'Attaboy. Get 'em grateful, that's my philosophy.'

'Are all your girls foreign then?'

'The only way to fly. And they're not so foreign-looking – blondes, half of them.'

'Do you not get accused of exploitation?'

'Bobby, Bobby, Bobby.' Truman leant close. His features grew dramatic under the spotlight, his voice fell to a rasping murmur. 'They're a naturally occurring resource, their willingness to play is a naturally occurring phenomenon. It's philosophically impossible to exploit naturally occurring resources – you merely manage their exploitation of you.'

'Well it's just that some people might –'

Truman put a finger to his lips, lowered his voice further. 'Did you ever hear the term "exceptionalism"? Memorise it for when some bleeding heart asks you what gives us the right to run the world. Because it's the answer. It means this, Bob: we didn't go out and force the world to want to be like us. We came up with such an awesome way of life that they're breaking their asses to be like us anyway. We're the exception to all human constructs, above all forms of governance, because we're not the only ones who think we're superior. By their desperation to buy into our dream, the rest of the world *admits* we're superior. And because we invented the dream, they have to come to us to get it.' Truman brought the heat of his breath to Blair's face. 'We hold the franchise on freedom, Bobby. Imagine the potential. Now let me tell you something about these girls: they're hungry in their own countries. The places are blown to fuck, they're bullet

163

farms. Girls' asses are being wasted on foreign drunks, Arabs probably, who –'

'Um – Arabs don't generally drink.'

'Work with me here, Bobby. Digest what I'm saying: they live in bomb craters. And if they're hungry, and in danger, and if it suits my interests to give them comfort, is that exploitation? No, it's not. It's called freedom: the inalienable right to go after something better than you had before. Truman leant back and stared, pausing for potential's weight to fall on Blair. Then he winked, 'And the great thing about these girls – they take it up the ass.'

Blair moistened his lips. His penis tingled. 'How do you find them, exactly?'

'Find them? I own them, Bobby, I own the towns they come from. They come looking for *me*, the exceptionalist. Look, lookit here –' Truman went to the desk and pulled a sheet of paper from a leather in-tray. On it were printed six hopeful young faces, calendar beauties on a good day. 'My next consignment. Best yet – check this one – I ask you, Bobby, am I dreaming? Globalisation: lay it on me.'

Blair studied the page.

'Now – as one of my new lieutenants, you may qualify for a little overseas action, in the interests of forward progress – a little global reconnaissance. Truth is, I could really use a man like you to take a look around, scare up a few ideas. Hear what I'm saying? Do you think you could spare yourself, for a couple days?'

Blair drew a deep breath. 'I think I could manage it, yes. In the interests of forward progress, yes.'

'You're my man, Bob. You're my real man. Although, your brother looks kind of antsy to me – will he go along? Will that need facilitation? I ask because your guy at the Home Office says we shouldn't split you up.'

'I can swing it. I can swing that old one, Sir – leave it to me.'

'Attaboy. I'll send you to the source, Bob. I'll send you to the dripping hot source of the sandwich applicator equation.'

'You mean – to where these girls are? Are they not dear?'

'Bobby, these are the dearest little foxes you'll ever see. If they came with three assholes they couldn't be more –'

'I mean, are they not expensive?'

'Bobby, Bobby, Bobby. Uncle Truman has all the fixes.' He plucked a card off the desk, scribbled a line across it, and stuffed it along with a handful of Howitzer sachets into Blair's breast pocket.

'Crumbs,' said Blair. He sat for a moment, looking around, sniffing the oncoming life of his dreams. He savoured the moment in a trance, eyes fixed through the window. A moving shape finally prompted focus. It was Donald Lamb, combing the crowd.

Truman followed his gaze. 'Lookit, there's our man. Let's haul him in.'

The pair left the office, and edged along the window towards a door at the end of the mezzanine. Truman threw it open just as Lamb passed the other side. 'Danny, you old dog!'

'Bloody hell,' Lamb blinked. His eyes crawled through the dark. 'I see you've met the lads – I've been all over the ruddy shop looking for them.'

'These are my boys, Dan – where do you keep guys like this? Come on up, we were just –'

'Actually we're just off – it's a bit awkward, but –'

'Don't run out on us now. Not now, Dan.'

Lamb peered through the doorway. 'Where's our Gordon?'

'Gents, I expect,' said Blair, cupping a hand over his crotch.

Lamb detected a buoyant ring in Blair's tone. A public school-boy's ring. He took in Blair's posture. 'I see you've tried the fizz, then?'

Blair smiled. He was approaching the crest of a glorious wave of inner normality as he had never felt before, empowering beyond all measure. He knew without a doubt it was the way he would feel if he were the person he longed to be.

And thus, suddenly – he was.

'I did have a tot of it, yes,' he said. 'And Don – I'm sorry about the turn earlier. It won't happen again.'

'What concerns me, Blair, is that when the effect wears off, you'll find yourself in the same situation you were in an hour ago. Let's not forget how that felt.'

Blair tried to recall his feelings of an hour earlier. They were gone.

Truman slapped Lamb's shoulder. 'Danny, let me tell you something: we've spent some quality time, internalised some new dynamics. Hear what I'm saying? I'm Vitaxis chairman now – healthcare's my game. He's going to be fine.'

'Yes, honestly, I'm fine,' said Blair. 'Quality time, it was.'

'I think we'd best track down your brother.' Lamb turned to scour the bar. 'Has he had a tot as well? There's only the dance club he could've gone to, I've looked everywhere else.'

'He'll not be in the dance club, believe me,' said Blair. He leant to Truman's ear to ask, 'Will Bunny be feeling like this too?'

'You bet,' whispered Truman. 'And wait up – the best is yet to come.'

The trio wandered to the dance club at the rear of the building. The latest Sketel One mix stabbed the air. Blair felt puffs of joy flow through him, spurts of truth and love and power. He spotted Bunny across the dance floor, propped at a shelf beside the bar. Three young women attended him. One giggled, and slapped him playfully on the arm.

'There he is,' said Lamb. 'Jammy bugger.' He led Blair to the pool of light where Bunny stood swaying like a sapling in a breeze. Truman stood back and watched them with a father's gaze. Then he vanished like a phantom into the dark.

The girls stared at Blair as he approached. 'Is that him?' asked a spotty brunette.

'That – as we say up north – is him,' said Bunny. 'My lacklustre other half.'

'I s'pose he does look a bit like you, without the hair and shades.'

Lamb tensed. He inspected the girls' faces, and looked to Bunny, noting a large gin in his hand. A plastic bag bulged with music discs at his feet.

Blair smiled at his brother. 'Surprised you're not up dancing.'

'Not my style, mate, as you know. Nowt worse than not knowing the things that make you look a twat.' Bunny reached into the bag. 'However,' he said, turning to the girls, 'now he's here, I'll prove it to you beyond a doubt. Tell the music man to pick a tune off here. Look – "La Cumparsita" – try that one.'

'Buns, are you sure?' Blair clutched his brother's arm. 'And listen – I'm sorry about the discs.'

'A tango?' chirped the girl. 'I can ask the DJ.' She sucked her friends on to the dance floor, away into the crowd.

'I forgive you for the discs,' said Bunny. 'Good thing they hadn't been scavenged from the bin, mind. I'd have played war if they'd been scavenged.'

Blair narrowed his eyes. 'By Christ, Buns – I don't deserve you.'

Lamb held up a hand. 'Perhaps we should just move on. How many of those have you had?'

'Not enough,' said Bunny, emptying his gin before turning back to his brother. 'Let's just do this one thing – come on, it'll be like old times.'

The disc jockey bobbed out of his console to spot Bunny through the crowd.

'Lads,' started Lamb – but the pair were lost to themselves.

The Sketel number faded early. Bodies on the floor jerked to a halt, standing for a moment before moving to the edges. 'Boys and girls,' came the disc jockey's voice, 'we've a coupla fellas think they'll show us how to dance.'

Blair clamped his lips. 'Buns – are we up for it?'

With an icy hiss, loudspeakers sent a lone accordion note rocketing high through a gale of strings and hovering wood-winds. Punters coagulated into cells beside the dance floor as an orchestral firestorm set out hacking ribbons from the air. Spotlights hardened through the dark.

'Too bloody right.' Bunny set his jaw, and leant to his brother's ear, 'I mean to say, check the lasses. You're well in there.'

Blair's eyes rolled left. Three girls stared up at him. Behind them more girls looked on, and whispered. A spotlight cut over the floor to find the Heaths.

Blair blinked at the girls, then at Bunny. 'A tragedy that must be danced?'

'A tragedy that absolutely must be danced.' Bunny threw his head high.

The pair strode to the middle of the floor. They made a tight ceremony of facing each other, then pressed themselves hard together at the abdomen, as if plugging in a single nervous sys-tem. Like two halves of a puzzle they clicked into one formidable being, the join between them lost in the black of their suits. Their heads snapped mechanically forward, eyes fastened over each other's shoulder. They clicked up their arms, locked each other in a formal grip, and froze erect for the length of eight quick beats. Then, as if pooled for use between them, their four legs began to effortlessly scissor, lattice, churn, and chop the air, tangling and disentangling in blinding flashes, seemingly independent of the torsos floating motionless above.

168

For the Heaths danced their own species of tango.

A dry, strict tango, as fast as a motor, with edges as sharp as blades.

Their feet gathered speed, flicking and flashing between each other's legs like eels in slalom, until they were all but invisible, until they were a single form flying like a light across the floor. The crowd tightened a circle around them and roared, cheering each dip and twirl until a moment, at the tango's screaming heights, when the speed and heat of applause and lights and brass and drums melted into a single celestial impulse, welding all present to the Heaths' giddy vortex, flooding the room with power.

'That's bloody scary,' hissed one of Bunny's girls from the side-lines.

'That's fucking magic,' whispered Lamb. He pushed his way on to the floor as the tango thrummed to a climax. 'Out!' he shouted to Blair as the last drumbeat sounded. 'Grab your brother!'

15

'You've killed him dead!' shrieked Olga.

She stood between Aleks's body and the inspector's torch beam. It glowed nearly as bright as his face with the triumph of flushing three skulking boys out of the darkness. Olga threw the blanket back over Aleks's head, and began an elaborate perform-ance of wailing that included bows and twists, the serving of sour meals to the saints, the random tossing-up of arms in despair, and the deft routing of invisible tears from the corners of her eyes, ending with a decorative flick of her fingertips.

'This man has been dead for some time,' the inspector said thoughtfully. 'Look at his belly, he's inflated with worms.'

'How can he be fat with worms!' squeaked Olga. 'Only ten minutes ago your own agent Lubov Kaganovich was chatting with him as if they'd met in the bread queue on a busy Tuesday morning!'

'I wouldn't quite say chatting,' said Lubov from the doorway.

'Or perhaps,' said Abakumov, 'these young brutes with the gun have killed him. Or else why would a dead man's body lie in a room where a man with a gun was hiding in the dark?'

'No, inspector, it can't be that way,' said Lubov.

'Come out, you with the gun,' Abakumov threw the torch beam on to Gregor. 'And tell me also why your mother has not, in all your years of life, written that she has three sons instead of one.'

'Those aren't my sons,' said Irina. 'This one here, Maksimilian Ivanov, is my only son.'

'Then,' said Abakumov, slowly eyeing each person in turn, 'where do these boys come from into your house with guns? Have we stumbled on intruders as well, at the split second that a dead man's body is found with the fat of a week's worms?'

Olga and Irina turned to glare at Lubov Kaganovich.

'These are my son and nephew,' said Lubov. 'They came for the voucher with me, knowing in no small way the nature of these Derevs and their wickedness. They were now investigating the mysterious and damning question of the dead man and his vouchers. Can you imagine! We come for routine business and find ourselves dropped in such a mire!'

'Ha,' Abakumov puffed without humour, 'I'm still to answer why you should be here at all, in such a dark moment – indeed, I find you up to your throat in the situation.'

'Surely you don't say to the front of my face –'

Abakumov held up a hand. 'What is clear is that we must converse. And while we converse, you all must prepare yourselves for some hard times ahead. Some very bleak times.'

The group moved slowly into the main room, hampered by Olga's wailing and her jerky, unpredictable flailing.

'Please stop,' Abakumov said as she flapped past him. 'You've had at least a week.'

'Mama, go to his side, go and pray for his soul,' said Irina. 'I'll deal with those who want to blacken our already worst moment in life.'

Abakumov went to sit on Olga's tin chair by the stove. 'The police will be shocked to their faces,' he shook his head in lament.

'Hoh, and you'll quicker see an elephant up here than a policeman,' snorted Maks.

'Then it's a mercy, for your sakes,' said the inspector. 'In fact, the police would be the last people to trouble with this news. Because this news – a dead man signing vouchers to obtain

171

money from the state, from the army fund no less – this news, like a hydrogen bubble, would float to the top of police command, or even the Kremlin. Such cases have been robbing our already gasping state for too long now, and such a man with his worms would make a fine example to all. I shouldn't wonder *Pravda* will come as well, this is just too spectacular a crime.'

'She killed him!' cried Olga, thrusting a finger at Lubov. 'With her jelly head. I told her not to disturb him, with her guns and her treachery.'

The inspector reached into his coat pocket, and pulled out a notepad and pen. 'So,' he said to himself, 'the body was found in a room with six people in attendance, one of these brandishing a gun.' He looked up at Gregor, who stood in the bedroom doorway with the weapon held across his chest. 'Is that firearm loaded?'

'Yes,' said Gregor proudly.

'Is it fed by a clip, does the armament hold more than one projectile?'

'It has a clip of bullets, yes.'

'And is it now, as you stand with it, full of the total number of bullets it can contain?'

'No,' Gregor frowned, looking down at the weapon. 'But it has bullets enough still.'

'When did the arm last contain a fullness of projectiles?'

'Last week, yes.'

'One of these brandishing a recently discharged gun,' Abakumov corrected into his notepad. As he scribbled, choice words smouldered through his breath into the room's nutty smoke. 'Wrong voucher,' he said. 'In advanced decay. Worms.' After a moment he stopped, looked into space, then snapped his eyes to Irina. 'Has the body's flesh been violated?'

'Jesus father!'

'Let me put it another way – have you eaten meat during the last week in this house?'

'We're not cannibals, Inspector! Your hideous filth!'

'Well,' Abakumov shrugged, 'it happens.' He looked back to his report. 'Potential crime against nature,' he said inwardly, 'evidence of bread,' and as he spoke, each damning implication squeezed a sigh from the lungs of the assembled, until Irina finally said, 'Look at me in my face. We have nothing in the world. I tell you now, so you don't accuse me later of wasting your time.'

'Not true!' said Lubov. 'They have a tractor!'

'No, we don't,' said Irina. 'Where around do you see a tractor?'

'Ha,' said the inspector. 'Now you try to bribe a public official at the scene of the crime.' He jotted furiously with his pen: 'Bribe. Public official. Tractor.'

'Inspector,' Irina said wearily, 'I spoke to your face, as a friendly gesture, so as to save you all this trouble. Let's understand each other – we have nothing to bargain with.'

Abakumov stayed quiet, scanning the notes in his book. Then, still looking down, he said softly, 'As you take such a frank approach with me, I'm compelled to reciprocate, though it may prove to my thorough disadvantage. I can say there are people who might help the situation of such a barbarous crime as this. I say it mostly because, as I look at the facts written hard on paper, I feel a tremendous sorrow for you all. Many of these cases don't even get to trial. Many don't even arrive to an official report, because it's proved easier in such unthinkable cases to simply shoot the suspects and save more offence to God.'

All present dropped their eyes to the floor and waited for the routine to play itself out.

'Yes,' Abakumov mused distantly, 'to my own great disadvantage I have decided to try and help you, as I see you are truly walking dead otherwise.' His eyes twisted thoughtfully into a corner of the ceiling. 'Of course, there will be situations to overcome which have some cost attached –'

'And what about me?' Lubov asked without looking up.

'Well,' said the inspector, reaching for his hat, 'you may come off worst of all, when this gets filed, as it was you who introduced the weapon into the dwelling.'

'But I did not, Inspector.'

'Well, yes, you did, because you have maternal dominion over the boy who holds the very recently discharged gun.'

'And so what of me?'

The inspector pinched the top of his nose, clenched his eyes under the weight of new responsibilities. 'I see you have a room behind the bar of your depot. A furnished room. I think the only fair thing is to make that room a headquarters for this ongoing investigation.' He turned to look at Irina, then Lubov, before parking his gaze on the door behind which Olga spluttered and moaned. 'I wish I could say to the front of your faces that this will be a straightforward procedure, such a dark and twisted situation as this.' He rose from his chair and moved to the front door. Stepping down into the snow, he turned and shone his beam through the doorway, across the eyes of the gathered women. They shone empty of pupils, mere orbs of gel.

'But I can't,' he said.

Ludmila secretly hoped to miss the bread train. Giving all her money to a stranger seemed wrong. But her only alternative was to travel with it herself, into war, into harsh scenes over her failure, into a feud with Pilosanov, if he lived, if she even lived to return there.

The second reason she hesitated on the station steps was to feel gently suspended some moments longer in the hammock of freedom, in the sweet limbo of having options above the grave. Because the money snuggled in her underwear gave her no more rest than a frenzied lover with its torrent of schemes. And, being at a certain lucid stage in her flowering as a woman, she realised the decisions she made about those schemes were first steps into a vigorous state called independence. A state after which there was nothing more to beg of life.

These thoughts and feelings had become beloved pets to Ludmila. She knew it, and knew they had to die. She straightened her coats, and went into the station. It was colder inside than out: a wind blew efficiently down the tracks on to the open concrete platform, sweeping up ice-dust and litter. She found the faded sign for the Kropotkin service. A grimy train stood quiet at the platform.

'Is this the train for Kropotkin?' she asked a passing porter.

'No, this is the last Kropotkin train, just in.'

'Well, what I mean is: is this the next train to Kropotkin?'

'Well, what I'm telling you is no, because it's late. The train is running at least one schedule late today, possibly more.'

Ludmila frowned, and shifted her weight from one foot to the other.

'Look.' The man stood up his trolley and leant on it, preparing for a long exchange. 'What is it you don't understand? If you're looking for the fourteen twenty-seven Kropotkin service, this isn't it.'

'Then what service is this?'

'This is the ten fifteen.'

'Going to?'

'Kropotkin. Did you not read the sign?'

'And what time is it now?'

The man hoisted a sleeve to consult his watch. 'Thirteen forty-nine.'

'Thank you,' Ludmila rolled her eyes, and stepped down the platform.

'You can't go down there without a ticket,' called the man. 'They'll stop you and give a fine.'

'I just need to talk to the guard,' Ludmila called without slowing.

'You'll not find him there – the train's not due out for an hour yet.'

Ludmila stopped to stamp her feet. 'And at what time then does a train depart, if not at the time of its schedule?'

'It's – Jesus father, if only you'd listen – this is the ten fifteen! It hardly matters when it goes out now, does it?'

Ludmila spun on her heels to face the man. She had clearly found a soulmate for her brother, and so felt well versed in his handling. She assumed her poker face, carefully handed down through generations. 'And listen to me: it will soon be fourteen twenty-seven. If the train has missed one schedule – at ten fifteen – it is most logical for it, having been made so late that it runs into the next schedule, to leave at the moment of the next schedule – at fourteen twenty-seven – because everyone will have timed their arrival to catch it anyway. Or did you miss that sort of learning at school?'

The man shook his head. 'Try and help some people,' he tutted. 'The guard will be in the café at the back, where the staff meet, is all I'm trying to tell you. You city girls think you know everything about everything.'

Ludmila swelled at the man's words. City girl. She waited until the porter creaked out of view before following his trail to the rear of the station. An alley led on to a back street, where a greasy café festered in what could have once been a garage. She peered through its dripping glass at a handful of men huddled around tables inside. Then, straightening herself up, she stepped inside. The air swam with burnt fat. A girl came to the counter, wiping red hands on a rag.

'Do you know if any of these men are train guards?' asked Ludmila.

'No,' shrugged the girl.

'Well, do you know any of them?'

'No. Don't you want something to drink or eat?'

'No,' said Ludmila, turning sideways to assess the men by the cut of their hair, the grime on their uniforms.

'Is that another one for the washroom?' a massive, sweaty woman called from the back of the kitchen.

'No, Mama, she's looking for a train guard.'

'Well, if she's not drinking or eating she should know what to do.'

'Darling light,' one of a party of three young men called to Ludmila from a table, 'I didn't see you there with your hair so full and beautiful.'

Ludmila turned. The man beckoned with his fingers, looking past her to the hippocerf in the kitchen. 'It's all right,' he nodded, 'I've been waiting for her.'

'So have I,' an old man coughed from the corner. 'All of my life.'

The young man stood and dragged another chair to the table. 'You're looking for business on one of the bread trains? Come, sit down. We'll talk about it together.' He shifted his eyes to the chair, and called to the kitchen counter: 'You can bring her a coffee.'

'No, thank you.' Ludmila sat on the edge of the chair, examining the man's face. He was a ruddy blond with a jaw that yawed sideways when he spoke, giving him a sheepish, friendly air. 'Just tell me about the bread train,' she said, settling back.

The man tamped down the tobacco in a cigarette by tapping it hard on the table. 'Depends on which bread train. But be sure, one of us can help you. You need a delivery made up the line, am I totally correct?'

'Perhaps.'

'Please hear me: don't be afraid – we see people like you every day. Do you think we live on the jokes the railway pay us? We only stay to nurture the false hope of seeing our wages from last summer. If you and I can help each other, so much the better. Because don't forget – if you send mail with us today, it reaches its destination today.'

The man's candour softened Ludmila. She decided to confide in him. 'I'm a pilot of aeroplanes. I need to send an important document, my aeroplane licence, in fact, on the train to Ublilsk.'

The man sat back in his chair, watching with quick eyes. 'Aeroplanes, you say? Then why don't you fly it there?'

'Well, not such small aeroplanes, actually.' Ludmila shifted her gaze around the room.

'And why not? I hear you can land a Tupolev 134 on the strip where the component factories used to sit.'

'No,' said Ludmila, 'you can't land a Tupolev there, of any model. I've tried it,' she added, to nail the theme shut.

A short, bearded man leant into the conversation. 'Well, the old Ilyushins used to go there all the time,' he said, eyes aloft, reminiscing. 'Every moment of the day or night they would go for new propellers at Ublilsk. And they're bigger than your Tupolev.'

'Look at me in the eyes.' The blond man slapped the tabletop. 'Her Tupolev is the biggest flying machine in the world. Don't argue me that.'

'Well, I hate to be the one that says you're wrong.' The swarthy man shrugged, showing that in matters of truth he was

178

just a herald. 'As a friend I can only try to save you from humiliation by pointing out the true facts.'

'Listen, never mind,' said Ludmila. 'It's too expensive to fly the licence there. I want to see about the bread train.'

'And it might not be as expensive as you think to fly it,' said the blond, 'after you hear what the Kropotkin service charges for that little journey. There's a war up there, in case you hadn't heard.'

'The war hasn't reached the junction,' said Ludmila. 'The Gnezvariks will have been stopped before then.'

'Ha! And I wish this was the same news we've heard with our own ears.'

'Yes,' a third man chimed in, 'we can tell you, although we're not the men from the Kropotkin train itself, that the bread service is about to be cancelled for good. So I don't know what you want to be doing sending your aeroplane licence there, when you can't even set down a Tupolev, or find a loaf of bread.'

'Hoh!' said Ludmila. 'And they can't stop the bread train, everyone knows that. While there are mouths waiting, bread must be sent.' She sent a stern toss of her chin.

The blond man leant into Ludmila's shadow. 'Look, I am close to sources who control operations for the Kropotkin service, and I can tell you that this man is correct in what he says. No more bread to Ublilsk. It's a matter of economics.'

'But while there are still souls to feed – ?'

'Well, no.' The man held up a finger. 'It's because there are not *enough* people to feed. You see? The service is private now, with foreign owners. They're not going to send a train, and send men to clean the track, for just a dozen loaves.'

'We clean our own track! And we push the wagon by hand for the last kilometres anyway, it's not as though you have to do anything!'

'Well, firstly, don't give me stone eyes, because I'm not the one

179

cancelling the bread train, or any other train. If it were for me to decide, I would carry you beluga roe in my hand every morning and float it on to your tongue while you dreamt.'

The café's occupants chuckled, and Ludmila turned to see that all had angled themselves to best enjoy the exchange.

'And secondly,' said the blond, with a wink to his audience, 'you can eat all the bread you want in your tremendous Tupolev aeroplane, so why suck gas from our mouths?'

Laughter jangled through the smog.

Ludmila scowled, and looked down. She barely cast a shadow under the café's fluorescent light; this made her feel alone. Days and nights without Misha had brought compensatory manias of hope that now began to falter. Still, she swept his image from mind, and assumed her best poker face. 'And listen to me: just where is the guard from the Kropotkin train?'

'On the way to Kropotkin,' the man shrugged, looking around to acknowledge a final titter from the diners.

'But the train is here at the platform.'

'Then who knows? What I'm telling you is that there's a war at Ublilsk, and he would take twenty-five per cent of any delivery.'

'What! He'll take it with a gun!'

'Think of his position,' said the bearded man, leaning in to Ludmila. 'On top of his regular costs and fees, he has wartime security to think about. And those sidings that hand over in the wilds, like yours, where strangers push the wagon without any rail official – imagine! He has to buy loyalty all the way down the line, and have the depot bought as well. Imagine it for yourself!'

'Then I could live a month off the price of one delivery.'

'So you must be sending over a thousand roubles,' said the blond.

'I'm sending my aeroplane licence!'

'For an aeroplane licence the cost is two thousand roubles.'

While Ludmila sat glaring at one man and the next, another grubby type opened the door, and slunk like a hyena into the café.

The blond stood from his chair. 'Sergei Leonov – we're talking about you.'

'Keep your filthy lies in your arse,' the man growled, and passed the table without a glance.

'We've a client.' The blond pointed to Ludmila. 'Another Ubli like you.'

'Hoh! Well it wasn't me who killed Aleksandr, so you'll pay in hell for saying that I did!' Maksimilian stomped across the floor.

'And kindly excavate your ears,' said Irina. 'What I said was: fetch back the tractor.'

'And are we living in different worlds? Was it not an instrument somehow strikingly reminiscent of my voice that told you the tractor has been traded? In a very lucrative deal that would have you weeping with nostalgia for your hardship if you would just let it take its proper course?'

'In God's name fetch it back!'

'Or bring at least ten thousand roubles!' Olga called from the far window where she sat, 'because that's what it's worth to a dead beggar, let alone a man who would pay its full value of twenty-five thousand.'

'The tractor's not worth twenty-five thousand,' snorted Maks. 'It's been around since three wars.'

'That tractor has kept its back straight for many hard years, Maksimilian Goose Ingrate. You've not tasted a day of the work that tractor's done!'

'Hoh, and there's some ripe logic! That doesn't mean it gets more valuable, it means it's living off the strength of its ghost.'

Irina stamped both feet. 'Watch me: if we don't burn this tick Abakumov off our backs he'll suck us to our graves!'

'Pah!' spat Maks. 'Abakumov isn't even a match for Lubov's cretins.'

'Hoh! Yes! But he has the state behind him, Maksimilian – we won't win! Just bring the wretched tractor, I beg you as a mother.'

Maks detoured past the table, the stove, the kitchen bench, slamming things, hurling them, using every opportunity to make crashing noises before leaving the shack. And his route through the yard's grey light found a few sharp noises still to make. Once on the track, he threw his hands into his coat pockets, hunched his shoulders into the wind, and stormed away trailing bubbles of vapour like a steam train under water.

He took care to stay out of sight of the depot. This meant climbing through the yard of the ironmonger's widow, and skirting the back of the village. He muttered to himself, crunching and scraping his way to Pilosanov's patch of town. Pilo was definitely to blame for their attracting so chubby a bloodsucker as Abakumov. Because if Pilo had honoured his deal correctly, and delivered the mobile telephones and the gun, the family would have been able to respond with proper speed to the situation. In fact, Maks decided, the situation would not have arisen at all, because Olga would not have had to sign a voucher. Lubov would have been alone in her misfortunes with the inspectorate, without such a clear track along which to push her parasite like a trolley.

Pilosanov was to blame, then. And Lubov for her treachery. Abakumov was merely an irritant, not the instrument itself.

Maks ducked as a shell whistled and thudded near by. He cocked an ear, but the air was too laden with chill to gauge its distance.

Turning on to the town's last road, Maks saw Pilo's door standing wide open. Then, as he approached over rocks and pustules of ice and mud, he saw the door was missing altogether. He took a step inside the house, slowed, and stopped. It was empty. Robbed even of its ceiling beams. Half its corrugated iron roof had collapsed into the main room, and ice coursed down its furrows into a frozen wall-to-wall pond. The stairs had vanished, as had the windows, and their frames, and the bricks around their frames.

'He's gone,' hissed the neighbour, old man Krestinski, through the next doorway. 'But he nurses your death in his pocket.'

'Nurses *my* death? I nurse *his* death, a thousand times, in my pocket. I couldn't witness more treachery if I lived ten years with a Gnez.'

'Well, you're like a mirror to his words. And I have to comment, looking at you through open eyes, that he seems to have come off the worse.'

'Hoh!'

'Oh yes. He wore some nasty cuts about his head, just the ones I could see were dreadful, never mind the harm he could have taken inside.'

'And he told you this?'

'No, I never spoke a word with him. My simple life is too brittle to get involved with such thuggery. I'd be squashed at the first step into your paths, if such cuts as I saw are a thing to go by. And for that reason alone, I say good day now.'

'Wait,' Maks followed the man to his door. 'Where did you say he is, the shitmonger Pilosanov?'

'I didn't say he was anywhere.'

'He can't be far, if he's taken his whole house with him. Whose lorry carried the contents of his house?'

'He abandoned the house, it was this way when he came back. Do you think the Gnez up the street would mind it for him to come back to?'

'Hoh. Well, they did leave it clean,' Maks kicked a chunk of rubble across the road. 'Did he travel on a tractor?'

'No, he came some long distance on foot. He hadn't the strength left to curse.' The old man shuddered at the mention of it all, and closed his door without another word. Maks stood deflated on the road. He went back into Pilo's house to spread the correct oaths across its air. Then he slid up its kitchen step into the back yard. He scoured the ground for tyre tracks. None were there.

Ludmila huddled in the station's shadows. Her pupils swam after the light on the back of the Kropotkin train as it swayed into the mist. It was a mist whose icy grain stretched far over the horizon, a smoky eiderdown Ludmila shared with Ublilsk. Tears warmed her lips, she sent prayers to the light: to speed her family's wealth to their door, to dislodge Misha Bukinov from the conflict and deliver him safe to her. The question of Misha's absence had grown from a pinhole of inner dark into a canyon that groaned as it grew in her mind. She mentally edged away from it, not because it offered senseless worry, but because in it swirled an air of reason, of truth: that nothing good could have held him back so long.

Tiny muscles on Ludmila's face made her skin seem to crumple and blister. Her face grew shiny, and red, and she hissed from her throat with the pain of his imagining. When she closed her eyes, she saw his arms reach out to her. Then, as the train's click and twang faded under the wind's murmur, he vanished into an evening as cold and solid as steel.

Ludmila sniffled herself upright. She stood for a moment, struggling to rekindle her heart-fire – Ubli fire, Olga fire, that made wretchedness a cause to rejoice. She dragged a sleeve over her eyes, took a deep breath, and set off up the avenue to complete her interim plan.

The technical store on Ulitsa Kuzhniskaya was still open. It was a technical store in that, along with goat's milk, detergent, chocolate, cheese and bread, it also sold batteries and cigarette lighters. And one of the notices taped inside its door promised two official photographs for half the sum of money Ludmila had left. She stepped inside, argued with the old man behind the counter, haggled and pleaded until his gasps and winces of disability beat her down, and she handed him the money.

A curtain hung on a shower rail. The man limped to draw it around a corner of the room, pointing her to a mirror while he loaded a cartridge on to his camera. Ludmila stared into the mirror. She looked flushed and tired. The room's warmth sucked rosy patches to her cheeks and nose, and brutal light made the streaks of old tears glisten down her face. She wiped herself on a sleeve, flicked fingertips through her hair, left a strand hanging over one eye, and went to a stool in front of the camera.

'Angels help me,' said the old man. 'You want to frighten people with your photograph? Is it to be an agricultural implement to shock birds?'

'You have your money. Just make the picture.'

'Surely you want to smile for me? Is it for a party membership? An identity paper?'

'No, it's to shock birds. Just make it.'

The man's eyes sprang wide, and he burst out laughing. So genuine was his laughter, and so harsh was her retort in retrospect, that Ludmila began to laugh as well; first hissing through her lips, then with a wet, open mouth. And as she struggled to restrain her features, the man snapped a picture.

'I won't even take any more,' he said. 'That's the juiciest picture anyone will ever take of you.'

'Well, I paid for two pictures.'

'Wait till you see it.' He unlocked the cartridge, pulled out the film, checked his watch and waited with the plate in his hand, smiling. After a few moments of tuneless humming, he peeled off a layer of paper, and beamed at the photograph. 'Look at that.'

Ludmila took the picture. Her face shone wildly out, head angled down, eyes sparkling up through a fringe of hair, with just the edge of a dirty smile beneath. Raw spirit shimmered off it. It almost had a smell.

'But look at my mouth,' Ludmila said to the man. 'Try again, the next one could be better.'

'Never! Anyway, what do you need two for? This one says everything you need to say, though I'll admit it's fiery for a passport picture.'

'I want two because I paid for two – do you think I'm Gnezvarik?'

'Tut,' the man folded his lips. 'None of that, when there's no problem to speak of. If it's for passport, I'll make another. But,' he smiled knowingly, 'if it's to go on to a computer, I can make you a copy on a computer file. That's two pictures, and all for the same price. I'll even give you the disk it goes on.'

Ludmila stepped out with her photograph and disk, and made straight for the Leprikonsi bar, knowing Oksana's uncle hadn't accommodated her out of the goodness of his heart, and that her cooperation with the internet scheme was expected in return for lodgings. Also, by flirting with Ivan's computer, she felt strangely closer to Misha. It was a kind of research she was conducting, into the visa situation, on behalf of both of them. A day or two's research, until he arrived and hugged the breath out of her, kissed the shine from her hair, regaled her with the brave improbabilities that had kept him away so long.

The Leprikonsi was quiet when she arrived. Sunlight had fled its glum façade. Inside, she declined anything to eat or drink, and asked after Ivan. The barman took a mop and rapped its handle on the ceiling.

After a moment, Ivan's swollen head poked from the stairwell at the end of the bar. 'Father Jesus,' he looked Ludmila up and down, 'you again.'

An old woman in black billowed in the stairwell behind him. 'I'm telling you, we're not sending another soul for the American. Not until he pays for the last lot.'

'Hsst!' Ivan waved her away behind his back. 'It's a client.'

'I have the photograph,' Ludmila craned around him to see the old woman. 'Look.'

The woman turned away muttering; the dark of the stairwell absorbed her. Ivan ambled along the bar, and snatched the photograph from Ludmila. 'Pah! And what do you call this? You look like you were hit by a train.'

'Hoh.' Ludmila snatched back the picture.

'Anyway, that's no use whatsoever for the purposes of the business we discussed – if you'd listened, and paid correct respect to what I said, you could have avoided this expense. What you now have is a dire representation to send home to your grandmother, who I hope, for her own safety, is blind.'

'Keep your hatch off my grandmother.'

'Well, it will cost you all sorts of money to put the image into the computer from its current format – more than the cost of the photographer I was going to recommend to you, that is, before I saw that you only wanted to play hard games.'

'I'm not the one who makes the games hard. Anyway, I have no money to pay, so you'll just have to take it out of the millions you get from romantic foreigners.'

'And where is all your money?'

'And who said I had any money?'

Ivan slid an eye down her face. 'You can wear a baby's cheeks, but I'm not fooled. I know when people speak from on top of a pile of money, remember we've drunk together. Nothing escapes me, and I could tell you had notes in your pants because all you mountain girls are the same. So don't, if you want to respect me in the slightest way, now tell me you don't.'

'Well, I don't,' shrugged Ludmila. 'I sent it away.'

'On some God-forsaken bread train, I'll wager, like an imbecile.'

'Hoh! And do you think I'd be as ignorant as all the other farm girls whose pants' value you seem to calculate so well?'

Ivan sighed dramatically, and shook his head. 'Stupid girl. Just make sure you've called the depot ahead of the train, in whatever rat's nest it is that you're from, because if you don't make a deal for their cut before it arrives, you'll end up with nothing.'

'I told you I never sent it on the bread train.' Ludmila sent a push of her chin. But the flowering of her pupils, and Ivan's subsequent nod, let them both know he had done her a favour with his advice.

Ivan summoned the barman and ordered himself a coffee. Ludmila waited until it had been served before ordering one for herself.

'And you who have no money, now drinking in the finest cafés!'

'Hoh, well. If you won't invite me one, even having wasted all my time and money with your clearly fraudulent scheme –'

'Pah! I won't even talk to you again. Not any more, because in fact you're the one wasting all of our time. Talk of a fiancé, talk of money, talk of the air around your tits. If you have no money for the very reasonable price of our legitimate and famous service, I'll say goodbye.'

'Take the photograph,' Ludmila pushed it along the bar without looking.

'Well, you haven't a way to pay for its computerisation! So that's the end of the whole sorry tale.'

'Here is the computerisation.' Ludmila tossed the disk on to the bar, and took a dainty sip of her coffee. She felt like slapping the man, but didn't. Restraint was a small price to pay for a bed overlooking the Kaustik.

Ivan stood watching her with tight lips. He tossed eyes at the barman, frowned again at Ludmila. Then he snatched up the disk and turned on his heels.

Ludmila tossed her chin after him. 'I'm free Wednesday to shop for houses and jewels.'

16

The door clicked shut on Lamb, the twins crept down their stairs. Then the weight and colour of their mood became clear. The moment was as breathtaking, as intimate, as the moment a jungle butterfly emerges for its fortnight of sweet life.

'Before we take another step,' Bunny gripped his brother by both arms, 'I've something to tell you.' He felt bone beneath the sleeves of Blair's old suit. The cloth hung large around him, seeming to highlight Blair's innocence in the face of new life, his vulnerability in a world that marched on without him, that came as a thunder of feet heard over the horizon. Looking at his brother that night, Bunny saw in him the purest human instinct – the simple impulse to follow, to roam cocky within the noise of his herd.

They had been islands. Now one of them wanted to form a peninsula.

Blair stood with thin, parted lips.

Bunny removed his glasses. Tears wobbled at the rims of his eyes. They didn't fall, but stayed sparkling like springs seen from above. Slowly his hands moved to Blair's shoulders, then to his head. He leant towards him, and planted a kiss on each temple, a peck as light as a scrape from a dragonfly's wing. 'I'm sorry, mate. For everything.'

'Don't, Buns. No. I'm the one that's sorry.'

'No, mate. Don't. I've lived my life through you, can you not see? You've been my charisma.'

Blair disentangled a hand, and held it up. 'No, Buns – you're the one that's kept us together all along. My only contribution has been this sense that you're somehow in the way. That you're somehow just an appendage, when in fact, even physically, specifically, we were born a team. I just want you to know –'

'No,' Bunny tipped his head to release a tear. 'Don't.'

'No, no, Buns, no –'

'No, no.'

'No.'

The pair stood within the haze of each other's breath, heads lowered, arms falling to dangle by their sides. A fox barked outside. A siren cried like a peacock in the far distance. The twins just stood.

'I'm going to show you something,' Bunny wound his eyes up to Blair's. 'Something Matron gave me when we left – I didn't have the bloody spine to show it to you then. I've been so afraid to lose you. I'm sorry, mate. I brought it tonight, in case you found your independence, like you wanted to. In case it was our last times together.'

Blair's eyes filled with tears.

'Don't, mate.' Bunny's hand trembled into his jacket's inside pocket. He pulled out a folded sheet of lined paper.

Blair opened the page, and read:

'Capistrano'
41 Sunnymead Close
Solihull
West Midlands

Dear Son,
   I hope you are chipper and that all is going as well as it can. Your mother and I are all right, in our way. It might be some time before you can fully understand this letter, but it is important for me to write it nonetheless. Because, although it isn't

191

mentioned much, and I don't want to appear to harp on unduly, I wanted to let you know that you are not alone in your disappointment at the way things have turned out. Much attention has been paid to your plight, and quite rightly so, as you will have to bear its most direct physical consequence – but it is only fair to tell you that your mother and I suffer at least as much as you, and very probably more. When we set out to create a little family of our own we could have never, in a thousand years, imagined the nightmare that would befall us. We have lost our friends, our standing in the street, our self-respect and, at the root of this sad but necessary letter, our respect and love for each other. I am very sorry to have to tell you that your mother is moving away, though we remain on civilised speaking terms.

Please don't feel that this is your fault, in a wilful sense, because it is not. I have never thought of you as a 'monster', as some people might say, or anything less than an 'innocent victim of forces outside all of our control'. Everyone else, including, I'm sure, the Nicholls next door (even after the unkind things we heard from them via Stan and Margaret in the early days), also feels this way; that it's just a massive accident of nature, a kind of nightmare from which we will never awaken.

But Son, these are modern, enlightened times. I won't say they're better, on average, than my day, but one thing that progress has brought to this country is the ability to clear the air, and say what's on our minds. Although it hurts me, or rather, further compounds my hurt, I know that writing these words to you is the 'healthiest' thing to do, and we should be thankful, I suppose, not to be living forty years back, when we might have avoided the truth for politeness's sake.

So, I'll get to the point, as I'm not making this any easier to read (or write!) by harping on. Because of the enormous

progress of our times, I am very confident that you will be well cared for at Albion. Our times particularly favour the handicapped, and the right systems are in place for you, according to the latest guidelines. As a long-standing taxpayer I suppose I'm pleased to see my hard-earned living go towards something tangible, because it's a lot of overseas holidays'-worth of tax I've paid over the years, in fact, an Andalusian flat's-worth, like the Nicholls's in Fuengirola, even a much bigger one than theirs, and closer to the shops. So, at least your mental constitution, and all your day-to-day requirements, will be well looked after by specialists in a great many fields. I could never offer as much because I'm not a specialist, and 'Capistrano' just isn't adapted for disability scenarios. And thinking in enlightened terms, with regard to all the unhealthy 'co-dependencies and enablings', and other scientific discoveries of psychology that can afflict people these days, I feel sure it would be better for me not to further complicate your lives by trying to create a façade of family life, or any such contrivance that might be difficult for you to rationalise later. Because, although I'll try and not harp on unduly about it, the truth is that you have handicaps that will keep us apart, and I think it probably best that you be left to find yourself, without any excess 'baggage' from me. I think it best for you to become independent now, and I'm sure you would thank me in future for making this very hard decision. Please have Matron read this to you, or at least see that she reads it. You know that all my very best wishes go out to you for the future.
    Ted.

P.S. Marjorie, your mother, insists I tell you that when I say 'Son' I mean both of you. Anyway, you are just one, in a way. Your mother is moving to Surrey.

193

Blair's eyes hit the last word of the letter and stopped, hanging glazed for some moments. Then he lowered the page and took his brother into his arms, sniffling softly on to his shoulder. Bunny sniffled in return, and brought a hand to Blair's back.

'That was addressed to me, wasn't it?' asked Blair.

Bunny's eyes dropped. 'There was only ever you. I was just a parasite. An accident of nature.'

'No, Buns. Don't say that. No.'

'No, it's true. I'm not saying it to be maudlin. I just want you to know I'm going to do every bloody thing in my power to give you the wind you deserve under your wings. Every bloody thing. I'm just sorry I've taken this long to come to my wretched senses, Blair. I'm so sorry, mate.'

'And I'm going to do the same for you, old friend. I'm going to do the same for you.'

The pair embraced until their sniffles grew occasional, and their breathing became slow and regular. Minutes were measured by clicks and slaps from the upstairs bedsit's cat flap.

Finally, Blair pulled his head back an inch, and whispered into Bunny's ear, 'Here – can you not sense a juniper-influenced restorative trend in the offing?'

There was a moment's silence. Bunny pulled back an inch. 'I can, as you mention it.'

As sunlight warmed London's haze like torchlight through a flesh-toned gusset, the Heaths set off for the kitchenette to carpet themselves in gin's warmth. Their original dose of solipsidrine hydrochloride showed no signs of abating. The better part of a bottle of Gordon's – Bunny's gin of choice – soon joined it in their bloodstreams, later shedding its tonic in the lavatory, and on the floor beside.

By the time car motors coughed along Scombarton Road, both men were naked below the waist. Blair's penis rose proud and

shining, Bunny's less so. They heard no birdsong over the thump
of Blair's Pirie Jammette disc, though they caught some harsh
footsteps from upstairs. The twins sang over them, writhing,
wagging wild fingers in the air, and as the song's climax
approached, they were simultaneously inspired to turn their
backs to each other, bend over double, and rub their bottoms
together, bouncing, chafing, glancing their skin till it glowed. This
would have been impossible just a year before. So they did it, and
danced in the strange, high-stepping way they had when not conjoined, buttocks wobbling in the gloom.

'We'll have a tagno next,' Blair puckered his lips to slur.

'Yes, my darlen,' said Bunny.

'You're my darlenk.'

'No, you're my daleks.'

Blair tried to wrest back control of his legs. Arms out-
stretched, knees bent, he found a fulcrum, and manoeuvred
himself to the computer chair. 'But look,' he said, thumping the
'On' button, and slumping on to the desk. A flywheel tried to
turn in his mind, and with its first uneven rotation, fragments of
urgent memory broke from it like sparks. He squinted, hung his
mouth open. Then he pulled from his jacket the card Truman
had given him.

He logged on to the internet, and began to tap at the keyboard: 'www.k –'

'Tits not found.' Bunny swayed, pointing over his shoulder.
'404 – Arse Not Found.'

'Non, no,' said Blair. 'Wait! There's grils in the thing.'

'Buds ony foren grils in the thing. Asian girls call Pong and Wee.'

'Nah, thiss Russian blons.' He tapped his penis clear of the
table edge, and it rested its head near the keyboard.

'Russan? Pork pies, like they. Theys right fuckin armred per-
sonnel carrers, summofm, big hard faces.'

195

'Nah, non, looket all them tennis girlies.' Blair hunched over the screen, forced his eyes to focus: 'www. kssnkz,' he tapped. His head swayed left and right over the keyboard. He deleted the line back to the first K.

'Get shot n fat the day after the weddng,' said Bunny, 'nwear black soscks for eternty. Called Lumbumla an Glom. Glomx.'

'www. kushnksgrils.'

'Anway, you're my darleng.'

'You're my darlan,' said Blair.

'I havet sleep now.' Bunny stumbled heavily around the bench, using it as a pivot for his trajectory to the nearest settee. He fell half on it. His sighs became snores, and he fell asleep clutching the lapels of his jacket over his chest.

Blair's eyes cut into slices. He drew back his finger like an arrow, and fired it at the keyboard.

'www.kuzhniskgirls.com.ru.'

Women leapt on to the screen. Women with hairstyles and poses unseen since the days of sheiks and flappers, against lurid studio backdrops of lakesides, beaches, and boudoirs.

And in the lower right-hand corner of that self-conscious assortment, one face shone out from the thick of a genuine life.

One wild, beautiful face.

Blair's penis twitched up to his hand.

17

'It's the imbecile Gregor!' Kiska shouted from the yard. A hissed reproach from Gregor came as an echo up the track.

'Shh!' Irina scolded through the door. 'Come away!'

'And I see you school your babies properly for this life,' said Gregor, trudging his gun up to the house like a husband late home. He flung open the door and stepped into the shack like its master.

Irina folded her arms, glaring from the stove. 'You tie your own noose, walking the mountain with your gun like that.'

'Well, I don't. Hear the war crackling outside, do you think this is the only gun around?'

Irina didn't answer, but barked a word through the door at Kiska, who was busy stalking the rooster with a length of fencing wire.

'Maksimilian is not yet back,' Olga tossed her chin at Gregor from the bedroom door.

'Then he's playing a big game with us, because I walked here with the feet on my legs, while he has a tractor to drive. Anyway, you should have brought the tractor direct to the depot and not wasted so much fuel moving back and forth to your rathole.'

'The tractor isn't always so reliable,' said Irina. 'He'll be back just now, you'll see.'

'He'd better be,' said Gregor, looking around the hovel. 'I have instructions to remove the chickens and the goat, and I'm not walking with them on my back.'

'Pah, but the goat is fleet of hoof,' said Olga. 'It would run ahead and be asleep waiting by the time you reached the depot. As for the chickens, well –' she shrugged, 'your cuckoos might infect them, they might lose the brains to travel at all.'

'Hoh, and just mind I don't pelt a lash at your hatch. Anyway, old woman, the inspector wants to know what you've done with the dead. He says if you don't register the death correctly then his job will be that much more difficult. It'll cost more than the tractor. Hoh. Now see what jokes you have after that sour news.'

'Then it's simple,' said Irina, sending a glare to her mother, 'because we have nothing more. You've taken it all.'

'Well, it's a pity,' said Gregor, 'because he said to remind you the likely outcome of such a case is that the little girl will be taken away. He said you might be judged not fit to care for such a youngster.'

Kiska stopped quiet by the door. Irina stared at Gregor. She fought the impulse to batter him till he was crushed. Somehow, after three wavering breaths, she squeezed the impulse into a sweet, confiding voice.

Olga picked up its edge. Her eyes fixed on her daughter.

'Gregor.' Irina stepped up to the boy. 'I don't suppose Ludmila contacted you? She asked for the depot number before she left, so as to call you in a private way.'

'Hoh! What?'

'Saints – what have I said, she'll die from shame!'

'Look what happens to you, Irina, when you open your stupid hole!' Olga wagged a finger through the smoke. She sliced her eyes at Gregor, and waited for reaction.

'No, tell me,' Gregor stood down his gun.

'Well, it's nothing,' said Irina. 'I should have kept my hatch cut. She'll despise me for saying a word about it.'

'But Irina, child, wait,' Olga said reasonably. 'The truth is that she has led us to think the boy already knew of her feelings.'

Irina let her eyes crawl across the ceiling. 'Well, and you might be right. God knows how many times I've washed her smalls over and over because she thought she might meet Gregor at the depot.'

Gregor stood still for a moment, images visibly churning behind the folds of his head. Then his mouth burst open. 'Haa, ha! Oh yes, you washed her smalls for me, the same day I turned into Yuri Gagarin!'

His mouth clamped shut. He shuffled to face the women with fresh disdain. 'A coloured goose's yarn. Now look with your eyes at the face of my watch, because ten minutes from where the hands currently sit I had better see Maksimilian Ivanov here with the tractor. Or else I have my instructions.'

'This boy of yours, Gregor, has made me very concerned,' said the inspector.

'But I say he'll be here at any moment,' said Lubov. 'We'll hear the tractor, if not the goat, coming into the road. The thing with Gregor, which is a good thing, if I myself say it as his mother, is that he won't come back with empty hands. As much as this evil family dishes sour platefuls to him, and tries to entangle him with their lies, he'll only pay attention to filling his hands with the required things.'

'I myself am quite tired already of these exhaustive examinations of the ledgers,' Abakumov leant against the bar of the empty depot. 'I feel I wouldn't fight away any tea that you made me, or any sandwich of bread.'

'Well, the bread train is only today reaching the junction, Inspector. Until Gregor returns to fetch it, there'll be no bread. Tomorrow we'll have some bread.'

'Then seeing as you ask, I'll share a vodka with you.' Abakumov stroked his chin, and gazed absently up at the ceiling.

Lubov pulled the old flagon from under the counter, and stood two glasses on the bar. The sound of the glasses brought a scruffy man's face to the door.

'Yes,' called the man, beginning to hoist himself through the door as if it were a submarine hatch.

'Don't bring another of your feet into my store,' Lubov shouted without looking up. 'This time you'll be for a beating.'

'Ugly sow.' The man staggered back on to the street. 'I shit on the graves of your dead.'

'Then you shit on your own grave, Papa.'

The inspector gulped down his shot, and gazed blankly over the landscape of tiles and shadows. 'Very, very concerned, I'm becoming. Highly disquieted. And where is the Derev boy? Why didn't he deliver his tractor straight here, knowing the situation?'

'Maksimilian? He's too wicked a boy to ever do what's good for him or his family. Listen to me when I tell you, Inspector, these are people who respond only to the hardest instructions. Dealing with them in any way is like whipping a pig without legs.'

'And are you sure that's all of them, in the hovel – certainly they must have other family, in the bigger towns? Nobody can survive on the mountain just like that.'

'They do have cousins, I believe, around Labinsk.' Lubov poured another drink. 'But I feel the cousins must be wise to them, they never appear around these parts. Why would they? So, yes, I'd say they survive like mice on the mountain. If you call that surviving. Of course, they have the older girl as well – a harder case still, if you listen to me on the subject.'

'And where might she be?'

'Uvila, or somewhere. She was seen riding out of the village. Some say Pilosanov, our local madman, took her, in which case anything could've happened since.'

'Well,' Abakumov studied the mildewed ceiling. 'It seems I could be here much longer than expected. Very much longer, as things stand, with this level of tangles.'

Lubov shivered at the news, and pulled from the moment's sleeve the only ace she had left. 'And I'm sorry for you, Inspector. Especially with the war so firmly on our doorstep! The very rooms we stand in may not be here for long, we hear the Americans might even come. Saints help us if that be so.'

'Ha! And come for what? Mother Russia hasn't been so ignorant as to get directly involved, neither any foreign power. Gnezvariks and Ublis are fighting a limited guerrilla war over a piece of wasteland, without life in it enough to support two goats. Invisible masters feed arms to the Gnez and stand back like impartial parents. It's one lesson well learned from our American friends: only show the hand that feeds – look what happened in Iraq, after all.'

'Well, but the Americans have moved their military from Arabia to Hayastan, scarcely two borders away – surely they have a purpose for that, Inspector?'

'And of course they do, apart from vacating the Islamic zones. But it would take a wild journey of imagination to think your patch of ice and mud held the least interest for them, when there are no resources here to speak of, and no reconstructions to contract. Rather, the Iranian border has sucked them up like wasps to a lover's perfume, I doubt they've even heard of such a rathole as this.'

'Still,' said Lubov, keeping an eye on the doorway where her father lurked, 'the Ublis are fighting for real, with Mozdoks and

Chechens arriving every day to help. You should know that every village between here and Azkua has been razed, and all the ethnic Ublis killed or driven out. We nurse our deaths to stay here a moment longer.'

Abakumov shrugged. 'You may nurse your death. I'm not ethnic Ubli.'

'No, of course.' Lubov was suddenly aware of her dusky complexion, and shifted back a little into shade.

'And if you listen to what I have to say on the matter, the ethnic question is just a ploy to attract international agencies,' Abakumov studied his fingernails one by one. 'The Ublis have painted a moth to look like a butterfly, so all the weeping herb-eaters of the world will publicise their misery. The truth is – and this is widely known at the levels of government I occupy on a daily basis – that no ethnic problem existed until the collapse of the union. The Ublis are fighting for money. That's all. And this is where the government could be more clever, in my view – because if they simply paid them their pensions and wages, they would happily go back to their fields. Instead they have, with the help of the Chechens, built a case for oppression, and thus a cause for them to fight for independence. They refuse to see that all Transcaucasia is in the same situation.'

Lubov listened, but didn't look at the inspector. Such school-book dogma was a common sound to her ears, heard daily over that very bar. She knew the first whistling bullets would add an urgent ingredient to the inspector's viewpoint.

'And,' Abakumov raised a finger, 'let's be honest with each other – what would they do with independence anyway? They've simply caught the fashion of the last two decades, where every village with more than two cats has to call itself a republic. Because, and you know this very well, sub-agent Kaganovich, there is no ethnic Ubli homeland. There never was a conquered state before. Your blood is just the grounds of the local wine, made over the years of Kabardine, Cherkess and Russian minority flavours. I mean – some Ublis are more blond than Germans!'

'Of course, Inspector,' Lubov tried to keep the tone minimally professional.

Abakumov gave a general sort of sigh. 'In any event, we haven't to concern ourselves with a war that may or may not fall at the door. What we need are other, more tangible things to fall there. And quickly.'

'Just now, Inspector, Gregor will be back, and things will look different. When Gregor returns just now, you can be sure he'll have every possible thing these Derevs possess. Anyway, Karel will be on his way there too, to see about the bread train. He will keep Gregor to schedule, you'll see just now.'

Maks sat on the rusted frame of a railway switch-box, beside tracks that once led to the village. The tracks now ended abruptly twelve yards from where he sat deep in thought. He was roughly half-way home, though he'd taken an oblique route.

His first thoughts were about the two remaining tractors in Ublilsk, tractors that he could possibly get his hands on. He didn't consider the mechanics of life after he'd stolen somebody else's tractor to present as his own, nor the explanations he'd give his mothers. Rather, he thought about how he could find, start, and remove the tractors from their yards. He even imagined how he might steal both tractors, and drive them both home. But soon after this thought, he knew no tractor would accompany him that day.

Maks spent some minutes cursing Pilosanov, and grinding his teeth, and tasting in his mind the vicious injuries he would award him. He even savoured the thought of killing him, and cooking him over an open fire to serve in crispy strips to the region's poor. That would be the first good anyone had made of Pilo's life, Maks reflected. Crispy strips, with onion and salt. As he sat with his dank thoughts, a lorry approached along the trail beside the railway line. It was slow, and moved with much noise, as though driving in the uppermost reaches of first gear. Maks looked up. As the lorry grew nearer, he saw it was full of men, crammed into the cab, and jostling in the tray at the back.

Fighters. Maks tensed, but as the lorry drew up he saw it carried Ubli freedom fighters. He cocked a hand in solidarity. The lorry hissed to a stop on the ice.

'Brother, is there a way around Ublilsk village from here?' a bearded man called from the cab.

'This is it.' Maks moved to the window. 'Keep going until the track disappears, then drive four hundred metres to the left and you'll be on the Uvila way. Are you coming from the front?'

'No, we're going *to* the front. Not tonight, though.'

'You're taking this way to the front?'

'We're carrying dead, a new boy. His parents will curse the sight of us, but what can we do? Can you confirm there are Bukinovs on the far side of the village, three kilometres or so outside?'

'Bukinov? Are you saying you carry Michael Bukinov?'

'We carry his body, saints keep him.' A murmur of amens rippled through the lorry. 'Can you confirm where his family have their land?'

It took a moment for Maks to respond. He stood gazing at the lorry's front tyre. 'Yes,' he eventually said, 'skirt the whole village, then take the last track to your left before the bridge on the Uvila road. A kilometre inside you'll find his uncle's lands, and a dwelling with Lukoil signage on the front.' Maks looked up at the driver. 'Can it be known how he died?'

'He took a bullet into the chest. He won't even have heard it leave the barrel.'

Maks joined another murmur of amens. 'It's good that you bring him all this way back.'

'He was a good man,' the driver paused for another murmur. 'Ordinarily we can't be carrying individual bodies all over the mountain, but he met his saints during some business we had at the junction, and we couldn't leave his body there to take the blame.'

'Hss!' the man beside him raised the back of a hand.

Maks watched them, and thought. He began to nod, slowly. 'You found the bread train.'

'Listen to me carefully when I tell you it isn't worth opening your mouth.' The bearded man brought up to the window a loaf of bread. 'Take this and stuff your hatch full of it. The free state will thank you and honour you in not too many weeks from now.'

Maks reached up for the loaf. 'I'm with you, all my soul is with you. I'd be fighting alongside you with my bare teeth, but for the household of touched old women I have to mind.'

The man reached down from the cab and ruffled Maks's head. 'The best thing I can tell you is to start moving them away. Gnez have their eyes on this theatre, with all its empty buildings. And I'll say to you, strategically, we have a mind to let them take it.'

A frown clouded Maks's face. He nodded to himself, and looked up. 'One thing to ask – have you left the bread carriage at the junction?'

'The carriage lies on its side. There's some iron you might be able to take, but nothing of real use – we have the chains and hoses.'

'And did the guard see you there?'

'Yes,' grinned a man from the back of the platform. 'And here he still is.' The men raised their rifles into the air, making an arch over the head of the guard from the Kropotkin train, who cocked a hand in salute.

Maks felt empowered by the soldiers' passing. Watching the

lorry bounce away, he felt a surge of emotional juice. With the air of higher destinies around him, and with the knowledge that the short term was growing shorter, Maks and his loaf marched for home. As a token of his now diminished regret over the tractor, he decided on his walk that he would not take any bite from the loaf, that his mothers would have first bite at it while he told them the sad news about the villain Pilosanov and his evil fraud. Even though he was hungry, he would save the loaf's honour.

This pact lasted two hundred yards, after which he could no longer bear the loaf's fresh weight any more. Anyway, who was to say he'd received it whole? A loaf was a loaf. They were lucky to have anything at all, let alone have it a day before everybody else in the district. As a mark of honour, a token of his earlier regret, he would break off pieces with his hands, not his teeth. And that he did, cramming chunk upon chunk into his mouth, struggling to find the spit to chew them with.

He waited until half-way through his last chew before turning the corner to the shack. Kiska wasn't on her usual sentinel duty, and his approach went unheard. He trudged up to the door, scraped his boots loudly across the frame, and stepped inside.

Irina and Olga watched him enter. Their eyes sharpened.

'A very silent tractor,' Gregor stepped from the shadows with his gun. 'You must've pushed it.'

Maks stopped at the threshold. His mother's eyes crept to him.

'And you have bread,' Gregor frowned.

'There's been a battle at the junction,' said Maks. 'The Gnez have spilt the bread. Even Misha Bukinov has been killed, attempting to defend the delivery.'

'What's that?' Abakumov turned an ear to the back room.

'It's the telephone trying to ring,' said Lubov. 'Sometimes it manages to make enough noise to be heard.'

'I'm surprised you even have a telephone.'

Lubov rolled her eyes as she stepped through the doorway. 'Inspector, it's only you who thinks this is a mud wasteland. Ublilsk was a thriving town for a century before you came.'

She opened the drawer containing the phone, and lifted the receiver.

'It's Ludmila Ivanova calling, with some urgent business for you at the depot.'

'So you live still,' said Lubov. 'I hope you have good and immediate themes to propose. I hope you're not swanning around the bars of Zavetnoye living the red life while we suffer every type of new consequence.'

'Listen carefully, and spare me your typical gas: I haven't long to speak, but you must know there is a letter coming on the bread train for my mother. It contains an important document.'

'And how many does it contain, because it will take more than one to fix up the mess you've left behind.'

'Well, forget your bitter pills, because I have a hundred roubles to give you for the trouble of delivering the letter.'

'Hoh, and you think I'll crawl so far out of my way for a hundred roubles?'

'Yes I do, because I know you'll send your idiot son with it.'

'You dare call him an idiot!'

'The second part of my message is this: to tell my mothers that I'm surviving, and will soon be able to help them. To you I have to say, with all the warmth I can gather, that I expect this letter to be delivered, and delivered quickly for the money I'll pay you, which my mother will give you when she opens it. Or else I'll come there tomorrow and make some type of trouble you will never have seen the likes of before.'

'Save your threats for the street dogs,' scoffed Lubov. 'When I see the thing, I'll know what to do.'

Ludmila hung up with a snort, and Lubov stepped back to the bar.

'Something interesting?' asked Abakumov.

'Not really.' Lubov reached for the vodka. 'A cousin from Zavetnoye. Expecting another baby, though the saints know she can't even wet the mouths of the ones she has.'

Abakumov narrowed his eyes. 'And she's sending this baby to you?'

'What would make you think that?'

'Haven't you just said you're expecting something? On the train, perhaps, that your son might collect? With some roubles attached?'

Ludmila walked back to Oksana's apartment. The question of foreign men entered her mind slowly, like a sand painting assembling from bottom to top. All her foreign men looked a bit like Misha: they were blond, burly types, but with high-pitched voices and too much money. She saw gifts arriving for her future babies, and these gifts she would sell secretly during the day while the lazy husband was at his work speaking English or German. She would sell them and make even more money to send home to her family.

The men in her mind smelt sweetly of women's perfume, though they would belch because they were gluttons, and used to eating too much food and conflicting varieties of it, particularly meat and cream. As she fleshed out their diet in her mind, a diet without subtlety of fragrance, she realised they might fart terribly, owing to poor digestion. This was why they kept so many toilets in their houses, because a cavernous fart of rotting meats could take them at any moment, a fart of too great a consequence to be aired in the common spaces of the home.

She reached the street of Oksana's apartment, and looked up

to find the window dark. Across the street, she peered through the glass of the Kaustik, hoping, as ever, to see Misha's broad back at the bar. Instead Oksana was there, watching television from a stool in the corner. Ludmila stepped inside.

'Did you see?' Oksana pointed at the screen. 'The train has been attacked up your way, in the war.'

'What train?' asked Ludmila. 'Fighting hasn't reached the railway yet.'

'Well, it has, because they've assaulted the train or something like that, some offence with the train. Assaulted it, almost certainly. The Kropotkin train, or part of it anyway, coming from here. Ublis are blamed, but nobody really knows as the guard has disappeared who was in charge of it. There are dead as well.'

Ludmila's eyes lost focus. She scraped a stool close, and sat slowly. Oksana's uncle turned from a conversation at the end of the bar and approached the girls.

'Here's a girl who knows when her rent's due.' He threw down his palms with a thud.

'Yes,' said Ludmila without turning, 'and when it's due, I'll pay it.'

'Listen to her,' the uncle tossed a laugh at Oksana. 'What did I tell you about this one? The rent is due today, but now she'll try to gain advantage over an old man already in his fifties.'

'The rent isn't due today, it's due Thursday,' said Ludmila. 'So now you try to gain advantage over a young girl, innocent from the mountains, where a single day is like half of your life for the hardships it brings.' She snorted disdainfully, and flicked her head away.

As she did it, the smile fell from the barman's cheeks. After a moment, he tore off his apron and stamped from behind the bar.

'Oh dear!' said Oksana.

'Come then,' said the barman. 'As your mouth is so clever you'll have no trouble finding your way, you'll probably end up president of your own republic with such a mouth.'

'What?' Ludmila looked up.

'Come and recover your luggage. After all we've done, and you still cut us down. I can find someone more grateful for the bed, who doesn't always put up such a smell about everything. Now come with me.'

Ludmila sat with her bag on the street. Snow fell, dusting her shoulders and hair. She cursed her pride, she should have bargained with Uncle Sergei, apologised, restated herself in a more positive way. But she didn't curse herself long, preferring to do what she knew was proper: curse Oksana's uncle. And Oksana herself, who hadn't said a thing against the sudden eviction. 'Oh dear!' Ludmila mocked bitterly.

She was truly alone, with less than the price of an insult. She had eaten her last pastry. And that was that. Suddenly, and for the first time since arriving in Kuzhnisk, she felt homesick. Not only for Misha, whose image strangled her every minute, but for the simple, familiar surroundings and routines of home, and for her family specifically. She conjured their images from the night's chill. They grew warm and plastic in her mind. Even her father's face came to her, because for all his wickedness, he had loved his daughters and spoilt them when he could, especially Ludmila, as Kiska had been a much later surprise, and was too young to respond to him. On even his worst days, his clothes starched stiff with old vomit, he would reach out a trembling hand, open it to reveal a gift, perhaps a ribbon, or a pebble from the Caspian where he roamed seeking work.

The images led to the day he was found with four rebel bullets in his back.

Mental pictures were soon overlaid with cries and shouts from Olga and Irina. A tear welled in Ludmila's eye. She looked up the street and imagined her stupid brother Maksimilian strutting towards her.

'Milochka!' he called, scowling over his latest scheme. 'You'll be thanking me in throat-kisses when you hear the new plan I have for us. And only because you're my sister by blood do I even risk to tell you such a money-spinner so early, because we'd surely be crushed under the feet of simpler minds if anyone knew of this scheme.' Ludmila's eyes searched the length of the street for Maks's swaggering form. The act of searching made her weep.

Truth was sinking in. Beneath her hard talk, she had not become intimate with the truth of her mission in Kuzhnisk – to simply save her family. Misha did not factor in that equation, nor Sergei, nor Ivan, nor Oksana, neither pastries, coffee, and vodka.

She saw her grandmother shine as she found Kuzhnisk soups bobbing full of meats, with salads like gardens beside them, and black bread as plentiful as summer beetles in Ublilsk.

'Best find bandages and ointment,' Irina would say, cocking an eye at Olga and her plateful of food. 'We'll tie the cut your grandmother must have in her throat.'

'Tie your own cuts!' Olga would snap. 'An old woman needs to eat! Not to mention an old woman in such advanced decay as you have let her become. Don't you know anything? An old woman's furnaces are not efficient, it takes more food to have even a mouse's chance of nourishment. You're lucky I don't demand your plates as well, as it's my right to do after being so miserably rewarded for bringing a family into the world.'

And so the old arguments would begin, arguments that, for all their poison, were as comfy as powdered scarves, having been played out so often before.

'If you had one working eye in your head you would've seen that man was no good!' Olga would end up saying of Ludmila's father.

'Yes,' Irina would spit, 'which is just what you told me on my wedding day, wasn't it! Those same words came over your lips in just the same order, didn't they!'

'It was too late at the wedding to even tell you anything, when you already had stupidly agreed with the man to marry him! What could I do but find a deeper pocket in which to nestle my tears!'

'Well, you nestled them all right, in a lake full of vodka!'

'What other consolation could there be for an old woman seeing such tragedy played out in front of her face!'

And so the wailing and slapping of hard surfaces would continue, the serving of sour meals to the saints, sometimes bringing the Derevs to inconsequential blows, sometimes, on very lucky days, turning into a single bitter force against some third party, most usually Lubov Kaganovich at the depot.

But that night Ludmila felt only the ghost of family turmoil. It played before her with less than the force of a snowflake hitting the ground, then was gone.

She knew it was a beacon, calling.

She would travel home. Misha would be there.

'Gregor's not here,' Maks leant through the kitchen window. On the floor behind him, Gregor lay dead. A crowbar wound bubbled at the back of his head. The crowbar hung warm from Maks's hand.

'He must be there,' Karel Kaganovich called from the yard. 'Where else is he going to be?'

'He went to the train,' said Maks. 'Or do you think he would leave the whole region starving for bread?'

'I don't think he went to the train at all.'

'Then don't come asking me where he might be – he's your kin, not mine. I tell you he left here to go to the train, and if you're not able to accept that, then I can't help you.'

'What have you really done with him?' Karel poked the yard's darkness with his torch.

'Such suspicions! You forget he has the gun, not me. What could I do against a loaded gun?'

Olga and Irina sat in the darkest corner of the main room. Kiska knelt between them, toying with their hems. Olga motioned Maks to get rid of the Kaganovich boy.

Maks shrugged helplessly, and leant back to the window. 'Didn't you hear they had a raid on the wagon tonight? The bread is all spilt, Misha Bukinov even died. Gregor ran like a rabbit to get there and salvage what he could. He said for you to run behind him, quickly, and help him staunch the flow of loaves.'

'What raid?' Karel called doubtfully. 'Let me inside to talk to you properly. And why are you now saying this, when it should have been the first thing you told me?'

'If you have ears attached to your head, then listen well to what I tell you: you've no business in here while my family's sleeping, you should go to the train where your cousin waits. I won't be to blame if you don't show up to help him, or if something terrible happens because you arrived too late to save it. I'll be telling him exactly how you were, deciding to stand here making lazy excuses, to spare you walking the track by yourself.'

There was a pause as Karel shone his torch around once more. 'Who told you there was a raid?'

'Ubli fighters passing on their way to the front. They told us to be quick if we wanted bread at all this week, because Gnezvariks had rolled the wagon.' Maks looked back into the gloom and rolled his eyes at his mothers. He skipped an eye over Gregor's swollen body, still lying awkwardly in smears of blood. 'And listen to me carefully,' he called back through the window, 'Gregor himself was the one who received the news. He acted quickly, as was proper for him to do, and I can't fault him on his reaction, as much as I'd like to. He immediately responded by departing to the junction. He had his gun carried in front of him, and he went straight away.'

'Then why didn't you go with him?'

'And leave the house here full of women, and a baby child?'

'I'm not a baby child!' Kiska shouted through the smoke. Her shout was met by a volley of low hissing.

'Aah! Aah!' called Karel. 'And you tell me the whole family is sleeping! There isn't a word that falls from your tongue that isn't a lie!'

'Ah! Ah!' cried Maks, 'and do you think a family of any sort could sleep through your diabolical rantings at their window? Even the dead would wake! The name Kaganovich has brought nothing but dismay and panic to this private house, I should step out and bang you down hard!'

Maks, Irina, and Olga froze quiet, waited for some shard of hope to emerge from the exchange. Maks had the power to repel the boy, because he then had Gregor's gun discreetly propped behind him. But to kill the last relation of an enemy was to invite a battle to the death. Not only that, it would be a battle that lasted generations, until both family lines were destroyed. While Maks was tempted to end the situation, he held himself in check, and waited for Karel to calculate the night's odds.

This was never going to be a fast procedure.

The Derevs willed Karel with their minds to do the obvious thing; set off for the junction, a round trip that would buy them the hours until dawn. Then all three Derevs would try to haul away Gregor's fat remains, because Maks alone had been unable to do it.

'Well,' said Karel.

The family held their breaths.

'It's clear I have to go back to the village for the inspector and his car. Otherwise I'll be hours on the track, possibly for nothing.'

'What do you mean, for nothing?' yelled Maks. 'I've told you what you have to do, in your cousin's own words.'

'And,' called Karel, 'I'll be telling the inspector to call past here first, so that he can hear all this from your mouth. I'll not be taking blame if it's a lie, as I feel it must be. Yes, I'll go for the inspector. Then we'll see.'

Maks turned, and widened his eyes at Olga. She frowned, and thrust her chin urgently at the window.

'Yes,' shouted Maks, 'and then I'll tell the inspector you were the one who delayed the whole operation until it was too late. If something happens to the bread, and to Gregor Kaganovich, you know whose fingers will be chopped. So go ahead and enjoy your lazy walk while you think of all this I'm telling you.'

'Be sure that I will,' called Karel.

When the torch beam disappeared around the corner of the track, the family leapt to action. First up was Olga, gathering her skirts. She hobbled past Gregor's body, out through the door to the patch of snow they called their toilet.

'Typical,' muttered Irina. 'Let's get him ourselves – you take his head.'

'Don't wake him up,' whispered Kiska, 'he might shout!'

'He won't shout,' said Maks. 'He has a worm.'

'Like Grandpapa?'

Maks grappled the boy's shoulders. 'Much worse than Grandpapa, who is the one most likely to shout.'

Irina and Maks carried the body three feet before dropping it back on to the floor. They had been trying to avoid drag marks of blood, but there was nothing for it.

'I'll just have to drag him,' snarled Maks. 'Help me this end, we'll drag him and try cleaning up later.'

'Then hurry,' hissed Irina. 'We've an hour at most.'

'My face has definitely been painted like a circus clown.' Abakumov looked at his watch. The seventh vodka had delivered him to the end of his restless tether. He suspected the Derev boy had absconded altogether with the tractor, and since Lubov's mysterious telephone call, he now suspected her of being party to some kind of deceit upon him.

Lubov sensed his increasing suspicion. Her helplessness was compounded by worry over the whereabouts of her boys. 'I honestly have nothing else to serve you for information,' she shrugged. 'If I knew the state of affairs I would tell you straight away, I'm not so ignorant as to delay you all the night waiting. Anyway, you've personally been here to see who's been instructed to do what. I have no explanation beyond what you know.'

Abakumov sucked a hiss through his teeth. 'This that you say is not true. You're a part of these mountains like any of its trees or birds, you know all the threads that tangle behind the story. I'm here just trying to skate on the brittle surface of the lies I'm being told.'

'No lies are being told, Inspector.'

'Then why is the story made only of words? No other action is taking place, except for these colourful promises like forest birds that you release flapping at every chance!'

'Inspector, I tell you with an open heart –'

'Enough!' growled Abakumov. 'We're going to drive to the hovel ourselves, right now. Come with me.'

'I will take an axe to this apparatus if you don't shut it up,' said the woman. She was a brusque woman dressed in black. She scowled at the computer in the box-room above the Leprikonsi bar. 'And why does it make the noises of a sick bird? I could more inexpensively procure a genuine sick bird, if this is all the infernal machine can do – this and eat up our money. Ivan? *Ivan!*'

'Father Jesus, Mama, what is it?' Ivan stumbled into the room wearing a large black dressing gown. He grabbed the bushy stub of a cigar from his writing desk, but his mother snatched it from his mouth, and hurled it into her mop bucket. Ivan rubbed his eyes, blinking to take in the computer, which hummed and chirped on its makeshift bench.

After a moment, he found focus. 'Mama – it's just another bite.'

'What?'

'A bite, I tell you. Look – from overseas. Somebody's taken the hook for a girl.' He fumbled to activate a flashing icon on the screen. It opened up a newly arrived e-mail. 'Look, there it is.'

'Well, can't you shut off the bird noises? The room is sounding like a jungle.' The woman leant to squint over the bench.

'Read it,' Ivan stabbed the screen with a finger. 'It must be in English.'

'Wait while I fetch my glasses.' She stood her mop against the window. Sunlight threatened to flood the room, giving both the nervy airs of vampires.

'No,' said Ivan, 'just tell me basically what it says, just look up close.' He pushed his mother to the screen.

'Well, and just pull back your dogs!'

'No, but –'

'Stop and catch hold of yourself, Ivan, for God's sake.'

The woman craned to within an inch of the screen, muttering to herself. 'It must be in very high English, I'm not even familiar with this type of spelling. "Gril",' she mouthed, '"margiagge, globsl makrets." It could be another one from the Liberty factory, the American seems to keep sending them.'

'Yes.' Ivan stroked his chin. 'Yes, and we must land this one like a prize beluga, land it firmly into our little boat and recover some costs. Now you'll see, Mama, that our investment in the letter, in those magical words and their devastating symphonic arrangement, will repay us a thousand times over.'

'And what letter is this?'

'I'm speaking, of course, of the letter of reply, from Kherson – don't you remember? The reply calculated to draw even the corpse of a man from his grave.'

'Well, you could have spared yourself the expense, any idiot knows the inquirer will now be waiting for more than words. The next promise must be concrete, it must throb off the page, and smell of perfumed sweat. The woman of his dreams corresponds with him now, shyly, uncertainly, with a simple picture of herself in a swimming costume, the smallest costume we can convince her to wear.'

'Yes!' Ivan thumped the bench. 'We'll do it now, immediately, and add it to the letter. Tell me which woman he inquires after!'

Ivan's mother leant back to the screen, and pursed her lips. 'Number sixteen, is it? Number sixteen – Ludmila.'

Ivan kneaded the red bikini in sweat-moistened hands. It had arrived like a message from beyond, through a chain of relatives and acquaintances known to Anya, his mother. How this chain had led to the smalls drawer of a slim young woman on the outskirts of town was beyond Ivan to imagine.

It took a moment for Oksana to catch his attention when she reached the top of the stairs. 'I'm here,' she finally said.

'Until now you show yourself!' Ivan glared at his watch.

'Only now Uncle Sergei came with the message, I ran here nearly all the way.'

'Yes, and this is why your breathing is slower than a walrus's, and your make-up dry and straight.'

'Oh dear!' Oksana squirmed at the door.

'Well, come in, come in – Father Jesus, I feel I have to come and manipulate your limbs independently to act! Sit, sit here. Here – look!' Ivan plonked his thumb-like bottom, a sort of uni-buttock, on the bench in front of the computer, and leant scowling into his niece's blank face. 'Now, here's the thing, the thing is this – I know what a hard case the mountain girl is, my mind goes numb conceiving the sour battle she would put up if I approached her myself, but the thing is this: you've lived some few days with her now, and if you're a clever girl, you will have found a way into her confidence, on a level of woman to woman –'

'Which girl, excuse me?'

Ivan's face blew open. 'The hard case – Ludmila!'

'Oh yes.'

'Well, good, and so, the thing is –'

'Well, but I can't say she has any doors open to gain confidence, in fact, because –'

'No, well, listen – just listen to me, will you! Whatever level it is you've found to deal with her on, I have the most important job of your young life to give you. I say it because I would certainly pelt slaps at her face after the first word she spoke – so listen to me, the thing is: you must induce her into this swimming costume for a photograph. You may even have to take the photograph yourself, if she ends up being as obtuse as I predict. Now, this is very urgent, it must be done immediately. Use any excuse you can find – do you hear the detail of what I tell you? Here is the camera, here is the costume. Photo. Do you hear? With her arse pointing out, make her poke out the arse. Now go, quickly, run!' Ivan lurched off the bench and shooed Oksana to the door.

She took the bikini, wet from his hands, picked up the camera, and scuttled as far as the stairs. Then she stopped. 'And so where will I find her?'

'What!'

'Well, after Uncle Sergei put her out of the apartment –'

Ivan's mouth fell open. His head turned this way and that. A finger shot from his sleeve, and lanced the bikini from Oksana's hand. 'Give me the camera. Take off your clothes.'

18

The known world ended at Heathrow airport. Tunnels connecting the underground railway station to Heathrow's terminals were an extension of London's damp innards, the vaginal tributaries of a lovely old whore, couching her punters all the way to the world's edge, not thrusting change so quickly upon them that they suffered shock. The airport thus started slowly, graduating itself from bare concrete to shopping-temperature light, to eventual angelic sunshine.

And beyond that, the heavens.

Military hardware surrounding the airport was not visible from the tunnel. This was a help to Blair, who tried to smooth his brother's passage to the departures hall. The Heaths moved uncertainly, washed along like sperm by a flow of people dressed for other places. Ahead white light shone on brushed steel. Ahead, through the light, lay a new world.

They would, for a time, voyage the heavens from this tumultuous, screaming place. They would jettison the diabolical and soar clean for a time, above the low, grey albumen of London's skies.

The airport was a cathedral.

Bunny's shuffle faltered in the tunnel. He twitched, and looked around. His shoulders hunched like a toddler's in sudden dark. 'I mean to say, Blair?'

Blair adjusted his crotch, bowing his legs slightly. 'Come on, Buns, we'll be fine. Come on.'

'We must be fucking mad. Mate? What in God's name are we doing?' Bunny's mouth pursed to form a canopy over lonely-looking teeth. Behind his sunglasses, wide, tremulous eyes cowered from a nominal horizon. His old plastic sports grip hung scuffed and crumpled from his shoulder. It slid on its strap to the crook of his arm, but did not swing.

'Buns – it'll be all right.' Blair sidled close. 'We'll be fine, I promise. And think of this – you'll be far away from the threat of terrorism. That'll be a bonus, won't it? You know how you hate your threat of terrorism.'

'I mean to say, though. What the fuck are we doing?'

'We're off on holidays, Buns. Our first holiday away. We'll have a right old laff!'

'Could we not just start with Scarborough?'

Blair soothed his brother out of the stream of travellers, and stood him against the tunnel wall. 'Mate – look at the broader picture. I'll bet anything they've done the same with other key patients, sent them off for a breath of fresh air.'

'But – for fuck's sake.'

'No, Buns, listen – there's nothing sinister about it. We're off on our hols. Mate? Right old laff!'

'I thought it's supposed to be a work junket – you're supposed to visit factories.'

'What do I bloody know about factories? I can just stick me head in and say hello. It's a gift, Buns – come on.'

'I think I'm going to be sick. The cocktail's worn off. Blair? It's fucking madness. We're barely a fortnight out of care –'

Blair grabbed Bunny's shoulders, massaged them with his fingertips, straightened them up. He coaxed up Bunny's gaze, and stared calmly, benignly, into his face. His reflection shone sturdy and bright in Bunny's sunglasses. 'We're not cripples, mate. Look at me – Buns – we're healthy young men. We're free.

The only restrictions left are in our minds. Do you hear?'

'Oh fuck. Fuck, mate, Christ. You're still pissed on that Yank bollocks.'

'Did you not have yours? I've had another this morning.' Blair reached into his coat pocket, and pulled out a sachet. 'Here, get this down you.'

'And when they run out? Blair? When we're left on our own, in fucking Spain, feeling normal?'

'The important thing is we'll have taken the leap. We'll be in the new world. Buns? That's what's important, my love: if we know it's conceptually right to move forward, we must use every possible tool to surmount our fears. Can you not see the way things are panning out, as if by coincidence?' Blair's brow suddenly rose, his face lightened implausibly, as a mother's would to her new-born. 'And it's all for a lovely holiday! We're not going to the gallows. It's a holiday! Buns!'

'But I'm not tired of the old world yet. I'd not mind a spell back at Albion, to be honest. Collect me thoughts.'

Blair looked around. The last carriage-load of travellers tapered past him up the tunnel. He was alone with Bunny in a cave of echoes and faint public-lavatory smells. He decided this couldn't be helping matters. 'Bunny,' he said softly, 'let's make a deal – there's a Legge-Deethog brasserie upstairs. Do you know what that means?'

'Trance music?'

'Full English breakfast.'

'Eh?' Bunny twitched.

'Full English and a pot of tea, Buns. We'll not go anywhere, we'll just sit and watch things flow past us. Over fried bread and bangers. Bacon. Just watch. And if, after a proper nosh-up, you still feel a bit dicky about things, we'll get a mini-cab back to the flat.'

'Full English, you say?'

'This is England, Buns. The very gateway. Do you think they'd not have the most cracking breakfast at the gateway to God's own Green and Pleasant Land? It's a matter of national pride, of national security. This must be the very wellspring of the proper fry-up, the home of Britain's three-dimensional flag, its edible glory. Buns: we're at the edge of England, looking out on to a poorer world. A world without bacon.'

'By, I'll not say I couldn't use some bacon. Me vein's going mental. I wondered if that tonic was a bit squiffy, I didn't want to say anything at the time. Tonic's quite an unstable beverage, in point of fact, now I think about it.'

Blair smiled, and closed his eyes. 'There's only one thing for it, Buns.'

'Fat?'

'Fat.' Blair hoisted the strap of Bunny's grip back on to his shoulder, and led him as if to his first day of school. The pair shuffled humbly in their black suits, up the tunnel towards the light.

'Will there be a gents?' asked Bunny.

'There'll be a gents.'

'Will they have proper butter?'

'Buns –'

'Aye, England. Aye.'

In the four minutes Bunny spent in the lavatory, a cocktail sachet emptied easily into his pot of tea at Legge-Deethog's. Blair stirred it until it cleared.

Bunny returned, ambling awkwardly and sat opposite his brother in their booth. He became transfixed by whorls of egg-streaked fat and the muddy oozings of fried mushrooms on his plate. He carefully sliced a blackened tip of sausage, speared and coiled around it a bunting of bacon rind, pushed these with his fork to the shores of his egg, and plunged them into the yolk. He examined their sticky helmet, took a swig of tea, nibbled a corner of toast, and popped the chunk into his mouth.

Bunny didn't look up until his plate was mopped to a satin sheen, and his cup had been emptied dry. And when he looked up, and sat back, and lifted his glasses – he was in a world laden with warm meaning.

'I think I'm coming good,' he said.

Blair reached across the table, and took Bunny's hand. He gave it a squeeze. 'You're looking good, Buns.'

Bunny glanced down, adjusted his lapels symmetrically over the visible white of his shirt, herded the worst of its wrinkles under his coat. 'Aye, well.'

He sat at England's synaptic gate, connected more than ever before to the rest of the world. All its people passed by him. All fizzed with a certain excitement. For the first time Bunny felt part of a race.

'Will we waste these air tickets then?' Blair casually tilted his pot of tea to weigh its remains.

Bunny's glasses dropped on to his nose. 'Are they to far away? We can always nip back, can we?'

'Of course – we can come back on the same plane if the place strikes us the wrong way. Might even just do that, honestly – have a laff on British Airways and nip straight back.'

'British Airways, do you say?'

'Aye, Buns. Full English Breakfast Airways. Endless Cups of Proper Tea Airways. Green and Pleasant Airways.'

'I mean to say. We could nip straight back, you know – they'd be sick to death of us, having a laff, on the way over – and then, when they thought they were finally safe in Spain, we'd be fucking sat there for the ride back!'

225

'You're the very devil, Buns. What's gotten into you? You're the lad, aren't you? We'd never do it, mind.'

'What d'you mean? Pass up a chance to take the widdle? The lads?'

'You'd never. Would you?'

Bunny filled his chest, dropped his voice an octave. 'Stand aside. It's the Heath louts.'

'Well –'

'Come on, we'll have a lend.' Bunny tottered ambitiously into the swirl of the concourse. 'Where is it we're going?'

'That set of desks, I think – over there.'

'I mean to say, what destination?'

'Check-in's generic, I think, Buns – we'll just head for Thank God We're British Airways. Anyway, I'm keeping it a surprise – you'll never guess.'

'Somewhere not too sunny, they'll have booked, though – won't they, your work? Not mad sunny, me eyes'd never take it. Just nice, sort of room temperature. Balmy, just for an hour, before the plane turns around. Not too damp, though.'

'Of course, Buns. It's overseas, isn't it?'

Check-in counters were set coolly, technologically, against a gleaming plastic wall beyond which sat the future. The wall didn't reach the ceiling, but had a gap over which promise flowed like floodlit vapour. Checking-in was to be their last act within the conceptual territory of Great Britain. Blair pressed his straining crotch against the counter, noting that Bunny seemed not to be suffering erectile abundance. Still, their breezing through security coincided with the high plateau of the Howitzer cocktail. They passed into the vast, strangely sunlit, godly space of the airside departures concourse. The first glistening shop they passed sucked them inside. As a token of their new rapport, Bunny made a thoughtful display of choosing a soft pornographic magazine for his brother.

'Bit hairy, that one,' Blair coughed.

'Is that not good?'

'Well, I mean – it's a bit continental.'

'Lasses have hair down there, mate.'

'Look, Buns, I'm chuffed –'

'No, no – you tell me what's in order.'

Blair ran his eyes along the top shelf of the rack, moved his bag over his lap, and leant into Bunny's ear. 'The thing is this, Buns, with these mags: if the picture on the cover won't get you off, chances are there's nothing better inside – in fact, you can almost guarantee the little two-by-four chatline ads in the back pages will be better than the girls in the spread. Look, there – bums are good, there's a bum.'

'I think I can feel a gin coming on. Can we nip out for a tab, and find a gin?'

'Can't nip out from here. Aviation fuel's the only environment outside here.'

'Might need a beer then. How long till we're there?'

'Not long, Buns. Not long.'

The brothers wandered the concourse like the anointed, lighter than perfume, shinier than warm ice. They bought a large tube of Smarties, for old times' sake. Bunny put it into his trouser pocket, and laughed when it outshone the bulge in his brother's trousers. The Heaths floated on, bags lightly nudging their laps with each step. Their ascent to Heaven wasn't contin-uous and bewildering, Bunny noted, but came in a series of ascents with adjustment plateaux in between. From the bleach-soaked tunnels of Middlesex, they rose through a series of tiers, each brighter, cleaner, and bigger than the last.

The next was the sky itself.

Blair took Bunny's arm, and guided him like a blind man over carpeted distances, through the departure gate, and on to the air-way bridge of their flight, shielding his eyes from the advertised destination.

Their last tunnel. Rubbery skirts gasketed the bridge to an air-craft door, protecting them from realities outside, of searing metal and hydraulic fluid, of crackling, raw, barbarous thrust and distension. Flashing red lights were the only clues to the forces that governed that windswept tarmac heath.

Bunny sensed a subtle change in the passengers as they boarded, as if something blew through the gap in the bridge's skirts, and brought with it a darker, more weighty fizz. Travellers' eyes scanned the tarmac, glancing first at idly spinning fan blades, then looking quickly up and down, making spatial calcu-lations to confirm their size in relation to the craft, and how far they had to fall to the ground. After this, they were absorbed into a foam of generator noise and cabin perfume, with notes of kerosene and coffee.

Blair and Bunny were silent. Music filled the cabin – not the expected music, but curiously empowering, other-worldly songs, strangely British in their effect.

'You Only Live Twice' played as they found their seats.

The twins had a row to themselves near the back. Bunny took the window seat. The cabin's strident hush conspired with the soundtrack to bring a curious calm upon him, till his breathing modulated, and his mouth fell into a smile. The soundtrack became newer, more daring, and seductive. Cabin attendants breezed and sashayed. The assortment of souls around him – some looking like miners from the Klondike, others swarthy and dressed for business – were on their way to join God in the sky, while society sucked soot, and scrubbed grime beneath them.

This was the air passenger's equation.

The aeroplane taxied some distance, bumping over cracks in the ground. Then its throttles opened up to a roar: rain turned to streak the windows sideways, utensils clattered in the galleys, and suddenly – the rumbling was gone. The craft shook sternly on all axes before rocketing through a lid of dark cloud on to a sparkling stage as big as the world.

Bunny opened the Smarties, and tapped a few colours into his hand. Popping a green one into his mouth, he turned to find Blair watching him, smiling like a biblical figure.

'The new world, Buns.'

Bunny took a long breath through his nose. 'Not bad,' he said. 'I've seen worse.'

Their hands met across seat 34E.

After a while, a feeling of damp made Bunny's eyes pop open and dart about.

A coffin waited for him, standing on its end by the door, visible from his old metal bed. Past it, he saw Blair approach in an old cardigan, a beige cardigan with brown leather panels down the front, and on the elbows. His sharply pressed trousers were an inch too short, something Blair fancied gave him a rakish, modern air, rather than the look of someone usually seen loitering with a school satchel at a railway station.

'Bunny,' he said, 'I mightn't be around at twelve, so I just wanted to say – good luck.'

The words struck Bunny Heath with the truth: his death had been scheduled for midday. The government had gone to some lengths to see that everything ran smoothly. Twelve was convenient for everyone, as lunch could be taken immediately afterwards, and minimum time would be wasted. This suited the spirit of New Britannia. There had been far too much waste at taxpayers' expense.

'Well, I mean, what I am saying to you' – Blair's eyes hung over the bed – 'is I just mightn't be around at twelve. I'm sorry if it's inconvenient, I'm sorry if I can't be everywhere at once. Anyway, be that as it may, I just wanted to say good luck, and –'

Bunny looked up at him, unable to speak. He looked up and waited.

'God bless,' said Blair.

He ran a hand over the engraved plaque on Bunny's coffin, patted it as if Bunny had made it himself at school. Then he stepped from the room, leaving the door open. Bunny's heart bulged with the moment's volume, but in the back of his mind he knew Blair had things to do that day. He could be a busy man, what with his lofty ambitions, his churning issues and causes. Bunny knew that perfectly well. If only he'd helped his brother with the burden of progress, he might have had more time to spare. If he had only been a proper person, not just a parasite, he might have shown a little more consideration.

'What was that?' Bunny woke with a start.

'What?' Blair awoke beside him, cocking an ear.

The captain was addressing the cabin. Bunny dropped a snaggle to Blair's face. 'Minus twenty-eight fucking degrees, did he just say?'

'Oh shit, Buns. Oh Christ. The thing's worn off. Can you still feel yours? Mine's worn off.' Blair prodded his crotch.

'The fizz?' Bunny scowled. 'I've not had any. This is just me.'

'You did take some. It was in your tea.'

'No, I drank from your pot in the end. Mine had a dodgy colour. Are you telling me you put fucking drugs in my tea?'

'Well, I mean, how else were you going to make it? You can't tell me you've come under your own internal gumption. You can't tell me that.'

'I bloody have, as it happens. I thought we were having a laff in Spain. Where is it we're going that's minus twenty-fucking-eight degrees?'

'Look, Bunny –'

'Where is it, Blair?'

'Yerevan.'

'Where the fuck's that?'

'Armenia.'

'*Ar-fucking-menia*! That'll be a fucking laff then. Eee, Blair, honestly.'

'I need a hit, Buns, I'm losing it.'

'Well, don't let me stop you. Honest to God, Blair – for fuck's sake.'

'The sachets are in the overhead locker. I'm not allowed, we're landing just now. I can't feel me cock at all, that's not a good sign. I'm frightened, Buns.'

'Serves you bloody right. I mean to say. We've been flying for over five hours, fuck only knows what time we'll get home. Knackered we'll be. Mad cunt.'

The plane fell through cloud into a hanging mist like frozen vodka. Buffeting stopped, and the craft sat still on its axes, descending with a gentle whistle, headlights making ectoplasm of the air. The nose buoyed up long before the runway appeared as a vague patch of grey carved through yards of ice and snow.

A chill new smell invaded the cabin.

Blair was silent and pale leaving the aircraft. He moved quickly, with short, twitching steps into the terminal. Bunny followed, shuffling. When the twins reached the arrivals hall, Blair flicked his eyes around the bare concrete space. Men in camouflaged jackets and military fur hats leant or stood or ambled with automatic weapons around a split-level hall with a meandering baggage carousel in between. Two small shops with bored women in attendance offered a hundred spirits in seemingly identical bottles. It was after midnight, local time. No other flights arrived or left. Bunny and Blair were among barely a dozen passengers from their flight who alighted in Yerevan. Only two of these – a red-headed girl wearing what appeared to be a sheep's carcass, and a tall, sleepy-looking man hung with cameras – seemed to be English, or even remotely western.

The improbability of the twins being in that freezing, bunker-like place suddenly sweetened the memory of their trip through the heavens. Red, white, and blue uniforms, East Anglian, Northern, and West Country accents. Cups of tea. Proper butter. Shortbread biscuits.

Blair rustled through his bag for a cocktail sachet. There seemed nowhere around to take refreshment, so he emptied it dry into his mouth. The crystals erupted on his tongue, making him cough. 'Well,' he sputtered, looking around.

'Well what?' said Bunny. 'How long till we have to be back on the plane? I'm gagging for a smoke, I hope there's at least time to nip out for a gasper.' He shifted his eyes around the sad, post-Soviet scene. 'Do you think they'll take proper money in the shop? We'll have to bring something back, just to prove we did it.'

'Um,' Blair wiped an exploratory hand over his crotch. 'I think we've ages yet, Buns.'

'We can't be the only ones off our plane, though?' Bunny watched two last passengers step out into the mist. 'Surely not everyone's stayed on the plane to go back? Blair?'

A soldier watched the men. Seeing them avoid his gaze, he wandered over and motioned them with his gun to a teller window. They went. It appeared to be an immigration kiosk. Blair tried to explain the men were in transit.

'In transit,' he shouted at the woman, 'continuing our journey.'

'Back to England,' Bunny added over his shoulder.

Blair flapped a hand. 'Shh, Buns, I'm dealing with it.'

'Just tell her we're off back, no need for a visa.'

'Well, but that's the thing – we're not off back, actually, Buns.'

'How d'you mean?'

'We're transiting on.'

Bunny turned to stare at his brother, arms dangling. His bag fell from his shoulder. 'Speak for yourself, pal – I'm off home.'

As he said it, a whine of turbines blew through the terminal doors. Blair tensed his mouth into a smile, widening his eyes in what he hoped was an encouraging way. The effect was that of an upholstered skull, begging. 'Well, but that's the thing – the ticket's to a place farther up the Caucasus, on the Russian side. Much more civilised up there, Buns, I mean – you didn't think I'd just park you somewhere like this, did you, in a corner of some foreign field? Just full of soldiers? May as well have stayed home, if I were just going to park you with soldiers and guns. We're off up to a proper place, and we'll be met off the plane, and taken care of. We've just a few hours in transit, to get used to things, poke around the shops. Here – you can smoke a car-ton of fags in that time, and we'll lay into some of the local rucking water, from the shop. Right old laff, we'll have.'

'I'm fucking off home.'

'Well, but, Buns – the plane's gone on to Tashkent.'

Bunny lifted his glasses, and hung his eyeballs on Blair. He stood for a while, hardly seeming to breathe. Then his jaw dropped. 'Tell me you're having a colossal fucking lend.'

19

'And where is this daughter of yours?' Abakumov paced a circle in the shack's main room. 'After all your sobbing, you prove to be an affluent enough family to send your young on holidays.'

'We don't know where she is,' Irina flicked an eye to Olga, who sat wheezing in the dark by the window. 'Her life is today visited by tragedy, as her intended has been killed at the junction, just as I told you. A bullet through the heart is the day's news, and it is no mark of respect that you then say she's on holiday – that news will destroy her.'

Maksimilian was outside throwing snow over Gregor's corpse. His mothers prayed he didn't stumble back inside with the gun.

Lubov nudged the middle distance with her chin. 'This is a worrying thing, the death of the young Bukinov. But it makes me ask, more importantly – where are my Gregor and Karel, and where is your infernal boy with the tractor?'

A moment's quiet followed, broken by the soft farting and hissing of the stove, and accompanied by furry flickerings of its light.

'Well,' Olga stirred in her chair. 'If that's all we have to say, I'll take my aching bones to bed.'

'Well, you won't,' Abakumov stepped into her path. 'Because although you've taken pains to fill your hovel with smoke, you've been unable to suppress the smell of rotting flesh. Which factor drives me to believe you have still the old man's corpse in your room – a factor describing yet another crime.' He turned to take in both Irina and Olga, and spread his hands out slowly to his sides. 'I've tried to be fair with you. I've given you every chance to respond correctly to the situation. But you've shown yourself too barbaric for even the simplest human respects. And on that basis, without need for further assessment, I deem you of too poor a character to exercise dominion over a young child. And I deem your natures and undertakings of life too improper to allow you to be proprietors or occupiers of property so near the border.' He paused a moment, letting the news fall by its own weight. 'I am therefore, and not without the greatest regret, forced to remove you to a place where you can be assessed and resettled. The youngest child will be found a suitable home.' The inspector turned to Lubov. 'Are either or both of your sons likely to appear? I may need some assistance removing such specimens as these.'

As he said it, the sound of voices came with a gust to the door. Lubov went to it, and squinted out. 'Hark! Even as you say it, Inspector, I feel they now approach.'

'Will you just unwind?' Ivan's mother adjusted a large faux-Persian medallion over the drapes of her lower neck, and pulled a face like a lizard into the bathroom mirror.

'I'm perfectly calm!' Ivan bellowed from the door. 'You take all the time you need, let our visitors, our clients – no doubt with friends at home waiting for recommendations of just such a service as ours, and with the American hovering to hear of their success – wait idling at the airport in Stavropol, with their thousands of cash dollars, in the cold.'

'You're worse than a used bride on her wedding night!'

'I mean, it's not as if the loiterers around Stavropol airport are in any way unsavoury types. It's not minimally as though they'd say anything whatsoever to get our clients into their cabs, and relieve them of any burdensome money which they otherwise would only unwisely spend with us, finding true love, and the gift of family life.'

Anya clattered out through the bathroom door, and gave her son a thump. 'I should've given you a girl's name when you were born,' she growled. 'Is the car even here to carry us?'

'You mean, is it *still* here to carry us?' Ivan rolled his eyes. 'Is it *still* here, or has Sergei died of old age waiting to hand me the keys, has the car now corroded into the snow?'

'Well don't get haemorrhoids over it – we don't even know where this Ludmila girl is, your thug cousin threw her on to the street!'

'And just for that shall we forget the whole business? Shall we leave the English millionaires to sit on their sculptured crocodile-leather luggage until the next flight out? Oksana is scouring the town, she's instructed not to stop until the girl is found. How hard can it be for a green-eyed mountain girl to vanish in Kuzhnisk? I could find her blindfolded, just by following the trail of injuries left by her tongue. Anyway, if for some reason she can't be found – well, love is a diverse agent, I'm sure they would fall for one of our other little treasures, even for Oksana herself, who, after all, matches the photograph we sent.'

'Hmph. Well, a part of her does. Listening to you, I can only advise that you take a heavy deposit before the men reach Kuzhnisk. A mighty deposit, looking at the mouse-circus you've prepared.'

'Well, the circus gets bigger and bigger waiting for you! If you don't put a bomb up yourself and get moving, we'll have no time to show them the factory!'

Ivan's mother paused to plump her hair with her fingertips. 'But is it sandwich-applicator week, or munitions week at the factory? The American doesn't send anyone to see munitions.'

236

'Well, how am I to know? If he's sent them today, then they'll see whatever's in production today.'

Poor weather turned spiteful as Ivan and his mother drove Sergei's car to Stavropol, along roads marked only by earlier tyre tracks in the snow. The old Gaz Volga whined and grumbled all the way, as did Ivan, and his mother. By the time they reached the first treated roads, and Stavropol's smoke hove into view, they had agreed that a party at the Leprikonsi – in truth Ivan's mother's bar – was the way to proceed. They would call past the Liberty factory on the return journey, and discharge their corporate duty. Then a party would be correct, in the company of Oksana and her friends. After all, the Englishmen would be tired, and would surely rather pursue the gift of family life fresh the next day. Moreover, the information Anya gleaned from them in the company of alcohol would better suggest the depth of their potential entanglement.

Ivan drove into the airport. He was late, and didn't bother parking. Apart from two shivering, black-suited men – one wearing sunglasses under an unruly mop of hair and the other self-consciously coiffed – only the expected local types were there.

'Only those two religious types.' Ivan wiped a handkerchief across the inside of the windscreen.

'Well, it won't be them,' Anya tutted. 'Look at the one on the left, the eyes. Clearly a crazed Evangelist, or Charismatic. As for the other one, your uncle Igor went to his grave looking better.'

Two more hours must have passed. Ludmila found it harder to ignore the sweaty woman in the café, who now hovered muttering, and clattered things on the counter. Pots and ladles banged like gunshots through the oily air.

Finally the woman huffed, and threw her pendulous arms to her hips. 'And will it be just another coffee, or will you find it cheaper to ask for water, or perhaps just air? Will I serve you a nice cup of air?'

Ludmila turned sunken eyes on the woman. 'And but listen, Madam: you're serving more than just coffee in your shop today. Because I am sincerely grateful to sit here, on a very hard day in my life. I won't be here for ever, and I beg nothing from you. But please realise that, the way my luck stands, these coffees are bought with money borrowed from my funeral.'

'Then do you want to borrow some more? Because you've been sat there all night for the price of four coffees, which makes this the cheapest funeral in the world.'

Ludmila's eyes darkened, but she held her tongue still. 'What type of soup do you have that isn't made entirely of water?'

'Potato,' said the woman. 'But a potato soup will only buy you forty minutes. An hour if you have bread. Some limits have to be set!'

Ludmila flicked her chin towards the counter. 'Then I'll have soup with cream and onion and bread, followed by coffee, and I'll not expect to hear any bile until the next train is through.'

'Look at me.' The woman pointed to her face. 'I told you last night when the train would come through, you should've left and come back again! Don't think just because you foolishly sent money on a bread train that you somehow belong to a club that lives in my café. No! The guard you dealt with may or may not be back, I've nothing to do with any of it. What I tell you is this: you're not the first person in the world to lose money on the bread trains, or to come sniffing around my kitchen for it!'

'I'm not looking for money, I just want a ride to Uvila, or Ublilsk Junction. I have to find my husband, who is a soldier, fighting to keep your miserable café peaceful, so that you might

238

continue to rant and insult consumers without a care. For the
scale of good business I gave the train guard, he should carry me
gladly.'

'Yes, and pineapples might grow in the snow. Are you eating
soup, and then leaving to wait in the alley, or are you just leaving to wait in the alley?'

'Bring the soup,' said Ludmila.

'Then put out the money.'

Abakumov and Lubov stepped on to the shack's front step,
searching the dark for the source of the voices. Splintered tones
seemed to be passing rather than approaching.

'Karel? Gregor?' called Lubov.

'Who is it there?' a man's voice called back.

'Come out, you who speaks,' Abakumov barked. 'Come into
the light!'

'No! You come into this light!' A beam lit the snow beyond
the fence. 'Move in front of the house!' called the voice. A
weapon clicked and crunched.

Abakumov and Lubov stepped into the yard and stopped,
hands not quite up, nor quite down.

'Is that Lubov Kaganovich, from the depot?' called the voice
behind the torch.

'Yes, it is.'

'Then be at ease.' The beam swung around to illuminate two
Ubli soldiers in the heaviest winter gear, machine guns over their
backs. 'We have to warn you in the strongest possible way to
move on – a nasty bulge is forming at the front, Gnez come
behind us looking to occupy just such properties on the mountain.'

20

'What in fuck's name have you done?'

'Deal with it, Bunny, for God's sake. Think of it as an adventure. Right old laff.' Blair adjusted a duty-free bag over his crotch, gasping as it scuffed the head of his penis. Bunny untied, and retied, all three dressing gowns, having donned them over his suit for warmth. The twins swayed shoulder to shoulder in the back seat of the Gaz as it bounced and yawed like a cannonball across the ice, Ivan brawling with the wheel while Anya screeched oaths and clutched dramatically at things. The drive to Kuzhnisk was a tense ballet, unhelped by a stench of Vaporub.

'What, in the name of fuck, have you done, Blair?'

'Well, it's not the end of the world – you've a cocktail here still to drink, if you feel yourself bottling out.'

'Every time I wake up from one of those fucking cocktails I find myself in deeper shite.'

'Well, but look around you, Buns – it's a holiday in the snow! A ski holiday, an alpine breakaway. Most lads'd kill for an alpine breakaway!'

'Firstly, pal, the word "alpine" implies alps. Secondly, I'll fucking kill you for it meself just now.'

Blair sucked in his cheeks, and readjusted the duty-free bag in his lap, provoking a sigh. The bag from the airport in Yerevan – plump with a gift-boxed Armenian brandy and two engraved glasses – had finally caught Ivan's eye after three laps of Stavropol airport. He remained sceptical about the men, even after Anya confirmed their identities in a shrill exchange through the car window. They must be very rich, thought Ivan. Incredibly rich, to expect young women to court them, looking as they did.

'What in bollocks name have you done?'

'Look – just have a nip, we've still two sachets left after that.' Blair hummed a crooked tune, and peered around like a schoolboy on a coach. Though he savoured the usual freedom from conscience brought on by the Howitzer, he found its effect weaker than before. He frowned, and hummed some more.

Ivan would occasionally leer over his shoulder, motion the duty-free bag, and cock a thumb into his mouth. Then he'd laugh. The twins would nod, chuckle, and raise their eyebrows. Blair's rose optimistically, to show Bunny they were in congenial hands. In a whispered exchange, he even said Ivan's gestures were a fine example of how strangers made friends across cultural and linguistic divides – that affable people everywhere fashioned jokes from whatever situation was to hand, and made them a point of reference for all future bonhomie. The brothers could expect more nudges, winks, and drinking of thumbs in the hours ahead, said Blair.

Bunny scoffed a click through his lips.

'I mean,' Blair returned a chuckle to the driver's seat, 'global relationships are my job now. It's my career, Buns. Surely you don't want to get in the way of my career?'

'Career my fucking bumhole. You're a sad little tosspot who's had to travel five hours on an aeroplane to find someone to knob.'

'Buns, Buns, Buns,' sighed Blair. 'Buns, Buns, Buns, Buns. What're we going to do with you? What are we going to do with old Buns?'

Bunny's brow dropped. 'Where's the card?'

'What card?'

'The cash card. Give it me here.'

'Why?' Blair rushed a hand to his trouser pocket.

'Give it me. I'm turning them around, going back to the airport, and buying a ticket home. You can do what you like.'

'Well, I'm sorry but you can't just come this far and bottle out. What about the lads? The laff? Mate?'

'Sitting in Spain eating chip butties and deliberately mispronouncing local words is a laff, Blair. Abduction to third-world permafrost shitholes full of dumpling-people with faces like old Citroëns is a fucking lend.'

'Well, I take exception to that.'

'Give us the fucking card.'

Anya turned a wary eye. 'Is not such shithole, once you accostume. Beautiful ladies here. After few wodka you accostume.'

'See!' hissed Blair, reaching for the brandy. 'For Christ's sake, break it to them gently.' He filled both glasses, and passed them to the front seat. Ivan roared with delight, and tossed his down his throat. Anya declined, scowling at Ivan. The brothers took a tot each.

'Now give us the fucking card.' Bunny made for Blair's pocket.

The sun was gone when the Gaz chugged into Kuzhnisk. Brackish light fell on verges of snow. Plumes of vapour and smoke reached into a brackish sky, showing that all was still, if not well.

There was an understanding in the car that Bunny would return to London. Much English had been hissed in the back seat, much Russian in the front. The Gaz hissed like a reptile house for over an hour. This made the ride uncomfortable for the Englishmen, prickly like the hot woollen pants they once wore at Albion House. Two stops were made for what Anya then knew as a widdle, or 'weedoll'. After the last of these, during a lull in the hissing, she began to shepherd the Heaths' attention into the journey's proper corner. 'So, well,' she said, 'still we must take cost for two persons, is late now for cancel.'

'Of course,' said Blair.

'When you pay now, in cash dollar, it have discount for twenty pier cent.'

'Yes, yes, of course.'

The car slid sideways around a corner on the edge of town, snaking down a lane to crunch into a snow bank. Ivan switched off the motor, waiting a few moments for its cough to die. The twins looked out, and saw they were beside a large warehouse. It groaned and clunked, and seemed to shudder on its foundations. A sign above its metal door read: 'Global Liberty Solutions.'

'Look, Buns,' Blair pointed.

The pair sat expectantly, but there seemed to be a problem. With a tissue, Anya wiped a peephole on her window, peering this way and that, and muttering in Russian.

'Pah,' said Ivan.

There followed an exchange between the front seats, of reproaches, and beads of saliva. A particularly explosive syllable finally propelled Ivan from the car, and he hurried the twins into the building, spitting words at a glum receptionist as they entered. The woman absorbed their tone without a twitch; even the sight of Bunny in his gowns failed to move her. She pointed to a large door, and held her finger pointed until the men jumbled through it. Inside, an apocalypse hissed and hammered, and spewed hot light.

'Is this the right place?' shouted Bunny.

Blair reached into a box beside the door, and pulled out a bullet. Its stamp featured a tiny design of either an eagle or a demon poised to swoop. As he studied the shell, Anya burst through the door behind him. Ivan rasped a curse. The twins turned to each other; from the corners of their eyes they saw Anya pelt her son a slap.

'What, in fuck's name, have you done?'

Ivan kicked open the door, tossing his chin for them to follow. Blair pocketed the bullet, and slid back to the car, arms aloft like a trapeze artist. Mists eddied after him, curling to make paisley patterns in the beam of a factory spotlight.

'I mean to say. I'd laff to see you try and apply one of those to a sandwich.'

'Leave it out, Bunny.'

The Gaz left a clean imprint of its driver's side wing in the snow as it pulled away, and had barely achieved a ferry's chug when Anya turned lipstick-flecked teeth on the twins. 'When you pay immediately, cash money, will be more big discount,' she used a cupped hand to shoehorn a bosom into the gap between seats.

'Yes, of course,' said Blair, 'but I mean, we'll have to charge it to a card, we didn't get to a bank on the way over.'

Anya frowned. Bursts of Russian crackled along the dashboard, rising in pitch. Then she rejoined her bosom to address the back seat. 'What is cash you have with you?'

'I've a fiver still, I think. How much have you got, Buns?'

'Sixty-one pence. Knock yourself out, stay a fucking month.'

Blair turned a smile on the woman. 'We've only got five pounds sterling, I'm afraid.'

Another tangle of Russian, sounding at first like the stripping of very small gears. It gathered weight, flowering into dark, guttural bubblings like the beginnings of a retch, before settling into clumps of swallowed noise like a newscast played backwards on a gramophone.

'Another brandy?' Blair dangled the bottle between the seats.

244

'Niet,' the Russians waved.

'Here is problem,' Anya levelled her eyes on the men. 'No card is take in Kuzhnisk. Not we, not nobody. No cash from card. Stavropol airport have card, have cash – but automobile is no petroleum for go Stavropol.'

'I see,' Blair pinched his chin. 'What you're saying in effect, then, is –'

Anya held up a hand, and closed her eyes. The twins watched her eyelids stick together like halves of burnt rarebit. 'Mister Bani has travel go airport Stavropol – only solution is go with him, and make cash from card.'

Bunny patted the back of her hand. 'That's right, love. We'll nip back. I'll get me ticket, you get your cash, and Mister Blah can –'

'Well, but, Buns, she's just said they haven't bloody petrol for the trip.'

'Then can I just say one thing – what, in fuck's name, have you gone and done, Blair?'

'Oh piss off.'

Bunny lifted his glasses. Speaking loudly into the woman's face, he set out to discover how to return to the airport. As he did this, Blair poured a tot of brandy into a glass, and emptied a solipsidrine sachet after it. He closed his hand around the glass, watching colours flash on to his skin.

'Is only train go Stavropol from Kuzhnisk,' Anya tutted. 'For that is need cash money.'

Blair leant to Bunny's ear. 'Can you not sense a grape-influenced restorative?'

'Give us it here.' Bunny snatched the glass.

The woman stood sweating behind Ludmila as she dawdled over her soup.

'What? It's very hot!'

'Well, if you would use the cream, instead of nursing it like a dying aunt, you would find it cools. Would you like me to insert the cream into your soup, at no extra cost?'

'And listen to me: have I not just given you the full price of this meal, including the price of a table to eat it from?'

'And just you listen instead to me: you're a loiterer – a loiterer and a vagrant, and my days are hard enough without having you occupy my place like a tick. I'll tell you this: even if the train guard walks through the door while you're eating, I'll eject you to speak with him elsewhere. Your situation is not my responsibility!'

'And let me identify a problem of yours, in the manner of your thinking,' Ludmila wiped her mouth on the back of a hand. 'You imagine a single span of time, a whole night, without punctuation. You see me here still, and think: she has been here all night for only four coffees and a soup. This, if you'll forgive me, is the wrong way to treat the concept. Because actually you weren't here in the night, I saw that another girl dozed behind a crack in the kitchen door. So, as far as you're concerned, I may not have even been here. And whether I was here or not, if you stay open at every hour of the clock, to profit from factory workers as well as railway staff, you must also expect night patrons to come with other reasons. Most importantly for you, I've consumed five things, making me your most loyal customer of the day – five times I've patronised your café, whether or not I went in or out of the door in a physical sense. And I've caused far less erosion to your shop and its fittings – especially the door – than the late shift who fell in from the Liberty factory.'

'Will you just conduct that soup into your mouth!'

'Hoh! Your best customer, and listen!'

'And it's only four times you've consumed, because the toilet visit counts in my favour, not yours. Admit it to yourself: all

246

night and half a day in a café is the work of a vagrant.'

'Hoh, well,' Ludmila arched her eyebrows, settling gently back, 'I suddenly see in this meal a great many individual consumptions. In fact, as a paying customer, it's now my greatest desire to eat each morsel of potato as a tiny sandwich, with its own tiny bread. I'll start to fragment it now, so that you can begin to see some progress.'

'Get out!' Sweat flew to the glass door.

Ludmila lifted the bread to her eyes, and began to strip the first scrap.

'Out!' The woman batted the roll from Ludmila's hand, and tugged her chair from the table.

'Then I have a suggestion,' Ludmila snatched up her bag, and detoured to collect the bread roll, dusting it on her coat as she was manhandled to the door. 'That you trap some of these clouds of grease, and use them to slide your café up your arse, where it will fit with room for a garden and a pond.'

The Gaz carved furrows all the way to Kuzhnisk station, sliding the last ten yards sideways. All sat quiet for a moment, unclenching their limbs. Then Anya sighed, and turned to her son.

'Well, so. You keep the eager-looking one, and I'll travel up with this one, the cave hermit, to Stavropol.'

'What?' Ivan's mouth fell open. 'You'll take them both! What would I do with either, when I don't understand a word they say?'

'And but listen, they haven't the price of a rail ticket between them, we're over-capitalising as it is. Do you propose to pay for them both on the train? You lay your mother's bosom under fate's pestle to invest in your wretched computer, and then, when paying clients arrive, we have to invest more capital still?'

Ivan turned up his palms, shook them at his mother. 'But it's not capital, it's cashflow! And you're the one with the language capability, it's up to you to see they're prepared before we leave the airport! Surely you don't think the outside world lives on cash? There just isn't space in their clothing to carry it all. Cards are all they use. You should know that, as an equal partner in the commerce!'

'Well, I'll tell you this one last thing, Ivan Illich!' Anya threw herself out of the car, wagging a finger back. 'I will travel with them both, but it'll be the last breath I waste on any of your lazy enterprises! You're more work than a new-born goat!'

'Pah!' yelled Ivan.

'Pah, pah, *pah*!' shouted his mother, steadying her wobbling bulk with her hands.

Blair crawled out of the car. Cold smacked away a lingering stench of Vaporub. He put his hands on his hips, bent this way and that, and sucked in a breath of dung smoke, gazing up the misty avenue with its chain of fizzing street lamps. Low clouds flew like zeppelins overhead. From Kuzhnisk, the world appeared faded, as if seen through a nurse's stocking.

Bunny left the car, refreshed by the brandy. He took a deep breath, and blew a funnel of rolling vapour into the dark. The idea of a Rothmans rolled with it. He reached through his robes to find one.

Railway tracks began to ping and buzz behind the platform. Anya tugged at Blair's sleeve, and the trio made for the platform stairs.

'If it's travelling from left to right, it's not the train you want!' Ivan shouted after them.

'Well, I know which train it is,' yelled Anya. 'I was riding these trains before you could crawl!'

A klaxon sounded hoarsely in the near distance, and the group billowed up the stairs like extras in *The Battleship Potemkin*.

The platform was empty when they reached the top. As they crossed the concrete space, Blair heard shouting from the dark end of the platform. He looked across.

Ludmila's eyes sparkled with tears. She left the fat woman bellowing behind her, and hurried up the alley with her bag clutched to her chest, biting chunks from the bread roll in anger.

The train hissed alongside the platform, and as she quickened her pace towards it, three figures swept across her path. One was clearly a priest, swaddled in robes. He kept moving, but another man in a black suit stopped, turned to her, and stared. She took another few steps, chewed twice more, and stared back. Ludmila had never seen such a stare as the man gave her. She squinted to invite recognition, or some gesture of intent. When none came, she dropped her eyes, and headed to the platform's edge. The train groaned to a stop beside her.

'Ludmila!' came a man's voice.

She turned. Both the priest and the old woman stopped, following the man's gaze. The old woman seemed familiar to Ludmila, and leant out of the shadows towards her. 'Is it Ludmila Ivanova?'

'Ludmila!' said the man.

'Wait here, don't move!' Anya shuddered into action, lumbering across the platform to the stairs. 'Ivan! I-*van*!'

Blair tingled. He moved his hands over his crotch. The girl was like a nineteenth-century waif in the station's brown light: smaller than he had imagined, more delicate, damp, and crumpled. Her eyes were deeply set, though big enough still to sparkle. She chewed, and stopped, chewed again, and stopped, parking a bulge in one cheek. The intermittent pulse of her chewing showed a lack of self-consciousness that made the reality of her sizzle through Blair's mind. For in reality's chill, where dreams traditionally die, Ludmila drew men's eyes up and down her, hunting evidence of woman or child, hunting any part of her more pronounced than her windswept black mane. And in that hunting, in the recalibration of eyes to her subtleties, hints of a woman emerged from beneath the coats, hints like storm warnings.

Even her eyes had a bite to them.

And when she saw men bitten, her lips grew slightly plumper.

Ludmila had another wary chew of bread. She looked at the priests, bowed her head in respect, and took off down the platform towards the guard's wagon. The black-suited man made after her, calling out as she ran, while the shaggy priest made efforts at seeming to follow, but clearly hoped the situation would resolve itself before his running made him a fool.

Ludmila reached the guard's wagon, and poked her head through the door. The guard almost collided with her as he made his way on to the platform.

'I'm a client of the bread service,' she panted. 'I need to beg a ride.'

'Which bread wagon?' The guard stepped past her to look up the platform.

'Ublilsk.'

'Pah! You're talking history.' The guard watched a figure in black pass the last box-car. Behind the man, some distance up the platform, stood another figure, clearly a senior man of God. Probably a famous seer, to have such hair, and robes, and dark glasses at night.

Ludmila flicked her eyes into the wagon. 'I'm not travelling far, I won't be bad company.'

The black-suited man arrived puffing, Ludmila didn't turn,

but wound doe eyes up to the guard. He nodded to the priest, and turned back to her. 'Are you travelling with the holy men?'

Ludmila turned to the stranger. 'Yes,' she said.

'Well, you'll not get far standing on the outside of the train,' the guard motioned them into the wagon. 'Quickly now, we can't be seen making deals on the platform. And I tell you in clear voice: you may be put off the service at any moment if an inspector comes by.'

While the guard unfurled a flag and took a whistle between his teeth, the priest shouted to his bushy comrade, now flapping towards them like a huge flightless bird.

'Buns – shall we just go?'

'What the fuck are you doing?'

'Come on. Right old laff.'

'I mean –'

'You have to catch the train anyway, don't you?'

'But I mean to say – what about Anya, and the bloke?'

'Buns – this is the girl! We don't need them any more – I've got the girl! She's done us a good turn, Buns, they were about to bleed us dry. Now we'll take her with us to the airport, to civilisation! You can nip back home, I might find a room for a night or two. You never know – I might bring her back with me after that!'

'Eee, fuck, Blair.'

The guard blew his whistle. The train hissed, clunked, and began to roll. Blair jumped aboard and reached out to hoist Bunny behind him.

Anya returned to the platform, head bobbing like a turkey's in search of her charges. The train gathered speed, and she looked up to see the men sail past her, waving through the wagon door. She recoiled with a shriek. Her arms shot up, and she waddled

251

after them, waving, all the way to the end of the platform, till darkness swallowed her.

Bunny turned a meaningful gaze on his brother. 'Me vein's going mental now.'

With the guard out of sight in his booth, Ludmila settled against a clutch of mail sacks in a corner of the wagon's inner cage. She couldn't think of a reason to interact with the priests, although it was curious that one of them knew her name. She kept tabs on them through the corner of an eye, and soon dozed to the train's gentle roll.

21

Blair watched Ludmila from the floor beside the guard's booth. Suddenly he had nothing to say. She was in her own world. He was not. The beginnings of all he wanted from her were hidden beneath layers of unknown culture, and language, and coats. The gap between them seemed immense. Still, he felt the adventure on the train could only draw them closer. She seemed to know he had come for her: a calm glowed from her, perhaps born of relief. Almost melancholy, her calm.

They had all the time in the world.

Blair nudged his brother. 'We'll have a proper nosh-up at the airport.'

'Bacon bap, they'd best have. Or I'm taking me holidays in Blackpool next time.'

'I could murder a burger myself,' Blair mused. He looked around the wagon, paused here and there, gently chewed his lip. After a moment, he poked unfocused eyes at the ceiling. 'Do you think we're getting closer, Buns?'

'Not if it's as far by rail as it was by road.'

'No, I mean us.'

'Eh? What makes you ask that?'

'Just heard myself fancy a burger. Quite unusual, that. Perhaps we're growing closer after all.'

'You've a long way to come after the smug tosh you've been scoffing lately. Anyway, I'm not the one who's grown apart. Same as ever, me.'

'But you enjoyed the flight? The airport?'

'I suppose.'

'No, you said you were dead impressed. New world and all that.'

'Blair, just get on with it. Introduce yourself to the lass, and stop talking crap.'

Blair walked his gaze like an ant over Bunny's face. 'You shouldn't be so niggly.'

'Why not?'

'You're on solipsidrine – I spiked your brandy.'

'I know, I'm fighting it.'

'Well, don't fight it, for Christ's sake – what's the point in that? Bunny? We need to stick together on this, show a united front. I mean, it's brought us really close the last couple of days.'

Bunny sighed. 'It's brought us to the floor of a frozen box-car, Blair. It was a laff the first time round, now it's a desperate lie. A cocktail of empty, sentimental rehearsal. You say it removes the impediment of redundant conditioning – I say it removes the impediment of fucking reason.'

'Shh, Buns. Don't put a dampener on things.'

'Listen: the qualities removed by your so-called cocktail are there for a purpose, Blair. They're the little voices that stop us raping and pillaging. It might suit your Yank mate to do away with them, but we're civilised people, from an ancient, civilised country. I mean to fucking say.'

Blair nursed a frown, and blinked a few times. 'Well, you sound just like Matron now. I mean, do you seriously think anything as dangerous as you say it is would be available in wild cherry flavour?'

Bunny turned weary snaggles on his brother. 'Will you just get on and pull your bird? The guard'll have her if you don't get cracking.'

Blair flicked his gaze into the shadows. Then he heaved himself off the floor, and slid down the wall to Ludmila. His stirring woke her. She looked up as he sat beside her, and held out a hand. 'Blair,' he said.

'Bleh,' she repeated. 'America?'

'English. Anyway, you should know, after that cracking e-mail you sent.' He leant close to her ear, sniffed the cold of her hair. 'I really like the picture, by the way. I suppose you had it taken in summer, I can't imagine you out in this weather in a bikini.'

She pulled back a little, perplexed, and studied him for a moment. 'Why you come Kuzhnisk?'

'Well – to find you.'

'Me? Ludmila?'

Blair blinked. It must be a game. They were treading the path of infants, learning by innocent play. 'Yes, you – Ludmila. Millie, I'll call you.'

She reached out to a lapel of his jacket, and shook it. 'You come help? From God?'

He thought a moment. Suddenly the cant of her face, the deference in her eyes, made a new kind of sense. 'No, no, my goodness. I'm not from God – it's just a black suit.'

Ludmila watched him watch her. He felt the exchange was a triumph, and shone from it. She shrugged, and looked down.

Blair put a hand to her shoulder. 'Look – I'd just like to know you. We've all the time in the world.' He paused to gauge her understanding. 'We can speak slowly – and just get to know each other. I won't move fast. Do you understand?'

She nodded into her lap.

'You're very beautiful.'

'Thenkyou.'

'Do you mind if I sit with you?' Blair cocked his head, as if reasoning with a puppy.

255

Ludmila flicked her eyes over his face, and tightened herself against the sacks, drawing her knees up to her chest. Then she rested her head on them, and closed her eyes.

Blair's heart raced. He looked down over a flow of black hair on to the side of one cheek – softer, fuller from that angle, and frosted pink – to the perfect dunes that slid down to her natural quarter-pout. Her face didn't move when she breathed. Blair's instinct was to wrap himself around her. He sat back, oscillating inside, penis straining hard. It concerned him that she hadn't engaged him in more conversation. Was she not curious? Did she not have anything to ask about England? About the time they would spend together? He would have to expand the edges of his mind to contain such new cultural responses to things. The young woman was clearly hardened by life, a silent heroine.

Then, a sudden thought: it was his place to engage her – he was the male, he would be expected to make the overtures, especially in such a rustic culture as hers. It was so clear. His breathing grew uneven, he felt a stab of panic. Here men would be judged by the strength and speed of their overtures. Perhaps he had already been judged. Her falling asleep was a sign of boredom, an unmistakeable withdrawal from the courtship. In less than ten minutes he had thrown the game away.

His mind went to work in colour, retracing her imagined steps that morning. She had woken early, excitement jolting her from sleep. Or, no – she hadn't slept at all. His eyes twitched over her body. She was unkempt, in a powerful sort of way. Which meant she'd struggled all night with her pillow, quarrelled with it, with him, but eventually succumbed to his strength, his post-modernity. His penis. She had flopped on to her belly in a snit, knowing it was an invitation, making it known by languorously stretching her legs, parting them till the silk between them rippled taut, stretched off her sex.

But Blair caught himself shivering as the truth skulked to mind: she had gone early to the station, scuffed her feet up and down the platform all day, thinking he would arrive on an early train. But he never did. And when, by a miracle, her beloved, her saviour appeared – all he could do was stand there open-mouthed. Make her stare, make her stand in the cold until her disappointment sent her running up the platform. And when he finally, lackadaisically, followed her on to the train – not with the decisive gallantry of the adventurer, but for the convenience of delivering Bunny to the airport – he allowed the guard to seat him away from her, without so much as a word.

Now – understandably – she feigned sleep.

Or perhaps she actually slept, having shut the pain out of her heart. Or, having such a profound capacity for pain, had kept it inside her to gestate, to ache and fester into hatred.

'She might fancy a Smartie.' Bunny nudged his brother, taking some time, and not a little huffing and grunting, to sit beside him. 'Before you run away with your fucking self.'

'I've buggered it, Buns. She's gone.'

Bunny clicked his tongue. 'Bollocks. Look here –' He pushed his glasses on to his head, tapped Ludmila on the shoulder, and held a flock of Smarties in his hand, cupped them as if nestling a baby chick. 'Fancy a Smartie?'

Ludmila sat up. She looked down at Bunny's hand, up at his mad smile, and grinned.

'Try a green one.' Bunny marshalled a sweet with his finger, parked it at the very edge of his hand, and pulled the face of a silent actor in peril as it teetered there. Then he brought his hand to her mouth, rested it between chin and lip, and tipped the Smartie in. Ludmila's eyes twinkled up, widening as he funnelled the rest of the handful on to her tongue. She struggled to chew between giggles, and waved a surrender when he reached for more.

Bunny displayed the Smarties tube. 'England,' he said. 'Magic.'
'Mazhik,' Ludmila nodded.

Bunny nudged his brother, and sat back. 'See?'

'Well, I'm sorry, you've completely ballsed it up now. You've totally misread the clues.'

'You what?'

'Well, it's just not as easy as you think, interfacing with such a fragile and complex culture. It calls for delicate psychosocial manoeuvring, you can't just barge in like a chat-show host. I'm sorry if that little fact doesn't mesh with your hail-fellow-well-met liberalist save-the-cat agenda.'

'*Save the cat*? It's your gob wants interfacing, pal. I mean to say. I'm only trying to help.'

'Well, don't trouble yourself in future. Honestly, and the last thing she needs is refined sugar, and colourings. It's taken you less than a day to start polluting the place.'

'Drink's worn off, has it? Your knob shrivelled as well?'

'Shh! For God's sake. These are crucial moments for imprinting, her senses are recording every fleeting sensation like a baby's first sights. You're doing untold damage to those impressions, and I, for one –'

'Get away, fuck off.' Bunny shifted sideways to catch Ludmila's eye. He dropped open his mouth, and pointed at his brother. 'He's a tosspot, isn't he? Right old Widow Twanky, worse than me fucking gran!'

Ludmila laughed at Bunny's face, and at the empowering spirit that flowed from his gestures.

He leant close. 'Can you say "Tosspot?"'

'I mean it, Buns – don't!'

'Tosspet,' said Ludmila.

Bunny pointed at his brother, scowling: 'Tosspot!' Then at himself, nodding solemnly: 'Champion lad.'

Ludmila smiled, and jabbed a finger at Bunny. 'Tosspet!'

His face fell. His lip dropped, trembled, and he turned away, sniffling.

'No!' She scrambled to kneel beside him, stroking him like a kitten. 'Nooo!'

Bunny sprang back, touched a finger to her cheek, and shuffled on his bottom to Blair's side. 'See? You have a try.'

'Piss well off.'

'Is brother?' Ludmila pointed at Blair.

'Aye, love – evil twin. Hasn't even got a proper belly-button.'

'Don't listen, Millie. Bad man. Bad, bad, man.'

'I like.' Ludmila turned her eyes on Bunny.

'Well, thanks a bloody lot, Buns, is all I can say. Thank you very bloody much.'

Bunny winked at Ludmila and, curiously, sent a push of his chin. Then he put an arm to Blair's back. 'Listen, mate – there's only one difference between you and me, as we sit here. And it is – I've not thought of shagging her.'

'Just don't talk to me, Bunny. You've binned it.'

'Crap, I'm the one flying home – you'll have as long as you fancy in some seedy airport guest house, with dodgy-looking neon letters swinging in the breeze – backwards sort of bollocksed-up letters like they have here – just you and her. Blair? I mean to say.'

Blair consulted his watch, and sighed. 'When will we get to Stavropol, Millie? Sta-vro-pol?' He pointed to his watch.

'Stavropol?' Ludmila searched his face, then Bunny's, before pointing to the rear of the train. 'Stavropol? You go?'

'Yes,' said Blair. 'Stavropol. Train. How long time?'

Ludmila shrugged, mused a moment with her eyes. 'Tomorrow,' she said.

'*Tomorrow?*'

Bunny frowned. 'Hang about – which way's Staverpool?' He pointed each way up and down the wagon. 'This way – or that?'

'There is Stavropol.' Ludmila pointed back.

'So where is this train going?' asked Bunny. 'Where's this way?'

'Uvila,' said Ludmila. 'Ublilsk. My house.'

Bunny turned to Blair, lifted his glasses, and stared. 'What, for the love of God, have you done?'

'You come my house?'

The night was black, and sharp with ice, when the train grated to a near-halt at Uvila Junction. It didn't stop, but merely slowed, while sacks were tossed into the wagon from the platform. The guard received them with a wave and a shout. Cold blasted through the door, bringing a scent of cleanliness, an aura of snow and its dusts.

Ludmila jumped from the wagon with her bag, running a few steps through the snows to slow herself. Looking over her shoulder, she saw the Englishmen at the door, preparing to follow. She stopped, shook her boots clean, and watched them bumble like old women with their bags. There appeared to be a reason behind their presence, though what this might be escaped Ludmila. Still, she would be thankful if they accompanied her on the trek to Ublilsk. Uvila was at the safer end of the Gnezvarik conflict, but there were kilometres of flats and foothills to cross.

Ludmila couldn't know the situation at home. Her hope was to find Misha there, guarding and consoling her family. Or to find him along the way, waiting, in despair for her loss.

Still, whatever the situation, it would be best if they arrived before dawn.

She heard a thump and a grunt behind her. The black-suited Englishman lay in two feet of snow, rolling to find his knees. The funny one, Bani, crouched like a gnome at the edge of the wagon's door, ogling the platform, frozen with fear.

'Jamp!' his brother shouted, waving as if scooping air out of Bani's path. 'Jamp, Bans!'

Bani jumped just as the platform began its incline to the ground. He rolled like a pair of urchins in a fight, robes and belts flying, and disappeared with a thud into a drift at the bottom of the ramp. Ludmila went to find him. She pulled him by the sleeve, brushing a wig of snow from his hair.

Whatever curious fortune had delivered the brothers to Ludmila, she decided they must be a prize. A strangely answered wish.

She had an inkling they would change the equation in Ublilsk.

'What in fuck's name have you done?'

The train clattered away, and all three souls watched its light sway off into the night.

Blair turned to Ludmila. He tried to set an intrepid, workman-like jaw. 'Best make a plan, then. When is the next train to Stavropol, Millie?'

'Mmm. Tomorrow. Or next day.'

'Right. Well. How far is the nearest town?'

Ludmila had to watch him hard, squint at him to understand. The expression she made when she did this stabbed him through the heart. 'Mmm,' she pondered, 'Ublilsk – ten kilometres?'

'Ten kilometres?' spat Bunny. 'How many fucking miles is that? About seven bloody miles! Are we trekking seven bloody miles through this shite?'

'It's not that far, Buns – there's a couple of kilometres to a mile, surely.'

'There's not, you know. It's fucking donkey's miles away.'

'Right. Well. What I'm saying to you is – there's nothing for it, we'll just have to press on. Ludmila – is there a road, to the town? Might we see a car?'

'Mmm. Car? No.'

'We'll bloody freeze!'

'Come on, Buns. Imagine a nice hot soup when we get there. Lovely cup of tea. Shepherd's pie!'

'Give me the sachets, Blair.'

'Hey, now you're talking.'

'I'm emptying them into the fucking snow.'

'Piss off – it's just a cherry-flavoured additive.'

'Mark my words: if I see your hand anywhere near your gob, I'll have your fucking balls off. And the first chance I get, I'm having them sachets away. This has gone too far now.'

With the confidence of a truffle pig, Ludmila skirted all the deeper drifts, found a path where there seemed to be none, and led the pair grunting, occasionally bickering, through the moonless night. Snow whipped their faces from time to time and, before long, the men lost all sense of time and space. The effect of the cocktails withered to zero, and strangely, in the dark of that alien place, the very idea of them was absurd. The cocktail belonged to a world of internal concepts and self-references; a bitter Ublilsk wind wiped these away like fluff.

Blair lost all feeling in his hands and feet. For the first time in his life he had no option but to carry on; they faced death but for that commitment, and might face it even so. What kept them moving was Ludmila. As the cold pressed down on them, robbed them of their senses, stripped their mind of all but the most essential, autonomous thoughts, their attention became fixed on the beacon that Ludmila became, walking as she did without fear.

After a certain point, the Heaths didn't bicker again. They barely spoke. The brothers couldn't imagine what awaited at

journey's end – certainly poverty, possibly squalor, and danger –
but they became, as they stumbled like ducklings behind her, less
a part of their own journey, and overwhelmingly a part of hers.
They were reduced to nervous systems alone, without conceits
or dreams. And they discovered that, while the tendrils of
Ludmila's being were entwined close to the basic rod of her
spirit, their rod was bare; without top-of-mind preoccupations,
without cups of tea, without medications, without food prefer-
ences, and music, and news – they were nothing.

'Are we close?' Blair eventually asked.

'Mmm. Maybe eight kilometres more.'

An artillery shell thudded near by.

22

Light flickered ahead. Blair wept quietly when he saw it. It appeared and vanished and appeared again, a handful of glowing fragments. He stopped, trying to establish depth of field. He saw that the light was in the far distance, behind shrub branches in the foreground. As he moved past the shrubs, the light popped out as big as a sun. But it was only a distant pinpoint, whose aura shimmered large through frozen tears.

He had almost grown used to the sound of gunfire and shelling.

Bunny hadn't spoken for some time. The sound of his steps in the snow were signs enough of life. He had dressing gowns, Blair had none, though he'd put a jumper on beneath his jacket. Ludmila had stopped several times to wait for them, and once to shake Bunny's arm, and pull him along, when he fell into lethargy. When Bunny last looked at her, she strode ahead undaunted, an even vapour flowing through her scarf. Blair didn't look at her any more. She was so clearly their superior on the trek.

They weren't to know she marched with an image of Misha in mind.

After a few hundred yards, the light multiplied into a handful of working street lamps in Ublilsk village. But no sooner had the men taken them in, and felt a surge of spirit, than Ludmila made a sharp turn, and led them away up a hill until the lights disappeared from view.

'Millie!' said Blair. 'Ludmila!'

She didn't respond. He said nothing more, and, groaning now at times, tramped behind her over steep dunes of snow. And so it was like a cancelled test from God when, having prepared themselves for the worst, the men saw Ludmila slow ahead of them, and looked up to see the form of a shack nestled barely thirty yards away into a fold of the hill. She held up a hand, and they stopped. Treading carefully, she moved to the wall and listened. Light glowed through a frosty window, and from a crack under the door. She approached it, and crouched. All seemed quiet. Without beckoning the men, she tried the door.

'It's Gregor,' said a voice from inside. It was Lubov.

Ludmila entered.

The Heath twins followed.

'Stop there, identify yourselves!' Abakumov woke suddenly in his chair.

The twins ignored him, and clamoured to the stove.

'Milochka!' Irina scurried to plaster her daughter with kisses. Olga began to wail, serving meals to the saints with her hands; not sour meals, but sweet ones. In the flurry of greetings, the serving of meals, and rolling of eyes, the two strange men were ignored for a while.

Abakumov stood watching them, eyes flicking up and down the black suit of one, and the collected robes of seemingly all three Wise Men on the other, as well as their matted hair. He shared a raised eyebrow with Lubov, who stood sullen in the dark. They watched as the men stumbled to the floor, tried to sit, then fell beside the stove, heads on their bags.

'So, the prodigal daughter.' Abakumov paced slowly around the clump of women. 'Clearly she has journeyed great distances to fetch such holy types to your hovel. But I can't say it ameliorates your situation in any way.'

265

'Who is this?' Ludmila asked her mothers in Ubli.

'State inspector,' said Irina.

Ludmila looked the man up and down, stepping over Blair's chest to remove her coat and hang it behind the door, as if her regular chores beckoned.

'Yes,' Abakumov went on in Russian, 'it's the state inspector. Before I outline the situation here – presuming you remain unaware of at least some of it – I must comment on the condition of these apparent priests in your company. What is their provenance, and how might they appear so ravaged?'

Ludmila looked down. The Englishmen lay like piles of shuddering laundry at her feet. 'There's a war, in case you hadn't heard. Their coats and hats were taken at gunpoint – we were thankful to escape with our lives.'

'I see.' Abakumov stroked his chin, studying the men. 'And I ask myself – what man would steal the hat of a cleric, and leave your own two coats in situ?'

'Hoh, the man you ask after is a Gnezvarik soldier, perhaps a person outside of your direct acquaintance. Or do you imagine he'll fight at the front in women's clothing?'

Olga cackled, glowing with pride that her tongue had such a keen successor.

The welcome spurred Ludmila on. 'Perhaps I should have offered the man my scarf and underwear, instead of the priests' clothes, because, after all –'

'Enough!' Abakumov snapped. 'I see you're as hard a task as the rest of your family, whose barbarity has already blunted me to the core.'

'Clearly not blunted enough, to be found skulking after my mothers in the very dead of a night.' Ludmila stood over the Englishmen, siphoning energy in a surge that made her eyes dance. 'Your passions must be prodigious to be found in such a

266

situation. I can't blame these men for hiding their faces in the floor, having witnessed such impropriety. An inspector, lurking alone in a house full of defenceless women!'

'Quiet!' Abakumov's face began to bristle. 'I'm in the process of removing your so-called mothers, and the little girl, for crimes against nature, and incidentally, against the state. Unless you can show reason why I shouldn't immediately proceed, you should stand aside and acclimatise yourself to the thought of going with them.'

Ludmila pondered a moment, narrowing her eyes. 'Then you should proceed while the faces of these men are hidden. Now, instantly. Because if they see their journey's incentive snatched away, they will surely summon the other men that follow them, with wide-ranging consequence indeed.'

'And what reason might this be? Now I feel you are painting my face like a clown.'

'Hoh! And why would it need painting twice?' Ludmila busied herself with the bag under Bunny's head, while Olga rocked and twittered gleefully on her chair. When Bunny stirred, Ludmila knelt down beside him. Ludmila reached into his coat, rummaged for his inner pocket, and, after a moment, pulled out his British passport.

Abakumov's pupils widened. He looked down, and chewed his lip. 'Well,' he said, glancing at each woman in turn. 'Well, well. You have introduced two more unknowns into this equation. I fear you'll kill me with all this official work. Stand aside while I perform an identity check on these men.' Sighing, the inspector began to rifle through the men's pockets. He came upon Blair's wallet, and pulled out a cash card. 'Now, well,' he said. 'Sub-agent Kaganovich – we must travel back to the depot, and ring the appropriate authorities.' Abakumov held the card like a laboratory specimen as he made for the door. Lubov joined him. They turned as one to face the room. 'Don't any of you leave these premises. I will be calling for men from the regional office to back us up in your removal. But I'll also tell you, in all fairness, that if, through my checks, and my subsequent return here this morning, it is made clear that these foreigners have come to help you in the correct financial way – in the only feasible way, in fact, the extent of which I will ascertain on the telephone just now – it may be – and I only say "may" be – that your situations can be slightly upturned.' His eyes panned across the smoky dark, passing each face in turn. 'Let us pray that, for your sakes, this might be so.'

'And,' said Lubov, as Abakumov opened the door, 'remember Gregor lurks outside, and Karel can't be far behind. Tell them to wait here for us, we won't be long away.' With that, she strode archly on to the step, and banged the door behind her.

Olga, Irina, and Ludmila stood quiet in the haze until the crunch of footsteps grew faint. Then Irina gazed over the Englishmen, now beginning to stir, and curled damp eyes at Ludmila. 'Nights and days we've had these leeches in the house,' she said. 'Yet within ten minutes of your return you've scattered them away like beetles under a broom. Your house welcomes you, Milochka.'

Ludmila disappeared beneath another cloak of hugs and sweet meals to the saints. In the eruption of murmurs and cries, the women didn't hear the door creak open. They only heard it bang. All stiffened. When they stood back from each other, they found a haggard Maksimilian on the threshold, Gregor's rifle dangling from his arm.

He scarcely acknowledged them, but tramped shivering to the stove, kicking aside the Englishmen's legs as he passed. 'Hoh! And how long did you think I would wait on the mountain for you to empty the house of enemies? I'm surprised you didn't marry them and invite them to live in the room, if you wanted me to die in the cold!'

'Cut your hatch,' wheezed Olga, 'your sister has made them run like puppies to milk. You're lucky to enter at all.'

Maks snuggled up to the stove, glancing testily at the bodies beside him. 'And how is the house now filled with musicians? Are we starting a band to celebrate our troubles?'

'Listen to me,' said Irina. 'We haven't much time, so hold your typical bile. We must move Aleks's body outside and cover him, if not bury him properly. We have the excuse that the inspector thinks our guests are holy men.'

Maks studied the men. 'Holy men now, are they? This one here, with the glasses, is clearly an albino. I mean – hoh! – let's be serious, do we actually know what or who they are?'

'They travelled with Ludmila, it's not important who they are.'

'Hoh, well.' Maks kicked the hairy one's leg. 'They at least look soft enough – homosexual enough, I should say. I'm pleased at least that you're in your right minds still, that your feminine logic is intact. If homosexual musicians arrive in the house, it must be time for a funeral.'

'Maksimilian! You'll do as you're told!'

'And,' Olga added, 'you'll bury Aleks properly, with respect, and with prayers. And far away from wherever you've put the mongol Gregor, saints rest his soul.'

Blair sat up. He clawed at the air, hunting a centre of gravity. A gun clicked beside him. His eyes snapped to the sound, and found the barrel an inch from his nose. Using its length to find focus, he saw a swarthy, hollow-cheeked young man scowling down it. The man's finger was on the trigger. Blair's hands shot over his head.

269

There came a shrill outburst from Ludmila, who stepped up to the gunman. He sent a loose outburst back, but lowered the gun, and eventually stood it by the wall behind the stove. Blair smacked Bunny's leg.

Bunny sat up, blinking. He looked around, wiped his eyes, yawned. Then he sighed. 'What in fuck's name –'

'Shut up, give me time to think.'

Ludmila knelt between the men. 'Halo,' she said. 'Are you fine?'

Bunny looked up. Behind his eyes, the night's story reassembled in icy pieces. 'I mean to say. Fine's putting it in a plush light.'

'Yes, Millie,' said Blair. 'I think we're okay.'

His tone brought a snarl from the young man, and the waving of hands towards the gun. Ludmila thrust her chin at him, and sliced a stream of words off her tongue.

'Hoh!' the man said.

'Hoh!' said Ludmila. Then a gentler clutch of sounds rolled through her lips, ending with the word 'English'. It came with a delicate, breathy space either side of it.

'English!' Another barrage of hisses, seeming to end with 'homosexual'.

'Hoh!' said Ludmila.

'Hoh!' said the man.

Maksimilian watched Bunny uncrumple himself from the floor, gazing around like a blind man through his glasses. He lifted them, and found the two ladies in front of him, observing with some interest.

The very old one shone her gums, and pointed him to a chair while she spat a mouthful of language at Maksimilian – who clicked his tongue, and threw back his head.

'Mind, I'd kill for a cup of tea,' said Bunny. 'Never mind the bacon.'

Ludmila watched him, head slightly cocked. 'Tea?' she said.

'Yes, and some food,' Blair stood, and ran his eyes over the women's faces. 'We can pay you. Is there something?'

Ludmila frowned. After a moment, she turned to the ladies, and made a plea. It brought frowns in return. Her tone rose, and an instant came when the women snagged on one of her words, and their brows wavered. They looked at each other, spoke briefly, then threw a finger at Maksimilian, attracting from him a tirade ending with 'Hoh!'

The fingers stayed thrown. Maksimilian picked up the rifle, pulled out its cartridge, and emptied it on to the table. A single bullet bounced out. He moved grave eyes over each woman.

The fingers stayed thrown. The women stared until he reloaded the gun, and stormed into the yard. A shot cracked through the dark. Blair saw a goat dragged past the step, heard a blade clinking on stone. Within minutes, the animal's skin was hung outside the door, its innards saved in a bucket, and the remainder, including its head and feet, were quartered and tossed on the kitchen benchtop.

Before Maksimilian could scrub his hands, his mother issued a sharp request, nudging a chin at the Heaths. The boy looked sceptically at Bunny and Blair, until an ancillary eruption, from the old woman, made him lead the twins to a door at the back of the room.

They entered to find a smell. Maksimilian stood by a bed, and pulled back the covers to reveal a body.

'Fucking hell.' Bunny jumped back.

Maksimilian motioned the pair to the body's legs.

Bunny gagged as they carried the corpse from the room. The old woman regaled their passing with wails, and the throwing up of hands. 'What in the name of fuck, Blair?'

'I mean, I'm sorry, Buns, but it's not going to get any better going on and on about it.'

271

'Aye, mate. None of the steps we've taken in the last forty-eight hours, and none of the signs at the place where those actions have led us, suggest we'll ever fucking get out.'

'Well, that's just absurd. You're just being absurd now, Bunny, frankly.' Blair could feel the body's skin detaching to float on a kind of slime under its trouser leg. 'And it's not in the least helpful to make dark of the situation, when we really should be getting our heads around it. I mean, it's just a bit new, that's all. Relative comfort will settle in, you'll see.'

The trio stumbled off the front step, and waded grunting through a foot of dry snow. Olga followed at an oblique distance, wailing. Blair's mouth flapped and clamped intermittently. 'What I am saying to you is that we mustn't be put off at this stage. We have the tools we need to turn things around. I think – and I mean this seriously, Buns – that now is the time to really calibrate our attitudes, orientate our minds for best results. Wasn't it Nietzsche who said, "If your model defeats you, change the model?"'

'"If your *ethical* model defeats you." I think you'll find he said.'

'Well, but what I mean to say is – we've two of these sachets left. I think it's crucial, in the interests of –'

'If you touch another of those fucking cocktails I will make you shag this corpse, Blair.'

'Buns, Buns, Buns! You're missing the point!'

Maksimilian shuffled a half-circle with the old man's head, and grunted to indicate they should drop the body where they stood, in a dune of snow by the yard's fence.

It sank with a puff.

Bunny rinsed his fingers in the snow, and wiped his hands up and down his sock. Then he sidled to his brother. 'I'm not missing the point. Every drink we've had has gotten us deeper into shit. And do you know why, Blair?'

'Well, Buns, just look –'

'No, no.' Bunny leant closer, stabbing his brother with a finger. 'You look. Do you know what this drug does? Do you know its single active quality? The suspension of conscience, Blair. Do you hear?'

'Oh for God's sake. It doesn't produce anything we don't already have. It's a facilitator, that's all.'

'And it'll facilitate us to our fucking graves.'

'Now look, what I am saying to you is simply this: we can make a sensible and orderly plan, and be on our way tomorrow. We weren't to know about the trains. I'll have a proper chat with Ludmila – I'll even pay her to take us back to the airport, and we'll carry on with the original plan.'

'And she'll be swept off her feet by hotel toiletries, and follow you to the ends of the earth.'

'Well, that's not what I'm saying at all. Anyway, I mean – she did advertise, Buns. She did write me that letter.'

'No, mate. Here's what happened: you got wafted away with one of these fucking cocktails and told me we were off to Spain for a laff.'

'Well, I take exception to that. I never said a word about Spain.'

'I'm too fucking cold to argue. At first light, I'm off home. And I'm taking the card – if there's only the cost of one ticket in it, that ticket's mine, Blair.'

'Yes, yes, yes.'

All the while they spoke, the weasel Maksimilian observed the pair, keeping them silhouetted against the shack's dim light, his stare lurking over their forms, weighing each shift and thrust, each breath beween them.

Ludmila came into the yard. She stood a moment beside Olga, whose wails had shrunk to squeaks and hisses, and whose meals were only served as far as her chest. Had the meals been real, they would have formed a pile around her boots. Ludmila hugged her coats, and stepped up to the men. Maksimilian took a lingering squint at the brothers, then strode off to fetch a shovel. He muttered as he dug a hole around the body. Ludmila didn't look at Bunny or Blair, but stood behind them.

Blair leant back, close enough to feel the damp of her breath.

'English!' Maksimilian barked. He held up the shovel.

'He's got you pegged,' said Bunny.

'Why?' Blair moved testily around the grave. 'I'm not doing anything!'

'Well sussed, he's got you.'

'Piss off, Buns.'

'Because, do you know what, Blair? Shall we just be honest for a minute? All of this has come about because you're a virgin who found the talent back home a bit daunting. You've managed to rationalise to yourself a string of conceits, like thinking the dirt poor will lay down at your feet for the whiff of a quid.' Bunny levelled his eyes across the snow at his brother. 'Face it: the lad's on form. You've come to knob his sister.'

23

'Is it that the financial instrument is bad?' Abakumov argued into the telephone. 'Or why will you not honour a perfectly routine transaction?' He put one hand over the mouthpiece, tossed another vodka down his throat, and leant across the table to Lubov, hissing to her, 'They say the transaction can't be completed without a merchant account – you must have a registration number, as a commerce, with which they can charge the money from the card.'

Lubov crossed her arms, leaning into the back-room door frame. 'Well I have conducted business here for many years without such a registration. I'm certain it's not something required by the state.' Her eyes fell under the weight of greater priorities: the whereabouts of Gregor and Karel, who had never taken so long to fetch the bread. Already a handful of villagers began to shout at her door. This, and the curious absence of soldiers on the street, despite the closeness of gunfire, disquieted her. All was compounded by fatigue from the ridiculous debacle of the Derevs' voucher.

'I'm not saying it's for the state,' Abakumov tutted, 'I'm saying it would have been helpful to have an account to charge the card to. It's all that stands between us and a workable resolution to this dire caseload, if we could just lubricate the process with the proper funds.'

'I'm sorry, we cannot complete the transaction,' a voice said down the telephone. 'You will have to approach the cardholder.'

'I see, I see. But then can you give me the status of the account, a balance of available funds, before we approach the customer for a resolution?'

'No, I can't, only the cardholder can access such information.'

'Well, the cardholder is here.' Abakumov winked at Lubov, gave the shrug of the incorrigible rogue. 'He speaks no Russian, he's a tourist, we're helping him out of a bind.'

The operator was silent for a moment, and the chatter of other operators could be heard in the background. 'Then I'll have to give you another number, we can't help you here, this is for transactions only.'

Abakumov motioned his empty glass, and scribbled a number into his notepad. He drank another vodka, and dialled the number.

'Only the cardholder can access account information,' the new operator said. 'Put them on, because we can process their request in English.'

'Ah well, but they've just stepped out. Can you anyway suggest how we might settle this account with them?'

'They can withdraw cash at an automat, or over the counter of a bank.'

'An automat, you say?' Abakumov motioned his empty glass again. 'Where might I find one such?'

'What is your location?'

'Ublilsk Administrative District Forty-One.'

'*Where?*'

'Uvila,' said Abakumov, taking another vodka, and geeing Lubov to keep up with him.

'Uvila? In the west? Then perhaps Labinsk or Stavropol will have machines.'

'And how would we operate the machine?'

'What? Listen, is the cardholder there? What is your name, please –'

Abakumov put down the receiver.

'And so?' Lubov looked up.

Abakumov sat back, closed his eyes. 'We must carry the foreigners to Stavropol.'

There came with the first fragile light a sense of goodwill around the Derev family table. Blue twilight bathed the starker pockets of the night, and in their weariness and warmth beside the stove, the Heaths took some leave from internal horror. With this, and the absence of death in the house, the Derevs also lightened; their words rang with new hope as portions of cooked goat were lifted on to the table.

A little girl called Kiska had been produced from her bed, and sat like a shining fairy, basking in the visitors' attention. She tugged at Blair's sleeve, and dangled a strip of meat in his face. He ogled it with mock terror, and she hissed a giggle through gaps in her milk teeth.

Bunny's whole face seemed to be deployed in chewing. He left his glasses off, finding the gloom acceptable. 'Mind, I'll have a word with our lass just now, about getting back. We'll need directions.'

'Well, I'll speak to her, Buns. You get some sustenance into you, it'll still probably involve a walk.'

'Aye. But, Blair – I'm off after this, I mean it.'

'All right, all right.' Blair smiled obsequiously around the table. Olga shone her gums. Maksimilian tossed his chin without hostility.

Soft remarks in foreign languages anchored the gentle slurp of a roasted breakfast that morning. The remarks themselves referred to foreigners, and each foreigner, in a way, understood without understanding, though the Heaths were also able to make out the words 'albino' and 'English'. Without a cultural tie to bind them, both groups had in common that lightening oasis amid outrageous days and nights before. Such was the relief of the morning that Bunny even managed a quip, referring to napkins as 'Soviets'.

When the sun flew clear of the horizon, it painted the haze with rectangular ducts of light. Some of these glanced off heads and shoulders, making hot photo-realism from a scene of faded impressions. As colour entered the room so did life, and all were lifted with it.

Ludmila relaxed, and tore strips of meat from a goat leg. Blair watched her throw back her head, swinging strands of hair off her face. A dazzling halo attached to her as she sat back. She caught Blair watching her, and smiled.

'When you're finished, Millie, can I speak to you outside?'

Ludmila turned her head to the window. 'In outside?'

'Yes, outside. Just for a minute.'

With a pair of words to the women, she rose from the table, and made for the door. A dainty bark over her shoulder stopped Kiska from joining them. The little girl slumped on her seat with a whine. Irina tutted, and tossed her chin at the meat.

The air was shiny beyond the shack's step, rinsing Blair's nostrils with ice. Ludmila loosened her shoulders, and looked to the sky, where an aeroplane's con-trail unravelled over the horizon, soaking up colour from its glow.

Blair followed it to the yard's far fence. He had no particular reason to go there, save to show off a purposeful stride. After stumbling twice, he slowed to a shuffle, then stopped, breathing deeply, seeming to have reached a destination some yards short of the gate. Ludmila passed him, stepping lightly up to the gatepost. Both looked around: Blair as if browsing in a foreign shop, Ludmila as if serving in that shop, but with only slight interest. The breeze made a nest for their silence, and when the quiet became painful, they stepped out of the yard, and moved over a crest that fell sharply into the foothills of Ublilsk. Mists rolled between dunes below them.

Then snow crunched near by. Footsteps. Ludmila squatted, pulling Blair down beside her. The pair saw two fur hats and the tip of a gun barrel bob towards the shack. A moment later, the shack's door burst open. Ludmila dropped flat.

A bone fell from Irina's hands at the sound of Kalashnikovs being cocked. The shaggy Englishman spun in his chair. Maks's eyes flew to the rifle propped in the kitchen.

'Hoh!' said the first man through the door. 'And what colossal species of goose am I that I forgot to walk in with wine!' He was a square man in heavy combat gear. A moustache like a sooty hedgerow fell from his lip into outlands of stubble. Gnezvarik insignia flashed from his epaulettes. He turned to the soldier behind him. 'Fabi, can you believe your face? Have we died, or can it be the saints have sent us to a breakfast party, on the mountain, where cooked meats lounge on a table?'

A plump lad with rosy cheeks stepped inside, scanning the haze with his rifle. 'Gavrel, yes. Roasted meats they seem to be, lounging.'

The larger soldier, Gavrel, approached the table, and poked the goat with his gun. He smiled, tossing his chin at the diners. 'Feasting on meats while their homeland falls around them. A thoroughly Ubli approach.'

Olga resumed chewing, and stripped another cable of flesh from the bone. 'Hoh,' she muttered. 'It's only the Gnez. For a moment I thought I might have to bid welcome.'

'Raise your hands,' said Gavrel. 'Move into that corner, all of you – there, by the door.' He flicked his gun to the darkest corner. Then he swung it back to Maksimilian. 'And you, young buck – it's no wonder you don't wear a military badge, your eyes chatter more than widows at a funeral. If I see you look once more at your weapon, for even a second, even by an accident of reflex, we both of us will empty a clip into you and your family, though they be our last munitions.'

'Hoh, and save your gas – the weapon stands empty.' Maks sidled to the corner behind the women, wiping his mouth with a sleeve.

'Check it, Fabi.' Gavrel removed his fur hat, and hurried the shaggy foreigner away from the table. He prodded the family into a cluster in the corner. 'Now sit – sit there – and put your hands on your heads.'

Fabi confirmed the rifle was empty. Gavrel arranged his hat beside the goat, its fats sparkling in a shaft of sunlight. He motioned his underling to cover the group while he settled on a chair, delving surgically into the light for the juiciest meats. Eyes shone like night creatures from the corner. Gavrel's gaze wandered over them as he chewed and grunted, lingering on the shaggy man in robes. 'You, with the hair,' he pointed. 'Are you escaped from the circus, or are you an ugly woman trying to enjoy a man's fortunes?'

Bunny twitched. His eyes bounced over the family. Nobody engaged them. Squinting painfully, he moved a hand to his breast pocket, and fumbled out his sunglasses.

'Don't move!' Gavrel snatched up his gun. He sent his comrade to fetch the glasses, and turned them approvingly in his greasy hand, before perching them on his nose. 'So, answer me, girly-boy.'

Olga cleared her throat. 'He's not from here. Nobody can understand him.'

The soldier leant forward, studying the Englishman. 'Well, and as you say it, he doesn't look like anyone from here. Even an

Ubli mother would've drowned such a thing at birth. So tell me about this stranger.'

Maks stirred after a moment's silence, feigning to stretch and yawn. 'All I can say is you'll wish you had combed your hair when the pictures come on the television, and in the English newspaper.'

The soldier's eyes twinkled. He stopped chewing, and smirked at Maks. 'So it's not alone your eyes that embarrass you, young buck. I see your mouth also falls outside of your control. Did you think I wouldn't have met such vacant cases as you? Did you think I was Ubli, who spent my days puffing high-blown talk about nothing?' The soldier's gaze bored through Maksimilian, chased his eyes to the floor. 'Well, so now. The price of such a typically Ubli mouth is that young buck has raised the level of seriousness in the dwelling. We hadn't originally come to kill, but simply to occupy the house, which, in a way, was to be a certain protection for you, as this morning heavy guns will train this way. But now your vacant buck wants me to believe the wrong kind of witness is among you.'

The soldier ripped another chunk of meat from the bone, and left his chair to saunter chewing around the group, his gun hanging from a finger. Chewing slowed as he narrowed his eyes at the foreigner. 'Are you English?'

'I am, yes. From England, yes.'

'This bad place for tourist.'

The Englishman's face lightened. 'Funny you should say it, I was starting to think I'd never hear English again. As you speak it so well, can I just –'

'From fishing. Long time in boats. Scotland, Ireland. You love Manchester United?'

'Actually cricket's more my cup of tea. Look, can I just ask –'

'Quiet now. Wrong day for tourist.'

'And listen to me, Officer,' Irina pleaded. 'Don't take the words of my boy as an offence. We are humble people of the land, in the hardest of times, without a wish for or against you, or your war. No gun has ever inhabited this house.'

The soldier tossed his head with laughter. 'Fantasy followed by lies! You mean to say no gun inhabits your house except the semi-automatic firearm that sits in your kitchen with the boy's eye attached like a jewellery chain!'

'Hoh, but if it's empty –'

'Don't say another word to dig your grave deeper. Already now I have two souls to dispose of, according to proper military practice, if one is a press journalist, and the other possesses a firearm. But I will first say to you: although you see me in the course of a righteous military action, I remain still a man of family, and not without human feeling. I even tell you my name is Gavrel Gergiev, and that I don't fight to make sour the lives of old women and children, or to make them shiver with fear as they sit. Our interest is strategic and purely military. We are on our last clip each of bullets – though be assured they are enough to kill you all, and another person still. So tune a close ear as I repeat: we don't come for your lives, or to inflict terror. But at the same time, we won't tolerate to play games along the way. If you sit quiet, and serve up no strife, we will give you cover to vacate the mountain after dark falls.' The man's mouth stayed open after his last word, light and fat making wet fruits of his lips. He leant his head to one side, and chuckled. 'A humorous thought – after tonight, you should always remember it was Gnezvariks who gave you cover from your own Ubli fire.'

'And we certainly will,' Irina trembled with relief. 'We will use our lives to spread word of your good characters in war. Yes, Officer Gergiev, if this is to be the case, then you have made the Gnezvarik struggle welcome in our minds. We will not forget.'

'Hoh! I will,' said Olga.

'Mama!'

Gavrel snorted. 'This old wheezer is just like my wife's mother. Keep her quiet, or my mood will turn.' He moved to the Englishman and poked him with the gun. 'You – come out.'

'What do you want with him?' spat Olga.

'He's not family, you say?'

'No.'

'Then it's too strange that a foreigner should be here, in the very arse of such a district. In fact, it's impossible. If he's a journalist, as young buck says, he'll have to be put down. You should have no concern, if he's not of your blood.'

'Well, but he's a guest of the house. What would it do to our hospitable name, if guests are slain when they call? Nobody would visit again, if death is what we garnered fame for serving.'

'And have I not just said you'll be vacating the house? The mountain is part of free Gnezvarikstan now – in fact, my very feet, wherever they tread, turn the ground into Gnezvarik homeland. You'll have to lay your table elsewhere.'

'Hoh! A fine set of choices you leave our guests, to either be killed, or travel to a different country to visit us. We'd never see a caller again!'

Gavrel ignored the woman, and jabbed the Englishman out of the group, poking him on all fours into the bedroom. The foreigner's eyes were puffed shut from the light, tears flowed down his face to drip from his chin. 'I mean to say,' he gasped.

'Shh, you English.'

'He's a holy man, not a journalist,' said Irina.

'Watch your hatch, I say. I'm doing you the favour of dispatching him out of your sight. Don't make me shoot him in front of the child.'

'Well, but I can vouch he's no journalist.'

'Hoh, just as you vouch the house is naked of guns! He won't feel a thing, trust me. His eyes are shut, he won't even see. And to be honest, looking at such a creature, who doesn't even like football, and trails tears like piss – or perhaps even now trails piss along the floor – he'll be better off with the saints.'

Ludmila didn't fight Blair's embrace. The cold drove him to snuggle obliquely into her coats, one arm over her shoulder. Twenty minutes passed like this, on a shelf of snow overlooking the world. A whiff of meaty smoke also found them, a single coloured thread in a weave of breezes fed by the snows of a dozen nations around.

Ludmila's faint warmth, and the wet from her breath's vapour, sharpened Blair's feelings to a pinpoint. For the first time since leaving Albion, perhaps for the first time ever, he felt desperately alive. Hopelessly so. He knew Ludmila sensed danger in the shack, and thought he ought to feel it more himself. But her ramshackle culture, the benign glare of sunshine on snow, the slap of blue skies, of breezes like medicinal oxygen, put him at one remove from any sense of doom.

Sunshine made danger implausible. Only Ludmila possessed the discipline of belief in it, and hence the discipline for its survival.

Blair's fingers found their way to her neck, and into her hair. She didn't pull away, but lay watching snow-dust fly like a fringe off the crest. He inched his head into the crook of her neck. Her breathing quickened.

As he rested open lips on her, sniffed the pubic ripeness of saliva on skin, the sound of a motor broke the still. Fragments of speech eddied with it. Ludmila hoisted herself on to her forearms, and peered over the crest.

24

Gavrel and Fabi also heard the sounds, and froze inside the shack. They waited until certain that the voices – those of a man and a woman squabbling – were approaching the dwelling.

Fabi trained his Kalashnikov on the door. Gavrel left the shaggy Englishman sniffling on the bedroom floor, and quietly shut the door between them, edging to crouch beneath the kitchen window.

After a moment, Irina cleared her throat. 'They won't be armed – it's a district inspector with the woman from the depot.'

'Tsst!' hissed Gavrel.

'No, it's true,' said Olga. 'It's the sow Lubov Kaganovich with her state parasite attached like an unfinished turd. Listen to them – more than a gun, you'll need garlic and a holy cross to ward off this pair.'

Gavrel raised his eyes to the window, then turned to the huddled family. 'Oh-hoh? I must say I'm finding it a leap of imagination to discover why so many disparate people spontaneously congregate in your house at dawn, in the middle of a war. And I have to warn, frankly, that making a soldier's imagination leap is something you should try to avoid.'

Olga sucked her teeth, and widened her eyes at the soldier. 'Well, but we can't be blamed for our popularity! Anyway, these are unwelcome guests, only slightly less than yourselves. I can tell you the inspector has been here sucking us for benefit, and he comes under the tutelage of the worst kind of person, a tick's navigator, the depot keeper Lubov.'

'Shh now,' Officer Gergiev raised his gun.

The door flew open. Inspector Abakumov stumbled in with a bottle of vodka in hand. He appeared to have enjoyed some already, and teetered a little on his feet. Lubov bustled behind him, face primed for an outburst, probably about her missing boys.

Both stopped dead.

Two cocked weapons levelled in greeting. 'Speak your business.' Little Fabi kicked the door shut behind them.

'I am an inspector of the state.' Abakumov drew himself up. 'And I serve you official notice that this dwelling falls under my auspices, as I am charged with the investigation of crimes herein.'

Gavrel recocked his weapon, and smiled. 'Are you indeed? And what state is it you speak of?'

The inspector recoiled. 'You know it as well as your own name, don't make the mistake of playing games. Put aside your weapons, before you find yourselves added to the catalogue of offences.'

Gavrel's smile held firm as he stepped up to the inspector. 'It seems the bottle has perverted your sense of geography, inspector. In fact, it seems the bottle delivered you to prattle nonsense in a corner of western Gnezvarikstan.' He turned an inch, calling over his shoulder to his comrade. 'Fabi – does it not seem we're landed with an illegal immigrant, on top of everything?'

'Gavrel, yes – an alien, unless he has the correct passport and visa.'

Abakumov blanched. 'I warn you once more –'

'Tsst!' Gavrel raised his gun, pressing the barrel into the inspector's throat. He tossed a wry glance at Olga. 'An unfinished turd, wasn't it, you likened him to?'

'Yes,' said Olga. 'And a goose's arse, and a leech.'

'A goose's arse, and a leech,' Gavrel repeated into the inspector's face. 'Indeed, one thing I have very much in common with these wretched Ubli souls is a long history of measuring the sags and wrinkles, watching the loss of hope itself, in the faces of loved ones who have had to deal with your species of lazy, pompous, state-sanctioned little gangster.' He stabbed the gun into Abakumov's gullet till he hissed.

'Good boy, Gavi!' cackled Olga.

Gavrel locked his eyes on the inspector. 'So now, Inspector Unfinished Turd – do you wish to beg asylum in the free Gnezvarik state? Is this why we suffer your face before us?'

The inspector gurgled, flicking his eyes around the room.

'Hoh!' Gavrel threw back his head. 'Fabi – can it be that we're faced with a plea for asylum? Even as we've forgotten to carry our official rubber stamps with us?'

'Gavrel, yes. Asylum he seems to be after, hoh.'

Gavrel beat the inspector's arms into the air with his gun, frisking him before motioning him and Lubov to huddle with the group in the corner. The pair shuffled over and sat, hands on their heads. Gavrel frowned after them. 'I am made increasingly suspicious, I have to say. What kind of party is this, that assembles in the dead of morning with roasted meats, that attracts drinkers even as the sun first rises? This is not right.' He turned to his comrade, threw his eyes through the kitchen window. 'It's not right, Fabi. Who knows how many diverse partygoers still lurk outside? Go out and secure the area. Something is not correct.'

When Ludmila finally stepped out of the kitchen, Blair had almost finished painting the window frames in their large suburban conservatory. She wore his oversized rugby jersey over French knickers, and, despite knowing what this did to him,

287

bent over double, in plain view, to retrieve the abandoned nub of his goat's cheese, wild rocket, and pesto panini.

A welcoming chasm strained the silk at her bottom.

Then a gun clicked near by. A voice barked after it. Blair's eyes snapped open.

A soldier stood over them, panting fog.

'A real Noah's Ark, this party!' Gavrel sat nursing a shot of vodka. 'I half expect acrobats and cosmonauts to arrive. If we were correctly coloured geese we'd be selling tickets.' He moved his eyes over Ludmila and Blair, then past them to his comrade. 'Sit the girl with her family.' His Kalashnikov beckoned Blair to the table. 'And you? English?'

'Yes,' said Blair.

'Journalist?'

'Well, no actually, I'm a global markets consultant for –'

'Love Manchester United?'

'Do I love them? Well –'

'You say – who has goal in last Chelsea game? Tell me this.'

'Well, um –'

'You journalist.'

'No, no, listen –'

'Quiet.'

'I mean –'

'Quiet!' Gavrel slammed a fist on the table, making the goat skip across its plate.

The Englishman jumped, which seemed to amuse the soldier. He chuckled, and reached for two more glasses from the bench. 'Fabi, put the journalist in the back room with his partner.' He filled the glasses, and passed them to Blair. 'Gnezvarik hospitality,' he said, pointing the way with his chin.

'Very decent of you, cheers.'

288

'Cheers to you.'

'And can I ask,' – the inspector raised his fingers off his head – 'is this a wholesale kidnapping, are we to sit here for weeks?'

'And does it look like a kidnapping?' Gavrel threw imbecile eyes at the man. 'This genteel buffet with vodka and meats? And do you think anyone would pay for your safety, such carrion as you are? Rather we would have to run a lottery to choose who had the prize of killing you.'

'Well, I only ask because –'

'Quiet. We are merely securing the property. Our commander comes behind us, and when we're installed here in the night, we will decide your proper fate.'

'Yes, but can a gentleman's use of the latrine be arranged? Nightfall is far away in the company of such fluids as I've taken.'

The soldier gulped his vodka down, staring at the inspector. 'You risk becoming tedious enough to just shoot.' He called to the bedroom, 'Fabi!'

'Gavrel, yes?' The soldier's head popped into the room.

'Take the Russian out to the latrine, stand watching him all the time.'

'Thank you,' Abakumov rose stiffly from the floor.

'And the Englishmen?' Fabi lingered uncertainly by the bedroom doorway.

'Leave them, there's no window there. I'll watch the door.'

'But together, with vodka? What protocol advises to feed them drink? Will they not conspire in their language?'

'It's a last drink, Fabi – an anaesthetic.'

25

Blair absorbed the floor's chill through his buttocks. He moved both vodkas against the wall, and shivered.

Bunny found his brother's leg with a hand. 'Is that you?'

'No, it's Worzel fucking Gummidge.'

'Steady on.'

'Just don't talk to me, Bunny.'

Bunny's eyelids flickered painfully. A scene from his earliest memory burnt into mind, of he and Blair at Albion House. They were toddlers still. Bunny was busy sticking and unsticking his fingertips to a patch of marmalade on his thumb, when a vomiting incident took Matron's attention. The twins shambled out of her orbit, down a corridor to the activities hall. They were not allowed in the activities hall. So they went.

It was vast. Birds chimed, tall panes bled a mottled glow like cold lamb's fat. The little Heaths were drawn to a mirror that covered the wall at the room's darkest end. They went to it, stood pressed together, facing each other in profile amid rods and beams of sunlight. As they watched themselves breathe in that cursory way that sparrows and infants have, other, older children swirled chattering into the room, garlanding the space with chalky echoes. The children flew giggling alongside the twins, pressing themselves together in similar tight pairs. Blair and Gordon shone to see others like themselves. But suddenly, in an instant as bright as a sun shower, those children burst apart. They leapt aside from each other, flapped up clouds of glittering dust, and blew away like chubby butterflies in spacious universes all their own.

While the Heaths stayed pressed together.

And, after a moment, began to cry.

By the time Matron scooped them into her damp aura, the moment had infected the twins.

Snatches of overheard talk rolled through Bunny's mind. Words fell from his childhood sky like sods into an open grave.

'They are among very few undivided monozygotes to survive their birth,' one tweedy man said who ushered white-coated people to their rooms one day. 'Can anyone name the specimen?'

'Is it omphalopagus?' asked a woman.

'Technically, yes. Omphalopagus with thoracic complications. And note the dominant twin is not physically the strongest – see this chappie here?'

Bunny swelled when that hand singled him out.

'If the egg's divisive progress had begun even a day earlier this little chap might not have been parasitic at all. And had it begun a day later, he might have been a redundant appendage, a growth on the healthy twin's body. He could have been excised. Can anyone guess why the parasite should be dominant in this instance?'

'Its instinct for survival is the stronger?' asked an earnest young man.

'Indeed,' said Tweed, 'and in two ways: yes, the body's reliance on its healthier sibling provokes a greater drive to safe-guard resources. But it also has to do with the means by which it achieves control. In being the weaker, it has developed an emo-tional and psychological grip on its twin.'

'So,' the young man faltered, 'has the healthy twin become a – a sort of beast of burden for the parasite?'

'In the most basic sense, yes, although I think the full breadth

291

of the parasite–host dynamic would only manifest if they were separated. And of course it's moot, because the parasite wouldn't survive.'

Bunny sighed, and pulled his mind back to his mountain gaol. Patting his pocket for a Rothmans, he found the old pack crumpled, damp with cold. He spent some minutes straightening a cigarette, brought out a box of matches, and lit it.

'Stay this side of the gate,' he whispered.

'Fuck off, Bunny.'

'Losing your rag'll not help. Why don't you nip out and have a word? I mean to say, we've nowt to do with any of this. The big lad speaks English – nip out and tell him something postmodern, make him feel part of a team. You're good at that.'

'Do you think so?'

'Aye. All your new world palaver.'

Blair sat back, shifted his tongue around his mouth. Behind his frown, thoughts scudded like clouds slowly cheering into vapour.

Then he detonated. 'Wait! The sachets! Buns? We'll give them a cocktail!'

Bunny didn't interrupt his drag on the Rothmans. He drew a quivering lungful of smoke, and sat quiet till it coiled from his nostrils. 'You'll never get them to drink it.'

'Why not?'

'If they see it flash, they'll know you've spiked it. If they don't see it flash, they'll wonder why you're giving the drinks back.'

'But if I spike them in plain view, casually, and drink one myself – they'll think it's just flavouring. Buns? We have to give it a try.'

'Mind how you go with that shite, I'm telling you.'

'Buns, Buns, Buns – it's wild cherry flavour!' Blair's gaze sparkled up to the ceiling. 'We can engineer a reversal, look how things are poised. We'll be home, Buns, all the wiser for our mad adventure. Millie there with us – a real reversal, everything hunky dory. By, we're mad as cheese, though, aren't we? What a pair of lads, we'll have a right old laff on the plane, we'll cack ourselves laffing, about everything. We'll be sat in a hundred million pounds worth of jet-propelled Union Jack, with posh announcements in English, clear and crisp as day. Lovely cup of tea, thank you very much, another gin or two, don't mind if I do, and proper voices around, northern lasses probably, good as gold, fresh as moorland heather, whiffs of Heathrow drizzle still bedded in their hair. We'll aim for that moment, Buns – visualise it, pull it out of the ether. We'll nibble smoked salmon, on British Airways –'

'You'll not get British Airways from Staverpool – only that manky Russian plane, like out of *Thunderbirds*.'

'Well, but it's only a hop to Yerevan, Buns. Then, so help me, we'll be larking about on British Airways, and we'll suddenly turn and look at each other. And we'll cack ourselves laffing. The snow'll drop away beneath us, war and poverty and strife'll just plummet away, for ever, beneath us, and we'll rocket into sunshine, laffing like schoolboys.' Blair jabbed his brother with an elbow. 'I ask you – what are we bloody like? What a pair of lads!'

Bunny's eyes had swollen into slits. He swung them at Blair. 'I just mean to say: mind how you fucking go.'

The bedroom door creaked aside. Gavrel's mouth froze open mid-chew; a nugget of meat poked out at Blair. A rifle followed.

The Englishman twitched. He held up the glasses of vodka. 'I thought I'd best ask –'

'What! Get back!'

'Well, it's just that I wondered –'

'Get back!' Gavrel gave two sharp chews, shunting the mouthful into his cheek. He raised the gun to his shoulder.

'Well, but –'

'Here, fuck, Blair,' came Bunny's voice. 'Don't push your luck, I mean to say.'

'All right, all right.' Blair glimpsed the huddle in the shadows by the wall, and glanced at the family, the inspector, and Lubov, before turning back to the door. 'I just thought, seeing as he was on about Manchester United –'

'Hoh, what!' Gavrel resumed his chewing. 'Manchester United, what?'

Blair stopped in the doorway. 'Well, it's just that we've a drink –'

'Manchester United?'

'Well, it's a flavour, and it flashes colours –'

'Come.' Gavrel waved a hand, lowering his rifle an inch. 'Fabi!'

Fabi approached, his gun trained on the Englishman. Blair looked at both guns, and at both soldiers' faces, and set the glasses down on the table.

'You funny man,' said Gavrel. 'What shit you talk!'

'Look, it's this – lovely.' Blair tore open a sachet with his teeth, and emptied it into one of the glasses. It flashed darkly, blue and red surging like venous and arterial blood.

Gavrel's eyes narrowed. 'Too many colour for Manchester United. Only red is colour.'

'Still, though – from England.' Blair took a sip. 'Wild cherry, it's lovely. And in a way it's almost local, because my company, Global Liberty, not only makes this, but makes your bullets as well, in Konjinch.'

'Kuzhnisk.'

'Kujints. So I mean – fancy that! What are the odds?' Blair rolled his eyes around the room. Ludmila's scowl bored through the haze to scald him.

'Drink.' Gavrel prodded Blair with the gun, lounging back to watch him take a mouthful. His eyes studied Blair's face, hunting the drink's effects. None appeared, save for a nod, and a smacking of lips. A pair of grunted words passed between the soldiers. Fabi lowered his rifle, reaching out to take Blair's glass and lift it to his nose, eyes blinking left and right in its vapour. Lighter words, rasped, came with a nod to his superior, before he tipped the drink over his tongue.

Gavrel's eyes swivelled up to Blair. He pushed the second vodka towards him like a chess piece.

The Englishman tracked the glass's approach, and glanced up at the soldier's face. Checkmate. He emptied the last sachet into the vodka. 'It's a soldier's little helper. Military mothers' milk.' He smiled like a debutante hostess, watching with the men as the drink flashed, and cleared, before picking it up to sip.

'Soldier need no help.' Gavrel snatched the drink, tossed it into his mouth, and slammed the empty glass down on the table. 'Pah! Is for woman. Is drink for little girl.' He reached for Blair's hand, laying it across his palm like a bundle of baby geckos. 'Hand soft like tits – see? Drink only help for little girl, for baby to play soldier.' His chin sealed the matter with a push: 'Hoh.'

Blair cocked a smile. 'Well, obviously I'd much prefer a pint. Still, beggars can't be choosers. We are in a war zone, after all.'

'Hoh! Baby English girl! What you know from war?'

'Well – just wait and see how you feel in a minute.' Blair clamped his mouth for effect. 'I think you'll find yourself agreeing that violence is ancient history, that the battle to win is the battle for hearts and minds.'

'Mines?'

'*Minds* – brains, heads.'

'History?' snorted the soldier. 'English countries always use violent. Always win. Typical English, use violent whole time, and cry like girl when other use violent. Want only monopoly for violent.'

'Well, but what I am saying to you is: the hearts and minds –'

'Listen to me: minds find enemy, then use violent. Perfect.'

'Well, no, I mean – you might suppress the people with violence, but you'll only truly win them with freedom.'

'Exact!' Gavrel thumped the table. 'Violent win freedom.'

Blair looked down to see the soldier's face growing ruddy, his brow beginning to relax. He approached solipsidrine's limbo, the minutes of rising confidence before self-consciousness passed away, before victorious music gripped his mind. 'I mean,' – Blair rested a hand on the table – 'answer me this: what do you want more in life – happiness, or misery?'

'Misery,' said Gavrel. 'Only from misery come happy.'

Blair chewed his lip. 'Well, but – surely you'd want others to be free from misery?'

'Yes. Free for misery.'

'Mmm. I think what you're saying is: you want them to be free. And do you know the incredible thing? You have the power. You have the power to bring freedom, because you have in yourself a bigger instrument than violence.'

'Power, yes.' The officer slumped forward, nodding. 'Bigger violent, yes.'

'You can do it – clear a path for freedom, for democracy. You have the power in your hands – even as you sit there, you have the power.'

The soldier's eyes grew moist. 'Yes, yes, yes,' he turned to mutter some words to his comrade, made a gesture of weighing the rifle in his hands. 'Power.'

In the corner, Inspector Abakumov cleared his throat, and addressed himself to the officer. 'And may I briefly remark that, at least from this angle of view, your exchange with the foreigner shows a heartening new direction? Indeed, you seem touched and uplifted in quite some measure. Perhaps you would impart to us the gist of his disclosures?'

Gavrel turned slowly. His gaze fell on Abakumov like a tissue on to a puddle, absorbing his terse, expectant smile, his false composure. Without blinking, or shifting his stare, he fumbled the Kalashnikov on to his knee, and flattened a hand over the barrel to level it.

Then he squeezed the trigger.

Flame spat from the muzzle. A blast shook the room. Kiska's little coats exploded in a shock of smoke. Irina screamed. The group tumbled flat to the floor.

'Shit,' sighed Gavrel. 'Oh no. What it is we call this, Fabi, officially?'

'Hoh, erm – friendly damage?'

'Yes, no, no – *collateral* damage.'

'Collateral, Gavrel, yes. Friendly fire is the comrade you kill who also has a gun. In this case, yes, collateral – because the child was killed instead of the gangster. And she had no gun.'

Standing, Gavrel waved a hand over the corner, addressed the shivering, blood-spattered faces. 'Now you see in brightest colour the nature of the so-called inspector, this gangster – look what he does to you, shielding himself with such a little one. This was truly an evil act. We must stand together and prevail over his like.' Gavrel secured his grip on the weapon.

Lubov gasped as a rivulet of blood found her bottom. 'But she sat two metres away! She was nearer to you than to him!'

The soldier ignored the woman, sweeping a glorious hand into the air. 'And in respect of such a grave insult to nature, it has to be said: if you don't stand with me, you stand against me. With the child-killer – the evil one.' Gavrel's mouth stayed slightly, smugly open, his eyes clicked knowingly left. 'I only pray this cannot be so.'

Blair sat ashen, hands clasped over his crotch. His trembling rattled the chair beneath him. Gavrel's eye caught on the Englishman. He paused, and flicked Blair's hands aside with the gun. Then his face sprang open, a guffaw roared out. 'Fabi, look!' He pointed at Blair's lap. 'Look, English little secret!'

Blair followed the soldier's finger to his crotch, looking down to find a bulge visibly throbbing, almost wagging.

'Ha! Haaa!' Gavrel poked it with his gun, mouth agape. He pulled his comrade over. 'Suddenly it is so clear! Look, Fabi, watch.' He swung his rifle on to the family, spread his legs for support, and fired a thunderous shot.

Abakumov slammed into the wall, and slumped on to his side.

The soldiers turned back to Blair, lifting him from the chair, pulling him into stronger light. 'Haaa! Look, it's bigger still! Oh Fabi, what species of miscreation have we discovered?'

'A sick one, Gavrel, yes.'

'Here, Blair, fuck,' came Bunny's whimper.

English didn't reply, nor did he struggle as Fabi tugged down his trousers. In the symphony of gagging breaths behind the soldiers, only Olga managed to wail.

Gavrel spun, raising the gun to his shoulder. Bang. The wailing stopped. He turned to see Blair's loin stir gaily. 'A real statesman we have, a great leader! Themes of freedom and power and death are like a girl's musk to him!'

'Like hot tongue on his cock, Gavrel, yes – for instance, look.' Fabi aimed his rifle into the group. A shot roared. Irina jolted, and fell still.

Both turned to study Blair's reaction. His eyes clenched pleated under wrinkles of skin, his teeth gritted hard. But his groin stood proud and jolly.

Gavrel tossed a glance at the corner. Amongst the shattered flesh, frozen in beauty, crouched Ludmila. Beside her Maksimilian hung his head. Lubov curled into a silent, quivering orb by the wall. 'Fabi, fetch the girl here,' Gavrel dragged the Englishman into the clearing between the table and the bodies, redirecting an approaching brook of blood with the tip of his boot.

Blair's sense had almost left him when he heard Ludmila's sobs. He listened to the soldiers' growled commands, heard the rubbing of different weights of cloth. And when his eyes opened, there, painted into the light, was Ludmila, naked, shining with tears. A line was drawn in shadow from her uppermost pubic wisp to a point between the hang of her breasts, a snug handful each.

Gavrel forced her on to a pile of her clothes, jamming a foot between her legs to keep them apart. 'So, English,' he said. 'Before you die.'

Fabi pushed the Englishman on to the girl, prising open his knees as far as his trousers allowed, carefully marshalling his penis with the tip of his gun. Ludmila bucked and squealed.

'Don't do it to her,' cried Lubov. 'After you've orphaned her, after her lover Michael Bukinov, with a sickly uncle to care for, has already taken one of your filthy bullets into his heart. Monsters! Your bullets and filth and love of death!'

Ludmila stopped gasping at the sound of Misha's name.

Fabi lifted his gun, firing before even focusing his eyes. Lubov's head snapped aside. Maksimilian moved a leg to accommodate her body.

Blair's shadow fell over Ludmila. She stiffened, arched as she felt him enter, growled and shook her head from side to side. Gavrel stood a boot on the man's back, shoved them both across the floor till Ludmila clawed for a handhold, scratched and tore at her clothes, at the table, at the ground. Her fingers found the

Englishman's belt, and when it flew free, his waistband, and trouser, and pocket, where metal shapes blended with the rancid butter scent of his sweat, the image of his skeletal grimace straining, nodding, panting over her face. She touched and turned the objects with her fingers, tried to connect with something less ugly than flesh.

'Hoh, and Gavrel, watch!' the little soldier beamed.

Blair felt the barrel of a gun between his legs. The soldier split apart the cheeks of his buttocks, and jabbed the gun in and out, grunting with each thrust.

Then, with each of the shack's survivors making their own unearthly noise, with all reduced to a state beneath the kingdom of animals, a radio crackled, and the front door flew open. 'Father Jesus!' An older soldier stormed into the room, gold flashing from his epaulettes, rifle held at the ready. He surveyed the scene with a slackening jaw.

Fabi looked up. 'The premises are secure, commander.'

'Withdraw your weapon!' The commander turned blinking to Gavrel. 'Do I dream it, Gergiev – or have you here furnished a bowel of hell?'

Gavrel chuckled softly, and raised a sheepish smile. 'We're delighted to see you, Commander. Indeed, I was now imagining the many things I wished to discuss with you, and praise you for.'

The commander's gun fell dangling by his side. He scanned every corner of the room, pausing to frown at the bulges in both soldiers' crotches. 'Did the dead show resistance? How are you here with vodka, meat, and so many dead? And are these female dead? Is that not a child, dead? Gergiev? Is that not three generations of a simple mountain family like your own? Dead?'

'They're free now, commander. No more poverty. No more war. They are liberated. We have prevailed.'

'Father Jesus.' The commander shook his head. Light filtered through steam as it rose to mingle from merging puddles of blood. 'Move away from the table, stand down your weapons. Who remains alive on the property?'

Gavrel nudged his chin around the room. 'These love-rats, the boy in the corner, and another English.'

'English?'

'Yes, journalists. Something like that.'

'*Journalists*? Shit. Gergiev – Father, Father Jesus. They witnessed all this?' The commander's head shook in an ever-decreasing arc. He pulled the Englishman off the girl, and watched him crawl hissing to the bedroom on his belly. The girl's hands fell to her sides, her head lolled sideways, eyes closed, twitching. The commander picked a coat off the floor, and spread it over her like a blanket, before turning to scowl at the soldiers. They looked down, lips clamped, like infants stifling a giggle. 'What can you have been thinking? Oh saints, oh my heavens. You have truly furnished here a scene from hell. We'll have to finish the job, there's nothing else for it – Gnezvarikstan will be a blighted name across the world if this gets out. You, Gergiev, pass me the munitions.'

'Munitions? Do you not walk with them yourself, commander?'

'Can you be serious? And why would I carry munitions from the rear, when you are here establishing a forward post?'

'Well, but – no munitions were given us to carry. We ourselves must be down to our last.'

'Hoh,' the commander tossed an ironic chin. 'As you've spent the morning cutting down innocent peasants. Then go, finish them yourself, though in honesty, looking at the ungodly result of your patrol, I'm very hesitant. You should feel fortunate I don't remove your gun and badge, and shoot you both instead.'

'I can finish them,' Fabi said hopefully. 'Anyway, both are in pain – one blind and crying from his eyes, and one bleeding from the arse – it's unfair to leave them to suffer.'

'And Fabi, you genius – how can one be a witness when he's blind?' The commander sighed, and led the men into the bedroom.

The English quivered there. Their spirits had left them, as spirits do when a certainty of death draws near. They sat like statues of dirty ice.

An aeroplane rumbled high overhead, full of people drinking tea, travelling west to somewhere vibrant. The Heaths shivered to their feet without a sound. They seemed to do it instinctively, independently, and the spectacle made the commander pause. He watched them face each other, seeming to sense their positions like new-born cubs. They fell into a hug that pressed the full heights of their bodies together, and one of them began to rub a circle on the other's back. 'Silly sausage,' he seemed to say.

The commander tossed his chin at the soldiers. 'Well then, quickly – it's not a play you're watching at the theatre.'

The soldiers lifted their weapons. Aimed, and squeezed their triggers.

Click.

Click.

'Shit,' said Gavrel.

'This is an emptiness of projectiles, Gavrel, yes.'

Blair turned, and opened his eyes. He saw the commander bark insults at the men, saw the men remove and examine their magazines. Then, behind them, fully clothed, came Ludmila. Her face was flushed and fresh, though her expression, and her gaze – a gaze like a stabbing with spears of young bamboo – didn't change. The girl moved past the soldiers and stepped up to Blair, shedding on him a scent of their sex. Without shifting her eyes from his, she moved a hand to his crotch, lingering there, radiating heat through the cloth of his trousers.

Then she plunged her hand into his pocket.

A bullet emerged. It featured a tiny design of either an eagle or a demon poised to swoop. She passed it to Gavrel, and stepped from the room, silent and aloof, into the light of the kitchen window, and beyond it, through the door, into sunlit snow.

Without a word, the soldiers watched her pass. Officer Gergiev clicked the bullet into his clip. He smacked the clip back into his gun. Raised the gun to his shoulder.

And fired.

Blood sprayed the wall behind the Heath twins.

3

AND WAS JERUSALEM BUILDED HERE AMONG THESE DARK SATANIC MILLS?

Much later

Ludmila paused to watch the sun idle. It just hung, tediously, shimmering as if through egg white. The night stayed an urgent eternity away.

A helicopter gunship drummed in and out of tune near by. Ludmila stifled a shiver.

'Try, please, for me, to climb back to your spastic senses,' said Maks. 'If you had so much as half an eye in your head, you would see that this one is bound to die, or is already dead. Or else why do you think he just lies there, not even breathing?'

'Of course he's breathing.' Ludmila reached out a fingertip. 'See? Do you think I have so much electrical power that I can make dead things jump? So don't spray shit.'

'Hoh, well, that demonstrates less than nothing. You could have disturbed him in his final breath, by the look of him. You could have just scared his ghost out through his nose.'

'Slap your cuckoo! There's nothing to say their conditions are any different – just because one twitches and one lies still. This one is more placid. You would see it if you had a brain behind your eyes.'

'And – hoh! – placid now, is it? Well, I can say death is the highest form of placidness all right. I can say if you're looking to have no trouble from him, then the dead one is for you. Very, very placid, he is. Permanently serene.'

'Maksimilian!'

A young Chinese girl in a shop-assistant's smock edged

around the cage, dragging Ludmila's gaze from the glass shopfront. 'Can I help you at all?'

'I wondered if they're from the same mother.' Ludmila pointed at the nuggets of black fur. 'This one looks slow.'

The girl smiled, nodding. 'Yes, they're from the same litter. They will sleep a fair bit at that age, in bursts throughout the day. Would you like to hold one?'

'Yes, I would like to.' Ludmila unhitched her bag from her shoulder, and propped it on the floor. She wore the red dress her father had bought her all those years ago, her princess dress, her escape dress – though she wasn't sure why she had chosen it on such a stifling day.

'I want to hold it,' said Blair.

'You can hold it after me – but softly!'

Maks spat a wad of breath. He checked his watch, and tossed his eyes this way and that. 'Can you just resuscitate one of them long enough to get on with the day? The car will be towed away just now.'

Ludmila didn't look at her brother. Her face broke like sunshine over cloud as the cage door creaked open, and she burrowed a hand under the sleeping kitten. It awoke on the way to her chest, and gave a plaintive squeak. 'It's divine,' she cooed, finding its neck with her fingers.

'Can I not hold it?' asked Blair.

'Why don't I go on ahead and collect the things from the house?' said Maks. 'We have to be ready in an hour.'

'And please speak in English.' Ludmila flashed a reproachful eye, following with a burst of mother tongue: 'You'll have to start some time – you don't imagine Blair will learn Ubli just to understand your goose's gibberish?'

'Bollecks.'

'Maksimilian!'

'Bollecks,' echoed Blair, reaching for the kitten.

Maks gave a sigh. 'Hoh then, I'm leaving. If you're waiting for a passionate response from the cat, you'll be here until November.'

'I'm buying the cat, will you just wait! In saints' name!' Ludmila lifted the kitten out of Blair's hand, brought it to her face, and blew on it.

'Well, you seem not to be making enormous strides towards just buying it. Rather, you seem to be making a bond with the shop, and its smell of incessant turds.'

'And just cut your hatch.'

'If you would just get it home, you could spend all the time you like squeaking at it like a gerbil.'

'I told you it's for the office, we won't keep it at home.'

'Yes, such an important enterprise now, the office – such a global operation, the office, with its cat. And what, in the first place, possesses your mongol senses to think of a cat for an office? It's not a children's farm.'

'It will give it a homely air. It will be more placid a place – remember what the doctors said.'

'Ah, ah, of course – I forgot the emergency medical procedure that says to buy a cat for English, that says to carpet our place of work with droppings and piss.'

'And just listen to me: if you make the day too hard I will cancel your Mastercard.' Ludmila paid for the kitten and, while Maks huffed and muttered to himself, pointed out a few more requisites to the shop assistant, including a furry carrying box covered with love-hearts. Maks rolled his eyes.

He scowled, carrying the kitten in its furry carrier down the High Street. Ludmila scolded him for swinging it, and threatening to loop the loop with it. Another angry gust came when Ludmila slowed at the entrance to Sainsbury's food store, and told Maks to wait outside.

'Hoh, yes,' he spat, 'I will hold the cat on the street, here, by the bus stop, by the screaming sirens probably coming, by the gunfire of terrorist police, so it can finish its journey to Heaven unaccompanied by peace, or lack of outright terror, and lack of food and water due to your now pathological involvement with every type of shop.'

Ludmila ignored him long enough to let him feel properly ignored. Then she said, 'We'll need something for the train, to eat.'

'Well, but surely there is food already to buy on the train?'

'Yes, at probably four times the price. You don't think I'm going to be captive to the prices on the train?'

'No, of course, as you're so poor. As you're so poor you can only afford cats and cat accessories. In fact, why don't you just buy some sauce to add to the cat? Some sauce, or batter – Kentucky Fried Kitten, we could have, the family box, but with fur –'

Ludmila was gone, absorbed into the blinding trap of the supermarket entrance. The red of her dress soaked into the light and evaporated as if dispersed to a dazzling Heaven.

Time was running short when Maksimilian finally slid the BMW on to the gravel behind the office. He jumped from his seat, activated then deactivated the alarm, and left Ludmila trying to conceal the kitten box under a shopping bag. Blair sat quietly in the back.

'It's going to squeak at the first moment he steps into the car,' Maks warned over his shoulder. 'You offend intelligence, thinking you'll keep such a noisy thing secret for the whole train journey north.'

'Hoh! And from the same mouth that's been telling me it's dead!'

'I'm telling you. Even dead, they will make noise. That's how stupid they are. Why do you think they no longer live in the wild?' Maks disappeared through a security door into a tired industrial block of two storeys. He made his way up a flight of linoleum stairs, along a carpeted corridor thick with muggy air. A cricket match wafted from a radio, ushering Maks into a small office split into two cubicles. Cardboard boxes, stacks of paper, a ream of plastic bags, and two point-of-sale displays for mobile telephones cluttered its approaches.

'English!' Maks rapped his keys on a cubicle's window. 'Big bollecks!'

It took a moment for the hunched figure behind the Perspex to respond. Two white hands carefully laid down a sheaf of papers. One hand went up to smooth a patch of white, short-cropped hair. And then he swivelled around in his chair, a pair of black glasses sealed like goggles on to his face. 'Aye, bollocks,' he sighed.

'Bollecks tosspet English fuck!' Maks gestured through the window. 'Wenker!'

'All right,' English prepared to hoist himself from the chair. 'I mean to say. Is Millie with you?'

'In car. Quick, bollecks!'

'All right, all right.' English shuffled to the door, turning to flick off his standard lamp, and collect his satchel from its hook beside the desk. 'Catch down your cuckoos, for God's sake.'

Such was English's weariness that he didn't notice one of Ludmila's shopping bags rustling and squeaking on the train. Even once the bustle of King's Cross Station slid away, once military emplacements gave way to countryside, and the trio sat quiet in the gently vibrating hush of their carriage.

'English, did we get for the pay?' asked Ludmila.

'Yes,' said Bunny, 'You'll bank about nine hundred, after everyone's paid.'

'Hoh,' Ludmila turned to Maksimilian, speaking Ubli, 'and if

311

you would stop driving like a pimp around the town, and go to recover the Fone-Bay debt, we could bank twice that.'

Maks tossed up his chin. 'Well, if you can advise what time in the earth's eternal calendar they will revisit their abandoned premises, I will go and smash down something highly resemblant of their heads and upper bodies.'

Ludmila frowned through the window at streaks and flashes of light industrial foreground occasionally peppered with military drab. 'And I'll tell it to you only once again: I will take the car back if you don't make it pay. Do you think it's a charity I'm running?'

'Is there a Scotch egg?' Bunny asked, as much to staunch the flow of Ubli, as to quell any peckishness.

Ludmila reached into a shopping bag, and pulled out three packaged products. Bunny perused them solemnly before pulling a Cornish pasty across the table.

'I want the pasty,' said Blair.

'I mean to say, Blair. You only want it because I want it.'

'Well, I just want it. Give it to me.'

'You ask for Scotch egg, English,' Ludmila reminded in a motherly tone.

'Yes,' Blair reached across the table. 'You asked for a Scotch egg, not a pasty. Give me the pasty.'

Bunny sighed wearily, and pushed the pasty to Blair.

'And I want the Scotch egg as well,' Blair wrapped a protective arm around the pasty.

'Well you're not having it,' said Bunny. 'It's mine.'

Ludmila swept both the pasty and the egg into her shopping bag, and crumpled it on to the floor. 'Then you both get nothing. Instead shut up.'

'I mean to say.' Bunny sat back with a sigh.

Blair's lip began to tremble.

A tense silence accompanied the group north, and in the taxi to Albion. During this time, the kitten squeaked loudly, and Bunny was presented with it. He stroked it, relinquishing it to Blair after he went on and on about it.

It was teatime when they reached the home. Matron swept the kitten into her office with a saucer of water, while Bunny went to linger on the spot he and Blair had traditionally stood between meals; the corner by the foyer and green lounge, with a view of the corridor that ran to the kitchens. He hung there as regular people hang anywhere familiar, anywhere habitual, as if waiting for a bus he'd caught every day for thirty-seven years; stood and mused like someone who looked back on the phases of their past with embarrassment and dismay, knowing that very moment would itself seem awkward when looked back upon.

It was a big day at Albion. A reunion coinciding with the fifth anniversary of privatisation. To the sting of antiseptic was added a layer of party feeling, a specially engineered saccharine that made the residents assertively coy. Its engineer was Matron. She had a lot of practice in this, as every Sunday at the institution was traditionally a free day. Whereas the home's tall spaces usually rang with clinks and clatters, Sundays brought Frank Sinatra. A rare gloss coated those days. Frank would flow from low-quality speakers across Albion's museum spaces, and a saturated light always seemed to glow through the sash windows; at least, it made itself noticeable in the soporific clearing of the day. There also came a mood, a relief, like that of elder statesmen having survived unspeakable intrigue, or like graduates on the last day of college, being warm and being noble where ordinarily they might not. The music, and the relaxation of routine that it caused, made the residents slide like silk, feeling as though they were part of a wider global flow. Even Matron was relaxed on Sundays. She usually wore a simple woollen dress and cardigan with no-nonsense shoes. Flecks of make-up would shine on her face, giving her the stipple of a half-restored painting.

Matron was proud of her Sunday atmosphere. From outside those grey walls it might have seemed a sad emulation of normality, but the loose emotion it stirred were lollies of genuine human spirit in every way.

Bunny soaked up the old Sunday feeling from his spot beside the foyer. It was one of Matron's typical Sunday affairs. Plus – there were balloons.

Still a nervous flutter ran through him. It was because he felt part of nothing. He was no longer a part of the Albion community. And still not a part of any community outside it. He stood alone by the shadow end of the foyer, watching Ludmila and Blair answer questions from Matron, bathed in light from the entrance. Still, unease persisted in him, and he realised it would stay until one of his old co-residents came past. He saw nobody from the old days. They wouldn't be expecting him back, though they knew the day also held a short memorial service for Blair.

Presently Matron came over, pulling little Blair Aleksandr by the hand. 'So much for the colour code!' she barked by way of hello. 'You want putting away, dressing him up like that.'

'You what?' Bunny fell from his reflections.

'More than a year since they banned red in schools, and here you are, in a care environment with antisocial problems of its own, parading the little soul like a ruddy ambulance light.'

'Well, Matron, I've not dressed him. He's not mine, you know. His mother's dressed him to match her, look.'

'But the lass isn't to know, she's not from here, Bunny. Honestly, you'll have to exert some influence, you can't just leave things happen. And in your brother's absence you should be paying the child more mind. You did marry the girl, for God's sake – at least try and make a go of things.'

'Well, but it was an immigration issue. I mean to say, I love her

314

to bits, and all her mad little ways, but I was only trying to do the decent thing, under the circumstances. I've not slept with her or anything.'

'Honestly, Bunny, what are we going to do with you? I've had no sense out of the porters since she walked through the door, you want thrashing for wasting such a lovely lass as that. Bloody thrashing, you want.'

'Well, but Matron, I mean to say –'

'It's not unhygienic, Bunny, so don't start. It's what makes the world go round.'

'I wasn't going to say unhygienic, actually.'

'Well, she'll not be foreign for ever, will she? She might not be from here, but she'll catch on, you'll see. For goodness' sake, start exploring your options – there's many a man'd kill to be where you are.'

Ludmila walked tall and erect towards the whispering pair, light finding exquisite hollows beneath her cheeks, dazzling reflectors in her teeth. Maks trailed behind her like a grave digger, trying to finish an exchange in Ubli.

'I tell you,' he said, 'we could buy the propeller factory back home – it's at least as big as this place, we could fill it with the same kind of cripples. Fantastic amount of money they must be making here.'

'In saints' name, can you not open your mouth without insulting?' Ludmila smiled as Matron saw her approach. 'Anyway, the place needs doctors and many other things than just a building. And it needs a government that will pay – do you think for a second the Gnezvar-Kuzhnisk government would give money for a place like this?'

'Hoh! Doctors? If you had the cell of one eye in your face you would see these types are perfectly healthy. A bit turned, is all. A bit of porridge and a television is all they need.'

The pair reached the corner where Bunny and Matron stood, little Blair dangling from Matron's hand like a monkey. Ludmila turned to hiss a final note to Maks, 'And if you can't spend the day in English, just cut your hatch.'

'Hoh, and the very next moment I'm having to deal with Qazaqs or Bengalis!'

'Tsst!'

The group strolled down a long corridor. Lumbering up it came Gretchen, a familiar face from Bunny's day. Each twelve paces were punctuated with a little dance; a locomotive wriggle of her behind, fists pushing and pulling at her side like levers on a wheel. Then, just before she resumed her walk, she would flash over one shoulder a smile of innocent confidence.

She passed Bunny by without noticing him.

The group made their way to the activities room, where a smattering of adult guests mingled in a heat that curled the edges of sandwiches on a buffet. Residents were excluded from the gathering, as gin was being served, as were wine, and warm beer.

Beside the gin stood Donald Lamb.

A younger man fidgeted beside him, who by his attentive blinking gave himself away as Lamb's assistant.

Lamb beamed when Bunny and Ludmila entered the room. 'Hello, hello,' he sang, moving to greet them. He crouched for a moment to comment on Blair's height, and his ferocious scowl, then he made affable chat with Ludmila. And when Matron finally drifted away to mingle with other guests, and Ludmila and Maksimilian took Blair to peruse the buffet, Lamb and Bunny made a start on the gin. It conspired with sunshine, and the sound of bees and flies, to provoke conversation about the morning's play in the test match at Lord's. And this parlayed into more sensitive musings, which the day's resonant airs seemed to call for, or at least allow.

'Always meant to ask,' said Bunny, 'if it was a ploy, sending us away like that?'

'I wouldn't say that,' said Lamb. 'I wouldn't say that at all. I don't mean to harp on, but the situation really is more complex. Very messy business, privatisation. Unpredictable. Let's just say we felt your interests were better served outside the glare of public interest.'

Bunny nodded gently. His eyes joined Lamb's on the floor beneath their gins. 'And it was you wrote that letter from our dad?'

'What would make you think that?'

'Harp on – you say that in the letter.'

'Well,' said Lamb, 'the situation really is more complex. Though actually, on that score, I've a bit of a treat for you tonight. Bit of an introduction to make.'

'Oh?'

Ludmila's voice rang out from the buffet. 'No, Maksimilian! No orange Fanta!'

And the subject melted into the eve. On and on the stifling air was moved around Albion by wandering English people, and standing English people who simply moved their arms. The warmth shifted in dusty clouds around the activities room, until the people moved away, up the hall to the foyer, past the room of a man said to have a brain like a jellyfish, with only a thin cap of grey matter suspended in cerebrospinal fluid. Presumably a nerve connected it to the body of this man, who everyone went to the trouble of addressing as Mister, went to the trouble of dressing, caring for, and speaking to, because there, but for the grace of God, go we all.

Gin flowed until dark, and still flowed after it. And when finally a rousing tango gripped Albion's air, only Lamb, his assistant, and Bunny remained in the large hall. Lamb checked and rechecked his watch.

317

Bunny stood himself upright in the middle of the room.

His feet began to scissor, chop, and flash to the tango, but within a few steps, and barely one twirl, he stumbled, and fell.

Lamb's assistant tensed, ready to spring to his aid. But Lamb stood still, watching quietly. This held the assistant back.

'Will I help His Royal Highness?' the lad whispered after a moment.

'Leave him,' said Lamb. 'He'll have to find his own feet.'

As the crumpled ex-parasite tried to find his balance, the sound of crunching gravel puffed through Albion's windows. A fleet of black cars swept up the drive.

Lamb was about to step forward, when Ludmila's head poked through the door. 'English!' she called. 'Come, let's go home.'

'I might stop a bit.' Bunny glowered at his legs. 'I might just stop here a bit – Millie? I mean to say. I might just stop back now.'

'Come, English,' she sharpened an eye on his gin. 'What you devour, devours you.'

Bunny turned, and gazed through his goggles like an albino fly.

Ludmila took another step into the room. She arched her back a little, pouting. One eyebrow rose.

'Come, English: Friday tomorrow – shepherd's pie.'

The End

Thanks:
Outrageous fortune, All who took me back,
All who kept me in, Authors, Capybaras, Quint.

(

Father Tom and the fine people of Aughnasheelin and County
Leitrim, where the stars go sleep at night.